SHIFTING SANDS

KIMBERLY GARDNER
ALLY BLUE
WILLA OKATI
BRENDA BRYCE
J.L. LANGLEY
JET MYKLES

mlrpress
www.mlrpress.com

MLR Press Authors

Featuring a roll call of some of the best writers of gay erotica and mysteries today!

M. Jules Aedin	Maura Anderson	Victor J. Banis
Jeanne Barrack	Laura Baumbach	Alex Beecroft
Sarah Black	Ally Blue	J.P. Bowie
Michael Breyette	P.A. Brown	Brenda Bryce
Jade Buchanan	James Buchanan	Charlie Cochrane
Jamie Craig	Kirby Crow	Dick D.
Ethan Day	Jason Edding	Angela Fiddler
Dakota Flint	S.J. Frost	Kimberly Gardner
Roland Graeme	Storm Grant	Amber Green
LB Gregg	Drewey Wayne Gunn	David Juhren
Samantha Kane	Kiernan Kelly	J.L. Langley
Josh Lanyon	Clare London	William Maltese
Gary Martine	Z.A. Maxfield	Patric Michael
AKM Miles	Jet Mykles	William Neale
Willa Okati	L. Picaro	Neil S. Plakcy
Jordan Castillo Price	Luisa Prieto	Rick R. Reed
A.M. Riley	George Seaton	Jardonn Smith
Caro Soles	JoAnne Soper-Cook	Richard Stevenson
Clare Thompson	Lex Valentine	Stevie Woods

Check out titles, both available and forthcoming, at
www.mlrpress.com

SHIFTING SANDS

KIMBERLY GARDNER
ALLY BLUE
WILLA OKATI
BRENDA BRYCE
J.L. LANGLEY
JET MYKLES

mlrpress
www.mlrpress.com

Published by
MLR Press, LLC
3052 Gaines Waterport Rd.
Albion, NY 14411

Visit ManLoveRomance Press, LLC on the Internet:
www.mlrpress.com

Cover Art by Anne Cain
Editing by Maura Anderson

ISBN# 978-1-60820-024-5

Issued 2010

The clack of insanely high-heeled—and insanely expensive— shoes bounced off the varnished wood slats of the walls in the upstairs hall. "You'll be sorry!" Yi's grasp of English had grown in the past year, but when she was angry, the Chinese accent kicked back in. Add in a flurry of pure Chinese and Daniel had reason to be wary of the little spitfire he'd married.

Stupidest thing he'd ever done. He still didn't know what had ever come over him.

"Yi, damn it, get back here!" Her heels smacked on the wood staircase. Damn, how could such a little woman move so damn fast? His legs were twice as long as hers and he couldn't catch up.

"You fucktard," she screeched back, filling the house with the sound of her fury. When the hell had she started using that word? He'd only ever heard Russell and Jud use it before. "I've had enough of you!"

"Yi!" he bellowed, certain the cows in the lower forty could hear her. Did the little drama queen have to involve *everyone* in their fight?

The answer, he knew, was yes.

He reached the arch leading from hall to dining room to find Yi standing at the end of the long, heavy table, hands clawed, pretty face twisted into the ugliest sneer he'd ever seen her wear. He cursed when he saw Judson, Mike and Cy sitting at the table, staring at her in shock. Half-eaten dinners sat before Mike and Cy, hat-hair telling him they'd only recently come in. Jud stood just inside the kitchen door, apron slung around his waist, a full bowl of mashed potatoes held before him.

"All of you! Gay, country faggots!" She screeched, whipping a red-taloned finger out to gesture at them. "You're not real men at all! I've had enough of you. You don't want me? I don't want *you*! I show you!"

"Yi, calm down. Let's go back upstairs and talk…"

A wordless shriek burst from Yi, a far louder sound than it

seemed a small, slender throat should make, then she spun and sped through the far door.

As always, Daniel had to pause a moment, completely dumbfounded by the actions of the stranger he'd married just six months ago.

The three men in the dining room shared his moment of shock, then turned as one to gape at him.

The sound of the front door opening and the screen door slamming against the outside wall got him going again. Cursing, he stormed around the far end of the table and headed out after her. "Yi! You get back here!"

"No! I leaving you pansy-asses behind."

The sound of that sentence in her broken accent nearly stopped him. But it wouldn't do to laugh at her now. It'd just piss her off more. He burst through the screen door and onto the porch that circled the entire house, stomping to the corner toward the carport. "Where do you think you're going?"

Yi was just flitting down the steps toward her shiny white BMW. It had been the sight of the expensive little tin can he'd bought her, packed to the gills with the designer luggage she'd insisted on for the shopping trip that passed for their honeymoon, that had sent him upstairs after her in the first place. "I'm leaving." She glanced at him, stuck out her tongue and flipped him off for good measure.

Again, if he wasn't so pissed, he'd have died laughing. "You can't leave."

"Oh no?" Having reached the door of her car, she spun, long black hair spilling down her shoulders. "You watch me. You bastard!"

She'd become entirely too fond of that word. "Yi, come back here and…"

Ignoring him, she turned toward the back of the house, opening that brightly painted little mouth. "Russell!"

Russell? Whatever words he might have been about to say

rushed out of his head as his brain tried to fathom what she was up to now. She thought too damn fast for him, no doubt about that, and he couldn't figure out what Russell had to do with her leaving.

The boy rounded the back of the house wearing his best jeans, his fancy boots and a brand-spanking new shirt and hat. Neither the black shirt nor the black hat went with the boy's freckled skin, in Daniel's opinion, but they did set off his flaming orange curls like they were fire spilling from behind his ears.

Daniel gripped the railing of the porch, watching the boy scuttle to the driver's side of Yi's car. Behind Daniel, the screen door opened and took long enough to shut that he knew all three men from inside had followed him out. But he couldn't bother looking behind him. Cold rage or icy fear—didn't really matter which—froze him on the spot. "Boy, what do you think you're doing?"

Yi planted her feet on the pavement beside the BMW's passenger door. "He's not a boy. He's a *man*. He's the only man here!" Some of her anger must be cooling because her English was clearer.

Suspicion wound a hard knot in Daniel's gut. "Russell." Yes, the boy was well into his twenties but Daniel had known him since he was a pup. There was no way he was leaving without an explanation. "Look at me."

Russell hesitated, head still down, fingers almost touching the handle of the driver's side door.

"Don't listen to him." Yi snapped her fingers. "Get in the car."

Wincing, Russell gripped the door handle.

"Russell, boy! You look at me and tell me what you think you're doing!"

"He's going with me, you barren old man!" Yi stated triumphantly, opening the passenger's door as Russell opened the driver's door.

Rage pushed Daniel away from the railing, propelling him toward the steps. "The hell he is!"

"No!" Mike's boots echoed right behind Daniel's.

"What the fuck?" This from Cy, right in line.

Daniel scowled deeper, hating to have the scene witnessed, but more intent on apprehending Russell. "Boy, you'd better explain."

"Stop!"

Yi's command froze Daniel in his tracks, halfway across the pavement between the house and the car. Scowling, he faced her, not sure what pissed him off the most: Russell, her attitude or the fact that his damn feet wouldn't move.

Slowly, Yi's sneer turned into a spiteful smile. "He's going with me." Her voice was steady and low, her porcelain skin nearly translucent in the light of the setting sun. Out of the corner of his eye, Daniel saw Ben and Gordy, the last of the hands who lived on the ranch, come around the corner of the barn but he couldn't take his eyes off a thick lock of Yi's silky black hair puffing up on a breath of wind to caress her cheek.

Wait, there wasn't any wind.

"Yi." His voice sounded strange, far away. He cleared his throat and tried again, sounding only a little more normal. "What's going on?"

Her smile hitched a bit more at the corners. "Russell, start the car."

Daniel's brows crowded his eyes as, on the outskirts of his vision, he saw Russell duck into the BMW and shut the door.

"You're no big, important man," Yi started. "When I heard you were a rancher, I thought you'd be a rich man like George Bush. Important. Powerful. You're not." She frowned. "I thought you'd have a place with hundreds of men, *real* men, cowboys." She sniffed. "Ha! Six men and only one of them worth anything. If I left him here, they'd turn him gay, too. I'm taking him before you make him a deviant, too."

Daniel would have responded to the direct attack but his lips didn't want to work.

Scrunching up her nose with a dismissive snort, Yi turned. "You," she pointed at Gordy, stopping him in his tracks, "and you," Ben stopped as well, "all of you!" she pointed at the men behind Daniel. "Perverted! Unnatural!"

The BMW purred to life as Russell started the engine.

She shook her head, putting on a sad frown. "You don't know what you've done. You don't know what I *am*!"

A strange tingle started in Daniel's shoulders. He shook them, reaching up to run a rough hand through his hair. Where the hell was his hat? And his feet still wouldn't move.

Yi's shoulders shook, the silk of her tank top shimmering in the golden sunset as she started to laugh. "I'm not what you think." Strange, her hair really did seem to be floating now. There still wasn't a breeze. "I could have been big help to you, made you something, but no. You reject me."

Daniel wanted to object. He didn't think he treated her bad. Still didn't know why he'd married her, but he'd been as decent a husband as he could. He bought her nearly everything she asked for, had started the house renovations she'd harped on. What more was he expected to do? He tried to open his mouth to say it but it was hard to talk when his skin was buzzing.

She shook her head, almost as though she knew what he was thinking. "It's too late. I'm done with you. And I curse you." She literally spat on the ground. No doubt about it, now her hair really was floating, strands of it nearly straight up from her head. Still, there was no wind.

Daniel tried to glance around, to see if he could figure out what was going on, but he couldn't move. That tingle in his shoulders had moved up and down and now every bit of his skin was crawling.

"I curse you, *all* of you, to live with your *true* natures." Yi tipped her head back, arms spread, voice raised in a strange singsong, her shrill voice seeping into his skin and making his eyeballs ring. A stream of Chinese—he never could remember which dialect she spoke—spilled from her lips, twisting them in ways that didn't seem quite natural. Maybe that wasn't Chinese? Then she lowered her face to look at him again. Her skin really did look like it was glowing. "You live with the truth of yourselves on this land you love so much. You're stuck on it until you each find someone who can live with what you are!"

A part of Daniel decided that, no, the last few sentences of what Yi said wasn't in English. That part wondered why he could understand it. Another part of him wondered why the hell he couldn't move and why his skin felt like millions of ants were crawling underneath it.

Laughing, Yi lowered herself into the passenger seat. Delicately, taking her time, she folded her shapely legs into the car and smoothed her skirt out over her knees. Somehow, none of that hair got trapped in the door when she shut it. "Goodbye, Daniel." She waved like a beauty queen, even blowing him a kiss as Russell started down the drive. "Enjoy yourself! *Y'all.*" Cackling, she pulled back into the car and continued to laugh as Russell drove off.

Daniel could only stare at the spot where the little white car had been, could only track the retreating vehicle out of the corner of his eyes. *What the hell…?*

Motes of dust danced in the air about his motionless form. No, not dust, too colorful for that. Too thick. His nostrils flared, panicked for a moment that he might not be able to breathe. But he drew air into his lungs just fine, drew in the colored dust. It filled his head, tickling the inside of his skull.

Something thudded softly on the porch behind him, followed by a tiny rodent squeal. A rooster squawked to his right, far away from where any chicken had been just now. He managed to roll his eyes to the side just in time to see Gordy disappear. Disappear?! No, wait… *Ho-lee shit!* The shirt and jeans Gordy'd been wearing ripped as a big ole black bull expanded out of Gordy's body. Gordy just kind of *grew* and re-shaped and, bang, there was the bull with the tatters of Gordy's shirt on its humped back. The bull stood with legs splayed, staring at the ground with big, dark eyes. A clatter of hooves on cement and a horse's confused bray came from where Ben had been standing.

Daniel would have looked, but that strange feeling eased down his neck just inside his skin, spreading down his chest and arms. He blinked and colors he'd never seen before replaced a lot of the normal ones around him. The ground was a rainbow of strangely muted reds and greens and the sky was an odd shade of lavender. His shoulders hunched on their own and he managed to twist his neck some. It felt weird. Like there was a lot more to his neck than there should have been. He blinked again. The barn across from him was shrinking. So was the bull that used to be Gordy. How the hell could he now see the roof of the barn?

Daniel blinked again, shaking his head. It felt funny. There was more to his nose than there should be, the crazy colors showing him a shining blue silver like the moonlight itself shone underneath his… snout? He jumped back, standing tall, staring at the top of the chimney of the house beside him. Shocked, he tried to raise his hands only to find that they weren't quite long enough to reach his face. He bent his neck to find there was a whole hell of a lot *more* of it. And his hand…was that his hand? It only had three big fingers and a thumb, with big talons. Turning his palm down, he stared in wonder at the scales that covered his hand, a hand that was a shape he didn't have. A shape he'd seen…where?

On that crazy painting Yi mounted in the main room of the house. The one with the twelve animals in it, though one of them sure wasn't a real animal. It was a dragon.

A dragon?

*What the hell…*he tried to say the words, his mouth opened, but the musical sounds that came out weren't any words his ears could recognize.

What had happened?

SNAKE CHARMER

KIMBERLY GARDNER

Cyrus Malone felt the first sign, an almost imperceptible wriggling under his skin, just as he was about to plunge his dick into the sweetest, tightest little ass this side of San Antonio.

Shitfuckpiss.

Keeping his hand on the hip of the slim, young owner of said ass, Cy glanced over his shoulder and up into the night sky. Dusk slid rapidly toward dark and the moon would soon rise. It would shine, bright as a silver dollar, its cold, clear light spilling over everything. It would light up the narrow alley behind A Bar Named Sue like it was midday. Cy could already feel it, and for just a moment he was sure he heard Yi's shriek—that hellcat Daniel had married—as she cursed them all to this god-forsaken fate. If only…

"Cy? Something wrong?"

Shoving the memory away, Cy turned from the moon's pitiless glare, a smile ready on his lips. "Nothing's wrong, darlin'. Just got distracted a minute." Realizing how that sounded, he added, "Thought I heard someone comin'."

Large gray eyes peered at him over a slim, denim-covered shoulder. The warm breeze wafting down the alley ruffled the young man's auburn curls. A pink tongue slipped out to wet full lips, still swollen from Cy's kisses.

"Somebody be comin' soon enough, I hope," Bobby Lee drawled, his Arkansas accent as thick and sweet as warm maple syrup. Still braced against the wall, he thrust his bare ass back against Cy's crotch and wiggled.

Goddamn.

The wriggling sensation intensified, crawling up Cy's spine and inching down his legs even as his cock swelled to near painful fullness.

Fuck if he was passing this up on account of that she-devil's curse. No fucking way.

Grabbing his sheathed cock, Cy lined up and pushed.

Bobby Lee whimpered and shoved back, impaling himself to the root. They both stilled, their breaths drowned out by the twang of steel guitars that still managed to reach them from inside the bar.

"C'mon, Cy, fuck me, man." Bobby Lee did that rippley thing with his insides, the thing that made Cy crazy, the thing he thought of when he was alone in his bunk with only his hand for company.

He pulled out almost all the way then shoved back in, giving Bobby Lee what he asked for, fucking that sweet little ass for all he was worth. It was pure, sweet heaven.

"Ah shit, baby," Cy groaned, his fingers digging into his boy's slender hips as he slammed his cock in deep.

"Feels so good, Cy. Ah, God." Bobby Lee rocked back, meeting Cy thrust for thrust. He bore down, squeezing Cy's dick like a velvety vise, dragging Cy's orgasm closer and closer to the surface.

And with it, other things came closer, too.

Shitfuckpiss.

Another thrust, another moan from Bobby Lee and Cy knew he wasn't going to last. "C'mon, darlin', I can't wait. give it up. Come for me."

Cy's hips sped up, his movements turning short and sharp as the crawling under his skin got all mixed up with the tingle in his balls. He reached around and gripped Bobby Lee's cock, hot and hard, like silken steel in his hand. Pre-come dripped from the slit and he imagined the taste of it on his tongue as he used it to slick the shaft.

"Harder," Bobby Lee moaned. "Do me harder. Fuck me deeper. I want it. I need it."

Cy tightened his grip on Bobby Lee's prick as his lover's channel sucked him deeper, working his cock with those internal muscles, like to rip the orgasm right out of him.

Sweat dripped into Cy's eyes and he blinked it away. How much longer did he have? And would it be enough?

"Now, Cy, now. I'm coming now, baby."

The muscles around Cy's cock clamped down, the dick in his hand pulsed as hot come spilled through his fingers and the smell of sex filled his nostrils.

Cy's dick swelled as his orgasm rushed over him and his beast reared up.

His incisors lengthened, curving into long, lethal fangs. His tongue split as the rush of blood in his ears turned to a deafening roar.

Not now!

He bit down on his lip to keep from saying the words aloud and tasted his own blood. Then he was coming. Thrust in to the hilt, he filled the condom with pulse after pulse of spunk.

Bobby Lee's ass milked him steadily, prolonging the pleasure, drawing it out the way only he could.

Goddamn.

Cy sagged. He felt like a wrung out dishrag. His knees gave out and he collapsed against Bobby Lee's back. But the man was stronger than he looked. Good thing, too, because right then Cy could not have stood if someone had offered him a million dollars to do it.

Panting, he fought to pull himself together, but his legs refused to work. That gummy, melted rubber-band sensation stretched from ankle to ass and was quickly climbing up his spine. Sure as hell it wasn't just the orgasm doing that.

Grabbing the base of his cock, he pulled out and dropped a kiss on the back of Bobby Lee's neck, careful to keep his fangs away from his lover's skin. He had no clue if his bite, even an accidental nick, could be poisonous. "I got to go, Bobby Lee. I'm sorry, darlin'."

Bobby Lee straightened and turned, yanking his jeans up and putting himself away as he did. His eyes widened. "Cy, baby, you all right? You don't look so good."

"Don't feel so good." Cy staggered back, first one step, then another.

Bobby Lee's hand shot out and gripped his arm, supporting him. "C'mere, baby, before you fall down."

Cy leaned against the wall, the vibrations of the music from the bar-band tingling along his spine. Or maybe that, too, was something else.

"I got to go." Cy fumbled at his fly but couldn't make his fingers work. He swore.

Bobby Lee brushed his hands aside. Removing the condom, he tied it off, then pitched it toward a nearby garbage can. With a touch as gentle as a mother's, he tucked Cy's cock away and did up the buttons on his jeans. Their eyes met and Bobby Lee's were filled with worry.

"Maybe we should go back inside and sit—"

"No," Cy snapped. Gentling his voice, he tried for a smile. Somehow he managed it. "I'll be fine. I just need to get home."

The line between the other man's pale brows deepened and he bit his lip. "You sure? I don't like letting you go like this."

Yeah, and you'll like what happens next even less.

He forced a laugh. "Don't be such a mother-hen, baby." Mustering the last of his control, he pulled Bobby Lee close and brought their mouths together. The kiss was sweet, if way too short, and left him feeling even worse as he released his lover and stepped back. Pulling himself together, he patted Bobby Lee's cheek and turned to go.

Somehow he managed to keep his strides steady until he rounded the corner of the bar, well out of sight of his lover. He broke into a run, staggered and nearly fell.

Shitfuckpiss.

Please, Cy prayed, please don't let it happen here.

A few more lurching steps brought him to his truck. Gripping the handle with fingers he could no longer feel, he yanked open the door and threw himself inside. He flailed a hand out behind him, missed the handle then caught the edge of the door, jerking it closed just as he lost his grip on control.

Shitfuckpiss.

He felt the elongation of his muscles, the dissolution of bones, or imagined he did. The others said it didn't happen like that, but Cy thought different.

"It won't be so hard if you don't fight it so much," Judson had told him once. And on the few occasions when he'd managed not to fight it, the change had gone a little bit easier. But only a little. Cy didn't think it would ever be easy.

A shaft of moonlight pierced the windshield. As sharp and cold as a knife slicing through him. Suddenly it was over and he was lying on the driver's seat, his serpent's body tangled inside a heap of his own clothes. He writhed, not sure how to move, still not entirely comfortable in his new form. It was always like this right after the shift. Then something clicked over in his tiny serpent's brain and he slithered free of the clothes. He slid down to the floorboards and curled up under the seat to wait it out.

Shitfuckpiss-ss-ss-ss.

Two

It was nearly nine the next morning when Cy turned his truck onto the access road for Shifting Sands Ranch. A warm wind whipped through the open windows, its song blending with the rumble of the tires and the voice of Merle Haggard crooning about doing time. Pulling into the gravel side-yard, Cy parked his truck. He started to close the windows, then paused. He sniffed and wrinkled his nose. The truck's interior reeked of snake. Or maybe it was him that stunk to the heavens. Leaving the window down, Cy got out. As he closed the door he sniffed again. It was definitely him that stunk, or his clothes anyway. Goddamn!

Stuffing his keys into his pocket, he made his way around to the back door of the main house. The sun was already blazing in a sky so blue it hurt his eyes to look at it. Arming sweat from his face, he pulled open the back door and peered cautiously into the kitchen. It was deserted. Letting out a relieved breath he stepped inside and let the screen door swing shut behind him. He paused a minute to soak up the blessed coolness of the house. The quiet whoosh whoosh of the dishwasher and the hum of the fridge were the only sounds he heard. He headed straight for the refrigerator and opened the door.

He was always ravenous after a shift. And now he'd missed breakfast. He was also late for work and would be hearing about it, sure as shit, as soon as Ben tracked him down.

Ducking his head, he stared into the refrigerator at a multitude of plastic containers. He'd spent the night in snake form, curled up under the driver's seat of his pickup. It wasn't great, but it was better than the last time he'd been caught out. At least this time he'd made it back to the relative safety of his truck. Snakes might be predators but coyotes were damn scary. Even now he shivered, recalling the night spent cowering underneath a bush, waiting out the shift and wondering if he was going to end up as some coyote's midnight snack.

"You ever get the AC fixed in that wreck you drive you won't have to stick your head in my fridge to cool off."

Cy turned. Jud stood in the doorway between the kitchen and dining room, arms crossed over his chest, spotless apron tied over his jeans and work shirt.

"I'm gettin' to it." Cy scrubbed a hand over his face and, reaching into the fridge, grabbed a round container and popped the lid. It was filled with leftover green beans. Not bothering with a fork, he began shoveling green beans into his mouth.

"Don't do that." Jud came across the room in a couple of long strides. Taking the bowl of beans, he replaced the lid then used the container to point to the table. "Sit. I'll fix you a plate."

Cy didn't argue. The kitchen was Jud's domain, and any man foolish enough to give him an argument risked getting the boot with no food in his belly for his troubles.

He sat down at the table.

Jud took two white stoneware mugs down from the cabinet. One had a red checkerboard pattern around the rim, the other blue. He filled both with coffee from the urn he always kept going and brought them to the table.

Cy sipped from his mug and watched as Jud went back to the fridge.

"You missed breakfast. But I got leftovers from last night's supper—roast chicken and mashed potatoes. Will that do?"

"That'll do fine."

Jud took out several containers and began filling a plate, his movements both economical and efficient—two things Cy himself had never managed to be in any kitchen. He popped the plate into the microwave, pushed a few buttons then came back to the table and sat across from Cy. Lifting his mug, he took a contemplative sip.

Cy sipped his own coffee in silence. If Jud had something to say he'd sooner or later get to it. He'd known the man long enough to realize that there was no rushing him.

After several long minutes Jud set down his mug. "Glad to see the coyotes didn't get you." His index finger traced the pattern around the rim. "This is the third time you been caught out."

"Second," Cy corrected.

"Hmm. Seems to me making it as far as the access road don't really count."

Cy shrugged but said nothing. What was there to say?

"Your boy know you turn scaly once a month?"

So here it was, the thing he had on his mind.

"He ain't my boy."

Jud gave a jerk of his shoulder, a sort of half-shrug as if to say *the hell he ain't*, but that's not the question.

The microwave beeped.

Cy scraped back his chair and started to stand but Jud waved him back down.

"Stay where you are." Rising, he went to the sideboard, gathered utensils and a napkin, then retrieved the plate from the microwave.

The delicious aromas of roast chicken and gravy made Cy's mouth water. He nodded his thanks as Jud set the plate down in front of him, then resumed his seat.

Picking up his fork, Cy turned his full attention to his plate and tried to ignore his friend's unnervingly intense gaze. But after only a couple of bites of chicken, he set down his fork and met Jud's eyes.

"I haven't told him yet." He heard his own defensiveness and grimaced.

Jud said nothing, just continued to drink his coffee and wait.

Shitfuckpiss.

"I'm goin' to tell him," Cy said when he couldn't take the silence any longer.

"'Course you are. Else one of these old days your timing's going to be fucked and you won't make it out of there before the shift. Then what do you think your boy'll do?" His lips twitched. "Be some kind of surprise finding yourself all cozied up with a snake, don't you think?"

"That won't happen."

"It might."

Of course it might. It nearly had. Cy didn't bother to say this. No need to throw fuel on the fire. Jud was cooking just fine all on his own.

Cy continued to eat, though he'd lost his appetite. All this talk about what he should and shouldn't be doing with his personal life had killed even the starvation that followed the shift.

He set his fork down with a clatter then shoved his plate away. Pushing back his chair, he got to his feet.

"Where you going, Cyrus? You left half your food."

"I lost my appetite."

Jud snorted. "Sit down and eat your dinner."

Cy didn't move.

"I said sit and finish your food." Jud stood, carried both their mugs back to the coffee urn and refilled them. With his back still turned he said, "It's your business what you do with that sweet young thing you've been chasing after. I won't say more about it."

Cy resumed his seat and pulled the plate back in front of him.

Jud returned with his coffee but didn't sit down.

"You're right," Cy said. "Okay? You happy?"

"It's not me needs to be happy."

"I'm goin' to tell him." Cy shoved a hand through his hair. "I just don't…"

"You don't want to scare him off." Jud's tone was gentle. "He that important to you, Cy?"

"I think so. Maybe."

Jud nodded. "You'll do the right thing."

This time the silence that fell between them was companionable. Cy finished his dinner, wiped his mouth and stood. He carried his plate to the sink and turned on the faucet.

Over the hiss and splash of water Jud said, "I'll get that."

"It's fine. I'll just—"

"Leave it." Jud nudged him away from the sink. "The dishwasher's already going and I ain't having you shove a dirty plate in with the clean ones. I swear, the lot of y'all don't know dick about using this dishwasher. It's easier for me to just do it than straighten out your mess."

Cy laughed and held up his hands. "Okay. Fine."

"You want to do something, go find Gordy. He was looking for you to ride out with him to check that fence on the south side. And Ben says there's animals need seeing to. That bay gelding Daniel picked up at auction's got a bad hoof."

Inwardly, Cy let out a relieved breath. They were okay.

And he'd told Jud the truth. He was going to tell Bobby Lee about the shifting. Now he just needed to figure out how and when to do it.

THREE

"I was surprised to hear from you." Bobby Lee picked up his beer and raised it to his lips. Tilting the bottle, he drank deeply.

"Oh? Why's that?"

Cyrus watched the muscles work as Bobby Lee swallowed. He wanted to lean across the table and press his lips to the hollow at the base of that pale throat, just visible in the open collar of his lover's chambray shirt. But this wasn't the time or place for that. Not that anyone in the bar would have noticed or cared if he had. As country bars went, A Bar Named Sue was pretty laid back and gay friendly. But seduction, as much as it appealed, wasn't why he was here.

Bobby Lee set down his beer and wiped his mouth with the back of one hand. "I just don't usually see you in the middle of the week is all."

"If you have something else you need to do—"

"No." Fingers lightly brushed the back of Cy's hand then twined with his. Bobby Lee grinned. "I'm glad for the chance to relax, tell the truth."

"I hear that." Cy studied their joined hands atop the table and felt his resolve slipping. But he'd come here to tell Bobby Lee the truth about his snake. And Goddamnit, tell he would.

"We had some excitement at the garage this afternoon," Bobby Lee continued.

Cy made a noise to show he was listening, though in his head he was rehearsing for the hundredth time the explanation he'd prepared as he drove into town.

"I was working on this old Chevy, you know, my ass up on the seat and my head crammed under the dash, messing with the wiring, when something brushes my arm. I look over and curled up right next to my shoulder there's this big old snake just looking at me like what the hell am I doing down there disturbing his sleep."

Cy's fingers flexed. "What did you do?"

"Screamed like a little girl and high-tailed it out of there." Bobby Lee laughed but there was an edge to it. "I'm kinda scared of snakes. Have been ever since I was a kid camping with the boy scouts. We went to sleep on the ground and I woke up with a snake sharing my sleeping bag."

Cy's heart felt like a lead weight in his chest. "Shit."

"I'll say. I nearly did, too." This time Bobby Lee's laughter was more relaxed. "Everybody started screaming and yelling 'stay still, Bobby Lee. Don't move, Bobby Lee.' But I was Goddamned if I was staying in that sleeping bag with a snake. My mama didn't raise no fool."

"Jesus. You get bit?"

"No. I tore out of there so fast that fucker didn't know what was what."

He squeezed Cy's fingers. "It wasn't even a poisonous snake and only like three feet long. But it freaked me out. You know how kids are. I had nightmares for weeks."

Cy returned the squeeze.

What the hell was he supposed to do now?

Shitfuckpiss.

"About a month after that," Bobby Lee said, not seeming to notice Cy's silence, "my big brother played a joke on me. He put one of them little garden snakes under my pillow right before bedtime. I yelled so loud, like to wake the dead. That little snake scared the piss out of me, literally. Our daddy was so mad. Johnny got his ass tanned good for that one."

Bobby Lee went on talking while Cy listened with only half an ear. He swore silently, all the while nodding and making hmm noises in all the right places. Wasn't this just one fine fuckerall? Why the hell did he have to get the snake anyway? Of all God's creatures he had to be cursed with the one that sent his lover into a tailspin. Why couldn't he have gotten a rat or a rooster or even a horse? So you might wreck some clothes during the shift, big fucking deal.

"Cy?" Bobby Lee was looking at him, brows lifted.

"Yeah, baby? I'm listening."

"I asked if you wanted to get out of here, maybe go somewhere…" Bobby Lee's lips curved in a wickedly suggestive grin.

Despite his worry, Cy's body responded to the hungry look in Bobby Lee's eyes. His cock stirred. They could talk then fuck, assuming the man hadn't run screaming by then. Or maybe they'd fuck first. Yeah, that sounded like a better idea.

They both pushed back their chairs and got to their feet. Cy tossed bills on the table.

"Hey, Bobby Lee?"

"Yeah?"

"What happened to the snake?"

They wound their way through the tables toward the door.

"Hmm? Oh, you mean the one today?" Bobby Lee slipped his hand into Cy's as they stepped outside. "Joe, that's the guy who owns the garage, he went and got his twelve-gauge out of the office and blew that son-of-a-bitch away." He laughed. "They said there was snake guts all over the place."

Cy grimaced.

"Tell me about it." Bobby Lee shuddered. "This one guy was pissed they didn't just cut off the head and save the skin for a belt."

"A belt." A wave of dizziness swept over Cy. The parking lot shimmered and swam before his eyes. He closed them briefly and sucked in a deep breath of the warm, moist air.

"You wouldn't catch me wearing no snake-skin. Gives me the willies just thinking about it."

Cy said nothing. And what the hell would his lover say if he knew how close he'd come to doing just that.

FOUR

"Let's take my car." Bobby Lee tugged Cy toward the ancient Cadillac, parked under the meager shade cast by a scrawny tree at the edge of the blacktop.

"My truck's right over there."

"Yeah, but you ain't got the AC fixed yet, did you?"

Cy shook his head.

"I keep telling you bring it in to the garage and I'll take a look at it. It might be something real simple." He paused by the Caddy's driver's door and dug in his pocket for his keys.

Cy walked around to the passenger side. "I'm gettin' to it."

"Yeah?" Bobby Lee laughed and unlocked the door. "When you gonna get to it?"

"Soon." Cy grinned. He loved the sound of Bobby Lee's laugh. No matter how shitty his day had been, that sound always gave him a lift.

"How about next week?" Bobby Lee slid behind the steering wheel. He leaned across and unlocked the passenger door.

Cy opened it and got in. "Yeah, maybe."

He'd never been in Bobby Lee's car before. Unlike the interior of his truck, the interior of the car was clean and well-maintained, especially considering its age.

"This car's got to be nearly as old as you, baby."

Bobby Lee stuck the key in the ignition but didn't turn it. "It was my nana's car. She had to stop driving last year so she gave the car to me instead of selling it."

"That was nice."

They both fell silent.

Bobby Lee rolled down the window and after a moment, Cy did the same. A soft breeze wafted in, bringing with it the whoosh of cars passing on the road and the quiet buzz of cicadas and chirrup of crickets.

The deepening shadows pressed in around them. Soon it would be full dark. Fortunately, the full phase of the moon was past and the encroaching night was no threat. Only Cy's own cowardice stood in his way.

"I'd like you to meet her some time, if you want." Bobby Lee spoke softly in the evening quiet.

"Who?"

"My nana." A pause. "Only if you want."

Cy laughed, a shiver of nerves making his stomach jitter. "Yeah, I can just see that, darlin'. How do, Miz Sonders ma'am. I'm the cowboy been fuckin' your grandson for the past couple months."

But Bobby Lee didn't join in his laughter.

"She knows I'm gay. My nana was the first person I told and she's okay with it." He took Cy's hand. Squeezed. "She'd like you, Cy."

Shit.

Bobby Lee wanted a relationship. Christ, he wanted to introduce Cy to his grandmother. Meeting the family was some serious shit. And Cy, God help him, thought he might just want that, too. But how could he start a relationship without telling Bobby Lee what kind of baggage he was bringing with him? He couldn't.

Bobby Lee started the engine and eased the Caddy into the flow of evening traffic on the interstate. They drove for a while in silence. Usually their silences were companionable, relaxed. Not this time, at least not for Cy.

He should have brought his truck.

Stupid ass.

Cy kept his attention focused out the window of Bobby Lee's ancient Cadillac at the other cars and trucks passing them on the highway. What the hell was he going to do if, after he broke the news about his snake, Bobby Lee put him out on the side of the road? He'd walk back to his truck, that's what.

The way he figured it, this could go one of a couple ways.

Bobby Lee would park somewhere out of sight, the way they sometimes did. They would fuck or maybe suck each other off. Then afterward, certainly it would be afterward, Cy had no illusions about that, he would tell Bobby Lee the truth about his snake. Just the thought of telling was enough to have Cy's stomach tying itself in knots. Once the news was broken, the next step was anybody's guess.

Would he be believed? And if Bobby Lee did believe him, would he turn away in disgust? In terror? Would he put Cy out on the side of the road? Oh, he knew being turned out for a lunatic was a distinct possibility, maybe even a probability. Most people, sane people, didn't believe in witches and curses and animal shifters. Hell, he wouldn't believe it himself if he wasn't part of it. If he and the men he cared most about, the men who had become his family, didn't turn scaly and furry and feathery each full moon.

Cy thought again about his truck sitting in the lot at A Bar Named Sue. "Stupid ass."

"What did you say?" Bobby Lee laid a hand on Cy's thigh.

"Nothin', baby. Just talkin' to myself is all." Cy covered Bobby Lee's hand with his. The heat of his lover's palm penetrated the worn denim of his jeans. Cy's cock stirred.

He should tell Bobby Lee the truth before they fucked. It was the honest thing to do, the honorable thing, his mama would say. Apparently he was not especially honorable because right now all he wanted was to sink his dick into Bobby Lee's velvety heat, to feel that mind-blowing pressure on his cock and, maybe for the last time, hear those sweet little noises his lover made when he came.

Bobby Lee slid his hand out from under Cy's and returned it to the wheel. He swung the Caddy into a parking lot and stopped just under a glowing sign that read "Tumbleweed Motor Inn." One of the e's in "weed" was out, so it actually read "Tumblewed Motor Inn."

Cy turned to his lover. But before he could ask what they were doing here, Bobby Lee spoke.

"We never done it in a real bed before, so I thought…" The parking lot lights flickered on. In the yellowish glow, his cheeks colored but his gaze remained steady.

Cy looked up at the sign then back into Bobby Lee's eyes. "What? The bed of my pick-up doesn't count?"

Bobby Lee laughed. "Not hardly." A pause. "It's all right, isn't it?"

Was it? Cy had no idea, but he nodded. "Of course it's all right."

Bobby Lee went in and rented the room and left Cy waiting in the car. While he waited, he tried not to think too much, tried like hell not to anticipate further than getting Bobby Lee naked between the sheets. The mental image of that sweet ass primed and ready for him was enough to have Cy's cock straining against his zipper by the time Bobby Lee returned with a key. He held it up and jerked a thumb toward the row of brightly painted doors that ran along a strip of concrete bordering the parking lot.

"We're in number six."

Bobby Lee led the way along the row of rooms. As they walked, Cy occasionally let his arm brush against his lover's. Aside from that small contact they didn't touch, even though the parking lot appeared to be deserted, save for the two of them.

They passed an ice machine that roared like a semi on steroids and a Coke machine that was nearly as loud.

Bobby Lee stopped in front of a yellow door with a black six painted on it. He stuck the key in the lock, turned it and the door swung open. A blast of arctic air hit Cy full in the face, bringing with it the nose-stinging smell of antiseptic and something else even less pleasant. He followed Bobby Lee inside and closed the door.

Inside, the room was typical motor-inn chic in shades of tan and brown. Shag carpeting had seen better days and cheap pressed-board furniture bore the scars of previous inhabitants.

Cy hardly had time to take all this in before he was shoved back against the door.

His breath whooshed out and he found himself pinned between the door and Bobby Lee's slender body. Their mouths came together so hard their teeth clicked. Bobby Lee's tongue thrust aggressively into Cy's mouth. He tasted like beer and like himself.

Cy wrapped his arms around his lover and took everything Bobby Lee gave him. His hat fell off but he hardly noticed as he cupped Bobby Lee's denim-clad ass and shoved his leg between the smaller man's thighs.

Bobby Lee rocked against Cy's leg, his cock a length of steely heat even through their clothes. Needy little sounds bled from his lips as his hands fisted in Cy's hair and he devoured Cy's mouth.

Cy broke the kiss, both of them gasping. "Jesus, baby, settle down. We got all night." Secretly he was pleased as punch with this aggressive side of Bobby Lee. Christ, the kid was so fucking hot he would have him shooting in his jeans like a damn teenager.

"Need you, Cy. Right now." Pulling out of Cy's arms, Bobby Lee caught him by the hand and dragged him to the bed.

Cy sat down on the edge and took hold of his boot. A tug and it was off. It hit the carpet with a muffled clunk. He repeated the process on the other boot as Bobby Lee stripped out of his clothes.

Cy paused as Bobby Lee bent to pull off his own boots, his jeans and underwear around his knees, his bare ass at eye level from where Cy sat.

Now that was a pretty sight. His cock jerked. Hurriedly, Cy shucked his own clothes.

Bobby Lee turned, stepping out of his jeans. His cock, fully hard and flushed dark with blood, glistened wet at the tip. He grinned.

"See something you like?"

Cy made a sound low in his throat, half growl and half moan, and reached for his lover.

His hands closed on slim hips and he drew Bobby Lee toward him.

"C'mere, baby. Let me taste that pretty cock of yours."

A bead of pre-come welled from the slit. Cy swiped it away with his tongue, savoring the salty, sweet flavor that had become so familiar.

Mmm. So good.

"Hang on a second, baby." Bobby Lee's words came out breathless and he let out a little laugh. "Let me get my shirt off, will you?"

He undid the buttons then shrugged the shirt off.

But as he half-turned to drop the shirt, Cy saw the bruises and froze.

"What the hell, Bobby Lee?" Releasing his lover, Cy stood.

"What?" Bobby Lee's smile faded, the laughter dying from his eyes. He tried to pull his shirt back on, but Cy grabbed it.

"Turn around," Cy ordered.

"Cy, it's nothing, really. Just let it go."

"I said, turn around." Cy kept his tone gentle but no-nonsense.

Angry bruises marched on an angle across Bobby Lee's back. Mostly faded to a sickly greenish-yellow, Cy could still see how bad they'd been not so long ago.

He traced the worst of the marks with a fingertip. "How'd this happen?"

Bobby Lee said nothing.

Cy waited.

Just when he was sure his lover wasn't going to answer, Bobby Lee spoke, his voice very quiet.

"A week or two ago I had some trouble with a guy at the garage."

"Who?"

"New guy. You don't know him."

Cy knew that Bobby Lee was out at work. He'd said that the garage owner and the other mechanics were his friends and all were okay with his orientation, which was why this thing—these bruises—were such a surprise.

"Joe know about this?"

Bobby Lee turned. He shook his head. "No, and I ain't telling him neither. I can handle this on my own."

Bobby Lee's gaze met Cy's, and Cy saw the challenge there. He kept his tone mild.

"Seems like Joe aught to know he's got a homophobe in his employ. Don't you think?"

Another shake of the head. "I ain't no tattletale." Bobby Lee folded his arms across his chest. Defensive. "I told you, I'm dealing with it."

Cy knew what that meant, or thought he did. He also knew, or thought he did, that Bobby Lee was not likely to listen to anything he said on the subject. Not right now, not with that look in his eyes and defensiveness writ large all over him. He knew, too, that not every gay man was as lucky as he himself had been. Finding a place like the Shifting Sands Ranch, and an employer like Daniel, was a rare blessing and he was grateful, especially at moments like this.

Swallowing the sick fury on his lover's behalf, Cy tried for a conciliatory tone. He held out his hands, palms up.

"Okay, baby. I reckon you know what's best." He reached once more for Bobby Lee, sighing with relief when the other man let him pull him close.

Cy played his lips over Bobby Lee's until he felt the other man's body relax, going soft and pliant in his arms. Cy drew his lover back to the bed. He sat down and positioned Bobby Lee between his legs with Cy's face right at crotch level. Holding his lover's hips, Cy pressed his thumbs into the twin hollows just next to those sharp-angled bones.

Bobby Lee's breath caught and Cy felt him shiver. Looking up, Cy locked gazes with his lover and slowly slid his lips over the head of Bobby Lee's cock. That silky, steely heat felt so good against his tongue.

Cy took Bobby Lee deep. The head bumped the back of his throat and he buried his nose in the curls at the base of his lover's cock and swallowed around the tip.

"Jesus, Cy." Fingers fisted in Cy's hair and Bobby Lee clutched at his shoulder with the opposite hand. "I can't stand up when you do that." He laughed. "Makes my legs all rubbery and shit."

Cy pulled off and chuckled. "Then get your sweet ass over here and lay down. Take a load off."

"Don't you mean get my load off?"

They both laughed, Bobby Lee's ending on a squeak as Cy tumbled him onto the mattress.

Kicking away the tangle of his jeans and underwear, Cy rolled on top of Bobby Lee. Their cocks slid together, so hot, so good. Cy crushed his mouth down on his lover's, pouring all his worry and need into the kiss.

What if this was the last time he ever had this, ever tasted Bobby Lee's mouth, ever felt that slim, strong body moving under him?

Cy shoved the thought away. If it was, then it was. Nothing he could do about it.

Except maybe not tell, a little voice in Cy's head whispered.

There was no full moon tonight. There wouldn't be another for weeks, so what was the rush?

Honesty, that's what. The need to tell the truth to the man he loved.

Yes, it was true, he loved Bobby Lee. Not that he'd said it out loud. Hell, he might never say it. What if Bobby Lee didn't feel the same? Or worse, what if he did? What if Cy said the words and Bobby Lee returned the sentiment only to take it back after learning about the curse and Cy's shifter form? That would be far worse than never having heard those words at all.

"Cy? Baby, what's the matter?" A calloused hand trailed down Cy's back and gave his ass a squeeze.

"Nothin's the matter."

"You lie like a dog, man." Bobby Lee laughed and wriggled underneath him. "You ain't even heard what I said, did you?"

"What'd you say?"

"I said, let me up so I can grab the lube and condoms, 'less you want to lay there and think all night instead of fucking me."

Cy forced a laugh and gave his lover a hard kiss before rolling off him. "There's nothin' I'd rather do than fuck that sweet ass of yours, you know that."

Rolling off the bed, Bobby Lee grabbed his jeans from the floor and rifled through the pockets. He produced a strip of condoms and several small packets of lube. Dropping the jeans, he tossed the supplies on the mattress.

Cy reached for a condom, but Bobby Lee batted his hand away. "Let me get you ready." Scooping up the condoms, he tore one off. "Gonna use my mouth."

At that news flash, all the blood left in Cy's brain headed south and all he could do was watch as Bobby Lee tore the condom open with his teeth.

"Lay back," Bobby Lee ordered. "Gonna make it so you can't think no more. Gonna slide this rubber all the way down with my mouth. Then I'm gonna ride that big cock of yours."

Bobby Lee bent over Cy's groin. He placed the condom between his lips then paused as his eyes met those of his lover.

Goddamn, that was a sight. Pretty Bobby Lee with his hair all mussed and his cheeks flushed, those beautiful eyes filled with desire so hot Cy could just about feel it scorching his skin.

Cy slid a hand into Bobby Lee's curls and guided his head down. As his lover's mouth closed over the head of his dick, Cy's breath caught. Bobby Lee's eyes rolled up as he smoothed the latex down Cy's shaft. He swallowed once around the head before pulling back and crawling up Cy's body.

Grabbing a packet of lube, Bobby Lee threw one leg over his lover's hips and straddled him, spreading wide as he opened the packet and squeezed its contents into his hand.

"Watch me, Cy."

Like he could do anything else. Cy chuckled, the sound ending on a groan as Bobby Lee plunged two fingers into his hole and began to work them in and out, in and out. A third finger was added and Bobby Lee's lashes fluttered down and he began to rock, fucking himself on his own fingers, making Cy crazy with wanting.

"Christ, darlin', you're gonna make me come just watchin' you do that."

The younger man laughed and opened his eyes. "Uh uh, no way. I want that pretty cock inside me when you shoot, baby." He scooted his knees forward, pulling the fingers from his ass.

Cy took hold of his own shaft and positioned it at Bobby Lee's opening. His lover slid down in a single smooth motion, taking Cy in to the root and settling his ass on Cy's hips before going still.

Cy closed his eyes, reveling in the exquisite heat and tightness of his lover's channel. He took hold of Bobby Lee's slim hips and just held on for a long moment. He couldn't let this man go, not ever, no matter what he had to do to keep him.

"Okay, baby?" Bobby Lee leaned forward, a lock of red-gold hair brushing Cy's cheek just before their lips touched.

Cy opened his eyes. His lover was so close, so warm, so everything he'd ever wanted.

"Just fine, darlin'."

They kissed. Bobby Lee opening for him on a soft sigh, his

tongue sliding past Cy's lips, his flavor flooding Cy's senses till he thought he'd like to drown in the taste of him.

"You ready, darlin'?"

Rather than an answer, Bobby Lee squeezed Cy's cock before rising up just enough to make his lover really feel it. He slid back down, a smile curving his lips and that was all the answer Cy needed.

He took hold of Bobby Lee's hips in a stronger grip as his boy began to rock, slowly at first, then harder and faster.

It was the best feeling in the world, better than anything Cy had ever known.

Sweat dripped into his eyes, stinging, and he blinked it away. He wanted, needed, to see his lover's face as his pleasure built and built. The flush that colored Bobby Lee's neck and climbed up into his cheeks then spread down his chest. The sweat that dampened the hair that curled around his face. The smell of that sweat and the sharper smell of sex coming off both of them. Cy was drunk on it, all of it.

"Shit, Cy, baby, I'm gonna come. Oh God, can't wait. Come with me." The muscles in the younger man's arms stood out. The heat of his thighs bracketing Cy's hips about seared him clean to the bone as need wrapped itself tighter and tighter in his belly.

Bobby Lee's movements grew shorter, faster, as he slammed his hips down again and again and again. His muscles clamped down on Cy's dick and milked him as Bobby Lee shot, spraying Cy's belly and chest with his spunk.

Cy's cock spasmed inside his lover's ass and he filled the condom, coming and coming 'til he thought he was just about wrung dry.

Bobby Lee collapsed forward on Cy's chest. They lay there, panting, hearts pounding, skin slick with sweat and cum.

Cy stroked a hand down his lover's back, enjoying the way Bobby Lee's heartbeat seemed to match his own.

I love you, Cy thought, and had to bite his tongue to keep from speaking the words aloud.

After what seemed like an eternity, but was probably no more than a few minutes, Bobby Lee sighed and levered himself up. Cy's cock slid out of his ass and he collapsed over to the side, molding himself along the length of Cy's body and pillowing his head on Cy's shoulder.

Turning his head, Cy caught Bobby Lee's lips in a brief kiss.

"Mmm." Bobby Lee tangled his fingers in the hair on Cy's chest and tugged gently. "You're so sexy. My sexy cowboy." He yawned and cuddled even closer, wrapping himself around Cy, one knee settling between Cy's knees, holding him there.

Now was the time to tell the truth and shame the devil.

Cy took a breath. "Bobby Lee?"

No answer.

"Darlin'?"

A soft snore was the only reply.

Relief flooded through Cy. It was colored with guilt, but Cy pushed that guilt away. Burying his face in Bobby Lee's hair, he inhaled the scent of sweat.

"I love you, darlin'," Cy whispered and closed his eyes.

FIVE

"So you finally decided to bring the old wreck in." Bobby Lee grinned at Cy. He pulled a rag out of his back pocket, scrubbed at the grease on his hands, then held one out. At the same time his gaze dropped to Cy's lips, lingered there for a fraction of a second while they shook hands, then skipped away.

It wasn't as good as a real kiss, not even close. But it was the only affection they would show here in the lot outside Joe's Garage where Bobby Lee worked.

Cy nodded and returned Bobby Lee's smile. "I told you I was gettin' to it. You got time to take a look at her today?"

Bobby Lee nodded. "It's a slow day. Shouldn't take too long. Not just to see what's the problem anyway."

They both fell silent. Heat baked off the parking lot surface under Cy's feet. He imagined he could feel it radiating up right through the soles of his boots.

"So is there somewhere I can wait?"

"You're welcome to wait inside. Joe don't pay no mind. But there's a diner right up the road a ways. Might be more comfortable waiting in there. The coffee's good and they got fresh-baked pies and cakes every day. I can give you a call once I take a look."

Bobby Lee pointed out the sign for Lu Lu's All Night Eatery and Cy headed up that way.

Inside, the diner smelled of coffee and fried food. Cy slid into a booth and removed his hat, setting it on the seat beside him.

A dark-haired woman in a pink polyester uniform approached, a menu in her hand, which she laid on the table. "Get you some coffee?"

Cy nodded. "Appreciate it."

He picked up the menu, glanced at it and laid it back on the table. He didn't want food. What he wanted was to talk to Bobby

Lee, to go somewhere, just the two of them, and talk.

Liar. Hadn't he had the chance to talk the other night and what did he do? Not talk, that was for damn sure.

He was a Goddamn coward and that was the truth. Judson was right, though Cy would be the last one to ever tell him.

The waitress returned with his coffee. She set the mug in front of him then pulled an order pad from her pocket.

"What can I get you?"

A set of balls would be good, Cy thought and felt his lips twitch.

"Just coffee, thanks."

"You sure, honey?" She cocked a hip and let her eyes roam over his face. "I'm sure we could find something that's to your taste." Then she winked.

Cy suppressed a sigh. "I don't think so."

"Suit yourself." She stuck her pad back in her pocket. "But if you change your mind…"

He watched her walk away, hips swaying. Why the hell were women always trying to get into his pants? He wondered what she'd say if she knew he preferred a hard male body under him than soft feminine curves. Of course that wasn't the sort of thing a man advertised, not in a town the size of this one. Being gay might not be a problem in Austin or Dallas, but here? If a man knew what was good for him, he kept his orientation to himself.

Cy sipped his coffee and looked out the window. That was one of the things he liked best about living and working on Daniel's ranch. His sexuality had never presented a problem, not for Daniel and not for any of the other men at the ranch. Come to that, the place seemed to be a safe haven of sorts. Though he had never openly talked about his orientation with anyone except Jud, Cy knew that at least five of the six men on the ranch preferred cowboys to cowgirls. And he often wondered about the boss himself. Not because of anything overt—hell, the man had been married to a woman for a time—but just a feeling he got from watching Daniel. The way the man looked at other men, not Cy himself but that young kid Russell? It liked to set Cy's gaydar pinging like a son of a bitch.

Too bad the kid had turned out to be such a little shit, fucking the boss's wife on the sly then sneaking off with her the way he did.

Not that Yi hadn't tried with the other ranch hands. He knew for a fact that she'd offered her favors to at least three of the guys. Hell, she had even tried with Cy himself.

🐎 🐎 🐎

He should have known what the little hellcat was up to, or at least that she was up to something, when she showed up in the barn—a thing she had never before done. And she was wearing jeans, another thing that was new, never mind those silly spike-heel boots she had on.

He was working with one of the horses, that new bay gelding Daniel had just bought. He was a real beauty, sleek and glossy with fine muscle tone and clear, bright eyes. But his right front hoof had gotten infected and not been properly tended, which had resulted in the horse going lame.

Cy was crouched down with the hoof on his knee when Yi entered the barn. She flipped her long hair behind her shoulder and leaned on the half-wall separating one stall from another. She watched him in silence for several minutes and Cy, always content not to talk, merely continued working.

Then the questions started. Not stupid questions either because Yi, whatever else you could say about her, was not a stupid woman.

Unsure what game she was playing, Cy at first kept his answers as brief as possible while still being polite. After all, Yi was Daniel's wife, and even if he had no regard for her, he did have regard for her husband.

Plus his mama had taught him to always respect women. He also suspected that she would soon tire of her questions and leave him to get his work done.

But she didn't tire. Instead she became more and more enraptured with the horse, or so it seemed, until she was crouched on the floor beside him and leaning in close enough that her perfume tickled his nose and her long black hair kept brushing his arm as he moved.

The tilt of her body and her closeness might, to another man, have spoken of seduction, but as soon as the thought crossed his mind Cy dismissed it. He was gay. Everyone, including Yi, knew he preferred cowboys to cowgirls, a thing he'd never made a secret.

So he concluded, mistakenly it turned out, that her interest was genuine. That after all this time of living on the ranch, Yi was finally making the adjustment to being a rancher's wife. And, God save him from his own naivety, Cy was glad. For Yi, sure, but mostly for Daniel.

After that, his explanations became more detailed, his attitude less standoffish, and she even helped him with a particularly hairy bit of business with the bay's hoof. Not that he let her do much other than hand him the things he needed to get the job done. And when Yi left the barn she was smiling, a rare thing indeed.

The trouble came a few days later, on Friday, when Cy had forgotten all about his encounter with Yi in the barn. As they often did on Friday night, several of the hands had gotten cleaned up after work and gone into San Antonio for a few beers or games of pool or what have you.

"You sure you won't come along?" Ben paused, his dress-up hat in his hand and the other hand on the doorknob.

Cy shook his head. "I'm just gonna stay around here. Maybe drink a couple beers while I watch the Rangers get their asses handed to them on the TV."

"Suit yourself." A grin tugged at Ben's lips. "What do you want me to tell that pretty little redhead if he asks about you?"

At the mention of Bobby Lee Sonders, Cy's cock perked up. *Down boy.*

"That boy's not likely to be askin' about me." When Ben

started to answer Cy waved him off. "Go on now. I expect you're keeping the others waiting."

With a shrug, Ben left. From outside Cy heard the sound of an engine starting up then the crunch of tires on gravel. He had the place to himself.

In his room Cy pulled off his boots and unbuckled his belt. Tugging his shirt free of his jeans, he stripped it off and with it, the sweat-stained T-shirt underneath. He needed a shower, bad.

As he reached for the buttons at his fly his thoughts returned to what Ben had said. Despite his denial, Cy secretly hoped that Bobby Lee would, if not ask about him, at least wonder where he was.

Undoing the last button Cy shoved his jeans and boxers down. His cock, which had begun to fill at the thought of the pretty redhead with the big eyes and the full lips, sprang free and he palmed it.

Mmm.

Sitting down on the edge of his bed, Cy kicked off his pants and underwear. He laid back, shut his eyes and wrapped his fingers around his swelling shaft. He spread his legs and began stroking, imagining those luscious lips wrapped around his prick, the big gray eyes gazing up at him over a mouthful of his cock.

Oh yeah.

Pausing, Cy spat in his hand then resumed stroking, the slickness of spit adding to the fantasy of how hot and wet and silky Bobby Lee's mouth would be. How sweet it would be to have that boy on his knees, Cy's hand buried in his curls and holding him there while Cy fucked his mouth.

Goddamn.

A soft sound had Cy's hand stilling. His eyes snapped open and he yelped in shock. Yi stood in the doorway to his bedroom, leaning casually against the jamb and smiling like she watched guys jerking off every day of her life.

Cy scrambled for something, anything, to cover himself.

Grabbing a corner of the bedspread, he yanked it over his lap. "What the hell are you doing in here?"

Her smile never even dimmed, in fact it grew brighter as she straightened from the doorjamb. "I could ask you the same." And the little slut walked over to the bed and sat down next to him, just as bold as you please.

Cy's face was so hot he thought his head might burst into flames any minute. He gathered more of the spread over him, though by then his erection was completely gone. "Look, Missus, I don't know what this is about but—"

"You know." Yi leaned toward him. Her breath wafted across his face. "I see how much you like me, Cyrus."

He should get the hell out of there, right fucking now. Except that would mean giving up his grip on the spread that was his only nod to modesty. His gaze darted around the room. His discarded clothes were too far away to do any good, and there was nothing else near to hand.

Shitfuckpiss.

Yi got to her feet and for a moment Cy thought she was leaving. Instead she straddled his legs and tried to put her arms around him as she rubbed herself against his thigh.

Too shocked to think, Cy stood up, dumping her off his lap backwards.

She squealed in surprise and landed flat on her ass on the floor. And that was the end of that.

Yi had jumped to her feet, shrieking at him in a weird mix of Chinese and English. He didn't understand half of what she said between her thickening accent and the tears that choked her voice. But one thing he heard quite clearly.

Just before she slammed out the door she turned back to him. Pointing one long, painted talon, she asked, "Why the hell were you so nice to me?"

And without waiting for an answer she stormed out, slamming the door so hard the frame shook.

✵ ✵ ✵

After that Cy had steered well clear of Daniel's wife and she of him. Most likely she'd turned her attentions to one of the others, all of whom, as far as Cy knew, had also rejected her. All except the kid, Russell.

The cell phone clipped to Cy's belt began to vibrate. Pulling it from the case, he glanced at the display and flipped it open.

"Hey, darlin'. That was quick."

Bobby Lee chuckled. "Hey, I'm good. What can I say?"

"True enough." Cy shut his eyes and felt the smile curve his lips as he reveled in the sound of his lover's voice and that sweet laugh.

Christ, he was so gone on Bobby Lee Sonders. It was not even funny.

"So you can come and get her anytime."

"What was the problem?" Cy reached for his wallet. He stood and threw some bills on the table. With the phone still pressed to his ear, he walked to the door.

"Busted connector."

"What kind of connector?" Cy opened the door and the heat slapped at him. A sheen of sweat broke out almost immediately over his face.

"You really want me to get into all the particulars, I can do that but…"

"Not especially."

Bobby Lee laughed. "I didn't think so." A pause. "All right then. I'll see you in a bit."

Cy flipped the phone closed as he made his way across the parking area to the road.

He was sure glad Bobby Lee had been able to fix the AC in his old wreck. The man was a good mechanic, no doubt about it. They could use someone out on the place who could fix stuff good as that.

Cy armed sweat from his face, resettled his hat on his head and turned toward the garage.

And who the hell was he kidding anyway? He'd just like to have Bobby Lee out at the ranch, no matter what the circumstances. Even if the man didn't know one end of a wrench from the other, or one end of a cow from the other, wouldn't make a damn bit of difference to Cy.

His boots crunched on the gravel shoulder of the road, the sound almost drowned out by the whoosh of cars and trucks passing at a breakneck speed and kicking up a scorching wind in their wake. As Cy drew nearer the garage, he let himself imagine it; Bobby Lee out at the ranch, living with them—with him— maybe sharing his room and his bed.

That would be sweet.

While he was still a half-block from the garage, Cy saw his truck. It was parked out front, the sun shining off its dull blue exterior. It would be hot as blazes inside and Cy once more spared a thought for the luxury of air conditioning and Bobby Lee's skill as a mechanic.

The scream of an air-wrench reached Cy's ears over the constant roar of traffic as he turned into the garage. Music blared from a boom-box. Some old country song about tears and beers and losing your baby to another man. He didn't know the singer, but the words struck a chord and he thought of Bobby Lee.

He scanned the men working in the bays. Where was his baby?

"Help you?"

Cy turned. It was Joe, the garage owner.

"How's things, Joe?"

"All right, I reckon. It's Cy, right?" Joe stuck out a hand, grimy with garage dirt, then seemed to think better of it. He wiped the hand on the leg of his coveralls, not much cleaner than the hand itself, and held it out again. They shook.

"That your truck outside?"

Cy nodded. "Bobby Lee was goin' to take a look at her for me."

"Havin' some trouble with her, are you?"

Cy nodded.

"If anyone can fix her up it'd be Bobby Lee. That boy's got motor oil in his veins."

Joe grinned and Cy returned the grin.

"Bobby Lee around?"

Joe glanced around the garage. "I think he's out back. You want I'll take a look or you could just go on out yourself."

"If there's someone in the office, I'll take care of the bill first, then I'll do that."

After settling up with the dark-haired receptionist who looked enough like Joe that she had to be a relative, Cy left the garage and headed around back to the small scrap yard Joe kept for spare parts. The garage dog, a black and brown mutt named Max, trailed after him.

Cy rounded the corner of the low building. He heard a grunt followed by the clang of metal against metal then the words spoken in a low growl.

"Watch it, faggot."

Sun struck chrome, momentarily blinding Cy, but not before he saw the two men. He recognized one immediately as Bobby Lee. The other man, a broad-shouldered stranger with dark hair and a plaid shirt, shoved Bobby Lee. Then, as the smaller man stumbled back, stuck out his foot. Bobby Lee tripped and went sprawling in the dirt.

The stranger laughed.

A wave of anger, sudden and hot, swept over Cy and he recalled the bruises he'd seen on his lover's body as well as the vague reference Bobby Lee had made to some trouble with a guy at work. So this was the asshole himself, big as life and guilty as fuck to boot.

Cy let out a hiss and lunged. He seized the bully by the collar, swung him around and slammed him into the wall.

"What the fuck?" The guy's fist came up, almost too fast for Cy to duck. Clearly this dickhead was used to mixing it up. Well, he'd mix him up, all right.

The punch glanced off Cy's shoulder. It didn't hurt, just fueled his fury.

Cy ploughed a fist into the other man's gut. Then as the guy doubled over, Cy hit him again with a hard jab to the face. There was a loud crunch of bone and blood poured from the bully's nose.

"Shit!" The man clapped a hand to his face. Blood dripped through his fingers. "You crazy son of a bitch! Get the fuck off me!"

But Cy wasn't finished, not by half. He drew back his fist, ready to teach this asshole a lesson he wouldn't soon forget. Hands gripped the back of Cy's shirt, strong hands, pulling him back and off the other man.

Cy twisted free rounding on the owner of the hands. It took a moment before he realized it was Bobby Lee. Cy swallowed, struggling to get a rein on his temper. Only when the red haze began to fade did he realize the intensity of the wriggling under his skin. He nicked his tongue on a fang and tasted blood.

Shitfuckpiss.

"What the hell you doing, Cy?" Bobby Lee's cheeks were flushed, his eyes bright with some emotion Cy didn't recognize, not at first anyway.

"That asshole hurt you." Cy glanced over his shoulder to where the bully now lay half-propped against the back wall of the garage, nose dripping blood, his face already swelling. "He's the one put them bruises all over you, ain't he? You tell me, Bobby Lee."

"Jesus Christ, Cy."

"What?" Shame had begun to creep in, blurring the anger, but

Cy already felt the scales forming, the dissolution of bones and elongation of muscles.

Christ, he had to stop this. Get control of himself and beat back the snake. He knew he could do it. He had better control now than when he'd first become a shifter.

Turning his attention from the man on the ground back to Bobby Lee, Cy realized that his lover was talking. His mouth was going a mile a minute, his hands gesticulating wildly. But Cy couldn't hear a word of it.

His hearing was all but gone. It was another manifestation of the snake.

Shitfuckpiss.

Bobby Lee jabbed the air with a finger. He pointed to the man who was wiping at his face with an already-bloodied shirtfront. The finger swung in Cy's direction, poked him in the chest, hard.

Bobby Lee had stopped talking and was staring at him, clearly waiting for Cy to say something.

Cy started to open his mouth, realizing only just in time that his tongue had already split. Between that and the fangs, he dared not even attempt speech. He'd learned through hard experience that if he did try, likely as not all that would come out was a hiss.

Not helpful.

He did the only thing he knew to do. He turned his back and walked away.

Please, let the keys be in the truck, Cy prayed as he staggered around to the front of the garage. Yanking open the door, he saw with overwhelming relief that the keys had been left on the dashboard. He climbed behind the wheel, slammed the door and grabbed for the keys. They fell from his numb fingers to the floor and slid under the seat.

Shitfuckpiss.

No way he was going to be able to drive if he couldn't even hold on to his Goddamn keys. Cy stared down at his useless hands.

What the hell was he doing? Running from the man he loved, from the truth about himself, because he didn't have the balls to just tell the truth and let be what would be.

Cy rested his head against the steering wheel and concentrated. He could beat back this Goddamn snake. He knew he could do it, had done it before once or twice. He forced his thoughts away from the snake and turned them toward how best to hold on to what he had with Bobby Lee. That was what mattered, the only thing that mattered. All the rest was just bullshit; the curse, the snake, his own cowardice, none of it mattered a wit if he lost the man he loved.

Someone tapped on the window.

Bobby Lee.

He motioned for Cy to lower the window.

Cy started to do it then saw that the scales had crept down his arms and now covered the backs of his hands. And what if he did manage to open the window? He couldn't talk, couldn't explain himself or his situation.

Meeting his lover's eyes, Cy shook his head.

Bobby Lee studied him for a long moment then he shrugged and turned away, but not before Cy saw the unspeakable sadness that filled his eyes.

Cy knew that sadness as if it were his own because, in a very real way, it was.

Six

They all sat around the dining room table, the remnants of their dinner having been whisked away, coffee and blueberry cobbler produced as if by magic instead of by Jud's talented hands.

"Great as usual, Judson." Daniel sat back in his chair at the head of the table. He covered his mouth and burped quietly.

"I'll say," Michael added, finishing his coffee and rising from his chair, cup in hand. "Can I get anybody more coffee?"

Everyone but Gordy, their resident caffeine addict, declined. Michael took Gordy's mug and disappeared into the kitchen, followed by Jud.

"What time's the moon come full tonight?" Ben picked up his napkin and wiped his mouth.

"Judson's the one always knows that." Daniel said. "He keeps track of that down to the minute."

Though they were all very aware of the phases of the moon, it had become something of an obsession with Jud, a thing they all teased him about even as they appreciated his knowing.

Returning with the coffee, Michael said, "It's cooled off considerably. It should be a fine night for sitting out on the porch."

The rest agreed.

As the months had passed since the whole shifting thing started, each of them had found his own particular place, some area of the house or grounds where he felt most comfortable when his beast came on him. After the time Gordy had accidentally shifted in the dining room and, in his panic had succeeded in breaking half the china in the cupboard, they had all agreed that it was just wiser for the larger men to make sure they were out of doors well in advance of moonrise, for the sake of the interior decorating if not for the men whose shifted forms made being indoors uncomfortable, if not dangerous.

"All right." Daniel got to his feet. "I'll be heading down to the creek, I think. Anyone need anything before I go?"

They all said no, they were fine, all but Cy who said nothing. He wasn't fine and hadn't been fine for weeks, not since he'd walked away from Bobby Lee that day at the garage.

Somehow he still wasn't entirely sure how he'd gotten out of there. After Bobby Lee had walked away, Cy had driven up the road apiece and pulled into a parking lot where he'd waited for the shift to take him. It hadn't, not completely anyway. Sure, his skin had turned scaly and his hearing hadn't returned for hours. And his tongue and teeth had stayed shifted until nightfall. But the snake, in all its reptilian glory, had stayed away.

And so had Bobby Lee, ever since that awful day.

"Cyrus?"

Cy looked up and found Daniel watching him. "Yeah, boss?"

"I asked if you were all right."

"Fine. I'm fine."

Cy pushed back his chair just as Jud swung through the door from the kitchen. "You ain't fine, Cy." Jud pointed at Cy's plate. "I never knew a man who was fine to pass up a perfectly good pot roast."

Before Cy could respond, Jud picked up Cy's untouched dinner and disappeared back into the kitchen.

Cy stood and, knowing he should steer clear, yet unable to make himself do it, he followed Jud into the kitchen. He was feeling just piss-poor enough that maybe mixing it up with Judson would set him back on track.

Hell, in a couple hours they'd all be shifted. Maybe he should wait till then and just take a big old snaky chunk out of his little rat's ass.

This thought had Cy's lips tugging into a grin, despite his ill temper. He would never harm Jud, not in a million years. Jud was like a brother to him. And though he loved all the men here at the ranch, there was no one he was closer to than Judson. Which probably went a long ways toward explaining why they were so good at poking at each other.

In the kitchen, he found Jud scraping the food from his plate into a bucket for the hogs. The spigot ran full force, the splash of the water filling the silence.

Cy waited, saying nothing.

Jud turned off the water. With the empty plate in hand, he turned around and saw Cy.

"You got something you want to say to me, Judson?"

Jud stacked the plate in the dishwasher. "Not unless you want to tell me what crawled up your ass and been eating at you from the inside out."

"Not particularly. Seems to me you're the one got some hair up his ass tonight." Cy turned away. He'd gone no more than two steps when Jud's voice stopped him.

"I'd think by now you'd have got accustomed to our situation." Jud paused but when Cy said nothing he continued. "It's been near two years, Cyrus. Ain't nothing any of us can do to change things. Brooding about it isn't going to help."

"I'm not brooding."

And he wasn't, much. Not about the snake anyway.

"The hell you ain't." Jud planted his feet and fisted his hands on his hips. He looked downright fierce. "For fuck's sake, man, I got a rat. At least you got a decent animal."

They glared at each other. Neither spoke. They might have stayed that way until the moon rose if Ben's voice hadn't interrupted.

"Cyrus," Ben called. "There's someone here to see you."

What the fuck?

Cy let out a breath and turned away, breaking the staring contest. Jud could kiss his ass. Fucking ratboy.

As he made his way to the front of the house he heard the clatter of plates resume in the kitchen behind him. He passed Michael in the dining room but didn't say anything. Stepping into the front hall, Cy froze. Bobby Lee stood just inside the front door, his hat in his hand, a tentative smile curving his lips. His gaze met Cy's. The smile tilted, then disappeared altogether.

"Surprise," Bobby Lee said, taking a step forward. He paused, uncertainty filling his eyes.

Cy stood still, unable to move or speak, only look at Bobby Lee as if he couldn't get enough. His slender frame clad in jeans and plaid shirt, his bright auburn curls tousled and his eyes filled with hesitancy. Something like a fist squeezed Cy's heart.

"I shouldn't have come." Bobby Lee spoke quietly. "I'm sorry, Cy. I just…"

He swallowed, his Adam's apple bobbed.

Cy's paralysis broke. He crossed the distance between them in three strides and pulled Bobby Lee into his arms. His hat fell to the floor, his arms winding around Cy's neck. Bobby Lee pressed himself close.

Cy kissed him.

Bobby Lee's mouth opened under his and he kissed back eagerly.

The taste of his lover flooded through Cyrus, filling every aching empty place inside him.

Breaking the kiss, Cy buried his face in Bobby Lee's hair and inhaled the scent of shampoo and soap and some light scent that he knew was just Bobby Lee himself.

Christ. He'd missed the man like breathing.

Not wanting to, but knowing it was necessary, he released Bobby Lee and stepped back. Cy scrubbed a hand over his face. "Jesus, Bobby Lee, what are you doing here?"

The smile that had returned after the kiss dimmed considerably. "I wanted to see you." A pause. "I missed you, Cy, and I thought maybe…"

Cy heard a sound behind him. Turning, he found Jud in the doorway. He scowled as darkly as he could manage but Jud didn't take the hint.

Jud's gaze flicked from Cy to Bobby Lee. "How do, son?" Jud came forward and held out his hand. "I'm Jud."

Bobby Lee took the offered hand. They shook. "I'm Bobby Lee Sonders."

"Nice to meet you. You a friend of Cy's?"

Bobby Lee nodded. "That's right."

Jud smiled. "Will you have some coffee and maybe a bite of cobbler? I think there should be some left if the starving mob didn't polish it off when I wasn't looking."

Bobby Lee's gaze cut to Cy then quickly returned to Jud. "Thank you, sir. That'd be nice."

"That's fine then." Jud clapped a hand on Bobby Lee's shoulder. "Though if you don't cut out the 'sir' stuff, I'm gonna have to kick your ass right and proper."

Bobby Lee laughed. "Yes, s—Jud."

Cy stepped forward. He had to stop this. Whatever the hell Judson was up to, he had to stop it right fucking now.

"Can I have a word with you?"

"Sure enough." Jud turned to Bobby Lee. "Right through that hallway, straight back is the kitchen. Make yourself at home and I'll be right along."

When Bobby Lee's footsteps faded, Cy turned on Jud. "What the fuck are you about?"

"Just offering some hospitality is all, since you don't seem to be."

"He can't stay here. When the moon comes full—"

"I know what happens when the moon comes full. But I'm Goddamn tired of watching you fuck up your life. That boy—"

"It's my Goddamn life," Cy yelled. He lowered his voice.

"It's my Goddamn life, and I want to fuck it up, it ain't nobody's business but mine. So fuck off with your meddling. You're bad as an old woman."

Jud started to say something then sighed. "Fine." He turned and started down the hall toward the kitchen.

Cy stared, speechless. It wasn't like Judson to back down like that. "What the hell is 'fine' supposed to mean?"

Jud stopped. He didn't turn, only glanced over his shoulder. "I never took you for a fool, Cyrus. But that boy, the way he looks at you, if you run him off instead of dealing with this thing…"

Jud shook his head then disappeared down the hall.

Cy pinched the bridge of his nose.

Well, shitfuckpiss.

Instead of going to the kitchen, Cy turned in the opposite direction. He needed a minute and he was Goddamn going to take it.

Shoving open the door, Cy stepped out onto the front porch. It was deserted, since everyone was around the back or off getting ready for the moonrise. Cy leaned on the rail and gazed off into the west where the sun was slowly sinking, turning the sky all shades of red and pink and orange. It was beautiful and dreadful. He remembered a time when the sunset was his favorite time of day. Now it only served to remind him of his situation, of all their situations.

In the yard, Bobby Lee's ancient Cadillac sat in a patch of late-day sunshine. Cy closed his eyes and thought of the last time he'd been in that car with Bobby Lee, of what Bobby Lee had said. Cy had held those words close to his heart, worn them like a charm over these past weeks even while knowing that they might be snatched away as soon as Bobby Lee learned his situation. Yet he'd known he couldn't let the words hang out there undealt with, unresponded to. Yet that was just what he'd done. Not for lack of sentiment—he felt it, all of it. The longing for something more than just sex. The desire to meet Bobby Lee's granny and to take the man home to meet Cy's sister and her big, noisy brood.

The need to say those all-important three words and hear them in return. But how unfair to want all that when he couldn't even be honest about who and what he was.

Cy scrubbed a hand down his face. He could tell Bobby Lee, should tell him and let the chips fall as they might. Or he could let him go.

Behind Cy, the screen door squeaked and someone stepped onto the porch. Cy opened his eyes.

"I shouldn't have come." Bobby Lee's voice was soft in the evening quiet. "I'm sorry, Cy. I'll just go now." He started down the steps.

"Wait." Cy straightened. "Bobby Lee, will you walk with me? I have somethin' I need to tell you." When the other man didn't answer immediately he added, "Please?"

"All right."

Cy led Bobby Lee around the main house and back toward the bunkhouse. They didn't talk; the only sound the crunch of their boots in the sandy soil.

Cy knew just where he wanted to do this. Outside his bedroom grew a large tree. He liked to go there and sit in its shade and think. It was where he'd gone just after they'd all learned about the curse, after that first awful full moon.

He took his lover to that spot. "Sit down for a while, will you?"

Bobby Lee looked from Cy to the tree then back. "Look, Cy, if you want to break up, if that's what you want to tell me, you can just say it."

"No." Cy pointed. "Will you just sit and let me do this in my own way?"

"You don't want to break up?"

"Christ, no!"

Bobby Lee sat and leaned his back against the tree trunk.

Cy sat beside him, his long legs stretched out in front of him.

He took his lover's hand and twined their fingers together.

"This place is special to me," Cy began. "This ranch and these men are special. They're like my family." He paused. "And what I have to say to you involves all of them because we all share something."

"You told me before that they're all gay. Does it have to do with that?"

"No. In fact Daniel, the man who owns the land was married to a woman for a time. It has to do with her, in a manner of speakin'."

With only a few false starts and more than a few hesitations, Cy told Bobby Lee about Yi and Daniel's marriage, how the woman had never really adjusted to ranch life, and how she had eventually left both the ranch and her husband.

"But before she left, she sort of…cursed the place and all of us along with it."

"Cursed? You mean like…" Bobby Lee's words trailed off and he waited.

"I mean she put a curse on us and on this place so none of us can leave here, not for long anyway."

"I don't understand."

Cy laughed. "Neither do we, really. We're only just beginning to know what it all means." He took a breath. This would be the hard part. "But there's more, somethin' that affects you particularly."

"Me? How?"

"Well, us. You and me." Cy squeezed Bobby Lee's hand. "You ever heard about shapeshifters?"

"You mean like werewolves?"

"Werewolves are one kind of shapeshifter. But I mean like men who shift into animal forms when the moon comes full. Because that's part of the curse. We all, the men who live and work here, we all shift every full moon."

Bobby Lee's eyes went so wide Cy thought they might just pop right out of their sockets. It was almost cartoonish and would certainly have been funny under other, less personal, circumstances.

"You mean y'all turn into a bunch of wolves once a month?"

"No, not exactly. We all have different animals, but none of us is a wolf." Cy ploughed on before he lost what was left of his nerve. "Our foreman turns into a horse and some of the others become a rooster, a bull and a dragon. And Jud, the man you met there in the house? He turns into a rat."

"What about you? What do you turn into?"

Cy shut his eyes briefly. He wasn't a praying man, mostly, but right then he sent up a little prayer to whoever might be listening that he would find some way to say this and have it come out right.

He opened his eyes. "I got a snake."

"A sn—" Bobby Lee swallowed. "A snake? You got a snake?"

Oh shit!

Cy clung to his lover's hand like a drowning man clings to a rope. "Bobby Lee, darlin', listen. It ain't what you think. I can—"

"No, Cy. Don't." The younger man shook his head. He glanced briefly up at the sky, just beginning to darken then his gaze returned to Cy's face. "Tonight's a full moon, ain't it?"

Cy nodded. He couldn't speak.

"So it'll happen tonight."

Another nod.

"Answer me something?" A brief pause. Bobby Lee seemed to be choosing his words with great care. "When you turn into the snake, are you still in there?"

Cy swallowed. "How do you mean?"

"I mean, are you still you even though you're wearing a snake's body? Would you still recognize me?"

What was Bobby Lee getting at? Cy had no clue, but he answered anyway.

"'Course I would."

"Then I want to stay while it happens. Tonight. Here, with you. Can I?"

They had a strict rule, really more like an understanding since they'd never spoken of it, that there would be no outsiders allowed on the ranch when the moon was coming full. Cy looked up at the sky. There was no time to find the others and ask what they thought. This decision was all his.

Cy turned back to Bobby Lee. "I thought you was scared of snakes."

Bobby Lee smiled and Cy felt that familiar clutch in his chest.

"I ain't scared of you, Cy."

"But why do you want to do this?"

"Because I love you."

So simple. So sweet. And so Goddamn humbling. He'd been such a fool and his foolishness had nearly lost him the only thing that mattered.

Cy reached for his lover and pulled him close. With no hesitation, Bobby Lee wrapped himself around Cy and rested his head on Cy's shoulder.

"I love you too, darlin'."

🐍 🐍 🐍

Cy offered to remain outside and let Bobby Lee watch through one of the bunkhouse windows, but his lover wouldn't hear of any such thing. So they sat together on the bed in Cy's room, not touching, not talking, just waiting as the twilight pressed in at the window and the moon began her ascent.

Cy felt it growing stronger, the creepy crawly sensation that he recognized as the stirring of his beast. It would come any time now, but for once the shift wasn't the utmost thing on his mind.

Cy watched his lover, studied him, acutely aware of every change in his breathing, every movement no matter how slight, right down to the flicker of an eyelash.

"It'll be soon, darlin". You ready?"

Bobby Lee nodded.

He knew exactly where the moonlight would fall, had positioned himself just there, ready to catch that first silvery shaft when it cut through the darkened window.

Cy's fangs descended and his tongue split. His hearing grew muffled as the beast rushed up, desperate for release with the moon on the rise.

"Cy? Baby, I feel funny."

Bobby Lee's words reached Cy from far away. But when he tried to respond, Cy found he could no longer form words. Instead what came out was a long hiss.

And suddenly the beast was on him. Cy fell back on the bed, the shift taking him faster than it ever had before. Cy found himself on the floor in a tangle of his own clothes. He twisted free, feeling the powerful undulations of his snake's body, all that graceful strength. It had never been like this, not for him.

Cy slid free of the clothing and raised himself up, searching for his lover, needing to see Bobby Lee's reaction.

What he saw was like a blow to the center of his chest, if he'd had a chest, that was.

In the center of Cy's bed, curled in a ball, lay a sheep. An honest-to-Christ, wooly, four-footed sheep with huge and oh-so-familiar, gray eyes.

Bobby Lee? What the hell?

The sheep opened its mouth. And though Cy's hearing was gone because, of course, snakes have no ears, he heard the sound in his head anyway.

"Baaaah."

ALL THE
MOON LONG

ALLY BLUE

Looking back, Judson Jorgensen figured his first—and possibly worst—mistake was laughing at Yi when she tried to seduce him.

He couldn't help it, though. It was just so damn funny. She'd come sashaying into *his* kitchen dressed like a high-priced whore, shoved her boobs in his face and offered to share her other girl parts with him. He'd cracked up. If she didn't already know he'd rather have a hot, sweaty cowboy than a pampered female wrapped in silk and reeking of expensive perfume, she fucking deserved to be laughed at. It wasn't like he'd ever pretended to be straight.

Wasn't like it was her first time trying to cheat on Daniel, either. Jud had caught her at it more than once. Any man coming out to Shifting Sands best have his guard up against one whip-smart beauty on the prowl for dick.

He'd found out pretty quick that the little hellcat had a thin skin and no sense of humor. Of course her cussing him out in that heavier-when-she's-pissed-off Chinese accent had just made him laugh harder. He hadn't even stopped when she slapped him across the face and stomped out in high temper.

He hadn't found out until after she'd gone that she'd propositioned every single hand on the Shifting Sands Ranch, and been shot down by all but one. Jud was the last, barring the fucktard who'd gone with her. She must've been pretty desperate by then.

If he'd known what she'd end up doing at the time she made her move on him, maybe he wouldn't have laughed quite so hard.

Then again, maybe it wouldn't have changed anything. Who the hell believed in curses, anyway? They couldn't have known what would come of their collective rejection.

Or maybe Russell did, he thought, not for the first time. *Maybe that's why the bastard went with her instead of telling her to go to hell.*

"Spineless little shit," Jud muttered, guiding his battered brown van off the narrow ranch road onto the highway leading into town. "Wish he'd show his stupid face around here just one more time. I'd give him the sharp side of my fuckin' teeth."

It wasn't that being a shapeshifter was so awful, really. There were fun parts, even if it had taken him a long time to get over himself and admit it. But dammit, why'd he have to be a fucking *rat*? Why couldn't he be a dragon, like Daniel? His first sight of his boss's alternate form had sent him scurrying under the house in abject terror, but there was no denying the coolness factor.

At least he didn't destroy a perfectly good set of clothes every time a fit of temper forced him into a shift. He'd been caught buck-ass naked more than once before he learned to control—or at least predict—his inner rodent, but he didn't mind that so much. The exhibitionist in him even liked it a little. He had a nice body, if he did say so himself, and he didn't mind showing it off.

Too bad the one man he most wanted to see him in the altogether didn't seem interested in moving past the maybe-I'm-flirting, maybe-I'm-not stage.

Speaking of which, Woody expected him at the shop in half an hour to pick up his order. He needed to shake a leg if he was going to get there on time. He pressed his foot harder against the accelerator.

The trip to San Antonio passed in silence, broken only by Jud's occasional off-key whistling. Jud hated country music—which was a mortal sin in Texas—and top-forty held only slightly more appeal, so he left the radio off and drove to town with only his thoughts for company. He knew from long experience to keep those thoughts clean, unless he wanted to face his friend-slash-secret-crush with a woody of his own.

Thirty-two minutes later, Jud pulled the van into the parking lot of Wee Bee Kitchen Supplies & More. He slid out of the air-conditioned vehicle into the suffocating July heat. Instantly, sweat beaded on his brow and upper lip and dampened the armpits of his T-shirt. He hurried to the low adobe building, pulled the door open and sighed with relief when the blessedly cool air hit him. He'd lived here for going on twenty years now, but he didn't think he'd ever truly get used to the heat. The Tennessee mountains where he'd been born and raised just weren't this hot. Especially not at nine-thirty in the damn morning.

"Woody!" he called, sauntering toward the back of the store. "You here, man?"

"In the freezer," the familiar voice called. "Come on back."

Jud skirted the counter and walked through the half-open door into the storeroom. His heart hammered against his ribs as he made his way through the maze of box-filled metal shelves to the big walk-in freezer at the back of the room. He shook his head, both amused and disgusted with himself. A forty-year-old shouldn't react like a hormone-crazed teenager just from the sound of a man's *voice*, for fuck's sake.

He found Woody inside the freezer, piling paper-wrapped tuna steaks in a big cardboard box. "Hey, JJ," Woody greeted him, flashing the dimpled smile that always made Jud's knees weak. "I'm just getting your stuff together now, won't be a second."

"'S okay, I'm not in any hurry."

Woody nodded and turned back to his work. Those molasses-colored eyes lingered on Jud just long enough to make his insides squirm with a need he figured was doomed to go unfulfilled. Leaning against the doorframe, he tried to stare without looking like he was staring. Though really, Woody ought to be used to it by now. He turned heads wherever he went. Long, lean body, skin the color of milky hot chocolate, jet-black hair that curled enticingly around his face and neck. He had his Scottish mother's sweet round cheeks and his Mexican father's big dark eyes, but the charismatic personality was all his own. It was that more than anything that drew Jud to him like a flower to sunlight.

Yeah, you and half the population of San Antonio.

"How's your mom doing?" Jud asked, partly because he liked Bea and wanted to know, and partly just to listen to Woody talk.

"She's good. Just left yesterday for a week-long trip to New York City with her Senior Singles group." Slotting the last two steaks into the box, Woody hefted it in both hands and headed toward the freezer door. "Could you shut the door for me?"

"Sure thing." Jud stood aside to let Woody pass, then followed him out, switching the light off and closing the door behind them. "I can't believe you got Bea to leave the shop for a whole week."

Woody laughed, sending delicious shivers up Jud's spine. "Me neither. But I'm glad I did." Out of the storeroom, Woody carried the box to the checkout counter, set it down and started taping it shut. "She loves this place, and it pretty much kept her going after Dad died, but she takes too much on herself. I'm thirty-seven, for God's sake, I'm perfectly capable of running the place without her."

Chuckling, Jud moved to stand as close to Woody as he dared. "You're damn good at it, actually. I wouldn't get my kitchen supplies anyplace else, I tell you that."

Woody turned to face him, dark eyes sparkling with gratitude and something else, something Jud was afraid to name. He gulped.

"Thanks, JJ," Woody said, his voice soft. "I hope you don't mind me saying so, but you're my favorite customer."

Jud licked his lips, which had suddenly gone bone-dry. Woody stood so close, Jud could smell his clean, musky scent. God, Jud wanted to touch him. Just reach out, lay his palm on that broad chest, run his fingers through that dark hair and see if it felt as silky as it looked.

He swallowed and looked up to search Woody's face. The lips Jud had dreamed of kissing for so long were parted just a little, the dark eyes heavy-lidded and full of a simmering heat. Jud's heart attempted a flying leap right up his throat. Was Woody coming on to him? Finally, after nearly seven years of low-key almost-flirting and innuendo?

Only one way to find out. Jud curled a hand around Woody's shoulder and pulled him closer. This close, he could see tiny flecks of gold in Woody's eyes. Jesus, but the man was beautiful. Wondering if he was being admirably bold or just plain dumb, Jud rose up on tiptoe, tilted his head and pressed his mouth to Woody's.

For a second, Woody's lips moved against Jud's, and life was perfect. Then Woody seemed to realize what was happening. He stiffened and pulled away, and Jud's heart plummeted into his feet.

"I'm sorry," Jud said, looking anywhere but at Woody's face.

"Um. It's okay." Hands shoved in his jeans pockets and shoulders hunched, Woody turned to lean his back against the counter. His head hung down so his hair curtained his face. "I, uh, I don't have your pressure cooker yet. It didn't come in with yesterday's delivery."

"That's okay. Don't have anything to can yet anyhow." *Stupid, Jud. Stupid, stupid, stupid. Way to royally screw up, fucktard.*

"I'll call you when it comes in."

"Yeah. Okay."

An awkward silence fell. Jud wished the ground would open up and swallow him whole. He stared at the wide plank floorboards, wondering if he should ask Woody to get the rest of his order or if it would be okay for him to go get it himself. He just wanted to get the hell out of here before he died of embarrassment.

Woody let out an impatient breath. "Look, Jud, I—"

The front door swung open. "Hello? I'm looking for Woodrow Villareal, I'm told he's the manager and can help me find what I'm looking for."

Woody scowled, and Jud almost laughed in spite of everything. The man hated being called by his given name.

"I'll be right with you," Woody called over his shoulder. He gave Jud an apologetic look. "Let me see what this guy needs, then I'll get the rest of your order for you."

"It's all right, I'll get it." Jud forced a smile. "I know where you stash my stuff."

"Okay. Yeah." Woody glanced at the white-haired man studying the cappuccino makers behind him, then turned back to Jud. "Um. Okay, so…okay." He swiveled on one heel and strode over to the other customer.

Jud shuffled into the storeroom, cursing under his breath. Of all the boneheaded things he could've done, didn't he just have to pick the one most likely to damage his friendship with Woody beyond repair. Dammit.

Grabbing one of the hand trucks beside the door, Jud rolled it to the shelf at the back where Woody kept the Shifting Sands orders. He loaded the boxes onto the cart and pushed it out of the storeroom and into the shop. To his relief, Woody was on the other side of the room, showing the old man the blenders. Jud perched the box of tuna on top of the rest, then maneuvered the hand truck out the door and across the hot tarmac. For once, he didn't rush through loading the supplies into the van in the blistering heat. Right now he'd rather melt into a greasy puddle than face Woody again.

Unfortunately, not going back in wasn't an option. He had to return the hand truck and he still needed to pay for his order. Maybe he could leave cash on the counter instead of paying with the ranch credit card.

That hope was blown to hell when the old man passed him in the doorway, carrying a professional-grade blender. He gave Jud a nod and smile, which Jud returned automatically.

There wasn't one other car in the parking lot. He'd be alone with Woody.

Half an hour ago, that would've been something to look forward to. Now, it sort of made him feel sick.

Steeling himself for the inevitable, Jud dragged the hand truck inside and forced himself to walk up to the counter where Woody stood. He pulled out the credit card and handed it over. Woody rang him up in silence. Jud signed the credit card slip and stuck it in his pocket along with the card without once meeting Woody's gaze.

"Thanks," he mumbled. "Let me know when that pressure cooker comes in."

"Uh-huh."

"Well. Um. Okay. Bye."

Jud was almost to the door when a warm hand on his shoulder stopped him. He turned and looked up, straight into Woody's wide, worried eyes. The smooth brow was furrowed, and the long fingers trembled. Jud stilled. He had no idea what Woody would say, and wasn't sure he wanted to find out.

"JJ, I think…" Woody trailed off, frowning.

"Yeah?"

Woody opened his mouth, closed it again and shook his head. "Nothing. Just…don't worry about anything, you know?"

Some of the tightness in Jud's chest eased. He nodded. "Okay. Thanks."

"Talk to you soon, JJ."

"Yeah. Bye."

Woody turned back to the register. Jud walked out into the sunshine with as much dignity as he could muster.

For the first time in…well, ever, as far as he could remember, Jud drove away from Wee Bee with a sense of relief. He'd made a colossal idiot out of himself. It was just damn lucky for him that Woody evidently wasn't going to hold it against him.

Of course, his damned impulsiveness had pretty much fucked up any miniscule chance he might've had of being more than friends with the man.

"Yeah, like that was gonna happen anyhow," he grumbled, swerving around a puttering Buick with rather more force than necessary. "You're a *rat,* for fuck's sake."

And Cy's a snake. But Bobby Lee loves him. He knows, and he loves him anyway. Even turning into a sheep once a month hadn't stopped Bobby Lee from loving Cy.

Scowling, Jud shoved aside the insistent little voice of hope. He wasn't in any mood for pointless optimism right now.

You need to get laid. It was true. He hadn't had sex in almost two months, and his skin itched with the need for a hard cock up his ass. The problem was, only one man appealed to him anymore.

He had to close his eyes and pretend he was with Woody just to get it up. The last time he'd been with anyone—that closet-case rodeo rider who'd only been passing through, thank Christ—he'd actually moaned Woody's name. That hadn't gone over well. Which was why he'd decided he either had to have Woody for real, or form a deep and meaningful relationship with his right hand and his dildo.

He snorted. Maybe he could name the dildo Woody.

🐾 🐾 🐾

"Full moon tonight," Daniel announced at breakfast two days after the debacle at Wee Bee. "Y'all make sure you got everything squared away before moonrise. I don't want any incidents this time."

Michael scowled at his plate. "Wasn't *my* fault the barn door latch broke right at sunset and I didn't have the part to fix it. Only one horse got loose, anyhow."

Daniel arched an eyebrow. "Yeah, well, we're all just damn lucky that mare was in heat, else she probably wouldn't've followed Ben back home."

"Don't remind me," Ben said, shuddering. "I had nightmares about that mare for *days*."

Everybody at the table laughed. Jud snickered behind his coffee mug. It *had* been pretty funny to see the mare lifting her tail and nudging her rear up against Ben, trying to get him to mount her.

Cy caught Jud's eye across the table. He didn't say anything, but Jud knew what he was thinking. This was the first time Jud had so much as cracked a smile in two days. In fact, he'd snapped and yelled so much the men were avoiding him, and Gordy had told him to quit acting like a hormonal girl. Cy's smile said he was pleased to see Jud laughing about something.

And he's probably wondering why I've been in such a rotten mood in the first place, Jud thought morosely.

If things had gone differently, Cy would've heard all about it by now. As it was, Jud didn't feel like talking about it. He could tell his friend was worried, but Cy knew better than to push him.

Jud forced himself to return Cy's smile. Cy gave him a nearly imperceptible nod before digging into his second helping of *huevos rancheros*.

After breakfast, the men headed out to their various tasks while Jud started clearing the table. Cy poured the last of the coffee into a thermos, taking his sweet time about it. As if he were actually going to take it with him, hot as it was outside.

Jud shook his head. The man had no subtlety.

"What's up, Cy?" Jud asked after the rest of the guys had gone and Cy was still fiddling with his coffee.

"Nothin'. Just gettin' some coffee." Cy leaned against the counter, pale blue eyes following Jud's every move. "What's up with you?"

Jud sighed. "I'm okay."

"Somethin' happen with Woody?"

Fucking hell. Never should've told him I wanted Woody. Jud set his stack of plates in the sink and crossed his arms. "I don't wanna talk about it."

Cy shrugged. "Might help."

"Yeah, you're probably right. But I don't want to."

"All right." Pushing away from the counter, Cy crossed the kitchen in a couple of strides of those long, lanky legs and laid a hand on Jud's shoulder. "You change your mind, just say the word."

Cy stuck his hat on his head and walked out without another word. Jud waited until he was alone, then slid into one of the empty chairs and buried his face in his hands.

As usual, Jud felt the twitchy, crawling sensation inside him hours before the moon rose. The change always worked that way with him. Creeping up a little at a time, until the moonlight actually touched him. After that...well, he'd learned pretty fast to make sure he wasn't in public. Turning into a rat in the bathroom at a bar was bad enough. Becoming human again while miles from home and bare naked was worse.

At least the one time that had happened to him, he'd managed to swipe a pair of jeans off someone's clothesline and hitch a ride back to Shifting Sands. Nowadays, he made it a policy to never *ever* leave the ranch on the day of the full moon.

Jud served dinner early, like he always did on That Night. No one said much. Everyone, including Jud, was too busy stuffing their faces to make small talk. Shifting used up a lot of energy. Jud took pride in making sure his friends—his family, really— were well-fed and as ready for the change as possible.

Daniel was the first to push away from the table. "Okay, I'm off. You boys stay out of sight and keep your noses clean 'til morning." Picking up his glass, Daniel drained the last of his milk. "Y'all know the drill. If there's an emergency and you got no choice but to find me, send Ben or Gordy out to the woods to get me."

"But only as a last resort." Gordy's mouth curved into a wry smile. "Don't worry, boss. There's not too many situations you need a dragon to solve."

That got a half-hearted laugh all around. Shoving his chair back, Jud walked over to the fridge and pulled out a pile of choice-cut steaks he'd thawed out the day before. "Here," he said, thrusting them into Daniel's hands. "For later, when your dragon comes out."

"I just ate enough for five people," Daniel protested.

"Yeah, but I bet it's not enough for one dragon. You're always more wiped out than the rest of us after you shift back." Jud shrugged. "I just figured maybe some extra meat might give you more energy. Make you feel better after."

Daniel gave him a smile. "You got a point there. All right, I'll give it a shot. Thanks."

Jud nodded. "Sure."

Daniel grabbed his keys from the hook by the kitchen door and stalked outside. As if his leaving was some kind of signal, everybody stood and scattered to get ready for the change. Jud took a pile of plates to the sink and scraped the small amounts of uneaten food into a pail for the hogs. He gazed out the window toward the west. On the horizon, he could just make out the dark line of the forest where Daniel went to hide during his shift.

He worried about Daniel being out there all alone—hell, they all did—but it was better than having an unexpected visitor show up and catch sight of an honest-to-Christ dragon. Daniel's animal form couldn't just blend in with the livestock or hide under the furniture like the rest of them.

By the time Jud got the kitchen cleaned and returned to his room just down the hall, full night had fallen. He undressed, switched off the bedside lamp and sat cross-legged on the colorful braided rug his Great Aunt Violet had given him when he first left home for the wider world. When the moon rose, its light would pour through the window in a silver-white flood and he'd be transformed faster than thought.

Leaning his bare back against his bed, Jud stared out into the star-speckled heavens. It was a beautiful night. Maybe he'd go outside for a while after he shifted. He loved exploring the great outdoors in rat form. The small dark places around the house and beneath the shrubs fascinated him. Sometimes he ran into stray cats, but he could fend them off easily enough as most of them would rather catch field mice than fight a rat nearly their own size. The only things he was really afraid of were hunting owls, and he'd be safe enough from them as long as he didn't go out in the open.

As the time approached, the squirmy sensation of the coming change intensified. Jud consciously relaxed his body, breathing slow and deep and letting the strange feeling wash through him. He'd learned not to fight it. If he just let it happen, it was so much easier. Not pleasant, no. Not by a long shot. But fighting it made it worse.

Finally, a sliver of white peeked over the edge of the window.

Jud shut his eyes. He felt the moonlight touch his skin, then the change tore through him, ripping his body apart and remaking it. When he opened his eyes again, the window seemed hundreds of feet above him and the bed was as tall as a barn.

Twitching his whiskers, Jud scampered out into the hallway. The house was deserted, the other men—animals by now—either holed up in their own hiding places or running free on the ranch. All the lights in the main house or bunkhouse were off, leaving the whole place pitch black. None of them wanted the house to look welcoming if a visitor should happen by. Uninvited guests were rare, especially at night, but you never could tell what might happen.

Jud headed for the kitchen, where he'd installed the world's tiniest pet door in the outside entrance when it became clear that this whole were-critter thing wasn't going away. He dashed across the kitchen floor, claws clicking on the tiles, and threw himself headlong at the pet door. A running start, he'd found, guaranteed he got the damn thing open the first time.

The second he tumbled onto the big covered porch, he knew something was wrong. Two tall denim towers rose directly in front of him. One of them was on the move, coming toward him, fast.

Jud tried to stop, but his feet skidded on the wide planks of the porch. The rubbery gray thing at the bottom of the tower slammed into his side. He went sailing through the air, hit the edge of the doorframe and fell to the porch. A startled yelp sounded from somewhere miles above him, just before the thing which had just hit him—someone's sneakered foot, he realized in a flash of insight—landed on his right hind paw, and he felt the bones crack.

The pain was so huge Jud couldn't even move. His lungs seized up, his vision went gray and spotty. He'd broken his arm once, but it hadn't hurt anywhere near as much as this. The tiny bones in his paw felt like they'd been ground to powder.

Above him, the denim-clad legs bent. A gigantic head and torso loomed over him, bringing with them a familiar musky scent.

Some of the pain faded in a dizzying rush of adrenaline. Darkness hid the person's face, but Jud knew that scent just as sure as he knew his own name.

Woody.

Jud didn't waste any time trying to figure out just what in the hell Woody was doing here. He had to get away, before Woody decided to add one lame rat to his collection of strays. The man had a crazy soft spot for animals. Jud had been out to his house once, about a year ago. He'd counted two caged squirrels, five beagle puppies, a goat, a pair of potbellied pigs and a three-legged white Persian cat, and that was just in the house and backyard. He didn't even want to know what all lived in the big barn at the back of the property.

Keeping his broken foot tucked close to his body, Jud turned around and hobbled toward the pet door. A sharp pain shot through his side where he'd hit the doorframe. Cracked rib, most likely.

Ignore it. Go. Get back inside. The door's locked, he won't be able to get you.

He'd reached the door flap and was wondering how in the hell he was going to get it open when a large swatch of fabric fell on top of him. It smelled like Woody. Big, gentle hands slid beneath him, wrapping the T-shirt around his body as they lifted him into the air.

"'S okay, little guy," Woody murmured, cradling Jud against his chest. "Didn't mean to hurt you. I'm sorry."

Jud stared up at Woody over the edge of the dark blue fabric swaddling him. The T-shirt kept his paws close to his body. Woody used one hand to support his spine while the other held the back of his skull in a firm grip. Jud could barely move his head, and he couldn't move his feet at all. He couldn't have bitten or scratched even if he'd wanted to, which of course he didn't.

Part of him was glad Woody had the sense to protect himself from what was, as far as he knew, a wild rat, which would hurt him if it could. A deeper part of him wished Woody knew exactly what it was he held.

"You're no wild rat, are you?"

Jud let out a tiny squeak of surprise. He knew Woody was smart, but *damn*. How the hell had he figured *that* out?

Woody started walking the length of the porch, heading around the side of the house and toward the front door. "We'd better find your daddy, little guy. I don't think he's in the house. Hell, I don't think *anybody's* in the house. And I gotta tell him about you."

Jud stared up at Woody's slightly stubbled chin, wondering what in buggering fuck he was talking about. Jud's *daddy*? As in, his *rat* daddy? They weren't running a rodent farm out here, for God's sake.

At the front door, Woody pounded the solid oak with his fist. "JJ?" he shouted. "You in there? I hate to bother you, but...um, your rat's hurt."

For a heart stopping second, Jud thought Woody *knew*. Then the realization hit him like a rock to the head, and he groaned inwardly.

Jesus fuck, he thinks I'm my own pet.

If Jud's rat face could've scowled, he would've done it. That's what he got for muttering about "my rat" in public once too often. Although to be fair, it was probably the pet door that gave it away. A wild rat *might* run out a suspiciously small door flap, but it probably would not try to run back in.

By the time Woody had skirted the house, knocked and hollered at the bunkhouse door and even poked through the barn, Jud had slipped into a Twilight Zone comprised of equal parts hypnotic movement, throbbing pain and the soothing sound of Woody's heartbeat in his ear. He had no idea what Woody would do when he realized nobody was home on the whole ranch, but there wasn't a damn thing he could do about it in any case. Once the adrenaline drained away and the shock of seeing Woody in this context wore off, the pain in Jud's broken paw had grown into an agony so intense he almost couldn't feel it. With most of the night still ahead of him, he figured he might as well rest while he still could.

At least the others had seen Woody carrying him around by now. Bobby Lee had bleated at them from the stall where he and Cy sometimes curled up together, and Jud had caught a glimpse of Ben staring over the rail of the riding ring next to the barn. Michael, in a rare display of spunk, had squawked and pecked at Woody's feet.

"Well, shit." Woody stopped next to the passenger door of the Wee Bee delivery van. "Nobody's here, little guy." A thumb tenderly stroked Jud's head, and for a second he wished he was a cat so he could purr. "Let's just go leave JJ a note, yeah?"

A note. Oh yes, that's great. What was he going to do, leave Jud on the porch with a folded-up piece of paper under him saying "Sorry I broke your rat"?

This night just keeps getting weirder.

Shifting Jud carefully to the crook of his left arm, Woody opened the van door, reached inside and fished a small notepad and pen out of the glove compartment. He laid the pad open on the seat and scribbled for a minute, then tore off the sheet.

As he backed out of the door, Jud caught a glimpse of a large box sitting just behind the space between the seats. The yellow glow of the overhead light illuminated a picture of a new model pressure cooker.

Damn. He came out to deliver the fucking thing himself.

Jud didn't know whether to feel happy that Woody still liked him enough to do that, or irritated that he'd picked *tonight* to do it.

Woody headed back for the porch, the folded note clutched in one hand. He walked around to the kitchen door, probably figuring that was the one Jud would be most likely to enter through, and wedged the note between the door and the frame. That done, Jud expected to be laid on the porch, or maybe settled into a shoebox or something. He steeled himself for a long, torturous night. Maybe Cy or Michael would come stay with him until morning.

Jud was surprised when, instead of leaving him, Woody cradled him closer, turned around and headed for the steps. *Where the hell's he going?* Jud hoped he wasn't about to be dumped in the barn loft in a misguided attempt to keep him away from the horses. The *real* rats that sometimes skulked around up there didn't much like Jud as a rodent, and he wasn't in any shape to fight them off.

"Fuck!" Woody stopped abruptly on the bottom step. "Jesus Christ."

All Woody's muscles had gone hard and tense. Jud squirmed, trying to spot what had startled the man, but all he could see over the fold of Woody's T-shirt was the Wee Bee van, and the roof of the barn behind it.

"Go on, now," Woody said, staring at something below Jud's range of vision. His body moved, as if he'd pushed something aside with his foot. "I won't hurt you, little fella, but I gotta get down these steps."

Woody moved again. This time, Jud heard a sound he'd become pretty familiar with since Yi's curse—the whisper of scales on thin, scrubby grass.

Cy.

Ignoring the way his paw screamed at him, Jud struggled until he had his head free. He craned his neck until he caught sight of Cy's snake, coiled in strike position at the bottom of the steps. Jud let out a couple of loud squeaks, telling Cy as best he could that he was all right and to *please* just let Woody take him wherever the hell he planned to leave him. Cy couldn't hear him, since he was deaf in snake form, but maybe he'd catch the vibrations. Jud could crawl into a corner somewhere after Woody left, he just wanted him to *go* already.

To his relief, Cy seemed to understand. He slithered out of sight under a lantana bush. Jud wondered if he imagined the worried glint in those black reptilian eyes.

Woody let out a whooshing breath. "Okay, *that* was something.

Almost like he was trying to stop me on purpose."

Jud tried to relax as Woody edged down the steps and started across the moonlit yard. He could sense his friends watching. They would gather around him as soon as Woody was gone, and protect him until morning. The thought was comforting.

Jud tried not to think of what would happen if Woody left him where none of his friends could get to him. Or if shifting back didn't heal his broken bones.

When Woody stopped beside the Wee Bee van, Jud was confused. Surely Woody wouldn't take him away from the ranch. Right?

Wrong.

Woody opened the van door and slid into the driver's seat. Holding Jud in one arm, he snatched a small cardboard box from the floorboard, dumped a pile of receipts out and set it on the passenger seat. "Here you go," he murmured, lifting Jud into the box with infinite care. "I'm sorry, it's not very comfortable, but it's the best I can do right now. I can't drive while I'm holding you."

Alarmed, Jud chittered up at Woody's worried face. Woody looked startled for a minute, then smiled. "Don't worry. JJ'll get my note when he gets home, and he'll call me. I'll get you back to him."

Fucking fuck. He's taking me home. What in the hell's he gonna say tomorrow morning, when the rat's gone and the guy who tried to molest him is bare-assed naked in his house?

Damned if Jud knew the answer to that, and damned if he had the energy to think about it right now. Exhausted, he shut his eyes and drifted into an uneasy doze.

🐀 🐀 🐀

Jud woke in the middle of his shift back to human. When he stopped feeling like he was two seconds from puking and his galloping heart settled into a trot, he aimed an eloquent stream of swear words at the ceiling fan overhead. This was why he usually stayed up to greet the dawn on the night of a shift. He *hated* being yanked from sleep by the none-too-pleasant feel of his body going from rat to human.

The pain in his side had gone away completely, so the cracked rib must've knitted during the shift. He lifted his right leg and cautiously wiggled his foot. It felt a little sore, and a bluish bruise spread from his toes to his ankle, but there was no real pain. The bones seemed to have healed well enough. Good thing, too. Limping all the way home on a lame foot would've sucked donkey balls.

Sitting up, he studied the room in which he found himself. Three of the walls were lined with windows, shaded by blinds that looked like they were made of river reeds. White-painted wood made up the fourth wall. A closed sliding glass door broke the line of the wooden wall a good ten feet to Jud's right. To his left sat a glider wide enough for at least four people. Long white hairs—cat hairs, Jud thought, remembering Woody's three-legged Persian—covered the blue cushions. A small top-loading freezer hummed in the far corner of the room. Beneath the wadded-up towel and the cardboard box Jud had mangled during his shift, a thin grayish-blue carpet covered a floor hard enough to be concrete.

After a moment's thought, Jud realized he must've spent the night on Woody's enclosed sun porch. Woody had converted the house's original outdoor patio into a sunroom several months ago. The memory of Woody's palpable pride when he'd shown Jud the pictures made him smile, in spite of the seriousness of his current situation.

Speaking of which…

Grasping the arm of the glider to steady himself, Jud pushed to his feet. The room spun around him for a moment before the post-shift vertigo settled into a familiar vague lightheadedness. To his relief, his bruised foot held his weight with no problem.

He glanced around, looking for anything at all he could wear. Woody's clothes would be too big for him, but hanging on to an overly large pair of pants was a damn sight better than hoofing it back to the ranch in nothing but his skin.

The little room was cluttered with battered sci-fi novels, pet care magazines, gardening tools and bags of cat litter, but no clothes. Jud was about ready to say fuck it and take his chances cutting across farm country in the altogether when he remembered the towel his rat form had slept on. Cursing himself under his breath, he snatched the towel off the floor and wrapped it around his hips. It barely covered the necessary parts and his left thigh peeked out through the slit where the ends didn't quite come together, but it would have to do. He could *not* let Woody catch him here. Especially like this.

A quick perusal of the room revealed no exit other than the sliding glass door. The door that led to the rest of the house.

Shit, I'm gonna have to go through the house to get out.

Jud looked around, but didn't see a clock. It must be early, though. He always shifted back as soon as the horizon began to lighten, and the light filtering through the blinds was still gray and faint. With any luck Woody would still be asleep.

Hanging on to his towel with one hand, Jud padded to the sliding glass door and peered through it. The kitchen and living room beyond were dark and empty. He eased the door open, slipped through and crept toward the back door. It couldn't be more than ten feet. Only ten feet between himself and freedom.

As he drew even with the kitchen table, his feet tangled in something warm and soft. He stumbled, caught his sore foot on a chair leg and went flying ass over teakettle. The chair clattered across the floor. Jud landed on the unforgiving wooden planks with a thud that knocked the wind out of him.

A pair of crystal blue eyes set in a sea of long white fur stared at him from inches away. "Mmmrrrrrow?"

"Damned cat," Jud wheezed, glaring into the Persian's placid feline face.

With a swish of her fluffy tail, the cat turned and made her three-legged way across the floor. She jumped into the battered old recliner, lapped at one delicate paw and swiped it behind her ears. Her smug gaze seemed to say *mission accomplished*.

Jud flipped her off. Like it was *his* fault she'd been shut out of what was clearly "her" porch all night.

"Jud?" Bare feet pounded across the floor toward him, long bare legs bent, and he found himself looking up at Woody's concerned face. "Shit, are you okay?"

Crap. Fucking goddamn crap. Wondering how in the nine hells he was going to explain himself, Jud gave Woody his best approximation of a smile. "Yeah, fine. Tripped over your cat."

Woody winced. "Sorry about that. Einstein loves to get underfoot."

"Einstein?"

"Yeah, well. It's ironic." Woody shot the animal a fond smile. "Not to put too fine a point on it, she's kind of stupid."

No shit. What kind of cat doesn't know a rat when it smells one? Jud snorted.

Woody slipped an arm around Jud's ribcage. "Here, let me help you up."

Jud allowed Woody to haul him upright, trying to ignore the effect Woody's nearness was having on him. Why did the man have to be wearing those stupid, sexy Jersey knit boxer-briefs, anyway? The damned things clung to his body in a way that left not very fucking much to the imagination. Jud gritted his teeth and hung on to his towel with grim determination, hoping the developing tent would go away before Woody noticed.

Luckily, Woody's full attention was focused on Jud's face. Jud stared at Woody's collarbone, unable to make himself meet Woody's intense, searching gaze. "So. Um. I should go."

Woody's hands clamped onto Jud's shoulders, holding him in place. "Please don't. Not until we can talk, at least."

Jud closed his eyes and hung his head. "Look, Woody, I know you're wondering what I'm doing here, and why I'm...you know." He indicated his barely-towel-covered nudity with a quick gesture. "But I really don't think I can explain it right now, so if it's okay I'd like to go home."

"Hey. Look at me."

Jud shook his head, eyes screwed firmly shut. It was a childish thing to do, he knew, but dammit, he could *not* look Woody in the eye right now. He couldn't.

Woody's big palm removed itself from Jud's left shoulder. Firm fingers grasped his chin and lifted his face. Then warm, soft lips met his own, and damned if that didn't make his eyelids fly up like a couple of defective window shades.

Jud didn't even have time to process the fact that Woody was kissing him—*kissing* him—before it was over. Woody pulled away with a shy little smile curving those perfect lips. Jud stared at him, unable to move or speak or even *think*.

"You don't have to explain," Woody said, his voice soft and heavy. His fingers moved, tracing the line of Jud's jaw. "I know why you're here."

Jud's stomach plunged to his toes, bounced and tried to fly right up his throat. *He can't know. How the bloody buggering fuck could he know?* "Wh...you...you know?"

"Sure I do. You got my note, obviously." Woody grinned, his gaze taking a leisurely trip down Jud's body and back up again. "Showing up naked might've been overdoing it a little, but I like it."

Jud tried to make sense out of that and couldn't. "Huh?"

Woody's brow creased. "JJ, are you sure you're okay? I asked you to come here. I just figured that's why you're here."

Just what was he supposed to say to that? If Woody didn't know Jud was a shapeshifter, Jud wasn't about to tell him. On the other hand, Woody was handing him the perfect excuse to be here.

Except you don't know what his note actually says, *fucktard. What if he just wanted to tell you he thinks you're great, but he doesn't want to ruin the friendship with sex?* Jud licked his lips, his brain going ninety miles a minute. "Ummm..."

Hurt flashed in Woody's dark eyes for a moment before he got his blank face on. "Seems like I've read this whole thing wrong after all." Wrapping both arms around himself, Woody stared at a spot somewhere south of Jud's left elbow. "I'm sorry for coming on to you like that. It won't happen again."

After so many years of wanting and not getting, Jud's response was born of pure instinct. Launching himself forward, he flung both arms around Woody's neck, pulled his face down and fused their mouths together. He took advantage of Woody's surprised gasp to thrust his tongue between Woody's parted lips. Woody moaned, both arms snaking around Jud's waist to pull their bodies together.

"I don't want this to not happen again," Jud murmured into Woody's mouth. "I want it to happen all the time. Every fucking day. But…"

"But what?" Woody drew back, panting, and studied Jud's face with lust-glazed eyes. "I want you so bad I can't stand it. You want me, too. So what's the problem?"

Well, sir, the problem is that I am a cursed shapeshifter. Not only do I turn into a rodent once a month, I can never leave Shifting Sands for any length of time unless I want to risk becoming a rat every time I get mad or turned on. Plus there's the whole possibility that you might catch the curse if you get too attached to me, like Bobby Lee did with Cy. If that's really what happened, because we don't really know, *and isn't that just fun?*

It was a lot to explain, and with most of the blood in his body currently filling his cock to near bursting, Jud wasn't up to the task. "I'm a rat," he blurted out, and instantly wished he'd kept his big mouth shut. "That is, I…I…uhhhh…"

"What, you're a rat for not telling me how you felt before? Yeah, but so am I, so we're even." With a sly grin, Woody slipped both hands beneath Jud's towel to cup his bare ass. "Enough talking. Let's fuck."

For a second, Jud was torn. He knew he should make a real effort to tell Woody the whole sordid story. Or at least enough for him to understand how Jud had *really* ended up naked in his house before the sun was even properly up. On the other hand, Woody wanted to fuck him.

Oh great jumping Buddha, Woody wants to fuck me.

The knowledge effectively canceled out Jud's good intentions. Promising himself he'd come clean with Woody later, Jud clenched both hands in Woody's hair and kissed him hard.

Woody let out a strangled moan. His fingers dug into Jud's butt. Before Jud could process what was happening, his feet left the floor to dangle in midair. A thrill coursed through his blood. He wasn't a big guy, but he wasn't exactly tiny either. The fact that Woody could pick him up with such ease made him want to swoon like a girl.

Thanking his lucky stars that Woody couldn't see his reaction—what with their faces being attached at the mouth and all—Jud tightened his grip on Woody's neck and wrapped both legs around his waist. He dimly registered the towel coming undone and sliding to the floor, but he couldn't be bothered to care. He rubbed his stiff prick against Woody's belly and lapped up the resulting whimpers. Damn, the man was so responsive. Jud thought he could spend hours just listening to those sweet little sounds.

Jud was so caught up in finally kissing Woody the way he'd wanted to for ages, he didn't even realize he'd been carried into the bedroom until Woody tossed him onto the bed. He landed with a skull-jarring bounce. His vision blurred for a second. When it cleared, the first thing he saw was Woody standing beside the bed, stepping out of that indecently clingy underwear.

Woody's cock bobbed into view, and Jud bit his lip. God*damn*, but that was a pretty prick, thick and flushed, with a wide head that was going to hurt so fucking good going in. Just looking at it made Jud's ass clench in delighted anticipation.

With an endearingly shy smile, Woody climbed naked onto the bed to lie beside Jud, propped up on one elbow. His free hand rubbed slow circles on Jud's belly. "So."

"So." Jud let out a soft gasp when Woody's hand wandered

lower to cup his balls.

"So, what do you want?" One blunt finger dipped into the crease of Jud's ass, barely brushing his hole.

Jud spread his legs wide. "I want your cock up my ass five minutes ago," he growled, canting his pelvis upward just in case Woody had suddenly stopped understanding plain English.

Woody's brown eyes went hot, his cheeks turning a beautiful pink. His hand still lodged between Jud's legs, he leaned over to kiss Jud's lips. Jud reached up to bury both hands in Woody's thick hair. Woody's finger penetrated his hole just as Woody's tongue pushed into his mouth, and *damn* it was good, in spite of the dry burn from being fingered without even spit to ease the way. Jud moaned and drew one leg up to his chest so Woody would have more room to play.

"God, JJ." Woody's lips traced a sizzling path over Jud's chin, along his jawbone and down his neck. "You have no idea…" Woody's teeth dug into Jud's flesh just above his collarbone, tearing a yelp from him, "…how long I've wanted to get you in bed."

The flash of irritation over the years they'd wasted not fucking dissolved when Woody's finger twisted deep enough to hit Jud's gland. "Oh Jesus," Jud breathed, burying his face in Woody's throat. "Woody. Fuck me."

A violent shudder ran down Woody's back. He drew back with a smile so brilliant Jud barely noticed the finger withdrawing from his hole. "I'm gonna get the lube and a rubber. Don't you move."

"I'm not going anywhere." Jud couldn't resist reaching out and trailing his fingers over the curve of Woody's ass when he stood and bent over to rifle through the bedside drawer. God, but the man had a gorgeous body, all smooth olive skin and streamlined muscle. *Beautiful.*

Woody straightened up, lube and condom in hand and a startled but pleased expression in his eyes. "Thanks. I could say the same about you."

Jud's face turned hot when he realized he'd spoken out loud. Thankfully, Woody flopped onto the bed and kissed him again before he was forced to say anything. Jud happily opened his mouth wide and spread his legs so Woody could settle between them.

"How do you want it?" Woody nipped Jud's lower lip, dipped his head and nuzzled the curve of Jud's neck. "God, I love the way you smell."

Personally, Jud thought he smelled like dried rat sweat, but what the hell. If Woody liked it, who was he to complain? Snatching the condom from Woody's hand, Jud ripped the packet open. "Want it just like this. Lift up a little."

Woody obediently raised his hips. His lips parted on a stuttering breath when Jud rolled the rubber down over his shaft. "Shit."

Jud understood the wild tangle of emotions in that one little word. He couldn't quite believe he was here, like this, about to get his brains fucked out by the man he'd been lusting after for so many years. The whole thing seemed surreal, yet at the same time painfully sharp and immediate. He figured the expression on Woody's face right now would be burned into his brain for the rest of his life.

Sitting up on his knees, Woody flipped open the lube and squeezed way more than was strictly necessary onto his fingers. Some of it dripped onto Jud's stomach, making his skin contract. Woody grinned and shoved two slick fingers into Jud's ass, smearing the lube inside him and around his hole.

"Ohmyfucking*Christ*," Jud breathed, one hand fisting the rumpled bedclothes while the other dug into Woody's hip hard enough to bruise. "Fuck. Now. Please."

Woody's brow furrowed. "You sure?"

Jud nodded so hard it made him dizzy. "Yeah."

The fingers pulled out, but the frown didn't go away. "But, JJ—"

"I got a dildo, all right? I use it kind of a lot."

Woody's eyebrows shot up. "Gotcha." Grasping Jud's right thigh in one hand and his own shaft in the other, Woody poised the head of his prick at Jud's opening. "Hang onto your hat, cowboy."

Before Jud could come up with an appropriately smart-ass reply, Woody's hips flexed, his cock slid into Jud's butt and Jud forgot how to talk. Woody fell forward onto one elbow, the other hand curling around Jud's prick. Jud hung on with arms and legs and grunted his approval as Woody pounded him into a higher plane of consciousness.

If it hadn't been so long since Jud had gotten laid—and if he hadn't had such a massive hard-on for the man currently fucking him to within an inch of his life—he might've been disappointed that it didn't last longer. As it was, though, he was glad Woody didn't last more than a few minutes. It made his own lack of stamina a moot point, and he was just proud enough to not want to have to explain why he shot like a fucking sixteen-year-old losing his cherry. He buried his face in Woody's neck and clung to him as their orgasms hit them more or less at the same time. The way Woody shook in his arms made him feel giddy with something he couldn't quite name, and wasn't sure he was ready to.

"Oh. Jesus." Panting, Woody pulled out, rolled off of Jud and flopped onto his back. He pulled the condom off and tossed it over the edge of the bed, where it landed with a wet splat on the floor. "Wow."

"You can say that again." Jud turned his head and shot Woody a grin he knew was goofy as hell. "Hadn't been fucked like that in ages."

Woody let out a breathless laugh. "Sorry it was over so fast."

"Hey, you weren't the only one going off fast, in case you didn't notice." Jud rolled onto his side, savoring the twinge of abused muscles in his ass. "Guess we both kind of needed a good fuck, huh?"

"I'll say." Woody reached over to touch Jud's face. "It wouldn't have been that good with anyone else, though. Not for me."

The sudden seriousness in Woody's eyes made Jud's stomach turn back flips. He curled his fingers around Woody's hand. "Me neither."

For a moment, they stared silently at each other, a maelstrom of unspoken thoughts swirling between them. Then Woody looked away, a faint smile on his lips. "Um. Okay. You want some breakfast?"

Jud returned Woody's smile. "I could eat, yeah." In fact, now that he'd gotten the getting-fucked part out of the way, he was starving. Shifting into a rat didn't drain him quite the way some of the other guys' shifts did, but it used up enough energy that he usually ate three times as much as normal after shifting back.

Jud winced. God, Daniel and the other guys were going to be worried sick. "Hey, Woody, can I use your phone?"

"Sure. You need to call the boss?"

"Yeah." Jud ran a hand through his hair. "I, um, didn't exactly tell him I was coming here. And I forgot my cell."

Chuckling, Woody leaned over and gave Jud a sweet, lingering kiss. "Go on and call him. You can use the phone in here, if you want. I'll get some breakfast together." Woody slid off the side of the bed and stood, shooting Jud a sheepish look. "I'm really sorry about your rat, JJ. I feel terrible that I broke his paw. I'm taking him to the vet this morning. I'll let you know what they say, and I'll pay for all of it."

Guilt needled Jud's insides. He sat up and crossed his legs beneath him, schooling his face into the best-puzzled expression he could manage. "Yeah, you know what, I didn't get that part. I don't have a pet rat." It was technically true. He really didn't have a *pet* rat.

Shock flowed through Woody's eyes. "Um. Okay. So…"

"So, I guess it was a wild rat you picked up. Or maybe someone else's pet," Jud amended, unable to bear the embarrassed flush in

Woody's cheeks. "Maybe you could put a notice in the paper or something. Somebody might claim the little guy."

Woody shrugged, looking lost, and Jud felt like a heel for lying to him. *I'll tell him*, he promised himself once again. *As soon as I figure out a way to make him believe me.*

On impulse, Jud rose onto his knees, grabbed Woody's wrists and tugged until Woody bent down. They kissed, soft and slow, and Jud swore he could feel Woody's rat-related tension draining away.

"It's so hot how you rescue strays," Jud murmured when the kiss broke.

Woody's lips curved into a smile. "Thanks."

"Mm-hm." Jud stole another kiss, swift and tongueless this time, before giving Woody a gentle shove. "Go start coffee. I'm gonna call Daniel, then I'll come help you cook."

"Looking forward to it." Woody held his gaze for a moment, dark eyes shining, then turned and strode off to the kitchen.

Jud sat on the edge of the bed and watched Woody's bare butt moving down the hall. He wished the ugly feeling in the pit of his stomach would go away so he could enjoy *finally* being Woody's lover.

That's what you get for being a lying rat.

Sighing, Jud flopped backward onto the mattress. What the hell had he gotten himself into?

🐀 🐀 🐀

"No." Daniel shook his head without looking up from the papers spread out across his desk. "Absolutely not."

Not the answer Jud wanted, but hardly a surprise. "I know it's a little risky—"

"A little risky?" Lifting his head, Daniel stared at Jud as if he'd just offered to dance naked at a nursing home Christmas party. "Jud, you want to invite Woody to stay with you tomorrow night. *Here.* When there will be a *full moon*. That's not 'a little risky,' that's batshit insane."

Jud scratched behind his left ear. "I can see where you might think so."

Daniel's eyebrows went up. "Can you? Good. Glad we got that settled."

Jud bit back a frustrated growl as his boss bent over the pile of papers again. He and Woody had been an official couple for almost exactly a month. Things were good between them. Wonderful, in fact. Better than Jud had ever dreamed it could be. But it wasn't enough. It had taken Jud a long time to figure out that the reason he still felt unfulfilled was because of the one secret he hadn't shared. And he hadn't been able to think of a single way to reveal that secret to Woody—not one he'd believe, anyway—short of a demonstration.

Of course, a demonstration meant Woody would have to be here at the ranch when Jud shifted. Which meant asking Daniel's permission for a visitor on Shift Night.

So far, Jud's plan wasn't working out too well. No way was he giving up, though. He couldn't.

Jud leaned both hands on Daniel's desk. "I have to tell him. I can't keep something that big from him forever."

That got Daniel's attention. His head snapped up again, sharp blue eyes boring into Jud's. "Forever?"

Jud heard the question in Daniel's voice. It didn't seem fair to tell Daniel before he'd even told Woody, but there was no help for it. Daniel had to understand exactly how important this was. Although, judging by the apprehension in his voice, he already knew what Jud was about to say.

Jud forced himself to stand up straight and meet Daniel's gaze. "I love him, Daniel."

A muscle twitched in Daniel's jaw. "You're sure?"

"Pretty sure, yeah." Jud fiddled with the loose belt loop on the front of his jeans. "Probably have for a long time, come to think of it."

Daniel nodded. Shuffled a few papers on his desk. Nodded again, turned sideways and peered out the window to where Cy and Michael were fixing a loose board in the fence. "And Woody? He feel the same?"

That was the real question, wasn't it? Too bad Jud had no idea.

"Don't know." Jud stuck both hands in his back pockets and tried not to look like the not knowing bothered him as much as it did. "But if he did, having him here tomorrow night might be for the best."

Understanding dawned in Daniel's eyes. "Oh."

Yeah, "oh." Visions of Bobby Lee's unexpected transformation had haunted Jud's sleep for days, ever since he'd finally figured out why he felt so damn giddy every time Woody smiled at him. If the same thing was about to happen to Woody, Jud wanted to be there for him. Not that there was a whole lot he could do, since he'd be a rat himself, but still.

The silence stretched on. Jud cleared his throat. "So. What about it?"

Daniel sighed. "Yeah, okay. Bring him out."

"Okay, great. I'll call him after lunch." Jud gave Daniel a grateful smile. "Thanks, Bossman."

Daniel nodded, one corner of his mouth hitching up. "Wouldn't want the boy to be on his own if anything happened."

Jud swallowed a laugh. Daniel wasn't *that* much older than Woody. Hell, he wasn't much older than any of the guys at Shifting Sands—except Bobby Lee, who was just a young'un—but he'd become a kind of father figure to everyone here. The fact that Daniel seemed ready to take Woody under his non-existent wing with the rest of their hodge-podge family made Jud feel warm inside.

Sauntering down the hall to the kitchen, Jud felt lighter than he had in days. He'd been pretty sure Daniel would agree to let Woody stay, once he knew what might be at stake, but it was still a relief to have that particular conversation behind him.

Of course, the granddaddy of all heart-to-hearts was still ahead. And Woody probably wouldn't take it quite as well as Daniel had, even if he *didn't* turn into a bear or a hawk or a goddamn armadillo.

He probably won't shift, Jud told himself as he set about getting lunch together. *What happened to Bobby Lee was probably just a fluke. Maybe he had it in him all along and Cy just brought it out somehow.*

Jud let out a humorless chuckle. No matter how many times he told himself that, he still didn't believe it. Bobby Lee had become a shifter because he fell in love with Cy. If Woody felt That Way for Jud, the same thing would happen to him.

Part of Jud couldn't help hoping for it. And just how fucking sick was that?

🐝 🐝 🐝

Curling his fingers around his headboard, Jud braced himself and hung on while Woody pounded into him. "Oh fuck yeah. Fuck yeah. Harder."

Behind him, Woody let out a low moan. His hands tightened on Jud's hipbones. "Goddamn, Jud."

Jud managed a nod and a swift smile over his shoulder before Woody's cock speared him so hard it knocked his ability to speak into next month. He angled his hips so that Woody's next thrust would nail his gland, then had to bite his tongue to keep from screaming when he got his wish. He didn't think anyone who might still be in the house would appreciate the sound effects.

Woody's big, warm hand wrapped around Jud's cock and started jerking him off. A hard shudder ran down Jud's spine. "Fuck."

An appreciative hum answered him. Woody's body shifted, his free hand planting on the mattress beneath Jud's ribs and his damp chest pressing to Jud's back. "That's it, JJ. Come on."

Woody's breathless rasp shattered any control Jud had left. He came with a cry he couldn't quite hold back, his whole body shaking. A few seconds later Woody groaned and let go inside him, that work-rough hand clenching around his shaft.

They collapsed into a sideways heap, Woody's prick still twitching in Jud's ass. Jud let out a deep, satisfied sigh. "Christ, I needed that."

"Horny bastard." Dropping a quick kiss on Jud's shoulder, Woody pulled out of him. "We fuck so much it's a wonder your ass still works like it ought to, but you still needed it."

Jud obediently rolled onto his stomach when Woody nudged him. "Yeah, well. Been kind of tense today. A good fuck takes the edge off."

"Mm-hm. It does." Woody slid two fingers into Jud's loose hole. "Something wrong?"

Jud smiled at the sensation of Woody's fingertips stroking his insides. Woody loved to finger him after they'd fucked. It had become practically a fetish ever since they'd decided to ditch the rubbers a couple of weeks ago. Jud figured Woody liked the feel of his spunk inside Jud's butt. Which was just fine with Jud. He liked having Woody's fingers in him. It felt so damn *possessive*.

"Nothing's wrong," Jud mumbled into the rumpled sheets.

"Then why were you tense?"

Turning his head, Jud peered out the window. The moon was already out. Had been for a little while, its light drowned out in the bright August evening. But the sun had nearly set, and the tingle that had crawled beneath Jud's skin all during dinner, and the subsequent sex, had become a near-painful itch. Pretty soon he'd shift, and that would be that. He wanted to at least try to prepare Woody before that happened.

Should've talked right after dinner instead of having sex, fucktard. It was true, and Jud knew it. But he'd never been good at talking, and if what was about to happen drove Woody away, Jud wanted one last mind-blowing fuck to remember him by.

Steeling himself, Jud pushed up on his elbows and turned to meet Woody's curious, worried gaze. "Hey, Woody?"

"Yeah?" The fingers pulled out of Jud's ass, smeared cooling semen around his hole and plunged back in again.

Jud chewed his lower lip for a second. "You remember when I told you I was a rat?"

Woody's lips curved into an indulgent smile. "I remember everything about that morning."

A giant fist closed around Jud's chest. "Well, the thing is, I meant that. Um, literally."

Woody's brows drew together. "What the hell are you talking about, JJ?"

Jud opened his mouth to reply—how, he had no idea—but the sudden rush of prickling energy through his body told him it was about to be too late for talking. He gazed into Woody's eyes, wondering if it would be the last time. "Don't freak out."

Frowning, Woody pulled his fingers from Jud's ass. Just in time. Moonlight poured unfettered through the window, and the change ripped through Jud's body.

When the world stopped moving, Jud crouched in the midst of the mussed and sex-scented bedclothes, with Woody's shocked face staring down at him. He twitched his whiskers and squeaked in what he hoped was a reassuring way.

"JJ?" Woody whispered, peering at Jud with panic in his eyes. "Oh, my God."

Jud squeaked again. He wished to fuck he could talk right now. Even if he made a mess of it, which he probably would, it'd be better than not being able to say anything.

Keeping his eyes fixed on Woody's horrified face, Jud crawled forward as slowly as he could manage. He wanted more than anything to be held against Woody's bare chest and let Woody's heartbeat soothe away the ache inside him, but instinct told him that startling Woody now would be a very bad idea.

Not that his caution helped any. With a harsh sound somewhere between a sob and a shout, Woody scrambled backward. He tumbled off the edge of the bed, regained his feet and snatched his pants off the floor.

Jud watched, resigned, as Woody yanked his jeans on and ran from the room with his zipper undone and his shirt clutched in one hand. The slap of bare feet on wood sounded down the hall. The front door opened and slammed shut. After a few silent seconds, Jud heard the engine of Woody's car roar to life, then a squeal of tires turning too fast.

In the silence left behind by Woody's abrupt departure, Jud went to the edge of the mattress and jumped off. He hit the rug with a jarring thump. Shaking off the resulting momentary dizziness, he dashed to where Woody's underwear lay discarded on the floor and curled up on top of it.

He was still there when Cy slithered into the room, who knew how much later. Cy coiled his lower body and lifted his reptilian head, tongue flicking out. Jud knew Cy would taste not only the residue of sex in the air, but the devastation tearing at Jud's insides. He also knew that Cy wouldn't leave him alone with his misery.

Unwinding himself, Cy glided across the floor to Jud. He curled his long body around Jud's and laid his head on Jud's flank. Jud rested his snout on one of Cy's coils. The physical contact with his friend comforted Jud, even though it couldn't ease the pain of knowing Woody didn't love him after all.

🐀 🐀 🐀

At first, Jud was sure Woody would come back. He just needed a while to adjust. After all, how much of a mind fuck must it be to find out your lover turns into a rat every full moon? Once Woody got his head around it, he'd come back. Jud was positive he would. Besides, he'd left his underwear, shoes and socks at the ranch. He'd *have* to at least call at some point and make arrangements to get them back.

Days passed, then weeks. Woody never returned for the rest of his clothes, in spite of the multiple messages Jud left on his answering machine and his cell phone voice mail. Jud made a supply run to Wee Bee, wanting to see Woody and dreading it at the same time. Some of the hope he'd held onto died when he found Bea minding the store instead of Woody. He left Woody's things with her and managed to smile and sound casual when he asked her to have Woody call him. He didn't much think Woody would actually call, but he asked anyway. The worst that could happen was nothing, and that was already happening.

When September's shift came and went with not a peep from Woody, Jud finally realized it was over. He did his best to accept it and move on. Nothing else he *could* do, really. He couldn't force Woody to come back. But damn, losing him hurt like nothing else ever had.

"Stupid to ever show him," Jud muttered to himself, shaking the kitchen rug off the side of the porch. Bits of dust sparkled in the morning light as they drifted to the ground. "Should've known he couldn't handle it. Should've fucking *known* he'd bail. Dammit."

"Jud, I swear to all that's holy, if you call yourself or Woody a fucktard right now, I'm gonna kick your ass. You been doin' that way too much lately."

Jud shot Cy a poisonous glare as he sauntered over and leaned his butt on the porch railing. "Maybe I should kick *your* ass for listening in on things that ain't any of your business."

Cy's eyebrows went up. "Quit talking to yourself all the time and I'll quit listening in."

Jud sucked his cheeks in and reminded himself how obnoxious he'd been to the men he thought of as family for the last month and a half, and silently explained to himself that Cy was just worried about him. They all were. Jud knew that. Hell, he'd feel the same way if it was any one of them going through this hell right now.

"Sorry," Jud said, keeping his eyes firmly fixed on the rug. "Didn't mean to take it all out on y'all."

"'S okay."

Silence fell, broken only by the drone of insects and the occasionally stamp and whinny from the foundered mare in the nearby barn. Cy turned sideways, crossed his arms and stared at

Jud so hard he could feel holes burning into his skull. For one terrifying moment, Jud thought Cy was going to offer him a hug, or something equally uncomfortable. *Jesus Christ, if he makes me cry I'll kill him with a spatula.*

The distant sound of an engine broke the moment, to Jud's immense relief. Cy turned and squinted down the driveway. "Isn't that Woody's car?"

Jud's stomach turned a few somersaults. Draping the rug over the porch rail, he peered into the plume of dust kicked up by the vehicle bouncing toward the house. The flashes of blinding orange told him all he needed to know.

Jud leaned on the rail, fighting off the dizzying surge of fear and—improbable though it was—hope. "Shit. Fucking goddamn *shit.*"

"Guess I oughta go check on that mare." Cy gave his shoulder a squeeze before crossing to the porch steps. "Good luck."

Jud resisted the urge to follow Cy across the yard to the barn. If Woody was coming back *now*, he must have a reason. Whatever he was willing to drive out here to say, Jud wanted to hear it, even if it was just "fuck you and good riddance."

Even if he couldn't help hoping for something better.

Ages later, Woody's ancient Subaru hatchback ground to a halt in front of the steps to the kitchen door. The driver's side door opened. Woody stepped out, swung the door shut and walked to the bottom of the steps.

They stared at each other while the car engine pinged in the background. Damn, but Woody looked good enough to eat, in spite of the dark circles under his eyes and the nervous hunch to his shoulders. Jud's gut twisted. Not so long ago, he'd thought maybe he and Woody would spend the rest of their years together. Seeing Woody again just reminded him of how stupid he'd been to believe in that particular pipe dream.

He'd be damned if he'd let Woody see how badly he was hurting, though. He straightened his spine and lifted his chin. "Woody."

"Hi, JJ." Woody crossed his arms, uncrossed them again and shoved his hands into his front pockets. "It's good to see you."

In the space of a breath, Jud tried on and discarded several different ways to answer. In the end, he decided he was just too fucking rattled for anything but the bare truth. "Wish I could say the same, but I can't. What're you doing here?"

One shoulder hitched up beneath Woody's yellow and black Wee Bee T-shirt. "I needed to talk to you."

"Yeah, well, I been needing to talk to *you* for goin' on six weeks. Why the fuck haven't you returned my calls?"

Pure anguish twisted Woody's face for a second. Jud ignored the urge to apologize. He knew he'd sounded harsh and angrier than he actually was, but right now it was either that or melt into a quivering puddle of need at Woody's feet. And that was *not* going to happen.

Woody's teeth dug into his bottom lip. He hung his head. "I just…it scared me, you know? When you…changed. And I just couldn't face you after I ran away like that, and then…"

"Then what?" Jud prodded when Woody trailed off.

Woody raised his head. Confusion, apprehension and longing fought for territory on his face. "Look, I know you're probably mad at me, and I can't blame you, but could we maybe talk inside?"

No. Too much. Can't handle it. "I guess. C'mon in."

Jud turned and strode into the kitchen without checking to make sure Woody followed him. His heart was doing its level best to hammer a hole in his sternum, and he figured if he didn't sit down in the next few seconds he'd pass out on the damn floor. And how embarrassing would *that* be?

He plopped into a chair just as Woody edged inside and shut the door. "So. Talk."

Woody sank into a chair across the table from Jud, hands twisting nervously together. "I'm sorry, JJ. For running away, and for avoiding you since. I acted like a fucking idiot, and I'm sorry."

The cold knot in Jud's stomach melted a little, but he didn't let that show. "Okay. Apology accepted. Was that all you had to say?" Jud gave himself a mental pat on the back for not letting on just how badly he wanted Woody back for good.

Woody ran both hands through his hair. "No. But I'm kinda scared to tell you the rest, 'cause I don't think you'll like it much."

Jud's pulse rate picked up, as if it wasn't already racing like a NASCAR champion. "Just spit it out."

With a deep sigh, Woody rubbed a hand over the side of his face. "IthinkI'minlovewithyou."

Jud's mouth fell open. He closed it with a snap. "Huh?" *He did not just say what I think he said. Did he?*

"You heard me." Woody looked up again, a determined fire in his eyes. "I love you, JJ."

"Then why the flying fuck have you been ignoring me?" Jud sounded a little too teenage girl for his own comfort, but it was the first thing to pop into his head after Woody's confession and, dammit, he wanted to *know*.

Groaning, Woody slumped over the table with his head in both hands. "Told you that you wouldn't like it."

"Who said I didn't like it?"

"I just thought—"

"You thought wrong."

Woody's spine snapped upright so hard Jud wondered if he'd hurt himself. "What?"

Jud had to smile at the sudden shine of hope in Woody's eyes. "I love you too, dumbass."

Stunned astonishment flowed over Woody's features. "You do?"

"Yeah. I was gonna tell you that night, but you ran off and I never got the chance." Jud pinned Woody with his sternest glare, trying to pretend his head wasn't spinning with the knowledge that *Woody loved him*. "I can understand being scared when I changed. But didn't you ever stop to think maybe I knew what I was doing? That maybe I wanted you to stay with me when I shifted because I wanted you to know? Because maybe I wanted more with you than just sex?"

The grin that spread across Woody's face was so glowingly happy, Jud couldn't find it in his heart to push Woody away when he jumped up, leaned right over the table, dragged Jud forward by the back of the neck and took his mouth in a kiss that curled his toes. Jud opened up and let it happen. He figured he couldn't have stopped Woody right then even if he wanted to. And he definitely did not want to. He'd get his answers later. Right now all he wanted was to drown in this one moment.

"I'm so sorry I ran," Woody breathed against Jud's lips when the kiss broke. "But I swear, JJ, if you let me come back I'll never run away again. Not as long as I live."

Jud laughed for sheer joy. "I'll hold you to that."

"I'm counting on it." Dropping a light kiss on Jud's nose, Woody straightened up, skirted the table and took Jud's hand. "Come on. We have a lot of lost sex to make up for."

Grinning, Jud stood and followed Woody into his bedroom. Lunch could just be a little late today.

🐾 🐾 🐾

Ten minutes later, Jud lay flat on his back, bare legs around Woody's waist and semen running down the sides of his hips from the puddle between his and Woody's bellies. They'd barely managed to get naked before falling crosswise onto Jud's bed and frotting like a couple of sex-starved teenagers until they both came. Anything more would have to wait awhile, seeing as how they weren't actually teenagers and Jud, at least, needed more recovery time than he had twenty-something years ago.

That's okay, Jud thought, burrowing his face into the crook of Woody's neck. *We have plenty of time.*

Knowing it was true made him feel more content than he had in years. Maybe ever.

"Sorry it was so quick," Woody mumbled against Jud's hair.

"That's what you said the first time."

"Mm-hm." Raising his head, Woody gave Jud a lazy grin. "Remind me never to go this long without sex again. I don't need to embarrass myself around you anymore than I already have."

"Trust me, I won't let you go more than a couple of days without at least a mutual blowjob." Jud raked his fingers through Woody's tousled hair. "I'm glad you came back, Woody. I was just about to give up."

The brown eyes shone with such happiness, it made Jud's throat tight. "I'm glad, too. I was going crazy without you. Especially when—" his mouth snapped shut, cutting off his words.

"When what?" Jud held Woody's face between his hands and frowned as fiercely as he could manage with his whole body still buzzing in the wake of his orgasm. "You don't get to hide things from me. Not now. Spill it."

Woody's cheeks heated beneath Jud's hands. "Well, see, on the last full moon…um, something happened."

Jud's heart started jumping like a frog on hot asphalt. He knew what was coming next—the gist, anyway, if not the particulars— and he couldn't quite decide if the churning in his stomach was guilty horror or guilty joy. "Wh—what." Licking his dry lips, he tried again. "What happened?"

"I…well…" Woody's brow furrowed. "To tell the truth, I'm not real sure. I mean, I know *what* happened, but not *why*."

Jud shut his eyes and counted to five in his head. Long enough to keep from losing it, but short enough to satisfy his screaming nerves. "Woody. Tell me."

The corner of Woody's mouth tipped up in an anxious half-smile. "I kind of turned into a monkey."

A monkey? Of all the animals Jud had half-expected, a monkey wasn't one of them. He threw his head back and howled with laughter.

Woody shook loose of Jud's legs, sat up and wrapped his arms around his bent knees. "It's not funny."

"Okay, okay." Getting himself under control with an effort, Jud rolled onto hands and knees, kissed Woody's cheek and plopped down next to him. "Sorry. It's just, I wasn't expecting a monkey."

"Yeah, well, if you were expecting anything at all, you're ahead of me, 'cause I was sure as fuck surprised." Woody gave Jud a narrow look, which turned into wide-eyed indignation when he saw the wince Jud couldn't quite hide. "You *did* know, you little bastard!"

"No I didn't!" Jud hunched his shoulders at Woody's glare. "I really didn't know that was gonna happen."

"But you said you weren't expecting a monkey. As if you *were* expecting maybe something else."

"But I *wasn't*."

Clamping one hand onto Jud's shoulder, Woody gave him a hard shake. "Jud. The second I said something happened at the last full moon, you knew I'd turned into an animal. How did you know that? Is this ability of yours contagious or something?"

The implied accusation in Woody's voice hurt, but Jud ignored it. Anybody'd be kind of pissed off in Woody's situation. "It's not contagious. Not the way you're thinking, anyhow."

"But I got it from you." Woody frowned. "The changing into an animal part, anyhow. Obviously I didn't get the rat part."

"Yeah, you got it from me. Well, not exactly." Jud drew a deep breath and let it out, trying to think how to explain it. "Okay, here's the deal. Just over a year ago, Daniel's wife ran off with one of the ranch hands. And before she left, she put some kind of curse on all of us, to change us into animals every full moon."

"Like a werewolf."

Woody seemed more interested than angry now. Jud smiled. "Kind of. Anyhow, not long ago Cy hooked up with Bobby Lee. And now Bobby Lee changes once a month just like the rest of us. Nobody's one hundred percent sure why, but we all think it's because…well, because of how he feels about Cy."

"Because he loves him."

Jud nodded, watching Woody's face. "We think that's it, yeah."

Woody's expression turned thoughtful. "Makes sense. I didn't change until I figured out I loved you."

Jud moved closer and rested his head on Woody's shoulder. "I guess I'd kinda hoped you wouldn't get the curse like Bobby Lee did. I'm sorry."

Woody slung an arm around Jud and rested his cheek against Jud's hair. "Well, nothing to be done about it now 'cept deal with it."

"I reckon so." Jud curled into the warmth of Woody's embrace, his hand coming to rest on Woody's bare thigh. "You can come out here on the full moon. We'll take care of you."

"Mm. Thanks, I might do that."

"Good." Jud sat quietly for a moment, gathering his courage to make the offer he was about to make. "Matter of fact, you could stay with me all the time, if you want."

Lifting Jud's chin with one finger, Woody stared hard into his eyes. "You asking me to live here with you?"

"Well, yeah." Jud blushed under Woody's intense scrutiny. "You don't have to."

"I know that." Woody's mouth curved into an endearingly shy smile. "I'd like to, though."

Warmth spread like a wave through Jud's insides, washing away a little of the guilt he couldn't help feeling. "I'm glad. Can't say as I want to spend another night away from you ever again."

Woody's smile widened, his whole face glowing as if he'd just won a million dollars instead of being saddled with a curse that turned him into a monkey once a month. "That's good, because I can't think of anywhere else I'd want to be than with you."

"You're taking this whole thing awfully well," Jud observed, studying Woody's calm face.

Woody shrugged. "No point in getting all upset about it."

"Guess that's so."

Woody's fingers traced the curve of Jud's spine. "You know, there's at least one good thing about turning into a monkey."

Jud smiled at the wicked gleam in Woody's eyes. "Yeah? What's that?"

Woody leaned toward him until Jud could feel the gentle puff of his breath. "Hot monkey sex," Woody whispered.

Laughter bubbled up in Jud's chest and spilled out. Hooking an arm around Woody's neck, he rocked backward until they landed in a heap with Woody on top. "You're a smartass."

"Yep." Woody kissed the end of Jud's nose. "And you love it."

Jud reached up and framed Woody's face in his hands. "I do." *I love it. I love you.*

The tender shine in Woody's eyes suggested he could read Jud's mind. Angling his head, he covered Jud's mouth with his. Jud closed his eyes and let the kiss carry him away. He might be a rat, and he might be involved with a monkey, but that was okay. As long as they had each other, they'd be just fine.

COCK OF THE WALL

WILLA OKATI

Oh, Lord. Michael looked up over the pages of his novel, horrified. From the sounds outside of someone trying to sneak into the bunkhouse and doing a piss-poor job of it, Yi was trying her luck again—and given how she'd chosen a moment when she had to know he'd be all alone in there, reading on his lunch hour, she'd set her sights on him now.

"Michael!" Yi trilled, flinging his door open. She sailed in, easy as you please, and plucked the book out of his hands while he stared at her, his mouth hanging open in dismay. She'd decked herself out like her idea of a Dallas socialite princess, complete with her pretty, glossy hair pouffed up in a Texas bouffant and sprayed into an impenetrable shell. She'd plastered on thick layers of makeup and covered her fingers and wrists with Diamonelle jewelry—very much minus her wedding rings, as he couldn't help but notice.

Hoping he could get rid of her fast, he asked politely, "Something I can help you with, ma'am?"

"Oh, don't call me ma'am," Yi scolded with a pouty moue of her paint-slathered lips. "It makes me feel old. I'd rather feel young and sexy." She kicked off her heels, ruby red with rhinestone buckles, and dropped down to sit on the bed. "Do you know what, Michael? I think," she said, bending to kiss his knee, "that you think I'm young and sexy, too. Hot."

"Is that a fact?" Michael tried to scoot back up, away from her. Yi scared him half to death. She'd get them all in big trouble someday, watch and see if she didn't.

"Tell me, Michael Clarence Reilly…" Yi purred coyly, her nails crawling up his chest while Michael panicked at her knowledge of his family, which he tried to keep secret. "Have you ever met a woman like me?"

"No *ma'am*," Michael replied, his tongue parched with uneasiness. *And thank God for that*, he thought fervently.

"Good," Yi crooned. She straddled him, flinging one leg over both of his and settling down with her full weight on his highly uninterested crotch without so much as a by-your-leave.

Michael almost bucked her off out of sheer surprise. He reminded himself at the last possible second that she weighed less than a third of him, and would go flying into the opposite wall without benefit of wings.

Trouble was, Yi interpreted his motionlessness as an indication of agreement with her plans. "Oh, such nice muscles," she said, petting him as if he were a dog and squeezing him like fresh fruit. "I think you and I are going to be good friends. I'm an excellent friend to have, Michael. You'll see."

"How are you at enemies?" Michael blurted.

Yi's plucked eyebrows drew together as she scowled. "You do not want me as an enemy."

🐓 🐓 🐓

And truer words were never spoken, Michael thought glumly, staring at the emptiness of his fourth beer bottle. All around him, from rafter to rafter of the Ryerson's great barn, a weekend-night party raged, good ol' boys and good time girls set to whoop it up until sunrise. Michael hated this kind of shindig and would much rather have stayed at home and read a good book, but it'd been boss's orders for him to get out and face humans. Said he was getting too sour to stomach.

Well, hell. He might have come to keep the peace, but now he was here, no one had said he couldn't hang out in a corner and stew.

Not literally. Good God, he'd never be able to look a dumpling in the face again.

Because while he'd avoided the worst Yi might have had planned for him when she launched her sneak attack, he'd known even then that he was acting like a great big chicken, running away from his problem instead of facing it.

Apparently, Yi knew that particular bit of American idiom. She'd brought it home to roost, pun intended. Turned him into a man who became a chicken at the full moon to mock how he could be such a cowardly chicken by the light of day.

Which left him here, apparently, trying to hide behind stacked hay bales in a barn that rang to the rafters with loud country music and shouting laughter while four ladies in identical Daisy Duke cutoffs were dangled over tin washtubs, bobbing for bananas. Cynical, Michael bet that even the losers would end up winners before the night was over.

Abruptly, something jabbed Michael in the side. Hard.

Michael looked over, looked down, and then looked down some more, something he was used to at six-foot-seven.

Beside him and beneath him, a crazy curly-haired guy with a pirate goatee waved up at him. He wore an earring made up of a pink feather dangling from a stud, his face—what Michael's momma would have called "a face with *character*"—wreathed in an impish grin. "What's a nice man like you doing in a place like this? In the wallflower's corner, even, where the disenchanted come to lurk?"

"Um…" Michael stared at the colorful little fella, too confused to make a proper answer.

His lack of response didn't seem to bother the guy. He'd already moved on to new conversational pastures. "Are you new in town?"

"Um…no."

"Didn't figure. I am. The name's Zan, by the way. Zan Jedrek." Zan nodded at the craziness of the party in full swing behind them. "Okay, so the mystery of the hunk in the corner. Not so much a three-piper, said Sherlock. Big guy, strong silent type, squinting a skosh when he looks at me, so probably a reader, not a partier… I'm gonna guess a shindig like this isn't your kind of thing, huh? The fine ladies of the banana bobbing don't really ring your bell?"

Good God, he talked fast, running all his words together without pause for breath until he ran out. "I'm sure they're perfectly nice girls…" he offered, uneasy. "Can I help you with something?"

"Sure. I'll take the world on a silver platter, some lobster puffs, and a night in which I use up a whole box of condoms and wake up in a foreign country, but short of that I have a few other ideas."

Michael stared at him, baffled by Zan's stream-of-consciousness babbling. "Excuse me?"

Zan propped his shoulder on the barn wall and waggled his eyebrows. "I'm not enjoying the party. You're miserable. So what do you say you and I leave it behind and go outside, around back?"

"What's out there?"

Zan laughed, a disbelieving sound. "You're kidding me, right? You're telling me a guy like you—" he paused to give Michael a detailed once-over, "—hasn't ever been asked *out back*?" He drew elaborate, exaggerated air quotes. "And seriously, if you don't like backdoors, I'll have sized you up completely wrong, though I don't think so, I'm usually pretty good at that."

"What?"

"I'm asking you to go have sex behind the barn," Zan enunciated. "As in right now. Are you interested in a quick or not-so-quick fuck or not?"

"Jesus!"

"Really?" Zan peered around, hand over his eyes. "Where?"

Michael grabbed Zan's arm and shook him once, firmly. "Lower your voice," he hissed. "You'll get your ass kicked."

Zan rolled his eyes and flicked the pink feather dangling from his ear. "Please. You think anyone around here doesn't already know or gives a damn? No one's going to throw me a parade, but I'm still here and I haven't been tarred or feathered."

Michael flinched.

"What? What did I say?"

"Nothing." Michael studied Zan, trying in vain to get his measure. Small, crazy, annoying, but…unquestionably sexually appealing too. Very lithe, very…agile-looking…and very eager. Hard, the thick outline of his dick apparent in his tight jeans. Zan looked at Michael as if he were a slab of rare prime rib.

As long as he's not thinking about barbecued chicken, Michael thought with a hysterical inner giggle.

Zan fidgeted. "Well?"

Michael circled right back around to his initial assessment of Zan as *annoying*, realizing Zan reminded him of one of those damn fool dogs, good for nothing but carrying around snuggled between two powdered boobs, yapping their prettied-up heads off at the highest possible pitch.

He knew it'd be a bad, bad idea to go with Zan. The kid probably topped from the bottom anyway, the kind of man who'd push too hard, too far when getting fucked.

Damn. It'd been way, *way* too long since Michael had fucked *anyone.* Before Yi, even, and after that he hadn't dared, lest he change into the kind of cock his partner wouldn't be expecting to uncover during a filthy, sweaty roll in the hay.

Michael tried to be subtle about adjusting the pressure of his dick behind his zipper.

Zan grinned cheekily at Michael, obviously not a bit fooled, and nudged him. "Lighten up, Paul Bunyan. You look like you're walking the green mile to a chopping block. If you're really not interested, then say so."

Michael shook his head, starting to be amused, much despite himself. What a nut! "Do you expect me to believe you'd take no for an answer?"

Zan favored him with another blinding smile. "Depends. Is that what you're going for?" His hand shot up and between Michael's legs, shamelessly cupping his dick. "There's a pretty obvious indication of interest here, even if you're playing coy."

"How old are you?" Michael asked, employing his last line of defense. Risky business or not, Zan's hand spiked his libido, long since squashed. He gritted his teeth in the hopes of maintaining a calm façade. When Zan started massaging his dick, however, he couldn't maintain the pretense. "Would you quit that before I embarrass myself?"

"Twenty-five."

The non-sequitur threw Michael. "Huh?"

"You asked how old I was. Twenty-five." Zan manipulated him skillfully, easing up to gentleness. "Look at you, big guy. You're already sweating. Been a while, huh? I figured. You've got that uptight, tight-ass, desperately-needing-to-get-laid vibe going on."

Michael winced. "Would you please tone it down? Someone'll hear you, or see—"

"So? Let 'em enjoy the show. Tell you what. If you're so worried about privacy, then come around back with me already and let's take care of this." He squeezed Michael's dick. "What do you say?"

"You really are a dog on a bone," Michael said. *And you have no idea how much I know what I'm talking about.*

"The bone part's right, but as for the rest of it, say what now?"

"Never mind." Michael gave up and gave in, relieved to be done with the struggle. "Okay. Okay, sure. Let's go." He took a breath, whipped up the nerve to ask like a proper cowboy would, and blurted out, "Top or bottom?"

"Oh, I know it's stereotypical, but I'm a bottom all the way. I'll fight you for the chance to top, though."

Michael blinked. "You against me? Are you kidding?"

"Nope. This is one of the times in which I love picking impossible fights and losing is the goal. Shake your tail feathers, would you?"

Michael flinched.

"Now what's wrong?" Zan asked, his mood shifting to concerned.

"Nothing." Michael cleared his throat. "You're really serious about this, aren't you?"

"Never more so." Zan's good cheer returned in the blink of an eye. "So. Top or bottom is the question. I'll be serious, though I might rupture something from the effort and you'll have to kiss it better later." He stuck his tongue out and waggled it at Michael. "In all honesty I was hoping you'd fuck me against the wall. I've been dreaming about your cock up my ass since you walked in tonight. But if you'd rather, I'd be just as good with saving a horse and riding a cowboy, if you know what I mean." He winked. "Giddy-up."

Michael found himself starting to grin despite, or maybe because of, his disbelief in Zan's outrageousness. "Does that line actually ever work?"

"Seems to be fine at the moment. Does acting like a scared prom queen virgin ever work for you?"

Michael's cheeks warmed. He looked away. "Not usually, no."

"Then try it my way. Follow me, Roy Rogers." With a flip of his hip, Zan sashayed out ahead of Michael, clearly expecting him to follow.

Michael waffled briefly, amazed at how people honestly didn't seem to either notice or give a damn, ninety-nine percent of them completely focused on Daisy Duke #7 and some random guy in a too-big cowboy hat and suede vest lifting her up over the crowd for a reason he couldn't comprehend. This place was *nuts*.

Okay, then. Michael headed out the door, surprised to find himself grinning and more, laughing quietly. *The guys back at Shifting Sands are never gonna believe it—stuff like this just doesn't happen to me.*

Not that he objected…

🐾 🐾 🐾

When they got there, the back of the barn was already fully occupied and by more than one couple, although they all appeared to be heterosexual and busy with that sexuality. The musky smell of hard-fucking sweat mingled with a mixed bouquet of hairspray and perfume. Michael pulled back, dismayed, not up for either exhibitionism or voyeurism. It'd been long enough since his last roll in the hay that he'd end up embarrassing himself, sure as the world.

Zan, on the other hand, watched in rapt fascination. Once the look on his face registered, Michael slapped a hand over Zan's mouth before the nutbar could let rip with the stream of color commentary he just *knew* would be on its way.

No way he'd let a speed bump like this stop him, oh no. Michael thought fast, scrabbling through idea after idea and discarding them just as fast—until, as with a sound of horny angels, the Lord smiled down upon him with what he could only call divine inspiration. If he remembered right, there'd be a brand-new, still-empty storage shed erected on the back end of the property.

Perfect.

Michael tugged on Zan's sleeve. "I know a place. Better than here for damn sure, and there won't be an audience. Come with me?"

Zan gave Michael a respectful once over. "I do like a man with initiative. All right then, cowboy. Lead the way."

"Good. Follow me."

Of course, that made Zan drag his heels. "Is that a challenge to a race?"

Michael started to say no—then stopped. Tonight had been all kinds of crazy anyway. Why quit now? "Yeah. Why not?"

"I like a man who knows how to have fun even more." Zan tagged him on the shoulder. "One, two, go!"

The short man took off at full throttle with a surprising turn of speed. Michael exclaimed in admiration, shook himself, and gave chase. "You don't even know where we're headed!"

"I'll know when I see it!" Zan hollered back.

Michael laughed, put his head down, and set to the task of winning. Zan's miles-per-hour ratcheted up when he seemed to realize Michael was serious about the race, looking back every now and then with his infuriating, challenging smirk. Even with Michael's long legs to his advantage, they were just about evenly matched.

Once Michael realized as much, he changed plans and favored lagging behind a pace or three, all the better to check out Zan's ass and the strength in his fast-pumping legs. He felt as light as a feather, giddy from the four beers he'd gulped down too quickly, and could not remember a time in which he'd had this much fun with a hookup.

Zan abruptly changed course and jogged backwards nimbly as a circus performer, passing Michael in the other direction. A wolf-whistle let Michael know exactly why Zan had done it. Copycat—or copy puppy, rather.

Two could play at that game. Michael turned on his heel and ran backwards his own self, careful not to trip while challenging Zan by ogling his sweaty chest. "Don't waste time, short stuff. You can look all you like as soon as we're there."

"Aggressive. I like it."

In Michael's opinion, a man who could still talk while either running or fucking wasn't being pushed hard enough. His opinion of Zan's stamina increased and inspired him at the same time to do his best to drive the man speechless.

Lucky for both of them, they'd nearly arrived, the woodshed appearing on the far horizon. "Yonder!" Michael called, pointing.

Zan whooped, clicked his heels together and cranked his pace up to eleven. Michael almost stumbled to a stop in amazement. "Jesus Christ, he's like Speedy Gonzalez on acid," he muttered. "You wanna leave me behind?"

"Hell, no!"

For all that, by the time Michael caught up and stumbled to a stop inside the woodshed, Zan had long beat him, not only there but jumped ahead to the next—much better—step, shucking off his boots and hurrying out of his jeans.

Michael reached for his own belt buckle, rushing it open. "In a hurry, are you?"

"You wouldn't be, in my place? Life is fleeting, my friend. Better make the most of it, huh? I'll show you. Like this." Zan tackled him without warning him first, hitting Michael in the manner of a cannonball shot to the stomach. He might as well have shouted "timber!" Michael went down.

With the breath half-knocked out of him, dazed, Michael lay still and let Zan get on with it. He sure did have enough energy for both of them, and then some, and Michael decided he didn't mind being manhandled, not a bit. Zan's deft, rapid handling made Michael's head swim. He palmed and massaged his dick to ease up the burning need for friction until Zan smacked his hand away in order to wriggle his jeans off. Zan himself was naked only from the waist down. Should have looked idiotic, but it didn't. Especially not when faced—literally—with the graspable length of his dick, a very fine dick indeed and impressively sized to boot.

For his part, Zan whistled in admiration when he tugged down Michael's briefs and his dick sprang free. "Now that's something to write home about," he said, taking it in hand to study reverently. "If I wanted to give my granny a heart attack. That's a fucking appendage, boy."

"Don't call me boy, and for the love of God don't talk about your granny right now," Michael said through gritted teeth. Zan's hand made it almost impossible not to come then and there. "Fucking appendage? I aim to please. Get down here and get with the fucking."

"I like appendages." Zan bent to kiss Michael, not a gentle kiss, their teeth clashing briefly before he shifted to a better angle and slid his tongue through Michael's lips. Soft lips, clever tongue. One kiss melting into another, Zan worked Michael's dick with light touches, the lack of firmness keeping him at the point of popping and craving more.

The moment Michael thought he'd have to warn Zan to either let go or get jizzed on, Zan straightened and twisted around, reaching for his discarded jeans. He rummaged through the pockets and came up with a sachet of lube and a condom.

Michael laughed, almost out of breath. "Pretty sure of yourself, aren't you?"

"You bet," Zan agreed, happy as a clam as he got to work tearing open the condom packet.

A slow light of realization dawned. "You planned this, didn't you? Knew I'd be at that damn-fool party. Came after me on purpose."

"I sure did," Zan agreed, leering at him. He dangled the sachet of lube before Michael's eyes. "What say you get me ready?"

"You're serious." Michael damned the uncertainty that made him hesitate even now. It wasn't vanity that made him consider his dick too large for most men's comfort. Facts were facts and he never topped the first time around with a guy, too scared of hurting his partners before they got used to him. "You're sure you can take this?"

"Damn right I am." Zan rolled the condom on Michael's dick quickly and efficiently, not tormenting Michael with more teasing than he could handle. "I can take as much as you've got to give. I want to taste this in the back of my throat when you fuck me, and cowboy, from the looks of you, you might just get there. Here." Zan passed off the lube and tapped Michael's mouth with two free fingers, plainly asking him to suck them.

Michael flicked his tongue over Zan's fingertips to enjoy the taste of Zan's warm skin. "Why are these here?"

"For the fun of it, and 'cause I want to see what you look like when you're sucking." Zan prodded Michael's lips. "Open up."

Michael did as he was told and drew Zan's fingers in his mouth, rubbing them with his tongue and sucking, paying special attention to where finger met palm. Those spots he teased, tickling them. And to prove he could be just as bad, while he had Zan good and distracted, Michael snuck a hand between them and teased under Zan's balls, dragging the pad of his forefinger over Zan's perineum, hoping he'd react like—

Zan threw his head back and hissed, then started to pant.

Just like that, Michael thought, letting himself enjoy a moment of "smug."

"That's it, big guy. No more playing around." Zan's eyelids were heavy, his lips parted.

"Hurry up, then," Michael goaded.

"All good things come to those who wait. Better things come to those who rush."

"Shut up and let me fuck you."

"About damn time." Zan agreed. He snatched the packet of lube away from Michael and ripped it open, dolloping half over Michael's dick and half over his fingers. "Get to work."

"Your wish," Michael grunted, eagerly moving to circle Zan's hole with his slick fingers, "My command."

Zan hissed when the first finger popped inside. Though it near about killed him, Michael made himself stop. "You okay?"

"More." Zan wriggled, impatient. "More. What are you, chicken? Respect the cock!"

Michael didn't even have it in him to cringe at the hot words, far more happily occupied with finger-fucking Zan stupid and silent. When he'd got three fingers in, scissoring them open and spreading them wide, listening with amazed delight to Zan's litany of eager curses and demands, he finally let himself believe this would be good for both of them. His fingers weren't small, and Zan sure did seem to love those.

About time he saw what Zan thought of his dick instead, hmm?

Zan fisted his own dick, angry red and leaking, slicking it with his own pre-come as it bubbled out. Copiously. "You're like a fucking sprinkler," Michael gasped, amazed.

"Yeah. But I can still paint your face when I shoot." Zan laughed at Michael's awe. "Watch and see if I don't. Hurry up, now. Do it, cowboy. Fuck me.

Excitement made Michael reckless. "Like this." He grasped the base of his dick and held himself steady. "You said you wanted to ride. So ride."

"You're on." Zan straddled Michael, found his balance and let Michael guide himself into place. He slid down without taking it slow, heading straight for ground zero with a rattlesnake hiss and his eyes rolling back in his head. Michael slammed his own eyes shut. He started to count in Spanish to delay the moment as Zan's tight, lube-slick heat surrounded him. There was almost too much stimulation to feel good, but thank *God* it stopped far short enough of overload to equal out as the best, most mind-blowing fuck he could remember.

Zan exhaled a long sigh when he was fully seated, his bubble-butt pressed tight to Michael's hips. "You're on, and now you're in." He rocked his hips. "Do something about it."

"Hang on tight, then." Michael grasped Zan's hips and thrust up. Zan gasped, filling Michael with a savage triumph.

Zan snapped his teeth at Michael after a second's recovery and raised up before slamming down. Michael was the one to hiss and swear this time. Even match.

On the third try, Michael fucked up exactly as Zan fucked down. Both groaned between tightly clenched teeth, caught that rhythm and hung on for dear life. Zan threw back his head and cried out when Michael tugged him forward.

"Hit the good spot?" Michael forced out without proper breath to propel his words.

"Mmm," Zan moaned in reply and leaned to tug at Michael's hair. "Harder," he demanded, sitting back to grasp his dick. He fisted it and pumped fast, milking from base to head, the swollen top barely peeking out. "Fuck. Close. Real close."

Oh, hell. The thought of watching Zan fly apart was the last Michael could possibly take. He groaned, the noise ripping from the bottom of his gut, and thrust, hips almost clearing the ground. Zan bounced and slammed down, finishing the both of them. His ass clenched around Michael's dick as he shot, slim ropes splattering over Michael's chest, one splash landing on his *chin*. Michael's balls contracted with a spasm of *good* near-pain as he let go. Fumbling for something to hang onto for the ride, he found Zan's waist and grabbed him tight, fingers aching with the pressure. Zan moaned and pushed out another spurt, this one streaming over Michael's cheek.

Goddamn, he's gonna kill me, Michael thought hazily, thrilled down to his toes.

Cursing fit to turn the air blue, Zan collapsed over him. Michael protested when the change in position forced him to pull out, but Zan distracted him nicely by pushing his mouth to Michael's and demanding a good hard kiss.

Apparently, Zan didn't mind lying atop a mess of come. Michael's dick twitched at the thought, trying its damndest to shoot a few final drops into the nearly overfull condom.

Zan chuckled. "I told you," he said drowsily before lifting his head to lick the come off Michael's face. Michael lay still for it, amazed and almost reverent.

So thinking, he looked up. Right at a crack between the old boards of the woodshed, where the gibbous moon looked back at him. The cold light brought him crashing down to earth, dismay rushing in to overwhelm his afterglow. *Aw, hell. Come* on!

Damn it!

It'd been a dumbass mistake, letting it go this far when he knew what'd happen to someone dumb enough to fall for him. Lord knew what kind of beast Zan would end up as.

He couldn't do that to Zan.

The trouble would lie in convincing Zan of that without actually telling the truth. Michael didn't fancy getting carted away to a psych ward that night, thanks.

Unfortunately, he was already sure and certain that it'd be harder than hen's teeth, no pun intended, to change Zan's mind about anything once the scrappy guy had made it up.

"So when can I see you again?" Zan asked between laps at Michael's chin and his throat. "God almighty, big guy. If you'd gone bareback, I think you'd have gotten jizz on the back of my tonsils."

"Zan…quit that, would you?"

"Uh-uh. I taste good on your skin."

Michael shut his eyes and groaned. "Look, about seeing me again…"

"Soon as possible, okay? A man like you, with a cock like yours? I'm gonna ride you raw every chance I get. When can we two meet again?"

Michael damned himself for the cowardice, but he *couldn't* wreck the life of a guy with as much to give as Zan had. He sat up, dislodging Zan, discarded the condom, and reached for his jeans. He blocked his ears to Zan's puzzled protests and did what he had to do.

He left.

Once outside and far enough away to be sure Zan wasn't following behind, Michael finally let it rip. He was mad enough to—to *crow*—and he needed to drive home to himself the reasons why he'd *had* to do what he'd done.

Letting the change happen, Michael shrank down to a *rooster*, of all the things, and cussed Yi up and down in chickenese. He fought his way free of the remains of his clothes, ran around in circles for a minute—certain conventions were too strong to be overcome—and flew like hell back to Shifting Sands.

TWO

"COCK-A-DOODLE-DOO!"

Michael-the-rooster lowered his wattled head and scratched viciously at the dirt. *This is so humiliating.* He hated every single crow that he uttered, but be damned if he could fight a natural instinct to let 'er rip.

Aw, shit, here comes another one. Michael could feel it rising in his throat. The other hands had told Michael cocks didn't really crow at sunrise, or didn't have to if they didn't want to. Michael supposed it was his usual luck coming into play, plus the city-boy's bred-in assumption that when the sun came up, roosters made a fucklot of noise.

Michael pecked angrily at the furrows he'd just dug and tried to hold it back like a cough, a sneeze, or an orgasm, hoping that this time—nope. With a tickle in his throat, he began to twitch and to shake. His damned *wattles* flapped, making it even worse.

"COCK-A-DOODLE-DOO!"

If chickens could roll their eyes to heaven in search of help from the almighty, Michael would have. His inner cock wanted to crow? Hate it or not, better to stand back, let it happen, and pray none of the guys were around to bear witness. He wasn't the only rooster on the ranch, and he could always blame the racket on one of the other dumb clucks.

Hell, it could always be worse, Michael reasoned. He counted himself lucky that he'd stayed male under Yi's curse, and didn't foresee the need to lay eggs. He hoped. Wasn't supposed to be possible, but then again humans weren't supposed to physically be able to transmute forms, so who knows?

"COCK-A-DOODLE-DOO!"

There. Michael tipped his rooster head to one side, considering the ebbing strength of his urges. *Good. Think I'm done for now.*

Speaking of which… With his duties fulfilled, Michael took a deep breath and thankfully, gratefully, sensed the beginning of the change washing over him. Sweet, sweet relief!

Wait. Where'd I stash my clothes? Oh…fuck!

Trying to keep his dignity despite his speeding change from human to rooster, despite swaying wattles and shedding feathers that clung to his butt and blew up with the morning breeze, Michael half-scrambled and half-strutted—strutted!—across the yard to the side of the porch, where he was always careful to stash a set of clothes on shifting night. Not much, just an old university T-shirt washed so often that the logo had mostly cracked off and a pair of sweatpants much the worse for wear after accidentally getting in a load of whites with bleach. Laundry wasn't Michael's strong suit.

Safer than before, Michael stopped fighting the partial shift and let it happen, all the while keeping his senses as alert as possible, all the better to observe the changes as they took place. He'd been keeping a very precise record of the transformation process, hoping to learn how to stop and start at will, or to control the shift by means of controlling his emotions.

Cock Zen, to coin an unfortunate phrase, a phrase Michael determined he would never, ever say out loud in front of the other hands.

Michael hadn't had any luck so far in controlling the full change process during a lunar cycle; but in this matter at least, Michael, the natural-born pessimist, firmly chose to hope.

Trouble was, it was damned harder to concentrate than it sounded like. The process of transforming was more than a little uncomfortable, driving Michael to think this had to be what a pincushion must feel like. Despite knowing they were simply disappearing, he had the oddest, creepiest sensation of feathers zipping under his skin as his body grew and stretched like gooey rubber on a hot day.

Michael stood, momentarily dizzy as he readjusted to his normal height of six feet and change. *Lord, that's better. Much, much better.* His head ached, reminding him of the folly of four beers consumed too fast, but Michael could deal with that.

Not so much with what he'd done when his judgment was impaired by those beers. *Fuck a duck. Zan.*

Embarrassed half to death, Michael tried to cover his shame and to distract himself by working out his aches and pains. He stretched his arms, cracked his neck, and arched for the sheer pleasure of enjoying human flexibility.

"Well, well. Who do we have here, up to greet the sun? Morning, boy!" Jud called from the porch. He grinned down at Michael.

Ah. Much better distraction. "Good morning," Michael replied stiffly.

Jud chuckled. "Ain't it a shame? Such a big man, yet such a little cock."

"Very funny, and you *wish* you had a dick half this size," Michael muttered, stepping into and pulling up his sweatpants.

"That's all right. Some men aren't show-ers. They're crow-ers."

Testy or not, Michael had to exert strong force of will not to laugh. Even he had to admit to himself it *was* at least a little funny. To save face, he pitched his voice in the "surly" range as he snapped, "Are we getting fed today or not?"

"You bet we are." Jud winked at Michael. "Chicken fried steak and eggs."

Michael wadded up his T-shirt and winged it—er—at Jud.

Jud caught the ball of cloth easily and tossed it back. "Don't you forget to eat, either. And smile, huh? Gotta keep your pecker up."

Despite his best intentions, Michael really had to laugh now. "I'll get you when you least expect it, Jud."

Jud shot him a one-finger salute as he headed back inside. "Promises, promises."

Michael chuckled as he finished getting dressed, tickled

through and through, his bad mood lifting. Okay, so what Yi did to them had its drawbacks. Lots of them, such as feathers and surprise nudity and watching the moon like—okay, like a chicken hawk—not to mention keeping marks on calendars, and the vow of secrecy they had taken among them to protect their secrets.

And then there was the dread of what would happen if they actually ever fell in love—which meant, for a guy like Michael, a life mostly comprised of celibacy. Lord knew what kind of crazy bug had bitten him when he went so wild with Zan.

Well, what was done was done. Michael reckoned he could handle damage control if any rose up. He had to be three times the size of tiny Zan, outweighing him by far, and none of his mass from fat. Not that he'd put a hurtin' on Zan, no, but if he had to be cruel to be kind…hate it or not, he would.

Michael grumbled, feeling mighty "fowl"—*goddamnit, now I'm making puns too*—and adjusted his *dick*, thank you, and stomped off in search of breakfast.

※ ※ ※

During his teenage years, when he'd shot up a foot and a half seemingly overnight and hadn't stopped there, Michael had endured considerable teasing speculation about what his parents might be feeding him besides Miracle-Gro.

If he'd been exposed to a cook as skilled as Jud, Michael reckoned he might be ten feet tall by now. Michael patted his full belly, enjoying the afterglow that came from devouring as many hot buttermilk biscuits with pepper-spiced gravy as he could eat.

"My compliments," he said, tipping his hat to Jud.

"You think you're fit for work, or do you need to explode first?" Jud looked as pleased as punch. Good cooks did love to see their food appreciated.

"Exploding's not out of the question, man." Michael groaned. "Lots to get done today. If you don't hear a great big *boom*, expect to see me again at suppertime with a fresh appetite."

"The pantry might never recover," Jud remarked dryly. "Go

on, now."

Michael found himself walking slow and feeling fine, mellow, satiation calming his nerves. He didn't even so much as shoot the bird to the one ranch hand who clucked in his general direction when he walked past.

Outside, the day looked to be promising. Hot, as was to be expected, the skies clear without a trace of cloud anywhere. A day in which he could bask in the honest sunlight and work up a good, cleansing sweat.

All in all, Michael figured he was a walking advertisement for "new and improved mood" when he ambled onto the porch to get his work orders for the day. Ben went kindly on him the morning after a shift, giving him something good and laborious to focus on, putting body over mind. Yes sir, he was on top of the world.

Or, he was, until he raised his head and laid eyes on the strangest, ugliest van in the whole of God's green earth, Ben leaning on the open passenger side window, apparently having a friendly chat with the driver.

"Summer time, you bet we've got odd jobs," Michael overheard from Ben. "Can't trust you with anything big, you not being a trained hand and all, but if you don't mind dirty work then sure, we can give you a trial run, see how you get along chasing after us." Ben laughed. "You said it was Michael who you knew?"

Michael drew up short, horrified, then stretched up tall. For him, that meant height enough to see over Ben's head. By means of craning at a chicken-hawk angle, he managed a clear peek through the window when Ben stepped back and pointed toward a place to park the van.

Zan. Zan Jedrek behind the wheel. Zan Jedrek spotting Michael and flashing him a blazing bright grin in company with a jaunty wave.

"Hey, sugar lips!" Zan hollered. "I'm coming over to play!"

🐓 🐓 🐓

Sure as shooting, the second Zan puttered off in his hideous van to park where Ben had directed, the heckling started.

"Well now, well now, well *now*," commented one of the hands. "Where do you know a peacock like him from, Michael?"

Michael ground his molars together. "Who says I know him?"

"Anyone who calls *you* 'sugar lips,' Mister Live-Like-A-Monk, has some deep and intimate acquaintance with yourself," Cy pointed out, not unreasonably. "Say, you did go to that hootenanny last night, didn't you?"

Michael growled, shoved his hat further down on his head, and strode toward Ben.

Ben regarded Michael with an air of stoic calm. "Friend of yours?" he asked, nodding at Zan's van as it clanked and groaned to a rattling halt. "He sure spoke highly of you."

"I don't think this is a good idea," Michael said without preface. "I do know him, yes, though I wouldn't say we're friends. We only met last night. And I don't think it's a good idea to have him around."

Ben didn't blink. "And why's that?"

"He's trouble. Talks too much, asks a fuckton of questions, and anything that isn't nailed shut, you can bet he'll poke his nose in there."

"Uh-huh." Ben narrowed his eyes at Michael. Michael had the odd sensation that Ben saw clear through his human self to the thrice-damned chicken inside. "Got some and then got cold feet, huh?"

"Now, that's not fair at all."

"Then tell me how it really is."

Michael's face warmed uncomfortably. He shuffled his feet and shrugged. "You can't tell me it's a good idea to have someone as nosy as Zan around—" he lowered his voice "—*all things considered.* And since when do we need any extra help?"

"Since I decided we do," Ben replied. "If Zan's all you say, and I suspect he is as he found this place all on his own, better to keep an eye on him than have him snooping around on his own, don't you think?"

Damn it. Michael couldn't argue with that.

"And who better to keep a look out than the one he's got a puppy crush on?" Ben continued, a faint trace of humor in his otherwise steady tone. "You carry him along on your work for his trial run."

Michael, though he'd never admit to making the noise, squawked in protest.

Ben held up one hand. "Michael. You know I wouldn't do you any wrong, don't you?"

Michael had no rebuttal for that either. Ben was a fine man.

"Then trust me on this," Ben said. "Zan's your responsibility, for today at least."

Michael opened his mouth to argue. Before he got one word out, Zan bounced up beside him, as excited as a half-grown spaniel hound eager for playtime. He looked up, up, and up at Michael, happier than a bucket full of clams. "So where do we start, boss?"

Michael's day had started off interesting, for sure, and the "interesting" kept coming hour by hour. For example, explaining to Zan the right end from the wrong end of a pitchfork and why it'd be a bad idea to go bouncing into the stall of a horse that didn't know you.

Then, as if to deliberately tweak his chains, the horses took a shine to Zan like rain to thirsty ground, nuzzling him and near about stomping him flat indeed—but with love. By the time Zan emerged from their slobbery displays of affection, half his hair was matted to his skull and his idea of work clothes, a tie-dyed T-shirt and old jeans, were covered in chaff from the straw bedding.

Recalling the night before and how getting dirty hadn't bothered Zan then either, and seeing once again how good Zan looked mussed and jubilant, Michael cleared his throat and looked resolutely away, thinking of cold showers and presidents past and present on the toilet to keep his dick calmed down.

"Something wrong?" Zan flicked his tongue over his teeth, the little devil.

Michael coughed. The tickle in his throat reminded him far too much of the feeling that heralded his cock's crow. "Nothing," he said, turning away. "Grab the damn pitchfork and get to work. The stalls won't clean themselves."

"Aye-aye, *sir*," Zan said, appreciation evident.

Michael kept his back turned, counting silently. Zan made it through four whole forkfuls of straw before he poked Michael in the back with what Michael devoutly hoped was the butt-end of the pitchfork. "So what was with the disappearing act last night? We were having a good time." He poked Michael harder. "Did you have to get back before midnight in case you turned into a pumpkin or something?"

Michael grimaced.

Taking Michael's silence as an invitation to keep yapping, Zan bounced around in front of Michael and leaned his pitchfork against the stable wall, out of harm's way.

Zan gazed up at Michael and tapped his chin thoughtfully.

Michael, who had an instant, uneasy feeling about this, attempted to casually back-step.

"Oh no you don't." Michael didn't see Zan coming. One minute, a ranch hand on his lonesome. The next, a ranch hand with a double armful of firecracker, Zan not just jumping him but damn well *climbing* him as if he were a jungle gym. It was either help out or let Zan break something, so Michael grabbed on and hung tight.

"Now that's more like it," Zan said, pleased with himself. At this height, he could look Michael eye-to-eye. "I come on strong.

I get that. I've never seen the point in not going after what I want. The direct approach works for me."

"You ever consider you're crossing the line into 'overkill'?"

"Michael, if you didn't make eyes at me and if your cock didn't give you away, I'd leave you alone. Thing is…" Zan wiggled closer, plastering their torsos together.

Michael's heart sped up and his lips parted, dry. "Thing is, what?"

"Lots of 'things,'" Zan replied. He wrapped his legs around Michael's waist and locked his ankles at the small of Michael's back, far too limber for his own good.

Michael groaned through his gritted teeth. The new position planted Zan's tight bubble-butt directly above his groin. Vivid recollections of Zan's pleasure when he took every inch of Michael's dick and the heat of Zan's body, to say nothing of the rigid proof of arousal wedged tightly to Michael's belly, were too arousing to resist. His dick swelled, aching for another taste of Zan's unique charms.

Zan pressed his lips to Michael's, slower, lingering. Michael opened for him and dug his fingers in Zan's narrow back. On an impulse he turned them, his shoulders flush to the stable wall, needing leverage to rock up and grind against Zan's tempting heat.

"You make me lose my better judgment," Michael confessed. "I thought I was just drunk last night, but this—"

"This is exactly what I was talking about." Zan undulated, teasing Michael with the rocking motion and the brushes of contact. "God, you're hot. I couldn't stop thinking about you. Had to come see if lightning would strike twice."

Michael closed his eyes. "You and me, we're a bad idea, Zan."

"So says your head." Zan kissed him without mercy. "The rest of you knows better, and I don't flatter myself. If you truly didn't want this, you could buck me off easy as a gadfly. But you aren't."

"Want it or don't want it doesn't change it being wrong."

"Wrong, or risky? Big difference there."

Michael kept his mouth shut. Arousal made him thick-headed. He didn't dare speak for fear of spilling anything he ought not to.

"Thought so. But as I started to say earlier... you don't *want* to have a 'thing' for me, but you do," Zan said. "If you don't want to tell me what's got your pinfeathers tweaked, fine. Fair warning that I won't give up, though. This spark between us—don't lie, I know you feel it too—could spell something good."

"You don't know more about me than my name. If you knew the truth—" Michael clamped his lips shut.

"I know you're shy, you're smart, and I know for a fact you fuck like a demon once you're past the song-and-dance. What else do I need?"

"You don't even know me, Zan."

"That's the main reason *why* I've got the hots for you, dumbass, and what I don't know I plan to take my time finding out." Zan planted a hearty smacking kiss on Michael's lips. He wriggled to get free and bounced lightly down in the straw. "Back to work?"

Determinedly pushing away both the urge to toss Zan on his back in the straw to get busy, and the wanting to laugh in exasperation over Zan's bulldog stubbornness, Michael snatched at, well, the offered straws. "Yeah. Work. Work is good."

"You're cute when you're flustered."

"Work, I said."

"I mean to get to the bottom of you, Michael," Zan said, picking up his pitchfork. "There's more to you than meets the eye, and I love a challenge."

Michael threw a forkful of dirty straw in Zan's direction. *Yeah. I bet you do, and like I told Ben, that right there is the problem.*

All the same, he couldn't hold back a smile. One thing was for certain—having Zan around surely did keep him on his toes, chicken or not.

🐓 🐓 🐓

Propped comfortably on the porch steps, Michael watched Zan and his god-awful van ride off into the sunset. He wouldn't be a hair surprised if Zan didn't come creeping back in the middle of the night, minus his rattletrap, and would not be in the least bit shocked if he heard pebbles rat-a-tat-tatting at the window by his bunk around oh-dark-thirty. Zan was nothing if not persistent. And nuts. And a pint-sized peck of trouble.

And fun. Michael clicked his tongue to try and disguise his quiet chuckle.

Jud dropped to the step next to Michael, wiping his forehead on a clean, white handkerchief. "What's got you smiling like you just got a clear shot at Yi and won the lottery to boot?"

Michael shrugged, trying for an impression of nonchalance. "In a good mood, is all."

"Huh. Doesn't have anything to do with that little spitfire I saw climbing you like you were a tree and yapping around your ankles all day long, does it?"

Michael went still.

"I didn't say that was a bad thing." Jud leaned back on his elbows. "It's not too healthy, the way you keep yourself all—"

"You say 'cooped up' and we'll have to have less pleasant words," Michael warned Jud, mostly kidding. Mostly.

"I would never." Jud looked offended. "Since when do I poke fun at you?"

"Sorry." Michael grimaced apologetically at the cook. "He gets me tangled up inside, Jud. I don't know which way I'm coming and where I'm going."

"I figured he'd be the type."

They sat in silence for a moment.

"Seems like he'd be good for you," Jud said.

Michael made a noncommittal noise, then added, "But I'd be bad for him."

"Depends on your point of view," Jud said, surprising

Michael. "Hasn't turned out so awful for the others, has it?"

"That's not the point."

"Then what is? A man like Zan, well, I don't see him minding his life taking a turn for the strange and unusual."

"I won't bring this curse down on anyone else."

"Bull. You, buddy, are bound and determined to live your life out being miserable instead of doing something about it." Jud stood, dusting off his britches. "You ask me, I'd advise you to give that boy a chance. He'd be good for you."

Michael pinched the bridge of his nose, squeezing his eyes shut. He waited for the sound of Jud's footsteps to fade out of hearing range before he groaned.

🐓 🐓 🐓

And be damned if I wasn't right, Michael thought fuzzily at three-thirty a.m. that night, or at least insofar as he was capable of thought beyond the surging rise and fall of lust burning in his belly. Zan had come back for sure, all right, and with one thing on his mind. Michael wasn't any too sure exactly how they'd made their way from Zan pinging pebbles on his window to fumbling clothes off one another in the stables, but with his libido doing 99% of the thinking for him just then, he didn't care.

Zan discarded the rest of Michael's clothing, mauling him with jubilant, exuberant smooches. Michael gave back as good as he got, tossing Zan into the fresh clean straw as he'd had a mind to do more than once during the workday.

Naked except for one sock and a smile, Zan caught his knees and drew them up to his chest. "Giddyup."

Michael laughed breathlessly. "Damn. Every time I think you can't shock me, you turn around and prove me wrong."

"Turn around, you said?" Zan let go, flipped over, and rose to his hands and knees, ass raised high and tempting. "Like this?" He rocked and moaned, giving Michael a peek at—

No way. No *way.*

"See something you like?" Zan teased.

"Oh my God." Michael fell to his knees, no more able to resist Zan than the moon's call to change shapes. Glistening with lube, the plug he'd apparently been wearing all along—the little devil—drove him nearly out of what remained of his mind. He twisted the toy, jostling it accidentally-on-purpose. Zan yelped, shuddering.

"Take it out," Zan invited. "Figured I should prepare myself for that monster of yours. And added bonus…ah, fuck!" he shouted as Michael slid the plug free.

"Holy—" Michael gaped at the size of the toy. "This damn thing's bigger than a stallion's equipment!"

"You ever look in the mirror at yourself when you're hard?" Zan wiggled his ass. "Fill me up, big boy. I don't need anything more but your cock in me. Now. Like that, just like that—*fuck!*"

Michael held still, balls deep and shaking in every muscle. Even as relaxed as Zan had been, he still gripped Michael's dick smoothly snug. He struggled to see past the spots clouding his vision.

"Move," Zan urged, low and hungry. He clamped down. "I can do all the work, but—*ah,* yeah, there you go. More!"

"Insatiable," Michael accused. He thrust hard, fast and reckless, astonished at how Zan took him so easily and ravenously. "You make me crazy. Crazy for you."

"That's—that's the plan." Zan's back arched. "Right there, again, God!" He turned his head, face twisted with pleasure, egging Michael on. "All you've got, big boy. Gimme."

Still buried in Zan, Michael dropped to rest his weight on his arms and sought Zan's mouth, awkward angle be damned. Zan writhed, stiffened, and squeezed Michael ruthlessly.

Michael swallowed every howl Zan loosed and traded roars when he shot hard and filled Zan to the brim. He could stay here forever like this. He *wanted* to. All Zan had to offer, so freely.

God almighty. Knowing that, how could he possibly make

himself let Zan go?

Dismayed, Michael withdrew and turned over, flopping on his back, out of breath. *Fuck me sideways. What am I supposed to do now?*

Zan collapsed, panting like a dog who'd spent half an hour chasing its tail out in the sun. He whooped and asked, raspy from the racket he'd raised and Michael had muffled, "So. You had something you wanted to talk about?"

Michael groaned and buried his face in the clean straw. Fine. He couldn't trust himself in Zan's presence. Only one thing to be done for it, and if it hurt him, then so be it.

He waited for Zan to start snoring, and crept out of the stables without waking him, went back to the bunkhouse and locked the door, and pretended deafness when a new rain of pebbles struck his window.

The sun came up right about the same time as Zan finally quit.

Michael ignored the ache in his heart and the weariness in his limbs. He had work to do.

🐓 🐓 🐓

Sunk in a morass of his own making, Michael didn't catch on, at first, to how the ranch hands ambling out of the bunkhouse ahead of him changed their tune as they went. From hushed and uncomfortable, sneaking looks at him that ranged between envious and dubious—Michael knew he and Zan hadn't been exactly quiet—they started to grin, then snicker, and by the time he stepped out into the hot, white sunny morning, they parted like the Red Sea to let him through.

To give him a front-row, unobstructed view of none other than Zan himself, perched on an old chopping block, chin in his hand, so obviously waiting for Michael to show his face that, if the hands hadn't closed in a solid barrier behind him, Michael would have turned and run.

Zan seemed to know as much, too. "Thanks, boys," he said,

waving at them with the hand not occupied holding his head up. "Michael. Long time no see." He pretended to check a watch, intently studying the bare skin of his slim wrist. "So how about them Mets?"

"The who?" Michael's ears buzzed. "Zan, what the hell? Can't you take a hint?"

Uh-oh. Michael sensed the undercurrent of disapproval from his fellow men. "Y'all got a problem?" He turned to face them, his back to Zan, ignoring the twinge of pain at the inherent rudeness, but hoping against hope all the same that it might help his cause. Though he rarely did so, Michael drew himself up to his full height and squared his shoulders. "Anyone?"

"Chill out," Zan said, sounding not at all miffed. Amused, on the contrary. "I got this one, guys. Go do ranch stuff."

A hand snorted. "City slicker."

"Yeah, but I make it look good."

Michael pinched the bridge of his nose. The ranch hands' ire softened, probably guessing accurately that Zan already had him whipped something fierce, and that Michael just didn't know he was beaten yet. Kind of like a chicken on that good old chopping block, hopping around in a crazy headless dance when it was already too late to run far enough. Some clapped him on the arm, some pounded him on the back; some chortled quietly and some had a few lewd suggestions.

When they'd gone on their way and left him and Zan be, Michael hesitated to turn about and look at the stubborn little man for fear he'd be dazzled by Zan's brilliance and, once again, lose sight of his common sense.

"Why're you here?" he asked instead.

"Last time I checked, I work here. At least for now, until they run out of odd jobs, and from what I've seen, there's a list that stretches from here to eternity and keeps on growing." Shuffling sounds told Michael that Zan had started to move around restlessly. "Look at me, would you?"

Michael couldn't. Or rather, he had the ability, but he didn't dare.

"I'm not going away," Zan told him. He sounded sorry for Michael. The pity burned. "We can be friends, or we can be enemies, or we can be a whole lot more either way. What are you so scared of, Michael?"

"I'm not—"

"Don't even try." Michael heard Zan hop off the chopping block. "You're terrified. It's like elephants and mice, no insult to you and no insult to me."

Or to Jud, Michael thought, his lips twitching involuntarily. "There's no taking a hint with you, is there?"

"Nope. Not in the slightest. I'm gonna get to work, Michael. Any time you want to come work this out, you'll know where to find me." Zan hesitated. "I won't bite. Whatever you think's so awful, Michael, there's not a lot I can't handle. Wish you'd trust me."

"I barely know you."

"And I'm offering the chance for you to know me much better. I'll be here when you change your mind, and I'll see you when I see you. I'll always—" Zan sobbed, throwing his arm over his eyes "—always remember Paris, and—"

Damn it. "Zan, for God's sake. Stop. Please?"

Zan turned, his grin blazing. "That was easy. But take it again from the top, without the 'stop' word in there. We'll both be happier and it'll save time."

"Why does this matter so much to you? What is it about me that has you so fixated?"

"Told you yesterday morning," Zan said, taking the question in stride. He rocked on his heels. "You're different. There's more to you than meets the eye. I love a man with layers, those I can unwrap with my hands—" he waggled his fingers "—and those who are riddles on the inside."

"So I'm a walking, talking, six-foot-seven Sudoku puzzle."

Zan laughed, free and easy, though no less eager for Michael's approval. "Not quite." He rubbed his chin, tugging thoughtfully at the tip of his goatee. "You want the absolute truth?"

"I'd be obliged."

"Boiled down to its finest point, Michael, when I saw you I knew my place was at your side."

"Knew." Michael digested that. "Knew how?"

"Can't tell you that—yet—but it's still true." Zan raised one shoulder. "Share and share alike is fair, Michael. Penny for your thoughts."

Michael hesitated, briefly torn. He *could* walk away. Could. Would it do any good, though? That was hardly a question, and the answer was "no." A man of Zan's determination would chase after his heels like a terrier on the scent until he'd worn him down.

And God help him, Michael liked the little twerp. More pity Zan for affixing so to a man with enough baggage for a month-long European tour.

He'd have to show Zan, up close and personal, how it would be better for all if he left of his own accord.

Okay, then.

"Not here," Michael said. He gauged the skies, imagining the progress of the moon. He'd change again that night, and if he didn't fight, it'd happen sooner rather than later.

"Then where?" Zan asked, accepting of the wait.

"Stables at midnight. I'll meet you here, and if you're still sure you want this, want me—"

"I'm not changing my mind. Midnight." Zan tugged a curl that'd fallen over his forehead. "See you then, Michael. If you're late, I'm coming to find you."

"I just bet you would, too." Michael heaved a long breath, the weight of secrecy laying a few pounds heavier on his shoulders. "I'll be there. I promise."

🐾 🐾 🐾

"You kept your word," Zan said, stopping with a scuff of his boots in the straw.

"I did." Michael tilted his head. He sat, legs crossed tailor-style, and Zan stood, but they were still almost of an equal height to look one another in the eye. "You sound surprised."

"Kind of." Zan dropped in the straw by Michael's side, limber as an acrobat. He plucked up a stalk, examined it for dirt, and stuck the straw in his mouth. "Ugh. What's the point in chewing these?"

Michael laughed, startled into the humor despite himself. "There isn't anything you won't poke your nose into, is there?"

"Nope." Zan spat the straw out and began to twine it around his fingers, wrapping rings over his knuckles. "One for one, Michael. How about the rest of it?"

Michael bit his lip.

"Would you quit that?" Zan poked him in the side. "What are you scared of? You could squish me with one thumb. Whatever's going on inside your head, I swear it can't be that bad. Not unless you're a chainsaw killer. Then we might have to revise our options."

"Running like hell, maybe?"

"More like making sure there's a good lock on the utility shed and swallowing the key." Zan rolled to his knees, facing Michael, and laid his straw-ringed hand on Michael's upper thigh, on the inside. Oddly, it didn't come across as a teasing prelude to jumping Michael's bones, but as comfort. "Dish it out, Blue Ox."

"Not yet," Michael said, working hard to keep his nerves steady. "Zan, I'm a coward. I'm a chicken. Okay?"

"I don't think so. You're here, aren't you?"

"Only because you made me."

"Uh-uh. You came because you wanted to." Zan shifted forward and brushed his lips lightly over Michael's. Michael chased the soft, spicy-scented taste, disappointed despite himself when he didn't catch the prize. "Means a lot to me."

"Again?" Michael asked, reaching for Zan. Zan let himself be snagged this time, even leaning into Michael's touch. "One more kiss to remember you by, and then no more games. One kiss."

"Anything you ask me for, Michael, you can be pretty sure I'll give." Zan scooted in closer, his knees knocking Michael's. "Just as long as you know you can't make me run away. I won't."

"I'll be surprised if you don't, after I've said what I—"

"Michael? Shut up and kiss me, or let me kiss you." Zan caught Michael's lower lip between his sharp teeth and tugged.

Michael was lost. Cradling Zan's face in his palms, he held the little spitfire fast and took his sweet time exploring Zan's mouth. He catalogued the flavor and texture, spicy coffee and mint, the roughness of a chipped tooth, and the velvety smoothness of Zan's agile tongue.

Zan rocked back as one drugged when Michael let go. He pressed his forehead to Michael's, breathing his air. "Now that's a memory I'll keep with me until my dying day."

A lump swelled in Michael's throat. Damn it, why'd Zan have to make him want this so much?

What had to be done, though, there was no getting around it now, and no more choices. The moon rose full and fat and white, and any second he'd—

There. The first tingles of transformation thrummed in Michael's limbs and through his fingers.

He stood, pacing five steps back and away from Zan, kicking up the straw.

"Michael?" Zan watched his regress, showing no sign of anything but curiosity.

"You know what time it is?" Michael asked while he still had a voice, pointing at the ceiling, and above it, the moon.

"Hammer time?"

Zan excelled at startling Michael into a laugh, and now was no exception. "You are something else indeed," Michael said, shivering from the force of the oncoming change. "Remember, you asked for this."

Seemingly slower than usual, feathers appeared on Michael's arms, soft bird's down covering his fingers. He splayed them wide for Zan to see before he doubled over, grunting with the twisting shock in his gut that never got less strange.

"Michael," Zan whispered. "Look at you."

Michael hadn't intended to meet Zan's eyes again, not before this was over. Compelled by Zan's tone, he shot him a pleading look.

Zan stared back, mouth open in a delighted grin, nearly aglow with wonder. "My God. I knew you were something special, but…what are you, an angel?"

Michael arched, wings bowing from his back. Of a size to match his human frame, they whipped the air above him, feathers long and swooping, brightly bantam. "Not—not exactly," he rasped. "Not done yet."

"You're gorgeous," Zan murmured.

He couldn't believe his ears. "You're not scared?"

"Not of you." Zan settled in the straw. "I'll still be here when you are what you become."

That made a wonderful, awful sort of sense that wasn't. Too late to argue now, with no human voice left. Michael let the change take him. Not painful, though it always seemed it ought to be, twisting six-foot-seven into less than two feet, joints bending in new directions, long toes narrowing to small, sharp talons and the worst of all, the molding of his face.

Michael kept his eyes closed through the last popping of a pinfeather and waited for the final shudder that signaled completion.

A gentle tug to one of his feathers coaxed him out of his breathless waiting. He peered *up* at Zan, far, far up, and was astonished at how different he looked through these eyes. Foreign, unfamiliar, and unthreatening as a sunny day. Smiling, not screaming, and staying, not running.

Though he was clumsy, Zan was sure as he smoothed Michael's ruffled feathers. "There. Was that so bad?"

No matter how good the petting and no matter how relieving the acceptance, there was only one possible comeback a peppery rooster and an indignant man had for the question.

Michael pecked him.

🐓 🐓 🐓

"Morning, big guy."

"Mmf?" Michael stirred, cramped in what felt like every muscle and aching from stem to stern. He spat out a mouthful of straw. "Zan?"

"Who else?"

Michael pushed his face against his feather-free forearm. "You're still here." He didn't remember much from the previous night, not once he'd fully transformed. Nine times out of ten, he kept his head just fine. When it mattered? Ha!

"Told you I wasn't going anywhere, and I meant it, too." Zan sounded annoyed, almost offended, and kept on coming. Even through the crispness of the straw, Michael could pick up Zan's unique smell and sense the warmth of his body.

Michael didn't dare look up at him. "Last night. What'd I do?"

"You mean besides shapeshifting?"

"For example," Michael groaned.

"You drew blood when you pecked me." Zan dropped lightly to the straw bed. "Not much, don't worry. Then you ate some worms, crowed a lot, chased me through the front yard, and oh, yeah, you tried to attack the weathervane."

"I *what* now?"

"Gotcha." Zan ruffled Michael's hair, sifting the strands playfully. "And behold. Still here, like I said. And I come bearing gifts. Get your head out of the sand, er, straw, and get a whiff of this."

Michael's nose twitched. Beyond Zan's personal fragrance, he thought he smelled…bacon? He lifted his head, squinting against the brightness of the new day, disbelieving.

"You brought me breakfast?" he asked, gaping at the small tray Zan handled deftly, holding it out to Michael in an offering.

"Probably only enough to whet your king-sized appetite, but I left my Mack truck in my other pants. Also, this was all Jud would let me have. Said you'd have to haul your carcass to the kitchen yourself if you wanted more. It's the thought that counts, right? Voila. Breakfast in bed." Zan waggled his hand. "More or less. Eat up while it's hot."

For once in his life, possibly the first time if you asked Michael, Zan held his tongue and let Michael get on with taking care of business, namely stuffing his craw—er, gullet—*stomach*—with hot buttered, jam-smeared biscuits and three slices of bacon. No eggs, thank God.

Chewing the final bite of the last biscuit, Michael became aware of Zan's observation, fond rather than frightened. Softer now, more affectionate. He swallowed and dared to look back. "What?"

"You've got some schmutz on you." Zan licked his forefinger and dabbed at the corner of Michael's mouth, then slipped the digit between his lips and grinned around it. "Grape," he explained. "Can't let any of it go to waste."

Michael huffed, putting the tray aside. "The guy you've been fucking turns into a rooster and your biggest worry is grape jelly?"

"Of course not. Idiot." Zan had to reach up again to do it, but he cuffed the back of Michael's head handily all the same. His good humor dimmed, replaced by an unaccustomed scowl. "You honestly thought I'd run screaming, didn't you?"

"Can you blame me?" Michael protested, indignant. "I *hoped* you would."

Zan's nostrils flared. "Okay. Want to tell me why?"

Michael had to make himself say it, the savory breakfast turning sour in his belly. "I'm trying to protect you."

"Uh-huh," Zan said, dripping skepticism. "How so?"

"This curse, it's a hell of a long story."

"So?" Zan settled back, studying Michael intently. "I thought it might be. Start talking. I've got nowhere else to be."

Michael gave up fighting before he began; it'd be of no use and since he'd started this, by damn he'd see it through to the bitter end.

By the time he'd finished, Zan had heard everything there was to tell about Yi, about the not-so-average Joes that worked the Shifting Sands ranch, about Ben and Daniel and Jud and Cyrus and even Michael himself…and what befell any man stupid enough to cleave to them.

Zan gnawed at his lower lip, still examining Michael intently as a bug under a microscope. The narrowed focus of Zan's concentration near about gave Michael a case of the heebie-jeebies.

"Well? Say something," Michael snapped.

"What am I supposed to say?"

"Goodbye would be good. If you're half smart enough to get up and move your feet, you'll get yourself out of this mess as fast as you can."

"Huh." Zan tipped his face to the sun. "You know what? No."

"Great. Glad we see it the same way. And I'll always remember—wait, what?"

"I said, no." Zan rested his weight on his hands. "Michael, for fuck's sake. Look at me. You think I'm scared of the strange and unusual?"

"I—"

"Hardly. Even if I was, let me tell you something, cocky boy. If you think you're the first shapeshifter I've ever seen, think again."

Michael's mouth fell open.

"My Uncle Pieter. My Aunt Lizabeta. My sister Iulia. There's a knack to it. I never quite picked up on the 'how' before now. You want me to go on?"

Michael had an urge to pound the side of his head to dislodge whatever had clogged up his ears. "You're not serious."

"As the grave." Zan flipped position and lay on his stomach, ankles crossed over him. "Big guy, if you want, you could ask the guys here and they might have a story to tell you about a dog chasing a rooster last night. Please note the key words 'before now' in what I just said."

"Zan?"

"Yep, there was a new puppy around here last night." Zan kicked his legs, wholly unbothered by that news which sent pins and needles through Michael. "Yappy little dog, a patchwork mutt with tiny legs and a great big voice. Sounds like anyone you know?"

Michael couldn't breathe. "Too late, then," he managed to say. "My God, I am so sorry—"

"Don't be. Michael, I'm *glad.*" Zan grinned hugely. "Besides which, I finally managed a shift. Maybe with a little help, but still. *No* complaints. Baba's gonna bust her bloomers, she'll be so thrilled to hear about this!"

"You're…" Michael struggled for words as he shook his head at Zan. "You're completely insane."

"Yep," Zan agreed, cheerful as ever. "And persistent. And a dog now, apparently." He popped up on his knees, closer than expected, and invaded Michael's space, close enough for Michael to count his freckles or to lick them, if he'd a mind to. "And I'm yours. Looks like you're mine, too, mate." He pressed his lips to Michael's, no rush in coaxing him open.

The last barrier crumbled quietly, giving way to Zan's insistence.

"Give it a try," Zan whispered over Michael's cheekbone. "I'll let you peck me again." He dropped to mouth at Michael's jaw. "All night long, if you want. Don't be scared of me. Of this. Us. That's all I ask."

"That and the world on a silver plate," Michael scoffed without heat or meaning. His pulse hummed in his ears. It couldn't be this easy. Not when he'd spent more moons wide awake than not haunted by nightmares, or refusing the company of even his fellow ranch hands for fear of getting too close to anyone. Could it? "You're really serious, aren't you?"

"And then some." Zan caught Michael by the back of the neck and refused to let him look away. "Caught you, rooster. You know what they say about terriers. They never let go. I never plan to."

And Michael believed him.

The relief was too much for him to react sensibly. Michael laughed, which Zan took as permission to make an exuberant leap. Zan's pounce knocked him over, toppling him on his ass in the straw. The bigger they were, the harder they fell, and Michael knew he was lost for keeps. He crowed, loud and glad, and flipped Zan over to cover Zan's smaller body with his much larger one.

Zan yipped. "So whaddya say—want to teach a new dog some old tricks?"

"I do believe I do." Michael traced Zan's nose with his finger, amazed. He'd wasted so much time on fear. He had months to make up for, and for a certainty Zan wouldn't let him backslide.

A full breakfast could wait. Other appetites demanded to be filled first, and Michael planned to enjoy his fill.

Cock-a-doodle-do!

HARE OF THE BULL

BRENDA BRYCE

ONE

It wasn't his day.

Gordy Phillips stared down at his profusely bleeding hand and sighed. It wasn't that he had sliced the crap out of his palm on a piece of sheet metal that he'd been bending to make a patch for a water trough, but it did burn his ass that he wasn't able to finish the job before dark. He'd have to get back to it in the morning. By then, his hand should have stopped bleeding.

He didn't even want to think about the fact that the injury was staining the new blue flannel shirt that he'd worn specifically because he was going to be working in sight of the big house… well, that just beat all.

"Come inside and get that cleaned up before it gets infected."

Gordy's breath stilled in his chest. Wouldn't it be his luck to have the one person he wanted to impress see him at his worst? Peeking through his dark brown eyelashes, he sighed.

Yup, there was hot little Tristan Neely standing on the porch, nearly hidden by the newel post at the top of the stairs.

Glancing down at his hand, he nearly said no. Before he could, the idea that he could use the minor wound to finally get some time with Tristan struck him.

"Yeah. But I'll need some help. I don't think I can bandage it one-handed."

The hand that Tristan had on the post whitened, but he nodded.

Gordy couldn't believe it. Had his luck finally changed?

Slowly, he climbed the steps and approached Tristan. Without making any sudden moves, he held his injured hand out to the smaller man.

"Think you can patch this up for me?"

Tristan quickly glanced up just long enough so that Gordy

could see his sea-green eyes, but that was all. That fast, Gordy was staring at the top of Tristan's head and all that light brown hair.

Yeah, he sure wanted to run his fingers through that thick cascade of hair and see if it could possibly be as soft as it looked.

Preferably while Tristan had his lips around his—

Christ. He was such a pig…no, that wasn't the right species. He was more like the bull in the proverbial china shop.

Big, dark, and freaking clumsy as hell. No style whatsoever.

Tristan, on the other hand, was smart, refined, delicate, sleek, and just plain sexy as hell.

Everything Gordy was attracted to.

And damned if he didn't want to make Tristan his.

If only the man wasn't so skittish. He found excuses to leave the room whenever anyone who was bigger than him came in. It was frustrating as hell, since all Gordy wanted to do was get to know him better.

And fuck him.

Well, that and spend time with him.

And fuck him.

Make a life with him.

And fuck him again.

Damn, now he had to think about something painful to get rid of the wood he was beginning to sport. Well, castration season was just around the corner. Yup, that did it. No more wood. Good thing, too, 'cause he'd followed Tristan into the house and they now stood near the large wooden table in the unoccupied kitchen.

When Tristan took Gordy's dirty, bloody hand in his, Gordy jerked as if he'd been struck by lightning.

Tristan was touching him of his own free will and Gordy was afraid to move, even to breathe.

He was actually getting kind of light-headed, but as long as Tristan was holding his hand and his warm breath was caressing him as he leaned over the wound to get a good look at it, Gordy wasn't going to budge.

"It doesn't look too bad. I think all it needs is a good cleaning and a big bandage."

The air whooshed from Gordy and he gulped his next breath. The subtle scent of the shampoo Tristan used infiltrated his senses.

"I gotta sit down."

Before he fell down.

Tristan's startled gaze met his, then his sun bronzed face flushed. "Oh, um, yeah. You don't look so hot. Sit down."

Practically falling into a sturdy wooden chair at the table, Gordy sighed and tried to stop the spinning in his head.

He peeked at Tristan and wanted to groan. God, he was such a dork. All he wanted to do was impress the smaller man, and here he was, practically fainting like a woman.

This was not the way he wanted to portray himself.

Gordy kept his gaze trained on Tristan as the other man crossed the wooden floor to the cabinet that held the emergency supplies and leaned against the light wood cabinets, reaching for the kit on the second shelf. When he couldn't grasp it, the kit being just out of reach, he stood on tiptoes and edged as far onto the granite counter as he could.

Unfortunately, that's when Gordy realized Tristan's ass was at the perfect height and he was leaning at the best angle for a kitchen quickie, and couldn't contain the groan that erupted.

Tristan turned, kit in hand and grimaced sympathetically. "I think there's something in here for the pain. Just let me get the cut cleaned out first and I'll put the pain reliever on it, then it won't be so bad."

When Gordy held out his hand, Tristan took it in his. Only the warmth and relative softness of the other man's hand could be felt, and Gordy was grateful that the lightning didn't return.

Gordy hissed and jerked his hand when Tristan touched a deep part of the cut and Tristan flinched. He shot away from the table and eyed Gordy intently, as if he were watching for any sign that the bigger man was going to lurch out of his chair after him.

"Sorry. I'm sorry." Tristan muttered over and over as he continued to back away, hands raised as if to ward him off, eyes wide and frightened.

"What the hell?" Gordy stood and Tristan practically ran to the wall and slid down it until he was curled up on himself, covering his head with his arms.

"Don't, please. I didn't mean it."

Gordy stopped moving immediately. It was as if he'd been hit in the chest with the hay bailer.

"Holy shit." It slipped past his lips on a whisper of air. He'd seen someone act like this before: an abused child.

Had Tristan been abused? He'd known Tristan was a tad skittish, but there hadn't been a clue that this had been lurking inside of him. Shy is how Gordy had thought of him, since he didn't talk much and kept to himself a lot. For weeks now, Gordy had been trying to get close to Tristan, and now he had a small inkling why Tristan had seemed so edgy.

Not wanting to scare him more than he already had, Gordy slowly returned to his seat, and without raising his voice, called out to the other man.

"Tristan."

When all Gordy could get out of Tristan was more frantic apologies, Gordy felt like killing someone, the someone that had hurt this beautiful man, and it took everything in him to sit in his chair and watch Tristan cower in absolute terror. All he could think was that he hoped none of the other guys came in from the fields, and that Jud and Woody took a little longer with the shopping so that they wouldn't walk in on this.

❀ ❀ ❀

Memories flashed in Tristan's mind as he tried to protect his head from the raging man. Flashing fists, loud voices, curses and kicks echoed in his head. Curling closer to the wall to protect his back and spine from the booted feet that always aimed at him, he curled his knees toward his chest and covered his head with his arms. The blows would come and he had to keep from getting another concussion. He could work with a broken arm or ribs, even a broken jaw, but not with a concussion.

The thoughts, fears, and memories ran through him so fast and frantically, it took him several minutes to realize he wasn't getting hit.

His chest hitched with the hiccups he'd gotten from breathing wrong, and he tried to relax enough to move his arm out of the way to see where Howard...no. It wasn't Howard, it was Gordy in the room with him. Gordy; dark haired, tanned skin, flashing gray eyes, big hands and feet...Gordy. Not Howard.

Slowly, Tristan moved his elbow only enough to see where Gordy was. When he located him, he was relieved to see him sitting at the table well out of reach.

Closing his eyes tightly, he lowered his arms. When he opened his eyes, he stared at Gordy, wondering what was going to happen next.

Gordy only sat in the chair quietly. He didn't say a word, for which Tristan was grateful, but the silence was becoming overwhelming.

He didn't say anything either. What could he say? Nothing. So he stood, went to the sink, and rinsed out the towel he'd held onto through the whole ordeal.

"Tristan?" Gordy's voice was soft, not wanting to freak him out again.

"Sorry about that. Didn't mean to go all psycho on you." He moved away from the sink and put the towel back on Gordy's hand. He couldn't help but remain tense and watchful, not to mention shaking like a leaf. He tried, but he was too on-edge to relax, but managed to put a little steel into his wobbly knees.

"Tristan—"

"Please don't ask, Gordy." He heard the pleading in his own voice, and hated it.

Gordy looked as if he wanted to argue, but luckily he kept his thoughts to himself until Tristan had cleaned and bandaged the cut.

Once the chore was done, Tristan picked up the mess he'd made and started to leave the room.

"Tristan, why did you help me?"

That quiet question had Tristan pausing in the doorway.

Not turning to face Gordy, he told the truth even though he had to fight through eyeball-deep embarrassment. "I thought I could handle it. I thought I was ready." He laughed bitterly. "Guess I was wrong."

He left the room before Gordy could comment and went to the supply closet. It was a large enough room because everything necessary for the entire house was in here. Need a sheet? You would find it here. Extra blankets? Here. Did an impromptu wrestling match break a dining room chair? There was an extra in this room. Everything a big house such as this would need.

Tristan used it as his hidey-hole. Being the housekeeper had its perks since he worked at his own pace, four days a week, and on a rotating schedule. Not only that, a trailer was rented to him for practically nothing and was situated right off the ranch property proper.

Slamming the door, he flung himself onto the chair. Damn it, why couldn't he react like a normal human being? He was sick of jumping all the damned time just because one of the men moved too fast. It was ridiculous.

When he heard the kitchen door close, he grimaced. No telling what Gordy thought of him now. He was probably going to be the one avoiding him from now on instead of the other way around.

Punching a stack of blankets, Tristan cursed again. All he'd wanted to do was get a little bit closer to the stunning man, but now he'd fucked it up by running scared. No way was Gordy going to want to deal with all the baggage Tristan had, and it was some pretty hefty stuff.

"Crap."

He was never going to get to have a normal relationship the way he was acting. He couldn't even have a fling, he wasn't the type. He knew he was an all-or-nothing guy, but if he couldn't even manage not tripping out when he was in the same room with Gordy, how was he supposed to get naked with him?

And, boy, did he want to see Gordy naked.

Smiling, he imagined it. Gordy was such a handsome man. Tristan pictured the big gray eyes, strong hands that seemed so gentle when they milked a cow or petted the yard dog, and the one time he'd seen Gordy without a shirt, he'd nearly drooled over the ripped abs. All-in-all, he was absolutely gorgeous. There was nothing about him that wasn't sexy as hell.

He sighed. The problem was that he *was* big and strong and muscular.

Gordy didn't seem the violent type, but neither had Howard.

"What the hell am I doing?" He stood and sighed loudly. Cleaning was what he got paid for and that's what he would do.

He gathered his carryall that had all the things he would need and left the room. Standing on the porch, he recalled what had started this whole mess.

He'd been taking a break after cleaning the house before he had to head out to the bunkhouse, and saw Gordy striding across the yard, muttering, and dripping blood. Naturally, the uncontrollable urge to help had pulled the offer from him.

Now, Gordy knew what kind of chicken-shit he was, and probably would walk a mile out of his way to avoid him.

Entering the bunkhouse, he started cleaning with a vengeance, taking his frustration and self-loathing out on the bathroom floor.

His one chance to make a good impression on the object of

his nightly masturbation sessions, and he'd blown it. Coming to work for Daniel at the ranch a couple of months ago had seemed like such a great idea. The boss didn't have a problem with him being a chicken-shit and hiding out half the time, which was a great thing, and he had the time and space here to remember who he was and get the old Tristan back. He'd always been happy with himself and with his life until he'd met Howard. Being with that jack-off had changed everything. Now he just wanted to be not so jumpy all the damned time. Less scared and, damn it, he wanted to get to know Gordy. He was just going to have to man up and grow some balls if he was going to ever get Gordy's attention.

Just thinking about how he'd freaked out was enough to piss him off. He had turned into a freaking wuss, and damned if he was going to let Howard-the-fuck keep running his life. Swinging the mop up, he dunked it into the bucket and gave it several good pumps. Wringing it out, he put his all into it. He didn't even bother with using the attached wringer; he needed to manhandle the mop to vent his anger.

Stupid, fucking Howard. "I hate him."

"Tristan?"

No, it couldn't be. There was no way he could face Gordy again so soon.

Maybe if he didn't turn around, Gordy would leave.

The scuff of a booted foot on the wooden bunkhouse floor came from just outside the door of the bathroom he was cleaning. "Tristan? Please, look at me."

Or, maybe he wouldn't.

Holding his breath, Tristan turned and glanced up at Gordy. He forced himself not to flinch as he realized how close the other man stood.

Apparently recognizing the problem, Gordy took a step back and tucked his fingers into the pockets of his jeans.

"I'm sorry if I scared you earlier." Tristan had heard the big man use the same gentle voice on the spooked farm animals during a thunderstorm. "Honestly, I didn't mean to give the wrong impression. I wouldn't have hit you."

Tristan looked deeply into Gordy's dark gray eyes. The eyes always told the truth even when the mouth spouted drivel.

Finding only honesty, Tristan tried to smile, but it was a bit lopsided. "It's all right. I didn't mean to overreact."

"I don't think you overreacted. But I do think something, or someone, caused you to be so skittish."

The laugh that emerged from Tristan was as dry as dust. "You think?"

Gordy's solemn expression didn't change. "Yes. I do."

"Let's just say I was in a bad relationship."

Nodding, Gordy seemed to accept that. "But he hit you?"

Refusing to answer that, Tristan only stuck out his chin defiantly and stared into Gordy's empathetic eyes.

"Is he in jail?"

Tristan drew in a slow, choppy breath and shook his head. "No."

"Well, why the hell not?"

Flinching when Gordy's voice rose, Tristan started to take a defensive step back, but paused before he moved because the broad-shouldered, big-fisted man in front of him only ran a distracted hand through his hair and growled out a cuss word.

"You're telling me this asshole is still out there running around free?"

Again, Tristan nodded. What could he say? "I didn't think I had a choice. It was get out, or get dead. I grabbed some of my stuff while he was out and didn't look back."

Astonishingly, Gordy's only response was to slowly step forward, wrap his bulging arms around Tristan's back, and pull him toward the massive chest for a gentle hug.

Tristan's head barely reached Gordy's chin, but Gordy seemed to find this a bonus. His stubbled chin rasped across the top of Tristan's scalp.

"Ah, baby, I wish I'd have known."

Being in Gordy's arms nearly had him panicking. The first thing that got through his automatic need to run was Gordy's scent. There was no pricey cologne or hair product odor that Howard always drenched himself in. Only the scent of honestly earned sweat and the outdoors. Maybe a little bit of laundry detergent and soap as well. Nothing offensive or overpowering. He was a very big man, even taller and broader than Howard, but the sensation of being close to him was totally different. He felt protected instead of confined. The soft rasp of the cotton shirt rubbed against his cheek and Tristan turned his nose into the open collar to draw in the scent of him. Conflicting emotions raced through his system. One second he was tense and frightened, the next, mildly aroused.

"You couldn't have done anything. Violence would have only made it worse."

Hands on his upper arms pushed him away from Gordy's warm body. The smile that crossed the full lips was teasing.

"Who said anything about violence? Do you think I handle all my problems with my fists? No, I might look like a big dumb ox, but I do have a little finesse. I might trample the opposition, but I try to use my mind instead of force." He seemed to contemplate his assertion for a moment. "Except when force is used on me first. Then I might get a little testy."

Tristan couldn't help but laugh. "A little testy. I could see you doing some major damage if you got 'testy.' And not once did I call you a dumb ox."

Gordy's smile dropped from his face. "All my life, people have either been scared of me and my size and avoided me, or wanted to prove themselves better than the oversized faggot. Usually with their fists. Since the day I came out, I've had to defend myself, so I have an inkling of where you've been. Only difference is, I've got genetics on my side."

Tristan was shocked. He'd never thought that others, especially someone Gordy's size, had faced what he had.

Laughter rumbled quietly from Gordy. "You don't believe me. It's true. It's why I'm out here, on the ranch, working. I lived in the city, but every dickhead who had a beer or two in him wanted to take me on to prove to his friends he wasn't gay. It got…tiring."

That pulled laughter from Tristan. Like molten lava in a volcano, he felt it building up from his stomach. It took a few minutes, but his stomach finally quit jumping around in fear, but the original stress still had it churning. The pressure grew and grew then erupted from his mouth in a cathartic explosion.

He laughed long and hard, not that what Gordy had said had been funny, but the emotions had to be released. Laughing was much better than the alternative. And then, damn it, he started to cry.

Tears ran down his face in rivers, and his body lurched with the sobs.

Arms tightened around his back and, once again, he was pulled against Gordy's strong chest.

Memories assaulted him of when he'd felt so helpless and unable to do anything about the situation. The beatings, the broken bones, the rapes. Each and every time Howard had taken his anger out on Tristan's unprotected body flashed against the back of his tightly closed eyelids. Despair tried to drag him back into the fear and apathy he'd lived with all those months when he'd been under the control of a madman. He cried until he had no more tears.

The first thing that caught his attention was the realization that Gordy still held him. He rocked them side-to-side, rubbing a big hand up and down his back, murmuring soothing words. Not trying to get him to stop, but to be his anchor as he encouraged him to let it all out. Gordy held him together when he felt as if he were shattering, while smelling of fabric softener, hay, and a hint of cow. It wasn't generally what Tristan would have thought of as an arousing odor, but it was a measure of comfort to him.

For the millionth time since setting eyes on Gordy, his cock started to swell. Talk about an inopportune moment. Gordy wasn't doing anything but being a nice guy and damned if Tristan didn't go and get a woody. There was no way Gordy couldn't feel it.

Tristan tried to move away, but Gordy would have none of it. His arms tightened and the hand that was rubbing his back stilled.

Neither man said a word, but apparently none was needed. Gordy had obviously noticed the giant boner that was rubbing between his thighs, and damned if Tristan didn't feel something very interesting against his abdomen.

Could Gordy really want him, or was it just propinquity? God, he hoped it was want and not that he was the nearest warm body, because Tristan really wanted a piece of Gordy. The one that was poking him in the stomach would be a good place to start.

Two

Gordy was sure he'd died and gone on to the great beyond. The very man he'd fantasized about for the last two months was in his arms. He didn't want to take advantage of it, since he was honestly trying to help out a friend. However, if the dual hardons were telling him anything, Tristan wasn't immune to him.

That was good, right?

God, he hoped so.

Since he didn't plan on taking this any farther, and Tristan seemed to have himself somewhat under control, Gordy gave the smaller man's back a final pat and stepped away.

"Are you going to be all right?"

Tristan looked up at him with those big, watery green eyes and Gordy nearly changed his mind about being patient.

"Yeah. I'll be fine. Thanks for letting me cry on your shoulder."

Gordy shook his head. "Don't worry about it. Everyone needs to blow off some steam every now and then. This was your time. I'm just glad I could be here for you."

"Me, too." He visibly collected himself, took a deep breath, put his shoulders back, and raised one eyebrow. "Haven't you got work to do?"

Laughing, mostly in relief that Tristan could get close to him and not freak out, he shook his head. "Yeah, and so do you, or do you think these barracks will clean themselves?"

"Do I have to get my broom?"

That got Gordy started again. Not uproarious laughter, but a good chuckle. He was so glad Tristan felt safe enough with him to joke, he grinned his way out of the building and all the way across the yard to the barn. Since he and Tristan were temporarily the only ones not in the fields or on their days off, he was monitoring the delivery of a young cow pregnant with her first calf.

He became quiet when he entered the section the boss had set up for the birthing pens, not wanting to startle the soon-to-be-momma. She mooed at him when he approached her stall, causing him to tense.

"Shit." He grabbed his cell phone from his side and dialed. "Ben, it's Gordy. I'm in the birthing pens and we've got a problem with momma. Can you come in from wherever Daniel has you so we can do this together? I don't think the vet's gonna get here in time."

"Yeah, I'll be there in ten." Gordy relaxed infinitesimally, because the next best thing to the doc was on the way. However, the cow was in distress right now.

Making an even shorter call to the vet's service, he gave the specifics while he scrubbed his hands.

Gordy stepped into the stall once the call was complete and ran his hand over the quivering hide of the cow's shoulder. Sweat coated, she mooed again.

The cow was in a lot of pain, and when Gordy ran his hand under her distended belly, he worried that the calf was in distress. He hoped the foreman got here quick so they could do something, or they were going to lose the calf.

Staring into the cow's eyes, he began to murmur words of praise. The cow didn't blink or turn her head, keeping her gaze locked with his. Gordy continued the low, monotone cadence of his words to keep the cow calm in the hope that it would keep the contractions from escalating.

The scrape of a boot along the hay-strewn dirt floor caught his attention, but didn't distract him enough to break eye contact with the cow. His nostrils flared and it wasn't Ben or the veterinarian he smelled. It was Tristan. His scent was so unique that Gordy thought he'd be able to pick him out of a crowd blindfolded.

It was special enough that it overwhelmed the scents of the barn. Tristan's cleanser over male musk had Gordy's body in a difficult state faster than a 450 hemi on a dry, flat track. Trying to concentrate on keeping the cow subdued and monitoring her contractions wasn't easy to do when all the blood in his body was rushing to his cock. He actually felt a little light-headed because of it.

Tristan had come near and leaned on the wall of the stall. His forearms were on the top of the wall and his chin rested on his folded hands.

"What are you doing?" he asked curiously.

"The baby is giving the mamma trouble." Running his hand over the rippling underbelly of the distressed cow, he checked that the calf was still moving. "I am keeping her calm so the baby doesn't asphyxiate in vitro."

Tristan was quiet for a moment as he watched him. Gordy could feel the pressure of his gaze as he stared at him.

The ranch foreman burst into the barn and started issuing orders immediately. Tristan was told to run and get the tackle box that held the ranch's medical supplies. Gordy followed instructions in rapid-fire order. Helping Ben get suited up and gloved for the exam, then handing tools, syringes, and other equipment out of the tackle box Tristan had brought in, had time passing unnoticed.

The sound the calf made as it took its first breath caused the tired men to smile goofily at each other. Just as they were watching the momma nuzzle her offspring, the vet walked into the barn.

"Birth is a miraculous thing, isn't it, boys?" The vet checked the cow and her calf to make sure neither had complications. "You did good. Momma and young'un are doing just fine. Y'all can go on about your business if you have to. I'm going to stick around for a little while and enjoy the sight of this little one getting his sea legs, but there is no need for y'all to hang around."

"If you don't mind, doc, I'll just stick around for a while myself." Ben looked at Gordy and smiled. "Thanks. I couldn't have done it without you."

Gordy looked down at his feet in embarrassment. "Welcome."

Without saying another thing and running the risk of sounding stupid, he exited the stall, made sure it was securely latched behind him, and went to the scrub sink.

Tristan came up beside him and Gordy tensed. Grabbing several paper towels from the shelf over the sink, he dried off. Turning slowly, he let his gaze rake up Tristan's body, from feet to eyes.

While still tentative, his expression begged for attention. Gordy could not ignore him, even though he knew Tristan wasn't ready for what he wanted. What he wanted was Tristan, and after what he'd heard tonight, he could force himself to wait until Tristan was ready for him and his needs, if necessary. But that didn't mean he wouldn't have to fight his body's reactions to him every second they were within sight of each other.

With a heaving sigh and the decision that he would darned well try to be patient and not let Tristan know of his struggle, Gordy tossed the paper towels into the trash and motioned to Tristan. "Let's go."

Once outside the barn Gordy stuck one hand in his jeans pocket and clenched it. "Are you done for today?"

"What?" Tristan asked. "With the housecleaning? Yeah. I'm done."

"Would you like a ride home? Ben is here now, so I don't have to stay."

Curious green eyes turned up to his, but he didn't ask any of the questions residing there. "A ride would be nice."

Leading him to the garage, Gordy pointed out his truck and pushed the button to unlock it. When they were buckled in, Gordy started the truck, but didn't put it in gear.

"What's wrong?"

Turning slowly, Gordy let Tristan see the need reflected on his face. "I want you, Tristan, but I don't want to scare you into leaving. If that's not what you want, I can back off. I won't give up on the chance of an *us*, but I will give you some space and time to think it over."

When Tristan only blinked and fidgeted in his seat, Gordy nodded and pulled the truck onto the road.

"It's not—" Tristan's voice broke and he paused to clear it. "Really, it's not that I'm not attracted to you, 'cause I am. Very much so." His hand twitched and lifted, but paused midair and dropped back into his lap. "I'm scared."

Gordy flinched. "Of me?"

"God, no." The vehemence of his denial relieved Gordy as nothing else could. "I haven't been with anyone since I left Howard. It hasn't been that long, only a little over six months, and I can't seem to get away from him. Twice now, I've thought I was safe and he'd given up on me, but both times he's found me."

"He's come after you?" Gordy could feel the rage building in him over the thought of that asshole getting near Tristan again.

"No, but he did make it difficult to keep my jobs. The phone calls and bullyboys he sent to harass my employers put paid to that. I pulled up stakes and moved on each time he found me." Tristan had interlaced his fingers and sat quietly for a moment.

"Do you think he'll come after you?" God, Gordy hoped so. He sure would like to get his hands on this dude for just a few minutes.

"No. Well, maybe." That was anything but definitive. Even his tone was unsure. "So far, it's been just the harassment from a distance and I haven't stuck around long enough after I found out he'd located me to find out if he would actually come after me."

"You're safe at the ranch, you know? Even if you're at your place, the hands are just a phone call away." Gordy parked in the drive at Tristan's trailer. "It's not like you're across town. It's only a couple of miles from the ranch house to here. I can run that in less than fifteen minutes. In the truck, it's a quarter of that."

Tristan shrugged. "I know, but I don't want you fighting my battles."

Feeling the hit, Gordy closed his eyes against the pain. "I don't want to fight your battles for you. I want to help fight your battles, at your side."

Actually, that wasn't entirely true. What he wanted to do was get a tight grip on this Howard character and turn him into mulch. But due to the fact that Tristan had already been subjected to too much physical violence, he wouldn't go that route. Although, he would be willing to hold Howard immobile if Tristan wanted to wail on him for a while.

Relaxing at his less than honest words, Tristan smiled and opened the truck door. "Thanks." He glanced at the single-wide, off-white trailer he lived in. "Um, would you like to come in? I think I might have some tea in the fridge."

Stunned, Gordy didn't think. He reacted. Unfortunately, he'd forgotten to unhook his seatbelt before trying to get out of the truck and got tangled up in it. Red-faced and wanting to curse a blue streak, he slowly unclipped the seatbelt and climbed out of the truck. Barely restraining himself from slamming the door, he rounded the hood and finally looked at Tristan.

The other man had waited for him in front of the truck, and without even a small grin, for which Gordy was eternally grateful, led him to the door.

The trailer was stuffy from being closed up all day, and Tristan crossed the room to the window cooler and turned it on. It wasn't a fancy house by any means, but Tristan had made it comfortable. There were blankets and pillows neatly laid out on the tan couch and chair, and while there was no television in obvious sight, there were books galore. From what Gordy could see, Tristan liked westerns, sci-fi, horror, romance, fantasy, some non-fiction, and even a few of the classics. He had very eclectic tastes, it seemed.

There weren't any pictures on display, and Gordy wondered about his family. Since it seemed a safe enough topic, he broached it. "Do you have any family that live nearby?"

"I've got an uncle in Mississippi, but I haven't seen him for years. I don't know of anyone else."

While he didn't sound sad, Gordy could hear the loneliness.

"Yeah, me either. I found out my family was homophobic the hard way."

Tristan nodded. "Yeah. Sucks doesn't it?"

"Especially when you don't have anyone to turn to when you're in trouble."

"Yeah." He didn't say anything for a moment, but then shook off whatever memories he'd been having. "Would you like something?"

Gordy couldn't help it. It just came out without any forethought. "You."

A startled laugh burst from Tristan. "Me? I was offering something to drink, or eat."

Shrugging, Gordy didn't answer. Since he'd blurted the truth, why start lying now?

"Please, sit down." Tristan waved him toward the couch.

Sitting, Gordy began to sweat. If Tristan asked him to leave now, he would. With an inward sigh, he realized all he could do was try to talk him into changing his mind.

Tristan sat beside him on the couch without letting any part of their bodies come into contact. Gordy took care of that by shifting his knee to touch the jean-clad leg of the other man.

"Gordy, I admit, well, that I'm attracted to you." It all came out in a rush, and while Gordy was excited at the news, he was afraid of what Tristan would follow it up with.

Sure enough, Tristan took a deep breath and exhaled slowly. "But, I don't know if I am secure enough to get into a relationship." He held up a tentative hand. "I want to, but the last man I went with...you know about that. I don't want to get to a point during sex where I might freak out. Not to you, and not to me."

"I would go slow, make sure you like it." Gordy leaned

forward. "If we, at some point in our relationship, have sex, I would ensure you didn't have one moment of being scared of me. I could never hurt you."

🐗 🐗 🐗

Tristan stared into Gordy's earnest gaze. God, he wished he had the *cajones* to do what he wanted. Even though he denied it, he knew that a relationship with Gordy would be everything he desired.

He was scared though. Getting past what Howard had done was more than he could do alone.

Eyeing Gordy thoughtfully, he wondered if the man in front of him could get him over the hurdle. Could he bring himself to start something with Gordy? Take the chance that he could freak out during a crucial moment?

As he watched Gordy watching him, he realized that if he didn't give it a shot, then he would never know.

Unclenching his fingers, he put his hand on his own jean-clad thigh that was closest to Gordy. While keeping his cautious gaze locked with Gordy's earnest one, he slid his hand over the slightly rough texture of the couch. When his fingertips touched thigh, he stilled and waited for a reaction.

While Gordy didn't move a single muscle, his eyes ignited. The flare of excitement that rocked through Tristan was like nothing he'd ever felt. He considered it for a moment to identify the emotion. It wasn't fear, but excitement. He'd gotten this far, but how far could he go?

Unable to look away from the intent regard of the larger man, Tristan took a deep breath and forged ahead. Placing his far hand firmly on the couch cushion, he adjusted his weight, and swayed closer. Lifting the hand touching Gordy, he smoothed his fingertips up and over the now flexing thigh.

Tristan felt his eyes widening in discovery. Gordy wasn't just toned, he was really, really muscular. Feeling what had to be every muscle in his thigh, delineated against his questing palm and fingers, Tristan flushed, swallowed noisily, and blinked several times to fight off a case of dizziness.

Safe, he was safe with Gordy and he wasn't going to chicken out now. He could do this.

Tightening his lips, he scraped his palm down the hard thigh toward the bent knee. The taught muscles under his hand jerked, then settled. Gordy's face tightened, obviously straining for control.

That sign of self-control actually enabled Tristan to relax marginally. It was apparent that Gordy was going to let him do what he wanted at his own pace and not take over or force him in any way.

It made him bold. Shifting the direction of his hand, he ran it up Gordy's thigh, fingertips tracing the inner seam of the denim jeans. Hearing Gordy's breathing become ragged, he glanced quickly up at the tense features of his face. The excitement raged through Tristan and the heat coming off the man beside him caused the fine tremors rippling over his skin to turn into a shiver.

"Gordy." In his own voice, he heard the want and need he'd been too fearful to act on. He was still scared out of his mind, but he had to take the chance. If he didn't, he'd always regret it, and if it turned out badly, then he'd leave. He vowed to never remain in a bad relationship for longer than it took to recognize it, but if he didn't even try—

Firming his resolve, he let his gaze drop to where his hand grazed high on Gordy's thigh. With careful consideration, he turned his hand to cup the straining, denim-covered cock.

Almost hesitantly, Gordy lifted his hand and touched his long, dark fingers to Tristan's jaw. Tilting his head and rubbing his cheek against the work-roughened palm, Tristan closed his eyes and savored the moment of gentleness. The first he'd had since he'd been a child.

"Tristan, I want you to be sure." Gordy's voice sounded as rough as gravel as he spoke. "I want you so bad I'm about to implode, but I don't want you unless that's what you want as well."

"I want you very badly, Gordy," he whispered. "But I don't know what to do."

"We can start small." Smiling tenderly, he leaned in and placed his lips on Tristan's.

Senses whirling, he leaned into the kiss, letting Gordy take the lead. He was more comfortable following than leading, and while he let go of the speed and direction of what was happening, he stayed alert to any sudden or violent movements.

He chastised himself mentally since he wanted to trust Gordy, but he was unable to lower those barriers. He didn't know if he was capable of that much faith in another human being.

Although, he might manage giving Gordy a chance to prove himself. Only one chance. He wouldn't go through the cycle of betrayal and forgiveness ever again.

Tristan inched closer to Gordy and wrapped his trembling arms around his narrow waist until his hands touched at the small of his back.

Reacting to the embrace, Gordy folded him into strong arms and pulled him gently into his chest and deepened the kiss. Tongues dueled, lips clung, senses reeled.

Tristan wanted more but didn't know how to get it. He'd never had to be the assertive one, and he didn't know where to begin.

He pulled back, breaking the kiss and turned an imploring gaze up at Gordy. "Please," he choked out.

Watching him with twinkling eyes, Gordy twisted his mouth in a grin. "Please what, Tristan?"

God, he was going to make him say it. Tristan flushed and stammered. "I need you, Gordy."

He nodded. "I need you, too, but I don't have any protection on me, or anything else for that matter."

Tristan knew his face went red with embarrassment, but that didn't stop him from offering. "I—I have stuff in my bedroom."

The fire that leapt in Gordy's eyes sent a shiver down Tristan's back. Excitement, not fear, had him standing and holding out his hand to the broad-shouldered man.

THREE

"Please." The one word was all Tristan could squeeze past the lump in his throat as he stood there waiting for Gordy's decision.

This time, to Tristan's amusement, Gordy didn't hesitate. He immediately put his hand out. Tristan curled his fingers around the offered hand and stepped back when Gordy rose to his feet. He walked backwards, not taking his gaze off the dark hunger that tightened the skin on Gordy's face.

Wending his way to the bedroom, he traversed the short hall, tugging Gordy with him, and soon the back of his legs bumped against the bed. His room was nearly dark due to the thick drapery. The room was functional, with a bed, dresser, two nightstands, and a closet, but it wasn't anything special with its discount store décor. Right now, all that mattered was that the bed wasn't too lumpy and it was big enough to fit Gordy's long body.

Tristan tried to smile, but knew it came out as a grimace. Huffing out a breath, he ran an aggravated hand through his hair. "Damn it. I feel like a fool. I know I want you, but don't know what you want. It's making me really nervous and I feel inadequate."

Gordy shook his head and gripped Tristan's shoulder lightly. "The only thing I want is for you to be yourself. As long as you do that, we'll do fine."

Tristan rolled his eyes in exasperation. In the darkness of the room, Gordy probably wouldn't see it, which was for the best, since he wasn't mocking the gorgeous, albeit dense, man, but he really wished they would get on with it. The suspense of not knowing how it would come out was killing him.

He wracked his brain. How could he get Gordy to take the lead? Maybe if he undressed the big lug. Naked is the first step, right?

With that in mind, he gripped Gordy's shirt where it entered his jeans and tugged it free. When Gordy inhaled deeply, but didn't take over, Tristan clenched his teeth and reached for the top button. He undid it and moved on to the next one down. Continuing until all the buttons were undone, Tristan parted the panels and sucked in a strangled breath. Even in the filtered daylight that came in through the cracks of the drapes, he could see that Gordy's body was a masterpiece. Of course, he'd seen him shirtless before, but not nearly at this close of a distance. The delineation of the muscles, the broad plane of his chest, the washboard abs all culminated in making the photographs of Michelangelo's *David* look like a wimp.

He couldn't help himself. His hand itched to explore, and without conscious thought, it did just that. His hand swept across the flexing pecs that were at eye level. The skin was hot and smooth. Silk covered steel.

Drawing closer to Gordy, Tristan leaned in and drew the masculine scent of the man before him deep into his lungs. His eyes closed involuntarily, savoring the essence, then shifted until he could drag the tip of his tongue along the indention that separated his pectoral muscles. Clean sweat and salt. Tristan groaned at the flavor of it.

Gordy's groan echoed his and Tristan felt strong arms wrap around him.

"Where are the condoms, Tristan? I don't want to get carried away, which would be easy to do with you, and forget something important."

The look Gordy graced him with was searing and sultry and danged if it didn't set him on fire. He wanted out of his clothes right now, and he hoped Gordy hurried and got him that way.

How he wished he could be a tad more dominant. Then he could have what he wanted when he wanted it, but for now—

"Over..." he had to clear his throat, "over in the nightstand." He pointed to the other side of the bed where the wooden nightstand listed slightly to the right, with only a lamp and a digital clock on top.

Gordy ran a caressing hand down Tristan's cheek, causing him to shiver in expectation, and shifted away from him to approach the innocuous piece of furniture.

The drawer slid open and Tristan heard Gordy's hum of interest.

Oh God, oh God. Tristan turned slowly, remembering what he'd had stored in that drawer.

"What's this, then?" Gordy lifted his hand, which was wrapped around the large blue vibrator, and waved it at him. "Is this what you use when you are alone?"

Tristan couldn't get his voice to work so nodded his answer instead.

Examining it carefully, Gordy hummed his appreciation. "Good. It'll make it easier for you to take me inside you."

Nearly choking on his own excitement, Tristan raised his hands and slowly started to unbutton his shirt. He may not be butch or an alpha or a dominant, but he didn't have to be any of that to know what he wanted and he was quite capable of giving broad hints.

His actions caught and pinned Gordy's attention, who stared at him until he reached the bottom button of his shirt. Nearly stepping toward Tristan, Gordy stilled, and reached back into the drawer. He pulled out several condoms and the lube that he found there, set the items on the top of the nightstand, then rounded the bed. Standing in front of Tristan, Gordy gazed down at him with lust-filled eyes, and it didn't frighten Tristan. He was too turned on to be scared.

While Gordy began to peel his own clothes off, Tristan fought with the button on his jeans. Tight jeans and a quick release apparently didn't go well together. Finally the catch released and he leaned forward to push his pants down, but Gordy stopped him.

Totally nude, he stood proudly erect in front of Tristan. Leaning over, he was quite aware of *how* erect Gordy was, and the purplish head on the very generous shaft had an inviting drop of pre-cum resting on it. Tristan couldn't restrain the compulsion that hit him, so he bent a little farther down and licked the drop off. It was like the sea: a little salty and came with a fresh, clean scent.

Finally, and Tristan thought that it was about damned time, Gordy lost some of his caution and took control.

Tensing slightly when Gordy grabbed him by the arms and lifted him bodily from the floor, he worried about what he'd gotten himself into. But when he was lowered to the bed gently, he relaxed minutely. Gordy was being careful with him, even though he was excited.

While Gordy stripped the jeans and shorts from his body, Tristan lay still, watching the muscles ripple under the other man's skin. Working on the ranch had sure been good to Gordy.

As Tristan reclined admiring him, Gordy shattered any further thoughts by climbing onto the bed between his legs, leaning over his body and taking his mouth in a shattering kiss.

Total domination over Tristan's senses. The only thing he could think about was the feel of the man whose skin brushed his, the taste of his mouth, and the continuous bumping and rubbing of erections.

He craved. That was the word that described his excitement best.

Arching his hips, he pushed the length of his own hard-on along the full expanse of Gordy's. The hot press of his cock sandwiched between Gordy's impassioned glide and the firm span of his own abdomen made him clench his ass and squirm uncontrollably. A quick flash of Howard's snarling visage appeared to him, but he threw it off. This was too good to think about that dickless freak. He wanted more of this, and nothing was going to get in his way.

"Gordy." He managed to choke out the name, but nothing further could be propelled from his throat. Only groans.

Not that it seemed to matter to Gordy. His groan drowned out the noises that Tristan was making.

"God, you feel good."

It might have come out gravelly, but Gordy had managed a full, coherent sentence. Tristan took that as a challenge.

Damn it, he knew he was testing Gordy and his control, but he couldn't stop himself from antagonizing him to his limits. He needed to know.

Going with the fierce desire to push, he tightened his grip on his own fear and turned his longing-filled stare up to Gordy's mesmerizing one. Tristan fought his own inclination to glance away, and steeled himself. He could do this and survive any fallout. He'd been strong enough to leave Howard, he could surely handle Gordy.

He hoped.

Spreading his thighs, he lifted his legs and wrapped them around Gordy's waist, placing his feet on Gordy's muscular calves while his hands went to the bulging upper arms. Tightening his own muscles, he lifted his chest against Gordy's. Their bodies made a rasping sound as they undulated against one another.

Gordy took his mouth in a hard, rapacious kiss and the muscles in his arm clenched as he reached for the lube.

Tristan started to shake. Not so obvious that Gordy would notice, he hoped. Though it was enough that he had to reinforce his determination to do this.

The sound of the lube top popping open rang in the quiet room, and brought a new stiffness to his body. Fighting not to tense in anticipation, Tristan waited for the first touch.

When it came, it was practically a relief. Gordy wasn't tentative while remaining gentle as he spread Tristan's ass cheeks and rubbed the slick liquid down the seam. The light pressure as the finger circled his hole had him panting, and when Gordy inserted the tip of his digit beyond the clasping ring, the air rushed out of him.

"Oh, God." Tristan's eyes opened wide when the finger went deeper, then even deeper. The stretching feeling grew when he crooked the finger within him and Tristan saw stars. "Yes! Right there."

Having found the sweet spot, Gordy rubbed at it with the solitary digit until Tristan thought he would come. Before he could, though, Gordy slid the finger out.

"No."

Even his thoughts stalled when Gordy pressed two fingers inside him. The twisting and separating of the fingers opened him and Tristan couldn't lie still. He wiggled and arched into the questing hand and dug his nails into Gordy's shoulders. "Please."

"Shh. Breathe Tristan. Just breathe." He dropped his head and Tristan took his mouth in a kiss that tasted of lust. He couldn't get enough of Gordy; he was nearly frantic to have Gordy's cock inside him.

Begging again, he lifted his hips as far as he could with Gordy's large body in the way and bit down on Gordy's lower lip.

Finally, finally, Gordy rolled over and onto his side, reached for the condom, and rolled it on. Tristan ran his hands over Gordy's chest while he did that. Then, with a quick kiss, levered himself onto his hands and knees.

Gordy's hand rested on his hip. "Not this way, Tristan. I want to see your face when you come."

Confusion penetrated the lust-filled fog, and he turned an inquiring gaze over his shoulder.

Shaking his head, Gordy put pressure on his side so that he rolled onto his back. The approving leer warmed him as it raked over his chest and pulsing cock.

"That's better. Now, lift these." Strong hands guided his knees close to his chest. "Good. Hold that pose for me."

Tristan reached up and held his knees near his shoulders. He glanced down his body and flushed. God, he was going to be able to watch Gordy as he stuck his cock into his ass. He'd never done it this way and simply imagining how it was about to be had heat waves crashing over his body.

He tightened the grip on his knees and flashed what he hoped was a *hurry up already, I need you now* look.

Gordy smiled softly and reached for the lube again. Tristan followed his every movement as he smoothed a generous amount onto his cock and even more on Tristan.

"Here's how we are going to do this." Gordy's hand moved slowly on his own cock and Tristan felt his stomach clench. "I'm going to make love to you slow and easy. You let me know if you feel any discomfort, or for any reason you aren't completely with me."

Tristan nodded, unable to get his voice to work. He could do that. Sure.

"While that's happening, I want you to jack yourself off, keeping the same speed as I am. If you want me to go faster, you pump yourself faster. Slower, you go slower. You will be in control of the pace we keep."

Feeling his eyes bug, Tristan exhaled gustily. "I've never been in charge."

"Then it's about time you were. Wouldn't you say?"

"Uh huh." And he couldn't wait. All the fear had left him as if it had never been there. All he had was anticipation and white-hot need.

"Are you ready for me, babe?"

He drew in a deep breath and nodded. More than ready, but he couldn't say it.

It didn't matter. Gordy understood. He leaned over Tristan, one hand planted on the bed for stability, the other hand wrapped around his cock as he aimed and rubbed the crown around the eager hole.

Tristan rolled his hips up as Gordy settled in place. One outward push, and Gordy was inside him. Just the tip, but he was so big the pressure pulled the air from Tristan's lungs.

"Breathe, Tristan. We won't go any further until you're ready." Gordy's breathing was irregular, and Tristan could hear the strain he was under trying to hold back.

Several deep breaths later, Tristan relaxed enough that the slight pain he'd experienced eased. "I'm okay. I'm okay."

The gray in Gordy's eyes darkened as he stared into Tristan's. He was looking for the truth, and Tristan smiled crookedly. "Really, I'm all right." He wiggled his hips again in invitation.

For a moment longer, Gordy judged him and his truthfulness, then smiled. "Then we'll continue. Remember you're in charge of our pace."

"Oh, yeah." Tristan let go of his knee with his right hand and wrapped his fingers around his aching cock. It was so tender to the touch that it caused his ass to tighten, which in turn made Gordy groan.

Control. For the first time in his life, Tristan felt as if he were in control. He could really do this.

Slowly, he let his hand glide down the shaft of his cock. Gordy watched and flexed his hips so that his cock slid into Tristan a little farther. Tristan felt full already, but the need for more erupted.

Again, he pumped his cock, slow and easy. Gordy followed, pressing a little deeper.

Over and over, they played the game, Gordy delving deeper with each gentle thrust until Tristan felt as if he would explode from the inside and Gordy's balls rested against the cheeks of Tristan's very full ass.

Digging the back of his head into the pillow, Tristan panted. "So full. So good."

Unable to help himself, the hand on his cock sped up the thrusts. He wanted to feel Gordy's cock pushing into him, wanted to feel the fullness and pressure.

Gordy followed the pace exactly, grunting when Tristan pounded his fist up and down his cock. "Faster?"

"More. Harder. Faster." Tristan wanted it all. He had no thoughts but that he was going to come any second, and Gordy was going to get him there.

Thrusting into his ass, Gordy covered Tristan's hand with his own large, strong hand and tightened the grip on his cock. Faster and harder Gordy pulled on Tristan's cock until Tristan's gut tightened and his balls drew up close to his body and he couldn't hold back any longer.

"Gonna come!"

"Yes. Come for me, baby." Gordy sped up both his hand and the thrusting of his hips.

Tristan arched and cried out. Staring into Gordy's eyes, he erupted. Come spurted from his shaft and Gordy cupped his hand over it, pushed Tristan's hand out of the way and finishing the job. That was all it took, apparently, to set Gordy off. His eyes closed and his jaw tightened. Pounding now into Tristan's ass, he swelled and came. Tristan could feel the heat from it infusing him and he closed his own eyes.

Gordy rolled to Tristan's side and gulped air. Tristan lay stunned, letting his legs fall back to the bed.

A moment or two passed, then Gordy lifted up on one elbow and ran an unsteady hand through Tristan's sweaty hair. "You all right?"

Tristan took stock. "Better than."

That drew a startled chuckle out of Gordy. "No freaking out?"

"Only once."

Trepidation flashed through Gordy's eyes. "What did I do wrong?"

His own breathless laughter sounded as he turned his exhausted body toward Gordy. "You did nothing wrong."

"Then why did you freak out?"

"I…" he closed his eyes, took a deep breath, and forged onward. "I wondered how to convince you to stay the night."

FOUR

Tristan worked steadily through the big house. He couldn't restrain the happy smile that covered his face as he thought about the night two weeks ago, when he'd gotten the nerve to talk Gordy into staying the night. It hadn't been a difficult task, since that was what Gordy had wanted as well, and he'd stayed over every night since.

He frowned when he thought of having to spend the next few nights alone, since Gordy was going to have duty watching the cows. Seemed the hands did this regularly and it was Gordy's turn. Oh well, that was the breaks when it came to working on a ranch.

Gordy didn't need him in his pocket anyway and he had said that he would come to the trailer the minute he was freed. Tristan had grinned at the phrasing, but was glad that Gordy still wanted to be with him.

The man was a Godsend. They'd spent so much time together, the other guys had begun to notice. At first, Tristan had been embarrassed, but they weren't the only gay couple on the ranch and that relieved any worries he'd had about that. Gordy was also bringing him out of his shell. Simply spending time with Gordy was having a good influence on Tristan. He was able to talk to the other hands without panicking and he didn't flinch anymore when one of them yelled or slammed a door.

Things were going great, and he laughed to himself when he thought of how butch he was becoming. Heck, just yesterday, he'd told Cy to not come into the barracks with his poop-covered boots unless he wanted to face the wrath of the broom across his head. The other man had given him a funny look then taken the fouled boots outside. He'd felt darned proud of himself for that small feat.

Tristan was happy. Gordy was the reason, and there was no denying it. Damn, he loved that man so much. Now, if only he could get the gumption to tell him.

The shrill ringing of the phone shattered the quiet of the house. Tristan crossed the room and picked up the receiver.

"Shifting Sands Ranch, this is Tristan speaking, how may I help you?"

At first, all Tristan heard was breathing, then a torrent of violence and anger spewed across the line. "I told you that you can't get away from me, Tristan. Get your fucking pansy ass back home. Otherwise, I'm going to go there and kick your ass all the way back. It'll be better for you if you come back on your own."

"Howard?" Tristan was nearly paralyzed with fear at the sound of the psycho he'd escaped all those months ago.

"Of course. Who the fuck did you think it was? God, you're such an idiot. How can I put up with you? I swear, you wouldn't be able to find your head if it weren't attached."

Tristan hung the phone receiver back on the hook. He couldn't think, he felt numb. Howard had found him again. The phone began to ring and he stared at it, shaking.

Every moment he'd been with Howard flashed through his mind. The verbal abuse, the physical abuse, the threats and the beatings…every vicious word, every agonizing punch. For what seemed like hours, he stood rigidly staring at the now silent phone until a hand landed on his shoulder.

Tristan lurched away, turning and raising his fists. "No!"

He wouldn't let Howard hit him anymore. He'd fight until he died before he would take the abuse as if he'd earned it.

"Tristan, chill." Jud stood in front of him, hands up in the universal surrender sign. "I didn't mean to scare you."

Clenching and unclenching his fists, Tristan concentrated on breathing and waited for his heart rate to slow. "*You* didn't scare me."

"Yeah? Well, something did." He glanced around the room and shrugged. "Anything we can do to help?"

"We?" Tristan echoed.

Jud gave him a look that said he thought Tristan wasn't real bright. "Yeah. We, as in, the guys on the ranch."

Tristan was nonplused. Jud was right. He didn't have to face this alone. The guys on the ranch backed each other up, and he was one of the guys. A warm feeling started in his chest and radiated through his whole body, burning away the cold sensation that Howard's call had generated. He wasn't on his own anymore. He had a safe place.

That gave him the strength, not to mention the backbone, to face Howard. "Jud I've got to take care of some business. I don't know how long I'll be, shouldn't be more than a day, but I need you to cover for me with the boss."

"What about Gordy?" Jud asked.

That gave him pause, but only momentarily. "I'll leave him a note."

Running most of the way to his place, he burst through the door and scribbled out a quick note to Gordy that said where he was going and when he would be back. In closing he wrote:

Don't worry about me. I'm sick of Howard's crap and I'm going to make it stop. You've given me the strength to face my fears and I'm not afraid of him anymore.

Love you,

Tristan

Tossing clothes into a bag, he jumped into his piece-of-crap car and drove off in a spray of dust.

🐾 🐾 🐾

Gordy read the note, filled with trepidation. Tristan might have become less afraid of bigger guys, but that was around the ranch. The men here wouldn't hurt him for anything, but Howard wouldn't hesitate if Tristan sassed him.

No way in hell would Gordy allow Howard to lay a single hand on Tristan ever again. Anger built up, and he saw red. If

Howard touched him, Gordy would teach him a lesson in treating someone who is smaller with some respect. The hard way, if he had to.

It was a good thing he'd gotten Tristan's old address from him, because he needed to follow Tristan and knowing it would save time. Time he didn't have. It was so close to the full moon, he could actually feel the pull of the bull and the moon on his system. It didn't matter, he was going after Tristan.

"Daniel," He said into the cell phone as he climbed into his truck. "I'm going to bring Tristan back. He went after that ex of his."

"Damn. What about the full moon? It's tomorrow. You have to be here to change, and the farther you go from the ranch, the more it's going to hurt." Daniel didn't try to change his mind, only warned him of the consequences.

"Yeah, I know. But this is something I have to do. Tristan is finally starting to relax. No way am I going to let that guy beat up on him again."

"I understand. Try to be home by dark tomorrow night. I don't like it when y'all aren't here when it's time to change."

"Will do, boss. Even if I have to pick Tristan up and bring him home forcibly, we will both be back on the ranch by dark."

Gordy put his cell phone in his pocket and jumped into his truck. Gravel flew as he tore out of the yard.

By the time he reached the street where Tristan used to live, it was dark and he was so upset his breath came in snorts. He'd nearly gone insane wondering what could be happening to Tristan while he was trying to reach him.

Driving up on the grass, he slammed the truck into park and leapt out, stormed across the patchy lawn, and stomped up the steps onto the porch. Gordy raised his fist and pounded on the door.

"'Bout time you got here." The door opened on that rude remark and Gordy clenched his fists.

Practically breathing fire, Gordy glared at the tall, broad-shouldered, heading-for-a-beer belly, dark-haired man. "You Howard?"

"Who the hell are you?" The man clenched his fist on his beer can and it crumbled under the pressure.

"Where's Tristan?" Gordy was having trouble seeing the man through the red haze of anger. He wanted this piece of shit to make a move so he could rip his head off. He wanted to stomp him into the ground. Just one little move and he'd turn him into dust.

A car pulled into the driveway and when the door opened, Gordy turned to see Tristan step out of the cab.

"Gordy? What are you doing here?"

He'd gotten here before Tristan. That calmed him. Seeing that he was unharmed and not in danger helped soothe his ragged nerves.

"You left without telling me."

Tristan paid the cabbie and sent him on his way then returned his gaze to Gordy, lips pursed, hands on hips. "I left you a note."

As Tristan strode across the driveway to the porch, Gordy raked his eyes over him. Unharmed. Tristan was safe.

"What are you doing here?"

Fists clenching and unclenching, Gordy shook his head abruptly to shake off the feeling that he had to get Tristan back to the ranch. It was safe at the ranch. His body was beginning to ache, and he wanted to go home. "I want to go home."

That made Tristan smile. "Me, too. First, I have to take care of something." He stood on tiptoe and kissed Gordy's tight mouth until it softened. "Let me take care of this and we'll go straight home."

"What the fuck?" Gordy glanced up at the outburst. Howard had watched as Tristan had fearlessly approached him and, he noted, had finally figured out that the man towering over both of them was who Tristan was now seeing. "What's going on?"

Spinning on his heel, Gordy made a huffing sound that had a threatening tone to it. Tristan smiled again, patted Gordy on the arm, which did little to calm his anger, and stepped around him. "Don't worry, honey. I won't let him hurt me again." Tristan ran a soothing hand across Gordy's massive, heaving chest, and Gordy saw the humor in his eyes. "If he tries it, all the ranch hands will come here and tear him apart. Hiding the body on the ranch would be no problem since it's so big."

A chuffing sound moved Gordy's chest in a low, grating laugh, but he didn't take his threatening glare off Howard. One wrong move, and Howard would be ripped to shreds. Gordy vowed this.

🐝 🐝 🐝

When Tristan saw that Gordy wasn't going to interfere, only protect, he took a deep breath, turned, and faced Howard, who stood in the doorway fuming.

"Well then, Howard. I have a few things I want to say to you, so keep your mouth shut and don't interrupt." When Howard opened his mouth and clenched his fist, Gordy growled. "Stop it, honey. He can't hurt me anymore. I'm not afraid of him."

Sending Howard his own glare, Tristan twitched his nose. "You look like crap, Howard. I don't know how I was ever attracted to you."

"You left and I didn't have anyone to take care of me. You wouldn't talk to me like this if the big dumb ox behind you wasn't here." Howard glowered at Gordy, who returned the look full measure. He wouldn't move on Tristan with Gordy standing there, but he looked like he wanted to.

"So, all I had been was your slave and your punching bag, and Gordy's not your business." Muscles quivered throughout his body. "I was so afraid of you, and for what? Nothing. You're nothing but a bag of shit."

"You belong—"

"Don't go there, Howard. I belong to myself. Get that through your head."

Howard turned his pissed-off glare to Gordy. "It didn't take you long to replace me."

That made Tristan smile broadly and lean his back against Gordy's unwavering chest. "It took some convincing, but Gordy here is very persuasive. And, he only touches me to bring pleasure. For us both. You on the other hand only brought pain. You need help, Howard, or you are going to kill someone and end up in jail where you will meet someone bigger than you. You won't like being treated like I was, would you?"

Skin itching, needing to move, Tristan started to pace between the two larger men. "Look. I don't want you to call me or bother me ever again. You hurt me and you need help. If you ever contact me again, I'll call the cops. This is the end. Do you understand?"

"You've grown some balls, little boy. I don't care what you want." Howard took a menacing step forward and reached for Tristan.

He must have forgotten about Gordy. Tristan couldn't fathom how he couldn't remember such a—in his own words—"burly ox" of a man. He never would, that's for sure.

As he hopped out of reach, Gordy wrapped his big, strong hand around Howard's arm, holding him in place. "Never lay your hand on him."

"Let me go." Howard struggled to remove his arm from Gordy's grasp but couldn't. No matter how hard he tugged and pulled, he couldn't release himself from Gordy's punishing grip.

"We're leaving now, Howard. I would suggest you move on with your life. I have."

With that, Tristan bounded down the steps and literally hopped across the driveway to his bag. Picking it up, he crossed the lawn to Gordy's truck. "Time to go home, Gordy. I'm done here."

Gordy nodded from his position on the porch, hand still wrapped tightly around Howard's arm. "Never go near him again."

Howard flushed. "You can't tell me what to do, faggot."

Gordy smiled. "Yes, I can." Tightening his fingers, he let Howard feel a little of the beast that lived within him. "Stay away from him or I'll beat you so bad, it'll make you wish you were dead."

Howard opened his mouth with the thought of arguing more, but must have seen the absolute need to open a can of whoopass all over him, and stilled. "Yeah, whatever. He wasn't good for shit anyway."

"Keep thinking that and we'll get along."

Gordy released Howard's arm as if he'd been touching vermin, and turned his back on him fearlessly. Howard was just a pissant who could talk big and take it out on anyone smaller than him, but he didn't have the 'nads to take on someone his own size.

FIVE

Tristan was in the truck, buckled in the seat by the time Gordy climbed in.

Gordy glared at him. "I'm still pissed at you for leaving without me."

To Gordy's astonishment, Tristan only laughed, leaned toward him, and kissed his frowning mouth. "Yes, I know."

More than any words could have said, that told him how much Tristan trusted him. Immediately, the anger began to flow out of his system. He still felt itchy and in mild pain, but he was on his way home, and Tristan was at his side, so everything was as it should be.

"Where's your car?"

Tristan huffed. "Darned thing broke down on me about twenty minutes away from the ranch. I had a tow truck take it home while I caught a cab to the bus station. It's been a long day."

"It'll be morning before we get home."

"I'll help keep you awake." Tristan promised.

Gordy drove the speed limit, no matter how much it hurt to be away from the ranch, and Tristan's twitching in the passenger seat worried him.

"What's the matter, babe?" Gordy finally had to ask.

"I think I am having an allergic reaction to something. It's no big deal. When I get home, I'll take an antihistamine." Tristan rubbed at his arm in agitation.

Knowing how he felt, since he was in a bit of distress himself, he let the matter slide. He needed to get back to the ranch. Quickly.

When they pulled in front of the trailer, the sun was shining. Tristan leaned over and kissed him. "I'll go take that antihistamine.

I know you have to go back to the ranch and get some sleep, since it's your night on the range, but I want to tell you thank you for showing up and helping me out. I could have done it without you, but I'm glad I didn't have to."

Understanding how he felt, Gordy wrapped his arms around Tristan and deepened the kiss. "I'll miss you tonight. I want you bad."

Tristan sighed. "I want you, too." His eyes twinkled when he glanced up at Gordy's face. "Got time for a quickie?"

Instantly, Gordy's cock hardened. "A quick quickie. Yeah."

Running into the trailer, they raced for the bedroom and turned to each other. Lips slid firmly across one another, tongues tasted, teasing, breaths mingled. It was nearly too much for Gordy and he fought against coming in his jeans.

Pulling Tristan closer, he gasped when chest brushed against chest. He could feel the hard nubs of Tristan's nipples pressing into him. Gordy wanted to actually see this physical proof of his excitement and pulled back.

Gratified at the inarticulate complaint Tristan made, Gordy broke the kiss.

"It's all right. Shh."

He looked down as he ran his thumb over one hardened nipple and smiled. "Yeah, baby. That's nice."

Tristan gasped and his head fell back. "God, Gordy. Pinch it."

Gordy's heart leapt in time with his cock and drawing in a shuddering breath, he did as instructed. Through the soft shirt Tristan wore, he caught the bud between his forefinger and thumb and tightened his grip, pinching lightly and twisting.

"Gah. Yes. Harder."

Fascinated, Gordy watched Tristan wiggle in his arms. When his hips seemed to be uncontrollably moving in time with the pinches and twists of his nipple, Gordy grinned. Turning Tristan so his back was against the wall. Gordy freed the arm that had been practically holding the other man up. Placing the newly emptied hand on Tristan's thigh, he squeezed lightly.

Tristan's leg flexed as his hand slid upward, causing Gordy to smile in delight. Tristan might look soft, but he was no twink. Gordy lost just a little of the fear that was reigning in his power. Up to now, he'd restrained himself in their lovemaking, unsure if Tristan was ready for his beastly side. Obviously, Tristan could take more than expected and wouldn't be hurt by a little rough handling. He'd become more confident in himself since they'd been dating, and Tristan had finally shed all his fears now that he'd confronted his personal boogieman. Slowly, while massaging the path he followed, Gordy pressed on Tristan's inner thigh to separate his legs. Caressing and squeezing, his hand slipped closer to his goal.

The curve of Tristan's neck beaconed for his attention, and Gordy was unable to withstand the call. He pressed gentle kisses from his cheekbone, down the side of his face. When Tristan tilted his head to the side and back, Gordy took advantage of the exposed skin and licked from jaw line to the collar of his shirt. He wanted more and if Tristan's reaction was anything to go by, so did he.

Tristan released the grip that he'd had on Gordy's shirt and fought with the buttons on his own shirt. Cursing a particularly stubborn button, he growled and popped it off.

"The undershirt. Pull it up." Gordy was surprised at the deep growl that was his voice, but the need that coursed through him when Tristan parted the panels of his shirt and dragged the wife-beater up his chest knocked all thought from his brain.

He was firm, muscled, and smooth. Not a hair marred the pale, hard plane of his chest and abdomen. Before they'd gotten together, Gordy had imagined him to be softer, less muscled, but this…this was much better. Each time he saw Tristan naked, he marveled at how beautiful he was. It was also further proof he wouldn't be hurt by Gordy's brand of loving.

Leaning down, he covered Tristan's cinnamon-colored nipple with his lips. Dragging them softly across the hard nub, he alternated between nibbles and licks. Tristan didn't seem to mind in the least. As a matter of fact, he seemed to appreciate all Gordy was doing to him. So much so, that his arms wrapped tightly around Gordy and the hands that gripped his hair pulled him closer against him.

Not being a stupid man, Gordy continued his ministrations at Tristan's chest. But he needed more. He slipped his hand over Tristan's rippling abdomen and down to the top button of his jeans. When he popped it free, it caused Tristan to arch his hips into him.

"Off. Now, off. Please."

Damn he was responsive. It only made Gordy hotter and harder seeing Tristan like this. Helping Tristan shed the jeans was a bit of struggle, but they managed. Carefully, belying his urgent need, he laid Tristan on the bed.

"Comfortable?"

"Huh? What? Who gives a shit? Jeeze, Gordy. Please, I'm hurting here. Fuck me already."

Once more, Gordy had to hold in a laugh. Tristan was a firecracker, and he couldn't wait to watch him explode, but damned if he was going to forgo some yummy foreplay. He knew Tristan's likes and dislikes now, and foreplay was at the top of the like list, even though he sometimes wanted to skip it and get right to the good stuff. Gordy, however, was in the mood to play.

Suddenly, panic rocketed through his body. They had used the last of the rubbers the previous night. He'd planned on getting some as soon as the full moon was over, but hadn't done so yet. Cussing quietly, saying several different words as if they were one, he reached for his wallet. The air whooshed out of him when he realized he did, indeed, have a single, solitary condom, which wasn't beyond its expiration date, surprisingly enough.

"Good to go." He tossed the condom beside Tristan's hip and reached for him.

Naked, Tristan was everything and more than he had hoped and dreamed. Even after they'd gotten together he'd dream about this man. Every freaking night since he'd come to the ranch to keep house, as a matter of fact. It was even worse now. The dreams involved a permanent relationship.

"Gordy, if you don't stick something in my ass right now, I'm going to beat you to death."

Tristan looked serious. How could Gordy fight that?

He couldn't.

Sighing as if ever so put upon, he reached his hand up to Tristan's mouth. "Wet my fingers if you're in such need."

Tristan latched on to his first two fingers as if he were a newborn calf first finding his mother's teat, sucking them as deeply and as strongly as he could. Gordy's cock twitched as he remembered that mouth there instead of his fingers.

Apparently, Tristan wasn't going to wait around for that, though. When the digits were wet enough for government work, Gordy pressed Tristan's leg up toward his chest and when the other followed it, it opened him in a way that exposed all the really interesting bits. Gordy slid his fingers around the grasping entrance into Tristan's body. Round and round, in a teasing manner, more to watch the expressions on Tristan's face than any other reason, Gordy tormented him.

"Damn it, Gordy!" Tristan arched up and in a surprising move, he tossed Gordy off of his body and onto the springy bed beside him. Gasping for breath, Gordy wondered what the hell just happened, but before he could, he felt Tristan's hands at his waist removing his jeans. "Taking too fucking long. I need what I need right fucking now. Get these off."

Gordy didn't say a word, just helped Tristan push his jeans out of the way. They made it as far as his knees before Tristan abandoned the pants and reached for the condom. Tearing the cellophane wrapper, he had Gordy wrapped in a flash and was straddling his waist.

"Holy fuck." Gordy grabbed Tristan's thighs just as he felt the head of his cock pop through the tight muscle of the body above him. "Slow down."

"No." Tristan's eyes glittered as he pressed inexorably down on Gordy, surrounding him in heat and moisture and tight muscles. He didn't stop until Gordy felt Tristan's ass press against his pelvis.

"Deep. God, Gordy, you're big." Tristan's eyes rolled in his head, startling Gordy into trying to lift the man off him, but Tristan only circled his hips in a grinding motion.

Both of them made gasping sounds at the sensation. When he caught his breath, he pierced Tristan with his gaze. "Do it again."

He did and both men groaned. After that, it was only sparks and flame. Tristan used his thigh muscles to slide up Gordy's cock, his muscles holding on tightly enough that Gordy thought his cock would pop right off to stay in Tristan's body, but then Tristan reversed direction and the friction almost killed him.

Gordy grasped Tristan's waist and, lifting his own hips, pulled Tristan down onto him. Cussing a blue streak, they eventually achieved a rhythm both enjoyed and rode it out until it bucked them right off the planet.

It took damned near forever for Gordy to float back into his body, but when he did, he smiled. Tristan lay on him, totally spent, gasping for air, and crying.

Crying?

Terror ripped through his system.

"Baby, what's wrong? Did I hurt you?"

Tristan lifted his head from Gordy's shoulder. "No, darlin', you didn't hurt me."

Wanting to grin at the endearment, but still worried about Tristan's tears, Gordy ran his hand over his back soothingly and frowned. "Then why—?"

His question was cut off with the application of Tristan's hand on his mouth. Tristan shook his head and dried his face with his free hand. "You didn't hurt me. Just the opposite. I love you so much, it overwhelms me sometimes."

"You love me?" Gordy knew he sounded stunned, but he'd expected that it would take a lot longer for Tristan to admit his feelings.

"It's all right. I'm not asking for anything."

Gordy covered Tristan's mouth with his own in as loving a kiss as he could manage. "I love you too, baby. More than anything on this earth."

"Oh, good. You had me worried."

He felt Tristan's smile against his mouth when they resumed the kiss. God, he loved him so much.

A wiggle of Tristan's hips made Gordy realize he was still deeply embedded in the other man, even though he was soft now. He carefully lifted Tristan off his growing erection and laid him on the bed beside them.

When Tristan reached for him, he grasped him by the wrists. "I'm glad I didn't hurt you, baby, but we can't do this again."

"What? Why? Didn't you like it?" Tristan's whole body tensed, which wasn't Gordy's aim.

"Loved it. Hell, it was the best I've ever had, too. I want more, but that's out of the question."

"Why?" Gordy wondered if Tristan realized he was practically whining.

"'Cause." He looked down his body at his spent cock, which was still covered with the used condom. "I only had one rubber, and I've got to get to work."

Tristan punched him on the shoulder as Gordy laughed. "I'll pay you back for that, shithead. You 'bout gave me a heart attack."

Gordy closed his eyes and promptly fell asleep. Tristan laughed softly, and curled up beside him and closed his eyes.

🐫 🐫 🐫

A pain-filled groan woke him.

Rolling over, he glanced at Gordy who groaned again as pain

ripped through him, arching his back.

Tristan watched as Gordy writhed in pain on the bed, not understanding what he was seeing.

"Gordy! What's wrong?" He could see the agony he was in, but didn't see anything that could be causing it.

Leaping out of bed, he ran for the phone. Without thinking, he dialed the big house. When Jud answered, he took a deep breath and let it out slowly. "Jud, we need help here. Something's wrong with Gordy."

Jud spoke to him calmly. "Where are you at?"

"Oh, my place. We're at my place." Tristan looked around confused. He could barely see in the dark room. The sun had gone down unnoticed. The sound of grunts and groans of pain coming from the bedroom frightened him. "He's in pain, Jud. I don't know what to do."

"He's got to get back to the ranch, Tristan. Do you understand me? On the ranch property."

Tristan looked out the window. He couldn't see it in the dark, but the fence to the western edge of the property wasn't more than fifty feet from his door. "That doesn't make sense."

"It doesn't have to make sense, Tristan. He's got to be on ranch property."

"Yeah. All right. I can get him there."

He hung up without saying goodbye and ran back into the bedroom.

"Jud said I have to get you onto the ranch. I can't do it alone. You're going to have to help."

Lifting Gordy's arm, he tried to pull the agitated man to his feet. Apparently realizing what Tristan was trying to do, Gordy rolled off the bed and climbed to his knees.

"That's good. Now, to your feet." Tristan levered his shoulder under Gordy's arm and lifted with all his might. He wouldn't have been able to budge him if the big man hadn't done most of the work himself.

Finally, they made it to their feet, and in a move that was closer to falling forward than walking, they lurched toward the front door. Tristan wrestled it open and they continued their staggering gait across the grassy yard.

"Fifty feet, Gordy. Jud said ranch property. That's right over there." He didn't know why Jud thought this would work. He was just going to have to trust him in this and hope that help came soon. Maybe they were going to meet them once they got on the other side of the fence. That's probably it. They would be able to drive a truck right up to the fence, which would save time.

Heartened by that idea, Tristan put more strength into keeping Gordy on his feet.

They would make it.

They *had* to make it.

He couldn't lose Gordy now that he'd found him.

The fence was only a few feet from them, and with a jerk and a lurch, they crashed into it. Gordy bent forward and literally threw himself between the railings of the fence onto the ground beyond.

To Tristan's astonishment, Gordy levered himself onto his hands and knees. His naked back arched and the muscles under the skin rippled.

He seemed to be in excruciating pain. Tristan climbed through the fence and crawled to Gordy. Pain wracked his own body.

Oh God, whatever Gordy had, he had it too!

They were going to die before help could get to them.

Pain ripped up Tristan's back and it felt as if every bone in his body was breaking and reforming. Never, not even when Howard had nearly killed him, had he felt this intensity of agony.

Gordy bellowed, and Tristan heard his own scream echo Gordy's in the night.

Slowly the pain receded, leaving Tristan lying on his side,

panting. He was alive, and he could hear Gordy breathing, so he was alive, too.

He hoped help got to them before the pain returned. He didn't think he could take another round of it.

Opening his eyes, he looked for Gordy. Not finding him, he set his eyes on the large black bull that stood in front of him.

"Gordy!" He lunged to his feet, scared to death that the bull had stomped Gordy. He'd eat that bull for dinner if he had laid one hoof on Gordy's precious body.

The bull slowly, and with a whole lot of grunting and sighing, lay down next to him.

He blew out a puff of air so strong that Tristan was blown backwards. Head over heels, he rolled.

Dizzy, he sat up and stared at the bull, who seemed to be laughing at him.

"Stupid bull. Gordy!" Calling out over and over had no effect, and since the bull seemed calm enough, Tristan rounded him to look on the other side.

"Freaking huge-assed bull." It seemed to take forever to get around him and once there, still no Gordy.

The bull swatted him with his tail and when Tristan lifted a hand to rub the abused area, he nearly passed out. His hand was deformed. Taking a close look at it, he realized it was a…a rabbit's foot. He frantically traced a path over his arm to the rest of his body. *OH SHIT! I'm a rabbit!*

Again the bull snorted as if in agreement.

What the hell is going on? He could smell Gordy. That masculine, outdoorsy scent that always hit Tristan like a two-by-four and was an instant cock-hardener. He tried to look under the bull for Gordy, but didn't see him.

The bull leaned closer to Tristan and he hopped backwards. It rubbed its head along his rabbit side and the scent enveloped him.

Every muscle in Tristan's freaked-out, rabbit shaped body stilled. "What the hell? Gordy, you're the bull?"

Shifting his frightened gaze up, up, up the body of the bull, Tristan drew in a sharp breath when he saw the gray eyes he knew so well. The giant bull winked.

Gordy was the bull. The bull was Gordy.

And he was a fucking rabbit.

Tristan promptly fainted.

🐂 🐂 🐂

When he came to, he was lying on the bull's back and Gordy was grunting, practically humming as he walked toward the ranch house.

Wha—?

Gordy turned his big bull head to look at him. A wicked-looking bull smile broke over his face. Tristan's stomach jumped. He was a rabbit and Gordy was a bull. But Gordy didn't seem bothered by it. Taking several deep breaths, he held on to his control by a thread and nodded. *Okay. I can handle this. It can't be permanent. If it were, Gordy wouldn't be so calm. Right?* He could wait it out and when he turned back into a man, he'd get some damned answers.

He stayed on top of Gordy and wondered about the extra animals that were on the ranch. At least, he'd never noticed the dog, the monkey, the ram, or any of the others that Gordy snorted greetings at.

The night was long, but not uncomfortable and when the dawn broke, Tristan felt a strange tingle in his lower spine.

He jumped off Gordy's bull back and clenched his teeth through the agonizing pain.

When he could breathe again, he ran his gaze over himself and sighed in relief. He was once again himself.

He wasn't the only one who was no longer an animal. Gordy lay on the soft grass next to him, breathing heavily.

"So, what the fuck was that?"

Gordy laughed softly and groaned. "Thanks for not bailing on me, babe. I was worried that you would leave me before I could explain."

"Hell no. I have got to know exactly how and why I turned into Thumper, and you turned into Ferdinand."

Quickly, Gordy spun a tale of a crazy woman who cursed all the men of the ranch because they wouldn't sleep with her. Tristan grimaced at that. Eww! As if.

"But you're gay."

He snorted. "We all are, but she couldn't take the hint. Well, she got pissed and blasted us with the curse of the zodiac. Each of us at the ranch were turned into one of the animals of the Chinese zodiac. I got the ox. They are practically bulls anyway, so I blend in pretty well."

"Okay, crazy bitch zapped you. So, why am I a rabbit?"

The tale was so nuts that it was believable. Well, the fact that he was a rabbit and Gordy was a bull was pretty substantial proof.

"You love me." Gordy sounded awfully proud of that fact.

"Yes, I do love you, but what does that have to do with me being a rabbit?" Tristan squirmed around and made himself comfortable on Gordy's warm, broad chest. It was a very comfortable place to lie, really. He could get used to it.

"The curse is that when the person we love, loves us back, even though we are beasts, they join us in the curse. I didn't mean for it to happen, Tristan. I couldn't help myself."

He sounded so dejected, Tristan couldn't help but love him more. "You know…this isn't so bad. I've finally figured out what you do on the full moon." When Gordy flinched, Tristan laughed. "Yes, I'd noticed, but figured it was some secret society thing like the Masons. Anyway, this is all right."

A random thought hit him. "Oh, hey! Could you understand me when I was a rabbit?"

"Nope."

"Well, then, why did you keep acting as if you did?"

"I know you babe, and the first thing you would do is try to find me. I would do the same if you disappeared."

"Yeah, you would." A startled chuckle burst from him when he thought of something. "So I can spend the whole night talking, once a month, and nobody is going to tell me to stow it?"

Gordy heaved a relived sigh. If he could joke, it was going to be all right. "Damn, I love you so much, Tristan. What did I ever do to deserve you?"

"You accepted me with all my baggage, helped me find myself, and taught me what real love is. That's all."

"That's all, huh?" Gordy's laughter unseated Tristan and he leapt lightly to the ground.

Tipping his nose up to Gordy's as he leaned his big head down, they touched in a sweet kiss.

"I love you, big guy. No matter what."

"And I love you back. Forever."

"One thing, though." Tristan looked down at his body. "Why did it have to be a rabbit? I've been working so hard at being butch and I'm still just a freaking rabbit. Couldn't I have been something tough like a Tasmanian devil or something?"

Gordy's laughter echoed across the fields. How could one feel cursed when he was so damned happy?

LOST
AND FOUND

J.L. LANGLEY

"Quit that wigglin' 'round. You ain't goin' nowhere till we say. You devil-worshiping witch."

Devil worshiping witch? Shay froze inside the burlap bag. Well, wasn't that irony at its finest? Because if he believed in any deity at all he'd be praying to it right now. On the bright side, at least now he knew why he'd been roughed up and snagged out of his cozy bed. Nothing good could come of this situation. He had to get out of this damned bag fast.

Testing the opening—or rather, where an opening should have been if it weren't taped—with his bound hands, Shay groaned. Whoever invented burlap should be shot. Not only did burlap itch, it didn't allow for much visibility, and it was dusty. He'd been coughing since being stuffed inside the bag. If he believed in Christianity, he'd have said burlap was the devil's fabric.

Extending as far as mobility allowed, he attempted to work out the cramps in his legs, but unfortunately, burlap also proved very effective in restraining a person. Specifically a short, dumb big-mouth, who actually fit in the damned bag. *Grrr...* if he got out of this alive, he was going to seriously consider taking steroids.

"I said quit movin', you damned Wiccan scum." A kick accompanied Charlie's statement.

Blinking back tears at the stab of pain in his wrist, Shay closed his eyes, thankful the boot hadn't connected with his face instead. Wiccans were *not* devil worshippers and he wasn't Wiccan anyway, damn it.

He should have just tossed out that pentacle with the pig on it that Moonbeam sent him in her last care package. Hurting her feelings by not wearing it would have been preferable to this. He'd told her over and over that he didn't believe in totem animals and even if he did, he'd have chosen something a lot cooler than a pig. *Stupid pig.*

Note to self: "I don't believe in religion" is not a proper response when caught removing negative energy from a non-Christian object—like the offending pentacle pig—with a salt water wash. Not only did the phrase piss off his Wiccan parents, it apparently enraged Christian cowboys. Purifying that damn necklace had been second-nature to him. He hadn't even considered how it'd look. *Stupid upbringing.* Why did he always have to learn things the hard way? *When in doubt, just shut the heck up.* If he'd thought of that earlier, he might not be here now. Here being, as the saying went, *up shit creek without a paddle.*

The wind rushed past the truck in a constant whoosh of sound that probably meant they were on the highway, but Shay could barely hear it over the blood thundering through his veins at the speed of sound. A slight tremble raced up his spine and he told himself it was the chilly night air whipping through the bag, not his fear. He was a big fat liar. He was scared shitless.

And the worst thing about the whole situation was that he'd really thought he was beginning to fit in. Why hadn't he realized the men he worked with were backward, God-fearing rednecks with a wide streak of intolerance? Well, he knew now, didn't he? How could he have misread them so badly? They'd all seemed like decent, hardworking men. They loved animals. Animal lovers were good people, weren't they? Perhaps this was some bizarre bonding ritual that ranch hands did?

One thing was certain, he had to get out of this feed sack. Stretching, Shay pressed against the burlap again, trying to tear it. The rough material stretched tight over his forehead, feeling like he'd dragged his head across sandpaper, but nothing else happened. *Good grief, what did they tie this bag with?* Duct tape *and* Super Glue?

Another kick landed. This time it hit Shay in the shin. He bit his lip to keep from crying out. No way was he going to give them the satisfaction, but damned if his lip didn't hurt now, too. The pain made tears well up in his eyes. He couldn't fight back in his current predicament and if he were still, they'd leave him alone…he hoped. Besides, it was best if he saved his energy for when they stopped. *If* they stopped. *What if they throw me over a cliff or something without even slowing down?*

"Weird little queer." Someone, it sounded like Tommy, shouted over the wind.

Shay let out a shuddering breath. *Don't panic, they don't know you're gay. Tommy just means weird.*

"That's reductant." Marty said.

"What? What're you talkin' about?"

"It means that weird and queer are the same thing." Charlie complained.

Redundant, you moron, Shay mentally corrected.

There was a slap followed by an "ow."

Moonbeam was right. Shay had moved to Bubbaville and landed a job with the redneck version of The Three Stooges. Provided he lived, he'd never hear the end of it.

"I meant he's an actual cocksucker, stupid."

Oh shit. Shay froze, not even daring to breath. It was bad enough they knew he wasn't a Christian. If they thought he was gay, too... Shay shivered. If there was one thing he'd learned over the past year, it was that quite a few cowboys didn't think too kindly of one preferring their own sex. Men had been dragged and...his stomach clenched. He was going to be sick.

"Are you sure?" Charlie asked.

"'Course, I am. He's a witch *and* a fag. It kinda goes together. Everyone knows witches are sinners. Besides, you ain't seen him with no girls when we go out have you?"

Under any other circumstances, Shay would've rolled his eyes, but the situation was serious. They'd already tried and convicted him with no evidence. Not dating didn't make him gay any more than a pentacle made him a witch. The fact that he *was* gay and a witch was completely beside the point. "I'm not—" Pain exploded in his gut and the breath whooshed from him as a kick landed on his stomach. Tears streamed down the corner of his eye and over the bridge of his nose.

"Shut up. No one's talkin' to you, homo."

Panic threatened to set in and it was all Shay could do to keep from screaming and thrashing like a madman. The only thing that kept him still was knowing he needed to conserve his energy and come up with a rational plan, or a good spell. Why couldn't he think of a spell right now? Oh man, too late, he was panicking. *Think, Shay, think.*

"Okay, he probably is a faggot, but you sure he's really a witch, Tommy? He said his mom was stuck in the sixties. Don't hippies wear pentagrams and stuff along with their peace signs?" Marty asked. "That necklace don't necessarily mean he's a devil-worshipper or a witch. He said 'imself, he don't believe in religion. Don't them Wicca people consider that a religion?"

Shay nodded. *Finally, someone with some sense.* He tested the strength of the rope on his wrists by pulling in opposite directions. It didn't budge.

"He threw a leaf in the air yesterday and babbled some strange words and the leaf floated around like a bug or somethin' and led him alls the way out to the east pasture. That's how he found Dixie's new colt." Tommy said.

Damn, damn, damn. So not good. They didn't just suspect him because of the necklace, they'd seen him cast a spell. He'd thought no one was close enough to see him do that.

"That still don't mean he's a witch, Tommy. It was pretty windy yesterday." Marty's voice was overly loud due to the truck slowing at that instant.

Right. Listen to Marty. Pleeease, listen to Marty.

"The leaf floated against the wind."

Shit, shit, shit. Bile rose up the back of his throat, but he swallowed it back. *Concentrate, Shay!*

The truck made a sharp left. Shay slid over the bumpy bed, jarring his body and rattling his teeth. A wave of motion sickness hit him and out of instinct, he floundered to grab something.

Instead of steadying himself, his fingers raked rough burlap. With the disorientation and the air howling by, he didn't hear anyone move, but the toe of a boot connected with his shoulder.

"Fuckin' devil-worshippin' cocksucker."

Pain shot through his arm. Curling into a ball, Shay sobbed in surprise. *Stupid horse. I hate horses.* If that idiot mare hadn't lost her baby; what kind of mother loses her baby? Even Moonbeam, as flaky as she was, always knew where Shay was as a child.

Another quick turn threw Shay to the other side of the truck and made him bite his tongue. He winced, wanting to yell but not daring. Where were they taking him? What were they gonna do to him?

The crunching and popping of gravel under tires finally registered through the fear. They were still in the country? That didn't bode well. In the country, no one could hear him scream. And didn't that just sound like a bad horror movie? Still it made his breath catch. There was no telling what they'd do to him if they thought that they could get away with it. Why hadn't he seen them for what they were? There were signs, there were always signs, but somehow he'd convinced himself they were just wary of him because he was a stranger and a yankee. He'd figured working hard and cowboying up, so to speak, would eventually soften their attitudes. He'd let his idiotic dreams of being normal—of being a cowboy—blind him.

The truck stopped.

Shay's stomach clenched tight, painful in its intensity. He may have even let out a little yelp.

Boots clanked against the metal truck bed, coming closer to him. If they knocked him out…no, he wasn't going to let that happen. Curling tighter into a ball, he tried to cover his head with his hands as best he could.

A creak and a thud sounded as the tailgate was lowered, making the truck bounce slightly. A door opened and shut, jarring the truck to the side a tad.

If he could just get out of the bag, he could at least fight back.

"Well boys, what we gonna do with 'im?" Hank asked. A spitting sound followed immediately after.

Shay crinkled his nose. *Nasty.* Hank and his chewing tobacco. Shay hoped he choked on it. "I have an idea. How about we let me go?"

The four men laughed.

Someone slapped something, probably a leg. Cowboys couldn't laugh without slapping their legs, it was some sort of unwritten rule. Shay had always found that funny. It wasn't funny now. Now the slapping reminded him of them cuffing him upside the head a good one when they'd stuffed him into this bag.

"You're hilarious, kid." Charlie said, still hooting.

"Come on, Tommy, help me get 'im out of there." Hank spit again.

Shay cringed, waiting for the hands to touch him through the bag.

They never did, instead they grabbed the bag, hefting it and Shay. And wouldn't you know the damned devil's fabric was strong enough not to rip. He really hated burlap.

"I say we burn him."

No! Shay went wild, kicking and punching, not caring if they dropped him. He had to get out of there.

"Son of a bitch!" someone yelled.

Someone else yelped.

Shay hit the ground so hard it stunned him for a few seconds. There was cursing and muttering, but Shay didn't stick around to hear it, he rolled. He had no clue where he was going. Couldn't even see, but he knew he had to get away. He hated fire just as much as he hated burlap…maybe more. Why did people always think burning witches was a good idea?

Ignoring the pain of little rocks digging into him, Shay rolled, or rather flopped, since his legs were bent up, over the unpaved road until he hit softer ground. *Grass?* He didn't know or care, he just kept spinning as fast as he could. The guys were still there, but they were definitely farther away judging from the sound of their cussing and the pebbles crunching under their boots.

"Get 'im, goddamnit!" Hank yelled.

Footsteps scrambled on the gravel and grew louder.

He needed out of this damned bag. A spell. He needed to do a spell. *Seams, smeams... Aurgh. That's dumb. Seams...beams? Yeah.* "Seams unravel now and let me see moon be—ow." Something stabbed Shay's shoulder through the burlap. It hurt like heck and pulled, ripping the feed sack, but Shay didn't stop rolling.

"Someone hold this fuckin' barbed wire out of the way!"

Barbed wire? He must have floundered into a pasture. Shay's heart raced and his stomach muscles burned. The rolling became easier and he gained momentum.

Another kind of fear set in as he left the ground for a few seconds. When he hit the earth again, his teeth slammed down on his tongue and blood flooded his mouth. More concerned about going down an incline way too fast, he barely felt it. As he barreled out of control, he lost track of the ranch hands. "Seams unravel now and let me see moon beams."

Still hurling downhill, a breeze hit his shoulder where something had jabbed him, then the burlap peeled away from his face, revealing a dark sky dotted with stars and a full yellow moon. Johnson grass tickled his face.

On the next revolution he flew into the air. Landing hard, the rest of the feed sack came away from his upper body, it allowed him to straighten out, but it wound tighter around his hips and legs. The world flipped end-over-end, not really coming into focus, but Shay could tell he was in a pasture.

Other than a large dark object just a few feet away, which was blurry due to his rolling, it was all grass. Was that a tree or—a person? "Help," Shay managed to gasp out.

He thought he heard a response but it could have been his wishful thinking. Shay held out his hands, trying to slow his decent, but only managed to jam his wrists and cause a tingling sensation to shoot up his arms.

Something shiny rippled below him. There were two moons. Or was he rolling so fast it just appeared that way?

Shit, the moon rippled. That was not the moon, it was a reflection of it. Even worse, it was water…a pond.

Leaving the ground again, he hit his head on the way back down. His vision blurred. There was a splash and he stopped spinning. The overwhelming panic left him as recognition set in, and a calmness swept through him. Shay gulped in a deep breath of air right before the warm water flowed over him, sucking him down into a dark abyss.

This was nearly as ironic as what got him into this situation; water had always been his strongest element for working magick.

Two

"Help."

With a mix of excitement and dread, Ben watched the body go barreling past him, headed toward the stock pond. The voice sounded young and male, but not familiar. On the bright side, now Ben wasn't likely to be bored. Usually the night of the full moon found him wandering around in horse form with Gordy, checking the fence and surveying the land. Often times he wished for something more entertaining to do. The monotony of the whole thing was only one of the things he hated about shifting into a horse once a month. Stupid curse.

Splash. The body hit the water.

Tonight looked to be anything but routine. Then again, judging from the group of men running after the rolling man, it may be more of a thrill than Ben bargained for.

"Pppppppftt…" *Well hell*. Being a horse sure made communication a bitch. Glancing over at Gordy, Ben flipped his head toward the four laughing men, hoping Gordy would understand to run them off.

Apparently, Gordy spoke horse, because he was on it like a duck on a June bug. He snorted, lowered his head and charged full steam ahead. "Mmmmmooooo…"

The cowboys stopped dead in their tracks, then just about fell all over themselves trying to backtrack. One slipped, landed on his ass and started hollering his fool head off, calling for his friends to help him. The other three didn't even look back, just kept on running. What great friends. It was pretty comical, all things considered. Too bad there was a guy drowning in the pond. Gordy would just have to fill him in on what happened tomorrow morning.

Ben searched the surface of the water. The kid was still face down but his body was clearly visible. Ben hurried his pace, he'd much rather pull a live body out of the water than wait for tomorrow morning and pull out a dead one. Not only would a dead guy in the stock pond contaminate it, it'd cause way too much paperwork. And he sure didn't want to try and explain to the local law how it happened. *You see, I was a horse at the time…*

The cool mud squished over his hooves, until it covered them altogether, but Ben kept moving. Wincing inwardly at the slurping sounds accompanying each step, Ben tried to ignore the little splatters of mud sprinkling his belly and thighs. He didn't mind getting dirty, hell he got dirty on a daily basis, it just disturbed him to wake up human and find dirt in places where no dirt had gone before.

Bubbles floated up from both sides of the man's dark head. That was a good sign, at least he was alive. Unfortunately, he was also bare from the waist up, wearing only a pair of brown pants. His wrists and ankles were bound together with rope. He had short dark hair and a black cord of some sort around his neck. A necklace maybe? His feet were also bare. *Damn. What was this guy involved in?* He was lean and not very tall, but his shoulders were quite a bit wider than his waist and hips. His body was petite and couldn't possibly weigh that much. He didn't appear to have an ounce of fat on him.

Ben nosed the man, trying to get a response. Pulling him out of the water, with Ben in horse form, was going to be a bitch.

The pale body didn't move.

Gordy snorted and men hollered behind Ben, but he paid them little attention. He had to get the man's face out of the water. Hoping he missed the skin, Ben clamped his teeth down on the brown pants. The way things were nowadays the guy would probably sue The Sands for being bitten by a horse. And wouldn't that just make Ben's night?

He pulled backward and started making his way out of the muck. Sucking sounds and small splatters on his legs and underside accompanied every step.

The body followed for a few seconds then turned over and

the fabric began to unwind. *Shit.* Those weren't pants. Whatever it was, it was wound around the man rather than fastened onto him. Ben tugged harder and the body rolled once more. *Fuck a duck.* This wasn't going to work. After another jerk on the material, the body flipped, getting the dark-haired man's nose and mouth out of the pond. Ben dropped the brown material and trudged further into the tepid pool. With great difficulty, he got on the other side of the man, took a deep breath, stuck his nose in the water and pushed.

It was slow going with his hooves sinking into the mud, but he managed to get the man mostly onto the bank.

Gordy appeared on the other side. He hooked his chin over the man's hips and moved back. The lower part of the guy's torso moved.

This could work. Ben stepped closer, put the bridge of his nose against a shoulder and pushed. The heavy weight shifted, moving with Gordy's help.

What the hell? Something slapped Ben's hoof. He stopped and backed up, trying to see what hit him.

A piece of black string stuck out of the mud. *Damn.* The kid's necklace had gotten caught under Ben's hoof and snapped off. Whatever the pendant was, it was now smashed into the mud under a hoof print.

He sure hoped it wasn't important, because he wasn't about to root through the mud with his nose to retrieve it. They'd have to get it tomorrow, once they were human again. Human? In the morning they'd all shift. What if this guy didn't wake up and wander off by then? What in tarnation were they gonna do with him?

Looking up at Gordy, Ben neighed.

Gordy cocked his head as if to say, *what?*

Fuck. He hated this not being able to communicate shit that came with being a damned horse. He wasn't fluent in bull. Ben snorted and shook his head at Gordy. *Never mind.*

They went back to moving the man out of the mud. As they managed to manhandle—or rather horsehandle and bullhandle—the body up onto the grass, a rip sounded. *Damn it all to hell and back.* Graceful he was not. Ben picked his foot up and glanced down, trying to assess the damage.

Oblivious to Ben's actions, Gordy heaved backward with his chin.

The man flopped over.

Shit. Now, the guy was face down again.

Stepping away, Gordy lifted his head, cocking it to the side. One bovine brow rose at Ben.

Ben ignored him and rooted his nose down under the man's side and lifted. The smallish body rolled, flopping the young man onto his back with his arms still bound, resting on his belly. This time the man rolled himself to the side and coughed, spitting out water.

Good, he was awake. Ben stepped back and glanced down, finally getting a good look at the hapless victim.

He nearly swallowed his tongue. He'd been right, the waterlogged man was young and…gorgeous. The slim—what Ben had always thought of as a rodeo physique—body, wasn't the only thing the man had going for him. He had the face of an angel, well his profile at least. It was kind of hard to see the rest of his face with the man hacking up a lung the way he was. Even with the five o'clock shadow, his face was all soft angles and youthful beauty except for the shallow cleft in his chin. His nose was straight and turned up.

Finally the man flopped onto his back and took a few heaving breaths. His bottom lip was quite a bit fuller than his top, like a man that dipped snuff. Those lips were sexy and would be perfect for sucking cock. He blinked up at the sky several times then held his hands up in front of his face, studying the rope. "Damn it." He dropped his hands to his stomach and continued to study the sky, his breathing still a bit labored.

Ben's gaze followed his arms down. There was a bit of

dark hair between his nipples that led to a thick patch below his navel. It trailed down—and speaking of cock, those wet boxer shorts might as well be transparent. They left nothing to the imagination. Even limp and soggy, probably cold too, that was an impressive piece of meat. Goddamn, the waterlogged stranger was something else. Best thing Ben had seen in a month of Sundays. Ben jerked his gaze up and met wide gray eyes. The man had lifted his head and was staring right at Ben.

Ben stayed there, transfixed by the amazing eyes. They were the color of rain clouds. Ben had always loved a good thunderstorm. A tingle started in Ben's belly and his stupid dick began to harden. *No, no, no!* He could not get an erection in horse form. *Jeesus.* He'd never hear the end of it. The hung like a horse jokes were bad enough already. He shook his head, breaking eye contact.

The stranger looked from Ben to Gordy. "I must be imagining things." A few more racking coughs followed before he shook his head. Closing his eyes again, the kid lay his head back down. "Damn, I'm tired."

Turning away, Ben ambled toward the big oak a few yards away. Why the hell did those asshole cowboys have to fuck with his evening? Couldn't they have picked a different ranch? Hell, Ben guessed he couldn't blame them too much; he didn't want the kid here, either. That kid was trouble. Ben could feel it in his gut. Those stormy eyes were… Ben shook his head—the kid had to go. With any luck he'd rest, then be on his merry way. A little niggling in the back of Ben's head whispered that he wasn't that lucky, but Ben ignored it.

As the night dragged on, Ben and Gordy took turns standing guard over the young man as he slept. Ben did his best to ignore the kid's appeal, but wasn't entirely successful. Which pissed him off to no end. He was pretty sure Gordy had seen the affect the near-naked body had on Ben. There were definitely more "hung like a horse" jokes in his future. He supposed it could be worse. He could have been a rooster, and gotten all the cock innuendoes, or a rat. Poor Jud was always getting called a rat bastard.

It was getting close to his time to stand watch again, so he headed back down the hill toward the pond and the big oak tree.

When Ben got to the top of the hill, Gordy saw him approach and mooed.

Ben neighed back. He had no idea what he'd said, but it seemed like he should acknowledge his friend. Then again, he didn't know what Gordy had said either, so he supposed it didn't matter.

As Gordy wondered off toward the house, Ben made his way to the bank of the pond. It was getting close to dawn, Ben could feel it. His skin itched and tingled. The shift was near. It figured. He'd gotten stuck playing watchdog. What if the guy woke up? Gordy better hurry back with some clothes. Not only did Ben risk the stranger waking and seeing him, but he was close enough to the fence that anyone driving by might see him wandering around bare-assed naked. It was a damned good thing he loved The Sands, because he really didn't get paid enough for this shit.

Glancing down at the man, Ben assured himself the guy was still sound asleep. Did he always sleep this sound or was it the ordeal he'd been through? Ben could kick himself for even wondering. It didn't matter. The kid wasn't anything to Ben and he wasn't gonna be. Ben should try and gnaw the ropes off the man's arms, but he was afraid he'd wake him. And it was too close to the shift to risk that.

A prickling sensation raced up Ben's spine making him turn his head toward the east. It was time. The first streaks of purple and red lit up the sky, forcing the air from his lungs. One moment Ben was staring at his hooves, then with a flash of blinding light, his fingers were there. A shiver raced up his spine and Ben climbed to his feet. He dusted off his knees and his hands before studying his surroundings. The dirt road behind the ranch was clearly visible. A swatch of brown fabric hanging on the barbed wire fence blew in the soft breeze. It was still reasonably dim out, but it wouldn't stay that way for long. *Hurry, Gordy.*

A sigh echoed up from below.

Jerking his gaze down, Ben froze.

The temptation at his feet stared up at him with wide gray eyes.

THREE

He'd had the strangest dream. This horse had rescued him and turned into the most gorgeous man. Not just any man but a tall, sexy, naked one with dark hair and eyes. Shay sighed and smiled. His cock was already beginning to stir at the image of the stranger in his head. *Mmm*…a nice soft morning breeze blew over him, smelling spring fresh and leaving chill bumps in its wake. *Breeze?* That couldn't be right. Had someone opened a window in the bunkhouse?

"Is he dead?" someone asked.

What the—? Shay snapped his eyes open then snapped them right back shut when the bright sunlight stabbed his brain. "Son of a bitch."

"Nope, he's alive." Another voice answered.

Something nudged Shay's side. "You okay, kid? You need a doctor or somethin'?" The deep-voiced drawl was sultry, sounding like something straight out of a John Wayne western. Not uneducated and uncouth, like the ranch hands he'd worked with, but definitely Texan. Oh damn. The ranch hands. It all came back to him now.

Shay blinked his eyes open, trying to adjust to the light and not doing a very good job. The morning sun was a killer. Its position this time of the morning made it shine right at him, like a spotlight. His eyes watered, clouding his vision. "Yeah, I'm good. Where am I?"

"Oh no, maybe he has amnesia!" The first voice said.

"Bobby Lee…" The second voice admonished.

"What? He doesn't know where he is. That could be amnesia."

"Darlin', you've been reading too many romance novels again."

"Cy, you aren't s'pose to tell people that."

"I'm sorry." A smooching sound followed.

That got Shay's eyes open. Those were all definitely male voices.

Two men in cowboy hats pressed together, sharing one of the most intimate kisses Shay had ever seen. It was almost embarrassing to watch. He felt like a voyeur, but at the same time he couldn't look away. There was so much passion there. Shay'd kill for passion like that.

The shorter—and younger man from the looks of it—was on his toes, arms wrapped around the neck of an older, lanky blond man. Shay squinted and sat up. He couldn't be seeing things right. Two cowboys, kissing? He'd hit his head harder than he'd thought. Cowboys did not—

"For christsakes, would you two cut it out? It's way too early for that shit." There was that deep, sexy voice again. Regardless of the statement, the tone didn't have a lot of heat behind it. The man clearly had no issue with the other men kissing and he didn't seem a bit surprised by it, either.

Shay swiveled his head around, searching for the owner of the amazing voice. *Ow.* His skull was pounding. Bringing his hand up, he pressed against his temples with his thumb and forefinger. After a few seconds, when his head stopped spinning, he let go. *Holy shit.* His jaw went slack.

The sun glowed behind the man, giving him an ethereal magical quality. It was the horse-man in Shay's dream. He was Native American, probably not any older than thirty, and one of the most arresting men Shay'd ever seen. His chiseled profile was breathtaking.

Smiling at the lovers, dream man looked down at Shay. His smile melted away and his brow furrowed slightly under the straw cowboy hat as he scrutinized Shay. After several minutes the man made eye contact. "Ignore them. That's typical. Ya can't slide a piece of paper between 'em." Shaking his head, his gaze shot back to the lovers before returning to Shay. He raised one dark brow. "Who are you and what the hell happened to you?" His voice wasn't exactly harsh, but it demanded answers.

Shay couldn't think straight. Between this gorgeous stranger, the throbbing headache and men kissing out in the open, he felt as though he'd fallen down the rabbit hole. He pinched the bridge of his nose. Oh, his hands were untied...and he was char-free. His circumstances were looking up already, even if they didn't make sense.

"You okay? Your face is all white. Look at me." The man pulled his hat off and fanned Shay with it. "Don't faint, kid. That ain't gonna help anything." A white streak of hair just to the left of middle stood out like a beacon in the short, jet-black hair.

Shay's gaze was drawn to it. It was elegant, distinguished. Yet another thing that made this man intriguing. "You're bea—" Oh damn, he'd almost told the man he was beautiful. He'd already gotten himself roughed up for being gay once in the last twenty-four hours, he didn't need to try for two. But maybe— Shay flicked a glance at the two kissing cowboys. "Are they really kissing?"

They pulled back and the older man grinned at the younger with a soft smile; his eyes nearly twinkled. Whoever they were, they were, without a doubt, in love. It reminded Shay of his parents, the way they looked at one another. Wow, this was real. They really *were* kissing. It was strange, almost too good to be true.

The younger man's eyebrows pulled together. "Do you have amnesia? That could account for why you don't remember things."

Did he? Shay shook his head. No, he knew who he was, but it would seem he landed in Oz or someplace similar, only instead of talking scarecrows and bipedal lions, this place had horses that turned into beautiful men and gay cowboys. Maybe the Native American guy was a shaman and Shay had unknowingly smoked some peyote. "No, I don't have amnesia. I know what kissing is, I just—who *are* you?"

A smile lit the young man's face. "I'm Bobby Lee, this here," he indicated his lover, "is Cy and that's Ben." He pointed at Shay's dream horse, er, man.

Ben? Just Ben? Shay was half disappointed that it wasn't something romantic and magical like Black Wolf, Soaring Eagle or Running Bear. Yeah, it was a little stereotypical, but still those names would have fit.

"I'm a what?" Ben glared.

"Huh?" Why was Ben glaring at him? Shay frowned, trying to remember what he'd said. He was confused. *This has to be a dream.* He pinched himself. *Ow. Nope not a dream.*

"You said 'You're' and then stopped." Bristling, Ben plopped his hat back on his head. Again, with the sun at Ben's back, Shay marveled at the mystical vision.

"Are you a shaman?"

The glare grew so intense, Shay actually shrank back. What had he said? He hadn't meant it as an insult.

"No, I am *not* a shaman." Ben spat on the ground. "All witches should hang."

"Amen to that." Cy held up his hand over Shay and Ben gave him an unenthusiastic high-five that appeared more of a habit than actual excitement.

Shay's heart skipped a beat. *Oh crap. Not good, so not good.* The gay thing might not be a problem with these guys, but the witch thing? *Oh shit, please don't let me still have that damned pentacle on.* Shay glanced down. The necklace was gone. Letting out a breath, he sagged a little in relief. *Wait.* Shay glanced back down. He was in his boxers. Good grief, he was sitting in a field with three really good-looking men and he was in his boxers.

"Oh, now that's endearing. Look at that blush." Cy chuckled.

Shay fought the urge to cover himself with his hands. It wouldn't do any good, just make him look sillier than he already did. He glanced up at Ben.

Ben glanced down Shay's body, then back up to meet his gaze. It was a squirm-inspiring perusal, but Shay sat still.

Bobby Lee stepped forward and offered his hand. "Don't mind them. Cy hasn't had breakfast yet, he gets ornery when he's hungry. And Ben got up on the wrong side of the fence this mornin'." He frowned at the other men before turning his attention back to Shay. "Are you okay? Gordy said you were dumped off by a bunch of cowboys. Said they had you in a feedbag and you rolled away from them. What happened?"

Wrong side of the fence? Shay took the slim hand and let Bobby Lee help him up. "I—who's Gordy?" The last thing Shay remembered was staring into big, dark brown eyes set in a long, black-hair-covered face, and poof, that face had turned into Ben. He looked at Ben. Ben didn't look anything like a horse. It had been a hallucination. In fact, he sorta resembled an angry bull at the moment. Shay shook his head before turning back to Bobby Lee. "Last thing I remember is Marty, Charlie and Hank saying they were gonna light me on fire."

"Oh! That's terrible. Why would someone do that?" Bobby Lee let go of his hand and walked around him, checking him out.

"Ummm…" No way was he telling these guys he was a witch.

Bobby Lee stopped walking around him and grabbed Cy's hand.

Shay glanced back at Ben. *All witches should hang,* rang through his head. "Because they found out I was gay?"

"Fuck." Cy muttered.

Bobby Lee slapped his hand over his mouth and his words came out muffled. "That's terrible."

Ben didn't bat an eye. "That so?"

Shay nodded. *Please believe me.* His head hurt too bad to sustain another ass whooping. It wasn't a lie, he was gay and that *was* part of the reason he'd ended up in that damned burlap bag, if not the whole reason. He stared at Ben, hoping the big man believed him. Why he even cared if this man believed him was not worth thinking on.

"Benjamin Eagle. Call me Ben." Smiling, Ben held out his

hand. "What's your name, kid?"

The world tilted on its axis under the power of that smile. It made Shay feel all warm inside. He couldn't help but smile back and clasp the long-fingered, dark hand. He wondered at the abrupt change of attitude, but was so thrilled to have this man's smile finally turned on him he decided to let it go for now. "I'm Shay Duncan. I work at—um, used to work at the Bar W."

"Come on, Shay Duncan. Let's get you dressed and get us all somethin' to eat then we'll figure out what to do with you." Ben let go of his hand and turned toward a chestnut horse. "You can ride with me."

Great, he got to ride behind the sexiest witch-a-phobe he'd seen in years. Shay glanced at Bobby Lee, who'd been nothing but friendly.

Bobby Lee climbed up behind Cy, wrapped his arms around Cy's waist and kissed his neck. Sighing, Shay followed Ben. "Do you have aspirin?"

"I'll get you some when we get to the house." Ben seated himself in the saddle and held his hand down to Shay.

Shay took his hand, put his foot in the stirrup and let Ben help him up. Ben smelled so good. Like a fresh meadow. He started to lean closer and take another deep breath, then stopped himself. *Don't be stupid Shay, the man hates witches.* And how many other cowboys on this ranch agreed with him? Cy sure did. "Ummm... how many people are going to be at the house?"

"Not that many. Just the other guys. There are only ten of us." Ben heeled his horse, following Cy and Bobby Lee. "Don't worry about it. No one on The Shifting Sands will judge you for being gay. They'll treat you with the respect you're due."

Somehow that wasn't entirely comforting, considering Shay was in his boxers.

FOUR

Ben glanced around at his friends and noticed all six of them, with the exception of Tristan who'd shown Shay upstairs to the shower, and Jud who was setting the table, were staring up at the ceiling.

As soon as the water started Bobby Lee cleared his throat. "We gotta keep him. He—"

Ben's heart climbed up into his throat. He didn't know if he could take the kid being around all the time. Not only was he a walking temptation, but Ben was fairly certain that Shay had seen him shift.

"Now, darlin'—" Cy held up a hand to stall his partner.

"No, we don't. What the hell are we gonna tell him about all of us, fucktard?" Jud sat a plate of scrambled eggs in the middle of the table.

Cy shot him a glare. "Do not call Bobby Lee a fucktard, fucktard."

"Cut it out." Daniel said in a steady voice. "No one is a fucktard." He turned to Bobby Lee as Cy took his seat. "Why're we keeping him?"

Noticing Daniel said "why're we" instead of "why should we," Ben suppressed a groan. Damn Daniel all to hell, he was as softhearted as Bobby Lee.

"I like him." Tristan walked into the kitchen and took his seat beside Gordy. "I loaned him some of my clothes."

Bobby Lee nodded so hard his head was liable to come off. "He's got nowhere to go, y'all. He was beat up for being gay. We can't not take him."

"So what? We're like a gay cowboy refuge now? Just because Tristan loaned him some clothes doesn't mean he suddenly belongs here." Grinning, Zan shook his head.

Tristan threw a biscuit at Zan.

Catching it easily, Zan took a bite.

Yeah, him being gay was another reason Ben didn't want him to stay. Shay was not an easy man to ignore and Ben didn't need the distraction. It had taken him most of the night to get rid of the Shay inspired boner. Not a fun thing to deal with in horse form. No hands and no privacy were a bitch and the pond water hadn't been nearly cold enough. Hell, he'd gotten hard again with Shay all snuggled up close to him on Ginger in nothing but his boxers.

Daniel took a sip of his coffee. "Where'd he work before? He sounds like a yankee."

"He is. He's from Pittsburgh. But he's an Aggie, too. He went to A&M and has a degree in biology. He went to work for the Bar W right after graduation, about a month ago." Tristan got up and began helping Jud put the rest of the food on the table.

"Biology? Like animals *and* plants?" Ben frowned.

Tristan shrugged. "'s what he says. Said he majored in agriculture and life sciences and minored in agronomy."

"What the hell is agronomy?" Michael asked.

"Crops." Woody took a drink of his ice tea. "Soil too, I think."

Ben nodded. He knew that, on account of he'd been looking into it on the Internet in his free time. He and Daniel had been talking about planting a garden for all of them and maybe growing some hay for their stock. Problem was, they couldn't even keep the tomato plant that Jud had planted by the back porch last spring alive. Heck, even houseplants didn't fair well at The Sands. Jud and Tristan had managed to kill every one of the houseplants Russell had bought before Yi cursed them and hightailed it.

"Hmmm…" Daniel looked at Ben. "What do you think? You've been awfully quiet. You and Gordy rescued him."

"Didn't figure you'd want a dead guy in the stock pond."

"Ben!" Bobby Lee leaned past Cy and swatted at him. "How can you say that? I know darn well you saw how hot he is."

"Bobby Lee…" Cy's brows pulled together.

"What?" Bobby Lee shrugged and blushed.

"Y'all dig in." Jud set the last dish on the table, sat down and started filling his plate. "The kid seems nice enough and the agriculture degree sounds good. Lord knows fresh vegetables sound like heaven, but that still doesn't answer my question. How do we keep him, and keep our secret from him?"

"Well y'all kept it from me." Tristan sat down and reached for the eggs.

Gordy nodded, then shook his head. "We didn't keep it from you for that long. And the only reason it worked was because you were living in the trailer and it's not close to the house."

"We could always give him the trailer now." Michael added.

"Tristan and I live in the trailer." Gordy snorted.

Ben took another sip of his coffee. Gordy and Tristan could move into the extra bedroom in the foreman's cottage, the place was too big for just Ben by himself. That way Shay could— *Fuck a duck*. It didn't help his own situation any, but it made sense, unless it was all for naught. He couldn't believe he was even considering it. The sooner they got rid of the temptat—Shay, the better. The image of those big, pretty gray eyes staring up out of a battered face flitted through Ben's head. *Oh hell.* "He saw me shift. We might not need to keep it from him."

Silverware clattered and everyone but Daniel shouted, "What?"

"He saw me shift." Ben set his coffee mug on the table. "Gordy had headed back to the house to send Cy and Bobby Lee out with a horse and my clothes. I couldn't just leave him there. He opened his eyes and stared right at me as the shift came over me. I thought he might have been dazed and not realized it when he closed his eyes and fell back to sleep, but then when he woke he was acting a little funny so I suspect he saw."

"Well, then that settles it. He's staying." Bobby Lee nodded and chomped down on his biscuit.

Cy turned his body towards Bobby Lee. "Should I be jealous?"

"Umm…no." Bobby Lee blushed and glanced around the table. "Look y'all, I just feel bad for him. He seems really nice and no one deserves to get beat up like that."

Yeah, Ben felt the same way. Shay was way too tantalizing, but damned if Ben wanted the kid roughed up anymore. Looking at that abused face and body hadn't sat well with Ben, either. "Fine. Gordy why don't you and Tristan move in with me and we'll give Shay the trailer."

"Oh man, thank you. I needed that." Shay walked into the kitchen, his dark hair still damp. He wore a pair of jeans and a T-shirt that molded to his sculpted chest. He glanced around the table, then his eyes settled on Ben.

Damned if Ben's breath didn't catch and his cock stir.

Jud pointed to the empty place next to Ben. "Come sit down and get a bite to eat."

Shay nodded and headed toward Ben.

Daniel caught Ben's gaze and raised a brow.

Well fuck. As if Daniel hadn't already decided—and Ben knew his friend well enough to know he damned well had—he acted like he was leaving it up to Ben. Ben glanced around the table, trying to ignore the nice clean scent as Shay settled next to him. He could actually feel the heat of Shay's body, he was so damned close.

Bobby Lee gave Ben that sad, puppy look.

Tristan smiled and nodded his head slightly.

Well shut my mouth! Ben nodded at Daniel and dug into his hash browns. Was it his imagination or did Daniel grin?

Daniel turned his attention to Shay, completely dismissing Ben's discomfort. "So, Shay. Tristan says you know something about agriculture?"

FIVE

On Tristan's phone, Shay dialed the last digit in his parent's number and hit call. With any luck, Moonbeam and Sunny wouldn't be home. He could always hope anyway.

The phone began ringing and a loud pig squeal nearly drowned it out. It made some of the chickens scatter and Shay jump.

"Shut up, stupid pigs. I'm getting there." Shay reached into his bucket, grabbed some more chicken feed and scattered it around the pen. "Here, chick chick chick. Dumb pigs should wait their turn."

"Hello?"

Damn, damn, damn. Luck just wasn't on his side lately. Shay tossed some more feed.

"Moonbeam? It's me, Shay."

"Shadow? Why aren't you calling me from your phone? What's wrong? Sunny had a vision last night. I've been trying to call you all day. Are you okay?" She paused for a two second breath. "Sunny! It's Shadow. He's on the phone. Don't book the flight yet."

Shay winced. It was going to take some fast talking to keep her and Sunny from flying out here. He dreaded telling them what happened, though. "I'm sorry. I didn't mean to worry you. I'm on a friend's pho—"

"Are you okay?"

Before he could answer, there was a click followed by Sunny's deep voice. "Shadow? Are you all right? I had a dream you were in some water, face down. Do you need us to fly down there? Moonbeam and I have been scared to death. What happened, son?"

That was the last thing Shay needed. And wouldn't you know, Sunny's visions were always right. Once again his parents had known something was wrong before Shay had told them. "I'm fine. I promise."

One of the hogs fussed at him again.

Stupid, loud and obnoxious pigs. The very idea of them as a totem was ridiculous. Moonbeam was off her rocker. "For the life of me, I can't understand why you keep sending me things with pigs on it. I really hate pigs, they're a bad omen for me."

"You're changing the subject. What's going on? Where's your phone and when did your ranch get pigs? I thought it was strictly a cattle operation?" Moonbeam demanded.

"I've got a new job. I'm working at a ranch called the Shifting Sands. My phone is...still back at the Bar W." Along with everything else he owned.

"Shadow, what happened? I know you aren't saying something. So spill it." Sunny used the "father" tone that brooked no arguments.

"I got beat up, stuffed in a sack and hauled off the ranch."

Moonbeam gasped.

Shay pictured her hand flying to her mouth.

Sunny groaned. "And my vision?"

"They were going to light me on fire and I made them drop me and I started rolling to get away. I ended up in a pond."

"Oh no! Are you hurt? Sunny, book those flights."

Shay's stomach tied into knots. He loved them but, darn it, they just didn't understand, they were suffocating. Which was just...confusing. Weren't hippies supposed to be really relaxed on their parenting? "Wait a minute. I'm fine. Really. There is no need for you to come all the way down here."

"I thought you were getting along with the men at the Bar W. Why would they do that to you?" Moonbeam asked, her voice sounded disbelieving, rather than condescending, as Shay had expected. She'd been telling him for months that he should work someplace where he could be himself.

"Well…" Shay glanced out over the pasture at the setting sun. They were going to start hounding him to come home and the lecture about how he shouldn't have to hide who he was, was going to come back full-force.

"Shadow." Sunny warned.

"They saw the pentacle Moonbeam sent and realized I was a witch, and…" Shay set the bucket down and pinched the bridge of his nose.

"And?" From the sounds of it Sunny was losing his patience.

"And they realized I'm gay. But this new ranch? There're gay guys here. They don't care about my sexuality. This is a great place. They're even paying me more than the Bar W." Shay had nearly swallowed his tongue when Daniel had taken him into the office this morning after breakfast and negotiated his salary. Actually, there had been no negotiation to it—the offer Daniel made was very generous. He was making twice what he had at the other ranch. Daniel had even offered him the whole day off. Shay had refused, gone and done morning feeding with Michael and insisted on taking his turn at night feeding today. He wanted to start off on a good note.

"Are you pressing charges on those men?" Moonbeam wanted to know.

One of the chickens started pecking at the feed bucket and Shay shooed it away and picked it back up. "No. I just want to forget it and never see them again."

"What about your things?" Sunny cleared his throat. "You can't leave your things there. What about your Book of Shadows? What about your phone, wallet and credit cards?"

Everything was pretty much replaceable, but Shay had to retrieve his Book of Shadows. It was a gift from Moonbeam's mentor, Shay's now deceased godmother. Not only was it precious to him and irreplaceable, but there were some powerful spells in it that Shay wouldn't want to fall into the wrong hands. "My Book of Shadows has a spell on it. If anyone tries to read it they will only see blank pages."

A pig squealed again.

"Okay already!" Shay dumped the rest of the chicken feed and headed to the feed barn. The sooner he fed the scourge of the ranch, the sooner he'd have a moment's peace to plan how to get his stuff back.

"What're you shouting at?" Moonbeam asked.

"Sorry. I'm trying to work. I've got to go back to the barn. Can I call you back tonight?"

"Are you sure you're safe at this new ranch?" Sunny sounded hesitant.

Unless they find out I'm a witch. "I'm positive."

Heading toward the barn, he glanced around. He liked it here. The guys were all so nice and seemed to accept him in a way that the Bar W's ranch hands hadn't in the three months Shay had worked there. The only awkward thing about the Sands was that everyone on it was gay. It was strange. Well, no, not everyone was gay. Shay had no idea about Ben or Daniel, but everyone else lived with their partner and, well heck, it was weird, but it was also pretty cool.

Moonbeam began making umm noises. "I think he should come home."

"I'm not coming home."

"Leave him alone, Moonbeam. We love you, Shadow. Call us tomorrow and don't you go after your belongings by yourself. You take some sort of policeman or sheriff, or whatever it is they have out there in the sticks, with you."

Shay walked into the barn and headed for the feed room. "I won't. I love you, too. I'll call tomorrow. Bye." Shay quickly hung up the phone before Moonbeam could start harping on how he was better off at home.

Stupid pigs. He could hear those squalling menaces all the way up here. They wouldn't shut up until he fed them. And to think, Jud had already fed them scraps after lunch.

"Shay?"

Shay jumped. His heart raced at the unexpected shout, until he realized who the voice belonged to. A shiver shimmied down his spine and he turned toward the other end of the barn, watching Ben's long, lean frame as it appeared in the door. "I'm here."

"Are you finished with chores?" Ben strolled up beside him.

"Just have to feed the hogs, boss man."

Ben nodded. "Okay, when you're finished, I need you to come to my place." He turned and walked out.

Butterflies started up in Shay's stomach. What did Ben want? And why the heck did the man's presence make Shay feel like a giddy teenager? He had to get over this fascination. Not only was Ben a witch-a-phobe, but he was also the foreman. Sleeping with the boss was always a bad idea...well, assuming that was even possible and Shay had his doubts. Ben didn't seem the least bit interested. Which was probably a good thing. It was going to be hard enough to keep Ben from finding out he was a witch. Shay sighed and got some feed for the hogs. There was only one way to find out what Ben wanted.

After Shay finished with the nightly feeding he made his way to the foreman's cottage with more than a little trepidation. As he knocked on the door, he pulled his hat down lower over his eyes. He sure hoped there was nothing wrong. He really liked it here, even if it had been only a few hours.

Ben opened the door to his home and smiled. He wasn't wearing a cowboy hat; the sexy streak of white really stood out in his black hair. It beckoned Shay's fingers to comb through it. Would it feel different from the rest of his hair? Shay grinned, hoping his infatuation wasn't showing. "Hi."

"Hi." Ben held the screen door open wide for Shay. "Follow me. I have something for you."

"For me?" What could Ben possibly have for him?

"Yes, you. Come on."

Entering, Shay looked around. The place was nice. Rustic and manly. It fit Ben. It screamed cowboy. And if Ben was one thing, it was a cowboy through and through. He could rope, he could ride…he could give Shay a boner just looking at him. *Damn him.*

As Ben turned down the hall, there was a grunt and a long drawn out moan. He stopped short and stared at the door to his left, then shook his head and continued. "Not used to living with someone."

Shay stopped, his eyes wide. *Was that?*

There was a squeaking sound, followed by another groan.

Oh. Heat shot up Shay's neck. *Gordy and Tristan.* Apparently, Shay and Ben weren't the only ones absent from the dinner table. It was one of the awkward things about living here. He'd walked around one too many corners lately to discover lovers lip-locked…or more. It was embarrassing.

Ben turned his head, his gaze drifted down Shay's body, and one dark brow rose.

Shay looked, too. What was wrong—*oh.* Shay's breath caught. He got a funny tickle in his stomach and his cock twitched. His gaze shot back up to Ben's.

Chuckling, Ben opened the second door and disappeared.

Stunned, Shay stood there for a few seconds. He wasn't sure how he felt about Ben flirting with him. It was as unsettling now as it had been the day before. Ben made it difficult to think. Shay hurried past Tristan and Gordy's door to the one Ben had opened.

The big rustic log bed with a red flannel comforter dominated the room. A TV sat next to the door and a dresser that matched the bed took up the far wall. There were two opened doors to the left, one had light coming from it.

"Ben?"

"In here."

Shay walked farther into the room, toward the open door.

Ben picked up a bag that looked suspiciously like Shay's, and held it out. "Check and see if it's all there."

Shay froze. "You went and got my stuff for me?" Why would he do that? Shay smiled, feeling all warm and fuzzy inside.

"Yeah. Didn't think you needed to go back there under the circumstances. Didn't seem safe. They'd beat you up once already. I wasn't about to give them another chance."

Oh no! What if the men at the Bar W told Ben he was a witch? Shay's stomach clenched and he felt like he was going to be sick. What if his Book of Shadows was missing? Shay unzipped the bag and dug through it, his heart racing a mile a minute. He felt jeans, shirts, even his belt. He groped frantically until his fingers grazed the familiar bound leather. Had Ben seen his book?

"What's wrong?"

"Wrong?" His voice came out as little more than a squeak. He took a breath and made himself relax. Zipping up the bag, he put the strap over his shoulder. His book was here and if Ben saw it, he'd think it was a journal, a blank journal that Shay had yet to write in.

Ben's mouth quirked and he came forward, stopping only a foot in front of Shay. He tipped Shay's chin up, making him meet Ben's gaze. "You look so young with that shocked expression on your face." He licked his lips and his gaze fell to Shay's.

"I'm not." Shay's heart hammered in his chest, the blood pounded in his ears and he got that nervous little flutter in his gut. Ben was going to kiss him. And damn him, Shay wanted Ben, too. It was the worst possible thing he could want. He didn't need the complication. Ben had been way too vocal about his feelings on witch—

Ben's warm breath fanned across Shay's lips as he dipped forward and captured Shay's lips in a gentle kiss.

Fisting his hands by his sides, Shay tried to remain motionless, if he didn't kiss back…

Ben's lips were so warm and firm. Commanding, yet gentle. It wasn't like any kiss Shay had ever shared. The tip of his tongue traced the seam in Shay's lips. He took his time exploring and coaxing. His teeth caught Shay's bottom lip, then released it. He inched back, his eyes heavy lidded. "Open your mouth, Shay."

"I—"

Ben swooped in for the kill, blocking Shay's protest. His tongue caressed the sides of Shay's mouth, his tongue, his teeth.

Shay was lost. He unfisted his hands and tentatively touched Ben's waist. He tilted his head for better access and tangled his tongue with Ben's. It was like they had all the time in the world. Ben didn't rush him or hurry him in any way, just explored and coaxed a response from Shay. Their bodies only touched at their hands; one of Ben's on Shay's chin and Shay's on Ben's hips. It blew Shay away. He'd had a lot of kisses, but this one was different. It promised more and it scared the hell out of him. He couldn't do this. He had way too much to lose if Ben found out about him. Pulling back, Shay let go of Ben. His back bumped into the doorjamb.

For several moments, Ben just stared at him. The he shook his head mumbling a curse word under his breath. "I'm sorry, Shay. I shouldn't have done that. You really are young, aren't you?"

Shay frowned. He wasn't that young. Okay, maybe he was young, but he was certainly not inexperienced, but maybe if Ben thought so he'd back off. "I turned twenty-one two months ago."

Ben nodded. "What do your parents think of you being so far from home?"

"They don't like it actually, but I didn't give them a choice. I graduated when I was seventeen and went right to college, so they're getting used to it." *Sort of.*

"How'd you end up at A&M with a BA in agriculture? Seems kinda weird for a northerner."

Shay shrugged. "I love animals and nature and…I've always wanted to be a cowboy."

Ben smiled, his eyes bright.

Shay grinned, feeling a sudden kinship. A kinship that didn't help his attraction any, but at least now Ben thought he was too young. That would help them keep their distance…he hoped.

Six

"Ben, I'm going to check the west pasture gate." Michael pulled his hat off and raked his hand through his hair before replacing it.

"Yeah, go ahead. I'm going to check the stock pond, then head toward the south pasture. Howard James called this morning and said it looked like a section of fence along Boone Road was about to go down. I'm going to go check it out. I'll call ya if we need to repair it."

"Kay boss." Michael heeled his horse and took off at a trot.

Cy sat on his horse, grinning like the cat that ate the canary.

"What?" Ben patted his mare and turned her toward the south pasture.

"I'm surprised you haven't spontaneously combusted." Hurrying his horse up next to Ben's, Cy cocked a brow. When Ben didn't take the bait, Cy continued, "The heated looks the two of you give one another from afar should come with a fire hazard warning."

"Fuck off, Cyrus."

"Tristan tol' Bobby Lee he keeps seeing Shay watch you while you work." Cy's smile got bigger. Damn him.

It was true. Ben had caught Shay watching him. He'd done his fair share of admiring, too. If it weren't for the damned curse... he should be shot for kissing Shay the other day, but Ben had totally lost his head. Shay had looked so lost, like he'd needed comfort. "I live with a bunch of gossips," Ben grumbled.

"Hey, I'm just saying, why fight it? You can't tell me you don't want him."

Ben growled, but Cy, as usual, didn't back off.

"I take it he hasn't mentioned you shifting?"

"No." Heeling his horse Ben took off at a gallop. He didn't

want to talk about this right now. Hell, he didn't even want to think about this right now. He wanted to hurry and get his work done so he could get back and rest before sunset. In another hour, Shay should be done with the herb garden and Ben wanted to be safely ensconced in his house before Shay was done. The temptation to go talk to the kid was overwhelming. Not that Shay would seek him out. Shay had done a good job of avoiding Ben, too. There was a weird sort of connection between them. Kinda like Cy had had with Bobby Lee and Jud with— "Son of a bitch!" Ben reined in.

Cy came to a halt beside him. "Figure it out?"

"Fuck you."

Cy laughed. "It's not so bad, Ben. Hell, it's not bad at all."

"I'm not—we're not—he—" *ah, fuck a duck.* Shay was a good man. He loved animals, even the pigs, which he constantly grumbled about, and he loved being outdoors. The man had taken to ranch work like white on rice. Ben felt a kinship with him. That was all, wasn't it?

"Trying to convince yourself it ain't true?"

Ben frowned at his friend. "He isn't going to shift. The rest of you were in love before..." Maybe it had nothing to do with being in love, but more like a soul mate thing? Maybe Shay was fated to be his? Ben groaned. Goddamnit, now his overly romantic friends had him playing into that destiny shit.

"True, but I think it had something to do with the proximity and how much time we spent together, too. Maybe even affection, not just lust. Jud and Woody weren't together all that long before Woody shifted."

Ben shook his head. "No, it's—"

"Un huh. And it's obvious to everyone that you want him. I think you care for Shay at least a little aside from the lust."

"I don't know Shay. We've barely spoken for crying out loud."

"That's why you still bitch about them cowboys on the Bar W and say you'd like to kick their asses."

Ben took a deep breath. He glanced out over the pasture, noticed some of their cattle grazing. He did want to kick those guys' asses but— "Don't you?"

Cy shrugged. "You know me. I like a good fight, but, naw, not particularly. They're pieces of shit and not worth the hassle. Long as they don't come here looking for trouble…"

Ben thought about it. He wasn't normally a violent guy. In fact, he pretty much kept to himself. Did he want to whoop them guys? Yeah, yeah he did. Shay hadn't done anything to deserve that. And if Gordy hadn't run them off, no telling what those assholes would've done to Shay. As it was, he'd nearly drowned. "Som'bitches." Ben squinted against the glare of the pond.

"I'm just saying I think you're fighting a losing battle. Shay is supposed to be yours. Why else would he just turn up on the Sands like he did?"

"He didn't just turn up. He was dumped."

"Yeah, but what're the odds? Especially given how far the Bar W is from here."

"Good God, you've turned it to a romantic sap. You been reading Bobby Lee's romances?"

Cy snorted and totally ignored the question. "You can be pissed all you want, it doesn't change a thing." Cy turned toward him, reining in. "Don't you think you should warn him?"

Ben sighed. He should tell Shay, but not because he thought Shay was gonna shift. He felt guilty lying to him. Shay had become one of them. All the guys liked him, he fit right in to their little family here on the Sands.

The water reflected right into Ben's eyes as they drew close to the pond. He brought a hand up, shielding his eyes. As they drew closer, Ben realized it wasn't the water that was glaring so bad, there was something in the mud. Ben pointed toward it and turned his horse. They needed to check that out. One of the cows would end up hurt on it. It was obviously metal and they'd cut themselves.

"I see it." Cy turned his mount, too. "What's his animal?"

"Huh?"

"Shay. Tonight when he shifts."

Caught off guard, Ben jerked on the reins. His horse snapped her head up and came to an abrupt stop. "Would you give it a rest? He's not going to change."

Cy hooted. Throwing his head back and laughing his fool head off. "Keep telling yourself that."

Ben shook his head. Fuck. What if Cy was right? Ben couldn't deny the pull Shay had on him. He was certain Shay, no matter how reluctantly, felt it, too. Guilt gnawed at Ben. He didn't want this for Shay. Throwing his leg over the saddle, Ben hoped off, strolling toward the pond.

"Look at the bright side, at least Shay isn't terrified of horses."

"You aren't helping, Cyrus." Ben bent to pick up the metal disc half-buried in the mud. There was a black cord attached to it. "What the—" *Oh.* "Shay's necklace."

"What?" Cy hopped off his horse, holding his hand out.

"The night we rescued Shay and pulled him out of the pond. I stepped on his necklace. I'd forgotten about it." Ben walked close to the edge of the water, crouched and swished the medallion in the pond. Scrubbing it with his hands, he got the mud off it. He'd clean it up for Shay when he got back home, but he could at least get most the muck off now.

"What is it?" Cy held his hand out again and snapped his fingers. Impatient bastard.

Shaking the water off the necklace, Ben stood. He held it up, looking at it. All the air rushed from his lungs. His chest squeezed tight. "Son of a bitch."

SEVEN

"I got one Shay. Shit fire and save matches."

Shit fire and... Shay stumbled over his own foot and caught himself with the hoe. Laughing for the tenth time since they started this conversation, he glanced up at Tristan, "What the hell does that mean?"

Bobby Lee chuckled and continued down the row on his knees, planting the oregano. "Don' know. I guess it means you can't believe whatever it is someone tells you. You know, kinda like saying 'holy shit you're kidding me.'" A devilish grin spread across his face. "Doesn't even compare to my favorite though."

Shay was almost afraid to ask. "All right. I know I'm going to regret this, but let's have it, what's your favorite?" Resting his hands on the top of his hoe, Shay squinted against the afternoon sun, looking out past the corral. Was that Ben coming back from the pasture?

"Taste so good, make you wanna slap your granny."

Mouth dropping open and eyes bugging, Shay jerked his gaze away from the tall, lean body atop the gray mare to gawk at Bobby Lee. "You're kidding me. That is not a saying."

"Oh yes it is." Bobby Lee giggled without looking up.

Tristan snickered. "That has got to be a Arkansas hillbilly saying."

"Is not! I've heard Texans say it, too. Don't you have a house to clean?" Bobby Lee brushed sweat off his forehead with his forearm and glared over his shoulder at a hooting Tristan.

Shay laughed, too. The look was priceless. Bobby Lee took as much ribbing for his "hillbilly" roots as Shay did for his "yankee" roots. Shaking his head, Shay went back to breaking up the big clumps of dirt and weeding. The camaraderie he felt with these guys had been a surprise. He got along with all the guys on the Sands, but Tristan and Bobby Lee were fast on their way to becoming his best friends. He's spent a good amount of time with everyone except Ben, who avoided Shay nearly as well as Shay avoided him. Ben was slowly becoming an obsession. Shay sighed. One kiss and he could hardly think of anything else. How pathetic was that?

"I'm done with my housework, thank you very much. Don't you have an engine to fix or something?" Tristan asked, with amusement still heavy in his voice and a smirk on his face.

Bobby Lee stopped planting seeds long enough to flip Tristan the finger.

All three of them laughed.

When they stopped cackling, Shay went back to work on the row. If they were going to plant hay, Daniel was going to have to buy some attachments for the tractor. No way was Shay going to till a whole field by hand. This was only a twenty-foot by twenty-foot area that had been tilled before and it was still taking a long time to plant this garden.

Shay glanced over at the package of seeds on the ground by Tristan. A few of those herbs could be use in witchcraft. He winced. Should he tell his friends? The longer he waited, the harder it was going to be. Could he keep it from them forever? No, no, he *had* to tell them. But when? The guys on the Sands had become close friends and he was fairly sure that most of them would take the news okay, but there were a few...he glanced out towards the corral again.

Ben and Cy were dismounting, leading their horses into the barn. Damn, that was a fine-looking man. Shay's cock stirred. Maybe he could convince Ben to spend the evening in bed? *Yeah right.* Not only was there the whole witch thing, but Ben thought Shay was too young. Then again, maybe it would sweeten Ben's disposition before Shay told everyone his secret? *Or it'd make him even madder.* Shay winced.

"What the heck does that mean anyway? Slap your granny? Sheesh." Tristan asked, breaking Shay out of his thoughts.

Shay bent down to retrieve a weed he'd just dug up, shook

the excess dirt off of it and tossed it into the pile Tristan was making at the end of the row. "Yeah, that's messed up. Why would someone want to slap their granny when they got good food? Wouldn't you hug your granny? Well assuming she's the one that cooked the meal, anyway."

"Beats the shit outta me." Bobby Lee shrugged. "Hell, half the sayings don't make a lick of sense."

"Ain't that the truth. Take 'Katy bar the door' for example. Does that mean hey Katy, as in some girl named Katy, bar the door! Or is there some obscure rod called a Katy Bar?" Tristan mused.

Shay laughed again. Goodness, he loved these Southern colloquialisms. Nah, that was only part of it, these guys and this place had him laughing and smiling a lot. The Shifting Sands had a great group of guys. He never ceased to have fun. He'd only worked here for going on a month but it felt like years. He belonged here. Not only did he get to be outdoors with the land and animals, he was learning things. He'd wanted to be a cowboy since he was five years old; not all that unusual for a boy, but the dream had stayed with him. He loved the idea of earning a living through hard work. Moonbeam had always said it was because of his upbringing in Wicca. But it wasn't that, Shay didn't have the same beliefs she and Sunny held. Maybe their respect for nature was embedded in him, too, and cowboys just held some romantic notion for him because of the books and movies he'd seen. It didn't matter though; he was still determined to be a cowboy and the Sands was the perfect place for him. For the first time, he actually fit in somewhere. *Damn it*. He had to tell them. He'd do it tonight, before he chickened out.

"How's it goin' guys? Y'all almost done?"

Shay's insides got all fluttery at the smooth, deep voice. He hadn't realized Ben had left the barn. Which was unusual, he seemed to be ultra-aware of Ben's every move. Glancing up, he met Ben's gaze.

Ben stood about five feet away, his attention fully on Shay. Damn, just damn. Those long legs were thickly muscled from all the time spent in a saddle. His arms were hard as rocks, emphasized by the yellow leather-work gloves and the denim shirt rolled up onto his biceps.

Tristan and Bobby Lee both nodded.

"Shay?" Ben raised a brow.

He went back to hoeing before he ended up with a full-fledged boner out here in the herb garden. "Yeah?" Shay tried to focus on the weed he was trying to get up and ignore the shadow that came over him, indicating Ben had stepped closer.

Shay's heart was going to pound right out of his chest and darn his hands were sweaty. What did Ben want? Shay popped the weed out of the packed, dry dirt. He bent to pick it up and came nose-to-nose with Ben who also reached for it.

Ben's warm breath, and the heat radiating off of him, touched Shay like a gentle caress. His gaze rested on Shay's mouth.

A flutter started in Shay's stomach and he licked his lips. His mouth was suddenly dry.

They held the weed between them, just staring at one another. A trickle of sweat dripped down Ben's temple, over his high cheekbone and onto his chin. Shay got the insane urge to lean forward and catch it on his tongue. It would be better than any bottle of water. He wanted to pull Ben's hat off and see that distinguished white streak of hair. It was the only thing on Ben that wasn't dark as sin, and it was sexy as hell. Even more alluring than Ben in a cowboy hat and that was tough to beat.

Ben's gaze lifted to Shay's. It was so intense and heated it made Shay shiver. His cock gave up the fight and got hard. A tremble started in his stomach before moving up to his chest. Ben had such nice lips. Leaning forward, Ben tilted his head slightly.

Shay cocked his head, too, his gaze on Ben's mouth.

Someone cleared their throat.

Blinking, Ben tugged the weed from Shay's hand, tossed it in the pile of weeds and frowned. "Shay, what in the hell is this?"

With his gaze still on Ben's face, Shay shook his head. *What?*

He glanced down. Held in the big calloused brown hand was the pentacle with the pig on it.

EIGHT

"Fuck." Ben flopped down on the couch and ran his hands up his face and over his hair, knocking his hat off. Didn't that just beat all. Shay with a pentacle. Not just a pentacle, but a pentacle with a damned totem animal. Ben was no idiot, he knew what it was as soon as he washed it off. He remembered stepping on it, so there was no denying it was Shay's. A friend of Ben's grandmother had been a witch. He knew a little bit about witches and shamans. Granny's friend's totem had been a dog.

"Ben!" Gordy let the screen door slam behind him rushing in like...well like a bull in a china shop.

Ben grinned despite his mood.

"What?" Coming to an abrupt halt, Gordy frowned. "I thought you were madder than an old red hen?"

"What?" Sitting back, Ben studied his friend. How had Gordy known he was mad? Cy was still out checking the fence.

"Tristan said you shoved something at Shay and stormed off."

"I didn't storm off." Well, not exactly. He'd been fuming inside, but he hadn't kicked up a fuss. He'd just handed Shay the pentacle. "And I'm not all that mad anymore." Now Shay's distance made sense, given Ben's very vocal loathing of witchcraft. It also meant Shay would understand about them shifting. Shay being a witch pretty much removed all the reasons he and Ben shouldn't get together, because there would no longer be any secrets they had to keep. And if Shay could break the curse, then there wouldn't even be the threat of him changing into an animal like the rest of them.

Nodding, Gordy moved Ben's hat to the coffee table in front of them and sat down on the couch. "So he's a witch?"

"Looks that way." Not that Ben had exactly waited around for answers. He'd told Shay to come here when he was done in the garden.

"He is. They were talking about it when I left. Bobby Lee was trying to get some idea at how good he is. Tristan wanted to tell him about the curse and see if he could break it, but I told him to hold off."

Ben groaned. "I'll tell him about it."

Gordy propped his booted feet up on the oak coffee table. "Think he can undo the curse? Ain't like he'd do any harm trying." He sat up, dropping his feet to the hardwood floor.

Yeah, Ben had slowly come to that decision on the way back from the garden. "I know, but I don't want to put pressure on him, either." He dropped his head back and covered his face with his hands. What a day.

"He'll want to help." Gordy sounded sure. He propped up his feet and leaned back again. "Shay's a good kid. Tristan and Bobby Lee adore him. He's already family, Ben."

"Yeah, but we—" Ben sat up, leaning his forearms on his legs. He wanted to explore this attraction he and Shay had, but he didn't want to put Shay in jeopardy of shifting into an animal. Thanks to Cy pointing it out, Ben couldn't ignore the possibility anymore. "What if he gets the curse? Maybe we should send him away."

"Personally, I agree with Cy. I think it's too late."

All the wind whooshed from Ben's sails. He groaned but couldn't help smiling, too. "Fuck you. When did Cyrus go running his mouth off to you?"

Gordy laughed. "Hang in there, buddy. This whole relationship thing takes work, but you can do it. Hell I've never seen two people try so hard to avoid falling for each other, but you both suck at it. You're both just about as attracted as can be. Ain't no way fate don't have a hand in it. So I reckon you should tell him about the curse pretty quick. 'Cause I'm not believing, for one minute, that y'all don't belong together. 'Sides, Tristan and Bobby Lee might single-handedly beat your ass if you fuck this up."

The screen door opened and banged shut.

Gordy chuckled and stood. "No pressure, though."

Ben snorted and glanced at the door.

Shay stood right inside, his hat in his hands and his gaze down. He looked young. *Funny.* Ben had managed to forget just how young Shay was over the past month.

"Well, I better go." Gordy slapped Ben on the shoulder. "I strongly suggest you not wait around about telling him what you ought to be telling him. Remember Woody? And Bobby Lee? And well, hell, just learn from all of our mistakes, 'kay? If I were a betting man, I'd say Shay's gonna need that explanation tonight, if you know what I mean."

"Fuck." A tingle slid down Ben's face, right down his neck and to his shoulders. He was lightheaded. "Fuck." Leaning back on the couch, he stared at nothing in particular. He hadn't even considered Shay changing tonight. It was way too soon. Wasn't it?

"Good luck." Gordy made a laughing exit, stopping to pat Shay on the back before he closed the door and left.

"Umm…" Shay shuffled his hat around and around in his hands by the brim. "You probably want me off the Shifting Sands, right? I can get my stuff and be gone in about a half hour. Bobby Lee says he'll drive me to town, and—"

"What?" Ben's chest tightened and his breath caught in his throat. A nauseous feeling crept up from his stomach. "No!" Shay couldn't leave. Not now, not when— "Fuck."

A grin flitted across Shay's face before being replaced with uncertainty. "That's about the third 'fuck' in a row." He began bending the brim of his hat back and forth. "It might help me figure out what's what if you tell me why. Fuck I'm a witch? Or fuck I'm still here? Or fuck something else? And what did Gordy mean about telling me something you ought to tell me?" Shay shrugged and bit his bottom lip. "Or should I just go and shut the heck up?"

"Come sit down." Ben smiled, trying to think past the jumbled feelings surging through him. He hated seeing Shay so unsure of himself. It reminded him of the day Shay came to the Sands. Not a bad thing, but Ben had grown rather fond of the self-assured, easygoing cowboy who wasn't afraid to pipe up with an opinion even if it didn't match everyone else's. That was the Shay that likely got his ass kicked and stuffed in a sack. Ben grinned. He really liked that Shay.

Shay sat down, his eyes on his hat, squished in his hands.

Ben turned, took Shay's hat and set it on the table. Taking Shay's chin in hand he made him meet Ben's gaze. "I'm sorry. I shouldn't have just left after I handed you the pentagram. I guess I should tell you how I knew it was yours and how I don't care, huh?"

Shay's eyes widened. "You don't care? I thought all witches should hang?"

Ben couldn't help but wince. "Not you. I thought about it and I know you aren't a bad witch."

Giggling, Shay blushed and bit his bottom lip. "I'm Glenda?"

Ben laughed, too. "Are you?"

"I don't use magick for malice. If that's what you mean."

"So you're like what? Wiccan?"

Shaking his head, Shay cleared his throat, shifting a little in his seat. "I'm an agnostic." He winced. "I was raised Wiccan, though. My parent's are a Wiccan High Priestess and High Priest."

"It's okay. I'm not exactly religious myself." Bending forward, Ben kissed Shay on the lips. "I've been dying to do that since right after the first time."

Shay smiled. "I know. So have I." He looped his arms over Ben's shoulders. "We have a lot of time to make up for." He slanted his mouth down on Ben's and took control. He didn't dabble, play or ask for permission, he took.

It made Ben's head spin and had him harder than a rock. He loved decisive men. Taking charge of everything got old. Ben did it day-in and day-out. His job was to be in charge, in control and lead. In sex? He had always been content to follow. What more incentive did he need?

After nipping Ben's bottom lip, Shay pulled back and stood. He offered Ben his hand and glanced down the hall, then raised a brow at Ben.

Ben took Shay's hand, debating with himself about why this might be a bad deal. If Shay wasn't going to turn into an animal, would this seal the deal?

Shay squeezed his hand and, for a split second, he looked unsure.

The look made Ben's gut twist. *Fuck it.* Ben tugged Shay toward the master bedroom. Cyrus was right, damn him. Fighting this thing with Shay was a lost cause. He just hoped Shay forgave him.

NINE

"My God…I've dreamed about this every night since I found you."

Shay hadn't thought it possible for the man to be any sexier than he already was, but he was wrong. That low, husky voice as Ben shut the bedroom door sent shivers down Shay's spine.

As soon as the door clicked shut, Ben pulled Shay into his arms and trailed heated kisses down Shay's neck, making goose bumps break out on his arms.

He went up on his tiptoes and let out a very undignified squeal. Dropping his head forward onto Ben's shoulder, he marveled that this was finally happening. He'd wanted Ben since the moment he woke up by the stock pond and saw him. And Ben was even better now than he was by the pond. His cock was clearly outlined through his jeans. He was huge and hard. Shay couldn't help himself. He'd never been one to shy away from taking what he wanted. It was a very impressive, mouthwatering cock and it gave him all kinds of ideas. He palmed it, squeezing.

Bucking into his hand, Ben released Shay's shoulder with a groan. "Bed, Shay."

"Uh huh. In just a minute." Shay unsnapped the buttons on Ben's jeans, pulling the lapels apart. He had to see if Ben's prick was as perfect as it felt.

A wet spot appeared on the front of the black underwear and Ben's cock jumped forward, begging to be touched again. "Mmm…nice." Shay shoved the denim down, leaving Ben in his black boxer briefs. Oh man, wasn't that nice? Dropping to his knees, Shay fastening his lips over the cotton-encased cock. He'd always loved the feel of a cock in his mouth. And this one was going to be quite a mouthful.

Groaning, Ben's fingers sifted through Shay's hair. "Bed… please."

Shay hooked his fingers in the waistband of Ben's briefs and pulled them to his knees to meet his jeans. Ben's heavy cock bounced free. *Oh wow.* It was so dark and shiny on the tip. Shay licked his lips and swallowed it down in one fluid motion. It stretched his mouth wide, but the smooth glide felt wonderful against his lips. Ben had a cock made for worshiping.

"Fuck!" Ben's hips bucked forward. His fingers tightened in Shay's hair momentarily. "Shay, bed, my legs aren't going to hold me up much longer."

Shay sank back down on Ben's cock, then came up. The precum was sweet and addicting. Shay was sure he could do this all night long. He removed his mouth from the luscious prick. "What? You don't like this?" He dropped his forehead forward, trapping Ben saliva-slick cock against his lower abdomen and Shay's forehead. Damn, the man's dick even felt good on his forehead. There was something seriously wrong with that. Shay groaned, wanting to rub it all over his face.

"Like is way too mild a word." Chuckling, Ben bent and caught Shay under the arms.

With one last lick, Shay stood reluctantly.

Catching him under the chin, Ben angled his face up and brushed a smiling kiss over his lips. For several seconds they just stood there staring at one another. Something powerful and unknown sizzled between them. Why had they fought this so long?

Ben caressed his cheek. His eyes were heavy lidded and sexy. When he spoke, his voice was soft, almost in awe. "I can't believe you're a witch."

"Does it bother you that much?" Shay whispered back, not wanting to break the connection between them.

"No, but there're some things I need to tell you."

Knowing that Ben's attraction was stronger than his reservations about witches was a heck of an aphrodisiac. It made Shay feel better about the situation. They could make this work. They'd be good together, Shay felt it way down deep. "Okay. Tell me after."

"Yeah, good idea." Ben nodded and stepped back just enough to free himself from his remaining clothes.

Shay should get undressed, too, but he couldn't seem to take his eyes off Ben long enough to do so. His cock was so hard and throbbing it was nearly painful. He adjusted himself, while Ben toed off his boots and stepped out of his jeans. Stepping closer to Ben he ran his hands down Ben's sides, resting them on his hips. He didn't want to stop touching Ben. Ben's skin was so dark. It made such a beautiful contrast against Shay's lighter hands.

Ben moaned and began placing small kisses against Shay's lips, his cheeks, his chin and nose. "Bed. You're making me crazy looking at me like that." The snaps on Ben's shirt made a muted sound, almost like stepping on bubble wrap but quieter, as he pulled the shirt apart, and shrugged it off his shoulders.

That wasn't the way to spur him into action. Shay stood dumbfounded staring at the magnificent chest. His stomach clenched in anticipation of feeling that fine body against his. He adjusted his cock again. He needed more.

Sitting on the edge of the bed, Ben crooked his finger at Shay. The long and lean muscles in his forearm flexed, showing off veins. Ben was gorgeous. A true cowboy, built and honed from hard ranch work. Shay had always had a thing for cowboys and Ben was the real deal. That, with the caring he displayed toward his friends, made him a dream man in Shay's estimation. Ripping off his shirt, Shay swallowed the lump in his throat. He had to have Ben…now.

Ben was laid out on his bed by the time Shay got his shirt off. One glance at that long, thick prick resting on that muscled abdomen made him move faster. He hadn't had near enough of Ben's cock. Looking his fill, Shay made quick work of his boots, then shucked his jeans and his boxers. Even the man's balls were perfect, tightly drawn with no hair to get in Shay's mouth. Oh yeah, he really had to get that prick back in his mouth. He moved so fast he practically bounced on the bed, trying to take his place back between Ben's legs. In one swift move he took that luscious dick back into his mouth.

"Shay, why don't you—holy hell..."

Shay licked a long line up Ben's balls to the tip of his cock. Damn, the man tasted good. Grabbing Ben's prick at the base, he took it in again. Nice and salty...sweaty from working all day. He closed his eyes on a blissful hum. He sucked Ben for several minutes, until spit ran down Ben's balls and Shay's hand. There was just nothing like the feel of a dick in his mouth or the glide of that soft skin dragging over his lips. Shay's cock jerked, his balls pulling tighter.

Slipping his hand down, he teased Ben's hole with his sopping fingers. He stared at Ben's passion-dazed face as he slipped one finger in, waiting for Ben's reaction. Shay liked to top, but given his age and size, he was pretty used to going with the flow. Most men took one look at him and mentally slapped a label on his forehead that said, "bottom." Which would be fine, he could deal with that, but there was no denying that he wanted to sink balls deep into Ben, had since the moment he'd imagined Ben shifting from a horse. It was fate. Because if Shay would have had to choose a totem animal, it would be a horse.

"Shay." Ben's eyes flew open, his head raising up a bit. The lock of white hair fell into his eyes. "What? You? Ugh..." He closed his eyes and dropped his head back, pressing down on Shay's finger. "Good lord, darlin', please get a condom outta the nightstand and get up here and fuck me."

"Really?" A tingle raced through Shay and he couldn't help but grin. He grabbed the base of his cock and squeezed, staving off the excitement. Ben just got better and better.

"Yes, really."

Oh yeah. Shay dove for the nightstand drawer, finding the condoms in record time. After he sat back up, a pang of nervousness hit him. This felt different than the other casual encounters he'd had. There hadn't been that many in recent years, he'd been too caught up in his studies, but this was noticeably unique. There was an odd sense of rightness, like Ben belonged to him. It felt like destiny. *Whoa.* Shay froze with the condom clutched in his fingers.

Sitting up, Ben snagged the condom out of his hand, then tipped Shay's chin up. He smiled softly and rubbed his thumb along Shay's cheek. "What's the matter? If you don't want to do this, you don't have to." His fingers trailed over Shay's jaw onto his neck.

Snapping out of it, Shay swallowed the lump in his throat. He wanted...needed to do this. He reached up and combed his fingers through the white streak in Ben's hair, like he'd wanted to do since the beginning. It was soft, but didn't feel any different from the rest of Ben's hair.

"Shay?" Leaning forward, Ben brushed his lips over Shay's. He sat back, studying Shay, looking like he had all the time in the world. It was Shay's undoing. At the moment he realized what Sunny and Moonbeam meant about soul mates. Ben was his.

"I'm okay. I just—this feels different. Like—" *like the beginning of something.* He shook his head. It was just too hard to explain and Shay didn't want to take the time to do so, but Ben seemed to understand. He lay down, taking Shay with him, and rolled over until the weight of his body rested on Shay. Once his hard prick nestled next to Shay's, he touched Shay's cheek. It was a tender action, one Shay was beginning to crave. "Have you ever done this, darlin'?" He dipped, nipping Shay's bottom lip.

Okay, maybe Ben didn't understand. "Ben, I'm not *that* young." Shay growled and bucked his hips up, showing Ben just how not young he was. The last thing Shay wanted was for Ben to treat him like some horny teenager who didn't have a clue.

Chuckling, Ben nipped his chin. "Just checking. You looked lost there for a minute." He sat up, straddling Shay's hips. His gorgeous, large cock pointed right out. A milky drop appeared on the tip and ran down. It was mesmerizing. Ben looked down, then back up at Shay. "Are you ready for me?"

"Oh heck yeah." Shay decided he could do without baring his soul and confessing his undying love. At least for a little while.

"I'm ready." He held out his hand for the condom.

Ben tilted his head, studying him for a few seconds, then he nodded. Tearing open the foil package, Ben gripped Shay's prick, holding it up. He grabbed his own prick, mashing them together. Shay's balls pulled tighter and they both moaned.

Ben's head fell back, exposing his long neck. His Adam's apple bobbed as he swallowed hard. "Damn, that feels good." Shuddering, Ben let go of his own prick and smoothed the condom down over Shay's erection.

In the six years he'd been having sex, Shay couldn't remember anyone every putting a rubber on him. It was kind of intimate... strange. The way Ben handled him with such care, such admiration, made Shay's chest ache.

After the protection was firmly in place, Ben cocked one dark brow, rose up on his knees and gripped Shay's cock. "Ready?"

Shay nodded a little too eagerly and hoped in hindsight that he didn't just reaffirm the horny teenager image.

Sinking down on Shay's cock, Ben let out a low, lusty moan that would have made Shay's head spin if the feel of that tight hole wrapping around him hadn't done just that. "Oh man." After that he couldn't think at all.

Ben leaned forward and caught his lip between his teeth before kissing him. Then he set to riding Shay's cock. It wasn't like Shay to babble incoherently, but he just couldn't seem to help himself. Ben felt so good and boy did he know what he was doing, Shay was so close to coming it wasn't even funny. And that would so not help his case any. "Close."

Nodding, Ben moved faster, raising himself up and down on Shay's cock. "Me, too." His voice sounded strained and he looked so damned hot with his thigh muscles working as he fucked. It brought to mind Ben on horseback. All strong and confident. He'd look stunning on that black stallion Shay had imagined him to be that first day.

Ben's whole body tensed, his hole squeezing Shay tight, and he threw his head back. The corded muscles in his neck stood out as he moaned low and deep. Then hot splashes of cum landed on Shay's belly, catapulting him over the edge, too. His hips arched up off the bed, nearly unseating Ben as he reached mindless bliss.

Falling forward, Ben braced himself above Shay on his hands. For several seconds they stayed there, staring into each other's eyes.

The simmering connection between them was as awkward as it was refreshing. They didn't say anything, just watched one another. Shay realized what he'd been hoping for the past month was reality. He *was* home. He'd not only found his place, but so much more.

Finally, Ben broke the spell by kissing him. He crawled off of Shay and began removing the condom. "Let me get rid of this and we need to talk."

As Ben disappeared into the master bath an uneasy feeling assailed Shay. Ben had not sounded too happy about "talking." Before Shay could ponder the change in Ben's demeanor, Ben came back with a washcloth and cleaned Shay's belly and his prick. Had Ben changed his mind about getting involved with a witch? Butterflies crashed into the lining of Shay's stomach. He didn't want Ben to regret it.

When Ben started to leave again, Shay grabbed his arm. "Are you okay?"

"Yeah. I—" He tossed the rag in the direction of the bathroom and climbed back onto the bed. He sat on the edge and turned his body to Shay, but didn't move any closer.

Shay's post orgasmic haze disappeared completely, replaced by panic.

"I've neglected to tell you something. And I'm not sure how you're going to take it."

Shay frowned. "Okay. What did you not tell me?" If his voice came out a little croaky Ben didn't seem to notice.

"You know that night those men ditched you on the Sands?"

"Yeah."

"Well…" Ben swallowed so hard his Adam's apple bobbed. "I was a horse at the time."

What? Shay sat up, looking directly at Ben. His dream. It was real? Ben was a horse. Shay chuckled, relieved that was all it was Ben had to tell him. *Wow.* He wasn't losing his mind. "I knew it. I knew that was you."

"You believe me?"

Snorting, Shay kissed his chin, but Ben didn't relax. "I'm a witch. I've seen some pretty crazy things." He tried to tug Ben into his arms, but Ben resisted.

"It's a curse."

Ah ha! Now it made sense. Shay pulled Ben harder, giving him no choice but to touch him. "That's why you hate witches? Someone cursed you?"

"Yeah, but let me tell you the rest. You may not want to be this close to me."

"I doubt there is anything that would make me push you away."

Ben moved out of reach and held up a hand, stalling Shay when he would've brought Ben back. "Tristan, Woody, Bobby Lee and Zan didn't shift until they fell in love with Gordy, Jud, Cy and Michael."

Shay's shoulders slumped and he sat back, thinking. Was Ben afraid Shay would shift? "What animals?"

"I'm a horse, Cy's a snake, Gordy's a bull, Jud is a rat, Michael is a—"

The Chinese zodiac. "I guess that explains the connection between us."

Ben's mouth dropped open. "What?"

Shay shrugged and pulled Ben into his arms, then laid them down on the bed, facing each other. "The curse started with just the original ranch hands?"

Ben nodded.

"It also includes your lovers. Sort of a destiny-based curse."

"You mean like soul mates or something?"

"Yes. I can't say I'm happy about catching the curse, but I guess it's a pretty fair trade off until I can figure out a way to lift it."

Laughing, Ben hugged him tighter. "So you're doomed anyway?"

"It would seem so. You feel the connection too, don't you?"

"Yeah, I feel it. Come here." Pulling Shay into his arms, Ben rolled onto his back. Once Shay lay on top, Ben cupped Shay's face in his palms and kissed him. It was slow and sweet, making Shay giddy. He could totally deal with shifting into an animal for this man. Maybe it'd even be fun.

After a minute, Shay broke the kiss and braced himself on his hands above Ben. What would he be? Maybe a tiger? No, he'd rather be a ranch animal, Gordy was a bull and Ben a horse. Maybe Shay could be the goat.

"What are you grinning at?" Ben caressed Shay's jaw, then ran his fingers over the shallow cleft in Shay's chin. "Do you think you can break the curse?"

Shay kissed his fingers. "I'll try. I'm gonna have to know more about it first, but even if I can't, I can deal with it if I get to keep you." He shrugged. "How bad can it be? Really? It actually sounds kinda fun."

Ben groaned and shook his head "No, it's not."

"I think it will be. I'll get to see the ranch in a whole new light. Talk about getting into nature." They'd be one with nature. They could run in the pasture together. Darn, it really was too bad Gordy was the bull. Oh well, he'd always been fond of dogs, or maybe—*oh shit.* "Please tell me someone else already shifts into a pig?"

A chill raced up Shay's spine at the exact moment he finished casting the spell. Which hopefully meant that it worked. Opening his eyes, he glanced up at the full moon just lighting the night sky, then down at his own nude body. He was still human. Had it worked? A fission of excitement bubbled up inside him. He picked up his athame, turned and froze. His excitement evaporated.

Just outside the circle stood a bull with a rabbit between his front feet, a lamb with a snake wrapped around his neck, a rooster leaning against a dog, a monkey holding a rat in his hands and a lone black stallion with a white star on his forehead.

"Shit fire and save matches! How come I'm still human?"

Ben's dark head cocked to the side and he neighed. He stomped his foot, then proceeded toward the closed circle, which Shay had directed him only to do if he were in animal form. Animals were pure of heart and could enter and exit a circle at will, humans could not. He had no idea if it would work with shifters, but he knew it wouldn't work for humans, hence the warning to his friends.

As Ben's hoof crossed the circle boundary it changed to a human foot. Slowly as each body part passed the circle it changed until Ben stood in front of Shay, fully human and completely naked.

"Whoa. That was wild. Felt like ants stinging me as I stepped in." Ben raised his arms studying them. "Why am I human?"

Shay's jaw dropped. How'd that happened? He'd flubbed that spell up big time.

"Put me down." Jud grumbled.

Pulling his attention away from Ben, Shay noticed his friends all in the circle, all naked.

Woody dropped Jud's feet to the ground.

"Holy shit, get off me!" Bobby Lee squawked.

Cy stood and held down his hand to a prostrate Bobby Lee. "Sorry, darlin', you ran for that circle so fast I didn't have a chance to slither down."

"You're heavy." Bobby Lee groused.

Tristan's hands immediately covered his groin.

Gordy grinned. "Next time, you need to make the circle bigger, Shay."

"Can you make the circle encompass the whole ranch? Or maybe the house next time?" Michael wanted to know.

"This sucks." Shay's dropped his head. Damn it, he was so sure he had it this time.

"Where'd Daniel go?" Ben wrapped his arms around Shay's shoulders.

"Took off after we all started changing." Zan shrugged. "Wonder if one of us should go get him and bring him into the circle?"

"Don't you dare leave this circle without me cutting you an opening." *Damn.* Shay's mood sank even further. He hated to break it to the guys but likely as soon as he cut the circle, they would all shift back. Unfortunately, he didn't have a lot of confidence in recasting a circle in pig form.

Ben lifted Shay's chin. Smiling, he kissed Shay's nose. "It's okay, sweetheart. You'll do it next time. This is definitely an improvement."

"Ben, we can't stay in this circle all night."

There were smooching sounds all around them.

Wincing, Ben grinned. "I'd say that's a good thing. As much as I like them, I'm really not looking forward to seeing everybody having sex and by the sounds of it—"

"Shay, can we, like, maybe take turns in the circle?" Jud asked.

Shay dropped his head to Ben's chest, trying to decide whether to laugh or cry. "They aren't seeing a problem with this."

Someone let out an overly loud dreamy sigh.

"No. They aren't. They're just happy not to be animals. We're going to have to break it to them." Ben tipped Shay's chin up again and kissed him. This time it was lingering and gentle. Not quite enough to arouse, thankfully, but full of love. At least Ben believed in him.

"What am I missing?" Wrapping one arm around Ben's waist, Shay carefully kept his athame close to his side.

Someone moaned.

"That's it. I'm so not into voyeurism when it involves my friends. And they're enjoying this small victory way too much." He glanced up at Ben. "You ready to go wander around the pasture?"

"Only if you're coming with me."

Shay nodded. As long as he had Ben, this wasn't so bad. He'd try again next month, but for now…

"Look at the bright side, sweetheart…you make an adorable pig."

Pulling the Dragon's Tail

Jet Mykles

The night faded. Although it couldn't be seen through the dull gray rain clouds, the full moon was on the wane. Daniel felt the beast's hold receding, so he unwound his body from where it was wrapped around the chimney. He was long enough in this size to wrap around once and half again. After two years, he'd grown accustomed to his elongated body, claws and hyper-clear sight. Just a few months ago, he'd discovered that he was capable of altering his size. Until then, he'd always spent Shift Night in the woods to hide a body that was taller than the main house. But now, when he could choose to be just a little bit bigger than Cy's snake form or anywhere in-between, he could stick a little closer to home.

A drizzle on the pre-morning breeze ruffled the fine white hair of the beard that lined his elongated snout. Perching clawed hands on the top of the brick chimney, he pointed his nose toward the east where the sky was just beginning to lighten as the sun approached. Beaded water slithered down his iridescent blue and green scales. He sniffed, drawing in crisp, cool air.

Something was wrong.

He trusted the dragon's instincts. From all he'd read about what he was, the dragon—the Chinese dragon—was a creature of weather and water with powers that varied greatly. He hadn't mastered all that a dragon was said to be capable of, but he reckoned that might have something to do with the fact that he'd only been one for about two years, and only once every full moon. But right from the start he'd had the instincts, the uncanny knowledge that something was happening that he needed to be aware of.

Trouble was, he couldn't immediately tell *what* was wrong.

After a few moments, he was no closer to knowing but his skin started that strange, subtle tingling that told him he needed to get off the wet roof before he was human and bare-assed naked up there in the cold. Delicately, he picked his way down the side of the roof toward the gutters. Just out past the barn, he saw Ben in horse form plodding toward the bunkhouse, Shay as a boar at his heels. Gordy stood right beside the porch steps, his big bull body pointed toward the east. Daniel's serpentine body poured over the edge of the roof and he caught hold of the drainpipe. A little thought altered his weight so he could easily shinny down the rickety pipe without pulling it off the side of the house. He switched from pipe to porch rail as soon as he reached it and wound himself down out of the rain into the shelter of the porch awning. There were some of the others. Tristan up on hind legs, long ears up, forelegs tucked in close to his furry chest as he stared toward the east like his lover. Bobby Lee rested on a rag rug in the corner, Cy's scaly body nearly hidden underneath his wool, clearly taking advantage of the warmth.

The tingling in his muscles increased. *Just in time*, he thought idly, pulling up onto his own hind legs right before the change took him. Scales morphed away, his tail receded. Holding up his hands, he watched the black claws shrink into human hands and felt the itch on his face that told him the downy soft white beard of the dragon was back to being his own salt-and-pepper chin covering. He blinked and the dragon's hyper-sight was gone, not to return until the next full moon.

The chill was immediate, his human skin far less adequate against the cold. Around him, his ranch hands, his family, stood and shook off their own shifts, each one naked as the day he was born.

"All right, boys." Daniel reached for the porch door to open it, "let's get some chow."

"There's an obvious pattern." Shay leaned forward, placing his forearms on the table to either side of the nearly full plate before him. One of Ben's old flannel shirts was way too big for him, but it matched the old, ratty clothes the rest of them wore. "Okay, yeah, the Chinese zodiac is involved but it has to be more than that. Why did the rest of us change?"

Daniel was now used to the youngster's enthusiasm about

"cracking the code" of the curse, as he put it. Although this boy, unlike the rest of them, actually had a shot at some good suggestions, being a witch. By "the rest of us," he meant himself, Tristan, Bobby Lee, Zan and Woody. Those who'd come after the initial six. Those who'd never met Yi, so had no reason to be cursed.

"Love," Bobby Lee stated firmly, reaching for the grits, his normally soft voice always full of conviction for that particular topic.

Right beside him, Cy's mouth curled into that warm little smile Bobby Lee seemed to naturally inspire.

"Yes," said Shay, pointing in his excitement, "that's the connection. But why? Why curse us all? She's obviously going for twelve of us."

"You mean she wanted twelve of us?" Woody asked, rising to refill the pitcher of orange juice before Jud could.

"Yes!" Shay ignored Ben as the older man dished scrambled eggs on his plate. "And if we can figure out what she had to gain, we might have a chance at breaking the curse."

"She was a vindictive bitch," stated Gordy with finality, cutting into his slab of ham with vigor. "She was pissed none of us would sleep with her."

Shay shook his head, not fazed by the ham any more than Gordy was fazed when Jud served steaks. Neither he nor Gordy would eat their respective meats, but they didn't begrudge the others. It just went to show that they weren't really the animals, despite the shapes they took on once a month. "I know that seems like a good reason, but she had nothing to gain by it. It took a lot of time and energy to set this spell. She had to have wanted *some*thing." He turned to Daniel. "How long were you married again?"

"Six months"

Shay nodded. "And you say she knew of you before you got married?"

"She said so, yes."

"She has to have studied you. Been watching you. She wanted *you* for some reason." He finally picked up his fork but used it just to toy with the eggs on the plate before him. "It's got to have something to do with the Sands, too. Otherwise, she'd 'ave taken you away and not come back." He tapped the fork tines on his plate, then looked up and around the table. "It's got to have something to do with the twelve. Six couples."

"There're only eleven of us now," Zan pointed out.

All eyes landed on Daniel at the head of the table. Aware of the attention, he sipped his coffee and waited for Shay to go on.

"Yes," Shay continued. "The key to breaking the curse has to be with Daniel finding his mate."

"Mate." When had they started using that word? It was probably Jud but all of them talked about each other like that now.

Jud laughed. "So what say you, boss man? Got any ideas who your mate might be?"

Yes. But he'd keep that secret, if he could. He just gave the thin little man a stare, which made the other cackle harder. *Unless*... to Shay, he said: "You think that'd break this curse?"

Shay nodded. "I don't see what else might. It's the way magic works. When there's a completion of some sort, then that's usually when things really happen. Makes sense that it would end with you since it started with you, you being married to her and all."

"What about Yi herself?"

"You think she's your mate?"

Daniel ignored the groans and snorts around the table. He still felt guilt for ever bringing that woman to the Sands, even without the curse. Least he could do was let them air their anger. "No. Do you think she might come back and lift it?"

Shay pondered, stroking his knuckles along the light stubble on his jaw. "Given reason, maybe. You know a good reason?"

"No." He'd been trying to think of one for two years. He glanced around the table, at the men who meant the most to him in this world. "Y'all seem happy with each other. Not all bad's come from this curse."

There were varying responses to that. Most started with shock, then some moved to thoughtful, others to denial.

It was Ben who spoke. "Won't deny Shay's one of the best things to happen in my life, if not *the* best, but I could've liked it to be without the horse part."

Jud nodded. "The rat thing can be neat sometimes, but it's caused more'n enough trouble."

Daniel nodded. They'd gone through some times, times that would've been difficult enough being that they were gay. The shifting thing just made it all the rougher. But they'd all made it. He believed the fact that their chosen mates got caught up in the curse was a measure of their love. Perhaps it was time he took his own chance. His gaze rested back on Shay. "And you think this can all end, the curse bit, if I'm with the one I love?"

The other man nodded.

Daniel nodded, lifting his coffee mug to his lips. "Then I'll have to give it some thought."

🐎 🐎 🐎

The door banged on the wall as Russell shoved it a little too hard with his boot. Yi would be pissed if it chipped the paint, but it couldn't be helped. His arms were loaded with plastic bags, the dry cleaning and the bag with his work clothes in it.

"Yi," he called, sidling into the kitchen, juggling a little so the frozen stuff in the bags didn't press too much on the expensive, just-pressed dress in its plastic, "I'm home."

No answer, but then he didn't expect one. She was probably in her room doing…whatever it was that she did all day while he was at work. *Hey, maybe she's cleaning house.* He snorted at that little joke. More likely she was watching the big screen television in her room, waiting for him to get home so she could complain that she was bored.

Dropping the bags from one arm onto the counter, he then held the dry cleaning with that hand as he slid the rest of the bags and his work tote onto the shiny blue and white linoleum. Knowing he needed to get *her* stuff out of the way before he did anything so trivial as unloading the groceries or starting the dinner she'd complain was late, he held up the dress and smoothed his hands down the clingy plastic, hoping against hope that the trip from Vera's Dry Cleaners to the apartment hadn't wrinkled it.

"Here, Yi," he said, rounding the corner at the end of the hall into her bedroom, "I picked up your…"

The room was empty. The television was off. The ridiculous pink and white bedspread was neatly laid over mattress and pillows.

"Yi?"

He crossed the room to her walk-in closet and hung the dress on the open door. From there, he had an excellent vantage point to see that her pink bathroom was likewise empty, the light off. Frowning, he glanced at her dresser. Nothing seemed amiss. Nothing was missing. Nothing was…w*hat?* He stepped up to the dresser and picked up the one odd thing. Her pink slide phone. She never went *anywhere* without her phone.

A nervous feeling crawled up the back of his neck. "Yi?"

He left her room and glanced into his across the hall. Not much chance she'd be there, but it and the hall bathroom were the only other rooms in the house. She wasn't in either. He returned to the kitchen that opened into the combined living room and dining room. Yi's cashmere cardigan was draped over the back of the couch. Most disturbing, her *purse* lay on the little table under the mirror just inside the front door. Cell phone and purse were in the house. Okay, it was just one of her many purses, but a quick glance inside showed her flashy white leather wallet and leather sunglasses case inside. Two more items she wouldn't be caught dead without.

That nervous feeling turned into cockroaches scuttling over

the back of his shoulders. In the two years he'd lived with her, she'd never gone missing like this. She was *always* home when he got home, demanding to know what he'd done during the day. He did the cleaning and the cooking and worked at the lumberyard. She kept him so busy he didn't have a social life and could barely function enough to finish what needed to be done before he went to bed at night. He couldn't even remember the last time they'd had sex.

His hand hovered over the cordless phone in its base right next to where he set down her purse but he stopped himself from picking it up. Who would he call? The cops? What would they say? He'd seen her that morning, sleeping in, as usual, with that ridiculous white mask over her eyes. Didn't you have to wait a day or two to file a missing person report? And could he report her? The woman was a witch, or whatever the Chinese equivalent was. She'd as much as told him that she didn't really exist in the true sense of the modern world. She had ID, but it was make believe. Maybe she'd just gone into a parallel dimension or something and lost track of time. She'd never done it before but that didn't mean she couldn't. Did it?

Frustrated, he circled the end of the sofa then sank down, bracing elbows on knees, his face in his palms. Could he hope that she was gone? No, best not to. Even though she'd never been gone before, always preferring to force him on any trip or whim she took at night, that didn't mean much. And she never confided in him. Hell, he still didn't know why she kept him or why she'd taken him from the Sands.

Call Daniel. His head came up, neck twisting so he could look at the phone. His fingers itched to hold the cordless. How often in the past two years had he wished for a chance to call Daniel? He wasn't allowed any personal calls at work and Yi kept close track of the few calls he made on the cell phone she insisted he carry. Besides, what would he say? "Daniel please come get me. I know I slept with your wife and ran off with her but she had me under a spell. She's a witch. Really. She made me sleep with her. She made me betray you. I didn't mean to. Honest. I want to come home."

Despair washed over him, forcing him to sink back onto the sofa, facing away from the phone. "Yeah, right. He'd buy that."

🐟 🐟 🐟

Daniel picked up his desk phone, eyes still on the contract in front of him. "Daniel Long."

"Russell is in trouble."

The contract slipped from Daniel's fingers when he recognized that high-pitched, accented voice. "Yi?"

"He's in trouble. You need to come get him."

"Listen here, what's this all about?"

"You know where he is. Come get him." The connection clicked, followed by a dial tone.

He punched his finger at the phone's switch hook. "Yi!"

No answer. She was gone.

Snarling, he slammed down the headset, then picked it up again to dial *69. For whatever reason, call return didn't work. He really shouldn't have expected it to. Again, he slammed the phone down.

Russell is in trouble…come get him. Was she serious?

Shoving to his feet, he snatched his cell from the holder on his belt and hit the speed dial as he headed for the door.

"It's Ben."

"Where are you?"

"North pasture. What's up?"

He rounded the bottom of the stairs then started to climb. "You alone?"

"No. Gordy 'n Cy are here."

"Shay?"

"No, he's with the foal in the barn."

"I need you here at the house. Get Shay and meet me here."

"On my way. Anything wrong?"

"I'll tell you when you get here." He punched off the phone. "Jud!"

He heard some clattering in the kitchen stop. "Yeah?"

"I need you up here."

He entered his bedroom and headed straight for the closet. He had his duffel open on the bed and was rummaging in the dresser for shirts by the time Jud made it to the door.

The smaller man took one look around and frowned. "What's up?"

"I'm leaving for a few days."

"What for?"

He paused, listening. The sound of hooves stopped at the barn. Ben was almost there. "I'm going to get Russell."

Silence. He glanced up to see Jud's mouth wide-open, eyes almost the same size.

Daniel tossed a few shirts on the bed, then went back for jeans.

"Are you serious?"

"Dead."

"What the Sam Hill for?"

Downstairs, the front door opened and shut. "He's in trouble."

"All right, I'm sorry to hear that but...so?"

"Boss?" Ben called.

"Up here." Daniel tossed clean jeans on the bed and went to the bathroom hooked to his bedroom while two sets of boots clomped on the stairs. "Jud, you got enough in the house account to tide you over for a few days?"

"Whoa, hey, how long you figuring on being gone?"

"What's going on?" Ben asked from the hallway.

Jud answered but stared at Daniel from the bathroom

doorway. "He says he's going after Russell."

"Are you serious?"

"That's what I said."

"Boss?"

Daniel pushed through Jud and Ben back into his bedroom. Shay stood just inside the door into the hall. "Russell's in trouble," he said, dumping his razor, comb and a new toothbrush into the bag.

"So?"

He glared at Jud, who glared right back. "So I'm going to get him."

Ben put a hand on Jud's shoulder to stop the cussing from spilling from his mouth. "How do you know he's in trouble?"

Daniel stopped, stood at the end of the bed, and put his hands on his hips as he faced them. "Yi called."

Three sets of eyes went big.

Ben recovered first. "Yi?"

Daniel nodded.

"When'd she call?"

"Just now."

"What'd she say?"

Daniel stared at the clothing and sundry piled haphazard on his bed, trying to decide if he had all he needed. He never did travel much, even before the curse. "That Russell's in trouble and I need to come and get him."

"That's all?"

He reached down to start shoving stuff into the bag. "Yep."

"Where is he?"

"Barston."

Jud stepped up to the foot of the bed and started to pull the clothes back out of the bag. "She told you that?"

"What're you doing?"

Jud gave him a brief glare. "You can't pack for shit, boss man." He quickly, neatly folded one pair of jeans. "How do you know Russell's in Barston?"

Daniel turned to the closet to see if he could find a bag to put the bathroom stuff in. "They've been living there."

"She told you that?"

Smart Ben. Never could get anything past him. "I knew."

Ben leaned a shoulder on the wall next to the closet. "How?"

He sighed, giving up the search. "I knew all along."

"What?"

Daniel crossed back to the bed and watched Jud fold clothes. "I agreed not to divorce her if she agreed not to move with Russell from Barston."

Jud froze. Daniel could almost hear Ben and Shay breathing. He stared out the window by the bed, trying to tamp down the urge to panic.

"You're still married to that bitch?" Jud's voice was soft, full of betrayal.

"Technically, yeah."

"To protect that little fucktard who ran off with her?"

Daniel spun around to see Ben holding Jud by the shoulders, both of them mad enough to chew nails.

"I don't blame you for being mad…"

"Mad?" Jud struggled in Ben's hold.

But the bigger man had always had a cooler head. "Why didn't you tell us, boss?"

Daniel nodded. It was time. "I wish I could explain. I wanted to forget, to move on. But I didn't. For two reasons."

Ben nodded. "First?"

"I figured since she set the curse, it couldn't hurt to at least know where Yi was."

Jud's nostrils flared but he calmed. Shaking Ben's hands, he bent over and picked up clothes, folding them angrily.

Ben watched him for a second before returning his attention to Daniel. "Second?"

Daniel turned to face Shay. The young man's eyes got wide but he said nothing.

"I've got this—" Daniel shook his head, hating how this was going to sound, "—feeling. I don't know and I can't explain it. I just know I couldn't lose track of Russell." That feeling had outlasted the anger, resentment, disappointment and, finally, despair that had followed Russell's leaving the ranch with Yi.

Shay stepped closer. "You think it's more than a feeling?"

"You tell me. You're the expert."

Shay screwed his mouth to the side. "Right." He wiped his palms on the thighs of his jeans. "You had this feeling since he left?"

"Yes."

"Does it feel natural?"

"Yes and no."

"How no?"

"I never felt like this for anyone else."

Shay exchanged glances with Ben.

"I know what you're thinking. I've been thinking the same thing. I'm just…" Frustrated, he ran a hand through his hair. This was more talking than he'd done about anything but cattle and horses in months. "It doesn't feel natural. It's too strong." He slapped his hands on his thighs, sitting straight. "But it doesn't matter. Russell needs help and I've never let him down. I'm not going to start now."

"Yeah, but boss…"

He ignored Ben, concentrating on Shay again. "Is it possible to put a spell on someone to make them do what you say?"

The younger man blinked. He blinked again and his mouth worked a bit before he could finally muster an answer. "Yeah."

"How long would it last?"

"Depends on the spell."

"How much has Ben told you about Yi when she was here?"

Shay glanced at his lover but Ben was scowling up a storm at Daniel. "Uh, some."

"You think she could have put a spell on Russell to take him away?"

"Oh come on, bossman," Jud exploded. "You don't think…?"

"Why not?" He faced Jud. "Why the fuck not? I didn't think so before either, but with some of what Shay's been saying lately, why the fuck not? She put a spell on us to change us into animals once a month. Who says she couldn't put a spell on Russell to make him go with her?"

That shut him up. Jud wasn't convinced, Daniel could tell, but now he'd started to wonder. So had Ben.

Shay glanced from Daniel to Jud to Ben then back at Daniel. "It's possible," he finally said. "Like you said, she changed you all into shape shifters. A spell to control one man for awhile should be something she could do."

A weight he hadn't realized was there lifted from Daniel's heart at the sound of Shay's words.

"I don't know about it lasting two years, though," Shay added.

Daniel shook his head. "Doesn't matter." He turned back to packing. "If I know that boy at all, the thought of trying to explain what happened and apologize would keep him away."

Jud snorted. "That's true enough." Daniel caught the small, reluctant smile on Jud's face. Him, Daniel and Ben had been the closest of any of them to Russell. Jud knew Russell's pigheadedness real well.

"But why would she take him?" Ben asked.

Daniel nailed him with a look. "Why'd she do this to us in the first place?"

Ben was watching him with a thoughtful frown. "You think she set a spell on you to get you to marry her?"

That stopped him. He'd given a lot of thought to it, but that particular angle hadn't struck him. The spell idea had only hit him since Shay had been with them, and that wasn't long now. He'd been so set on finding a reason why Russell would betray him, he hadn't looked at his *own* actions. Which was kind of stupid, come to think of it, but too late to regret it now. "Maybe so."

Ben nodded slowly. "Would explain a lot."

Jud nodded, too, as he set the last folded shirt into the top of the duffel bag.

"But why?" Shay asked.

Daniel shook his head, standing. "Won't know unless I ask her."

Ben grabbed his arm to stop him. "Let me get this straight. Yi calls, tells you to come and get Russell, and you're just *going*?"

"Yes."

"Don't you think…?" Ben stopped, clearly at a loss for words.

"What?"

"That it's dangerous?" Jud piped in.

"I don't know what's she's got in mind for Russell. I need to go."

"She could be lying."

"She could be telling the truth."

"You know this spell thing might all be wishful thinking. It coulda been exactly what it looked like. He could have *helped* her."

Daniel scowled. "No."

"No. Just because you don't want to think it, you say no?"

Daniel shoved Ben away and snatched up the straps for the duffel. "Russell wouldn't do that. There's no other explanation."

"Damn it. Then let me go with you…"

"No." Angrily, Daniel hauled the bag onto his shoulder. It seemed too light. "*If* you're right and something does happen to me, then you need to stay here and take care of the Sands."

Three bodies blocked his way out the door, with Ben's big body planted right in Daniel's path. "This isn't right. You're not thinking it through."

"I don't need to. You're in charge. You do what you need to…"

"Daniel, *quit* it! I'm worried about *you*."

He paused, giving each of them a long, measured look, ending with Ben who stood between the other two. "I need to do this. I need to know if Russell is the one."

Ben blinked. "You think…?"

"Maybe."

A wealth of feeling passed between them in that next moment. He'd known Ben since they were young men and trusted the man with more than anyone, save maybe Jud. There were good reasons he trusted these two.

Ben nodded and stepped aside. "You call when you get there. And you *call* if you need help."

Daniel started down the hall toward the stairs, all three of them at his heels.

"And don't you let that woman do anything to you," Jud warned. "You want me to pack you a dinner real quick?"

He reached the front door under a load of questions and warnings. Shay peeled off once they got to the porch but he returned in a hurry once Daniel had started his truck. By then a few of the others had reached the front and had to put in their two cents.

Shay waded through all of them, then grabbed Daniel's hand and shoved something in it. "Here, take this."

Daniel looked at the cord with a little leather bag tied to it. "What is it?"

"It's a spell ward. I don't know if it'll work against her magic, specifically, but it's better than nothing."

Without pause, Daniel looped the cord over his head, then smiled at the younger man. "Thanks."

"Your best bet is to just stay away from her, if you can."

Daniel nodded. "Anything else?"

They were all quiet now, watching Shay. The flush to his neck said he knew it, but he took a deep breath and bore it. "Be careful."

Daniel gave them all a look, smiled, nodded. "I'll be back in no time."

🦎 🦎 🦎

Hellfire, he was going crazy! Russell couldn't shake the feeling that there was something alien crawling around under his skin, just itching to get out.

Grumbling to himself, he paced into the apartment's living room. Off-white couch and matching love seat, delicate little feminine tables, a stupid white carpet that was an absolute *bitch* to keep clean. The cable and television had been his best friends on lonely nights for well over a year now, a subscription to NetFlix well-used. Easier to let himself be distracted than to deal with Yi and her demands. Still grumbling, he paced back into the kitchen and flung open the refrigerator. Mostly empty. He hadn't gone shopping much since she'd disappeared, so stores were down. No one for him to cook for except himself anyway and his appetite had been lacking. Tonight he was hungry, but there wasn't anything there for him to salvage.

He couldn't say he missed Yi. It was kind of a relief to be free of her constant nagging and demands. But having her just up and disappear like that had him on edge. He didn't know what to do. He'd decided he couldn't call the police. He really did need to figure out the finances. She was the one who'd held the purse strings, she was the one with full access to the bank accounts. His salary from the lumberyard might be enough to pay the utilities but not enough to pay the rent, too. What would he do if she never came back? He really should be looking at his finances, paying bills, making sure he wasn't going to get kicked out of the apartment that he never really liked in the first place. But he couldn't concentrate. He was able to keep it together at his job at the lumberyard, but once he got home, the silence ate at him.

"Have to go out," he muttered, closing the refrigerator. Shower, shave and he'd go out to that sports bar down the street and have dinner while watching a game or two. Yi'd only let him do that a few times in the two years she'd held him here.

Dumping his work clothes in a corner of his room, he grabbed a towel and went to the bathroom off the hallway. Unlike Yi's room, he didn't have his own bathroom. He should go in and use hers, just to be ornery. But he didn't. He'd have to get rid of all those fake pink flowers and stinky potpourri first and it just wasn't worth the effort. Hated her choice of decor. Hated the whole damn apartment. He wanted to go home!

Stepping under the spray, he just stood there for a moment, battling vivid impressions of life back at the Shifting Sands. If he didn't open his eyes, he could imagine he was in the bathroom upstairs, two doors down from Daniel's room. Instead of dingy white, the tiles would be blue and green. But as soon as he picked up the soap, he knew it wasn't that strong workingman's soap, meant to cut through the worst of ranch dirt and grime. It was just regular soap and the shampoo had a slight floral tang to it that wouldn't have ever made it into Jud's shopping cart.

Jud. Sarcastic Jud who was more of a brother to him than anyone. Ben, another brother—well maybe more uncle—who'd always looked out for him and had swatted his ass for being bad more than once. Quiet Michael who he suspected had deeper depths. Big ole' Gordy who was the most fun to be with outside of Jud. Suspicious, biting Cy who really had a heart of gold if you dared to hang around long enough to look for it. He missed those guys so much. Missed dinners around the table. Missed all the animals. Missed camping out for days on end sometimes at the far reaches of the ranch, watching the cattle.

And Daniel. Just the thought of the man in his vulnerable state made Russell light-headed. He had to lean forward to slap a palm on the tiles before him, bending his head into the spray to let it stream down his back. He missed Daniel the most. In unguarded moments like this, he'd admit why, at least to himself. Oh, he missed him because Daniel had always been there for him, had taken care of him. But he also missed the closeness of him, the physical *him* that had always been a balm to Russell's heart. Shortly before Daniel had gone off and married Yi, Russell had thought that maybe he was in love with Daniel. Wasn't like he didn't know what being gay was all about, surrounded by gay men and all. He'd heard the guys talk about other guys and realized that he felt that way about Daniel. He watched him like no other. The sight of Daniel would make Russell's heart patter. The sound of the man's voice went straight to something low in his belly.

Compelled, Russell palmed his cock. It was hard as a rock already, like it always got when he thought of Daniel. All right, maybe he might not be in love with Daniel, but he certainly was in lust with him. It had to be the reason that he'd slept with Yi in the first place. Yeah, she'd been persuasive and damned pretty, but Russell was pretty sure it was the fact that she was Daniel's. And wasn't that just cold-hearted and wrong of him? Desperate not to lose the hard-on, he tossed thoughts of Yi from his mind. Better just to think of Daniel. Better to imagine the cuts and curves of Daniel's muscles. He'd seen the boss man naked a few times and boy howdy did he want to see more! He ringed the head of his cock with thumb and forefinger, stroking and squeezing as he opened his mouth, ignoring the water in favor of imagining Daniel's cock sliding past his lips. He'd never sucked cock before but he'd jump at the chance to choke on Daniel's. Groaning, he let his hips give in to involuntary thrusts, pumping his shaft faster. Daniel would fuck him. He couldn't imagine it the other way around. Daniel would take the cock that Russell had never seen hard—damn it—lube it up and shove it deep inside. In Russell's imagination—fueled by assurances from Jud—it was the best feeling in the world. He'd seen some gay porn, had imagined himself on all fours, bracing while the boss man pummeled him from behind. It did it for him, had him going, had him… "Aaaaahng!" Spunk splashed the white tiles as he opened his eyes, refusing to allow himself to finish the dream since he knew he'd never have it.

🐎 🐎 🐎

The drive to Barston gave Daniel too much time to think.

"Damn fool idea," he muttered, running calloused fingers through his short brown hair. He left the truck windows down, letting the humid Texas air rip through the cab. Idly, he scratched at the whiskers at the side of his jaw. He'd shaved this morning but the beard the beast insisted he had always came right back by afternoon.

"Damn fool idea," he repeated, resting his jaw on his fist as he stared at the long, open road ahead. Fool idea but he was excited just the same. For two years he'd convinced himself to leave Russell alone. For longer than that he'd kept his own feelings at bay. Maybe part of the whole problem of this mess was because he *kept* hiding things. Time to stop that.

He hadn't always had a thing for Russell. That'd be absurd and just not right to think it. At first, he'd just helped out the kid where he could and been happy to do so. He wasn't sure exactly when he'd started looking at Russell *that* way. He was man enough to admit it was before he probably should have, when Russell was young. He wouldn't have acted on it, of course, but how could he not notice that Russell'd filled out into a fine looking young man? Hair the color of a cheerful campfire with wide set hazel eyes set into a good strong face filled with the most fascinating freckles Daniel had ever seen. Freckles that had been adorable on the kid, and still were adorable on the man he started to be but…well, a different kind of adorable.

He did remember when it had hit him so hard that he couldn't deny it to himself anymore. Russell had been seventeen, in the paddock with Ben and Cy when they were breaking a new filly. This particular filly was Russell's from birth, a present from

Daniel. Russell wouldn't be persuaded away from helping to break her himself. To his credit, Russell had taken it all very seriously and listened to every word Ben and Cy said to him. Even so, Russell took a fall and scraped up his arm pretty bad. Daniel had been there when they brought him into the kitchen for Jud to help clean him up. The boy took his shirt off and Daniel remembered standing in the door, frozen in shock. Goddamn it if the boy wasn't a man, complete with some ginger hair on his chest, curling around pert little nipples. The urge to go hug the boy had been strong, but not so much to see he was okay. He knew he was okay. Russell had been hurt worse before. No, Daniel had wanted to hug him just to feel that bare chest, to pinch those nipples while he sucked on the lower lip the boy was biting while Jud cleaned the scrape.

Very wrong. The boy was his responsibility. Not his son but definitely his legal ward. Daniel shouldn't have thought of him like that.

But the thoughts didn't go away. They got stronger. He caught himself watching the way the boy sat his horse, thinking about that fine little ass polishing the saddle. He nearly lost it once when he looked out his bedroom window to see Russell, bare-chested, dunking his shirt in the trough at the side of the barn. Mesmerized, he'd stared as the boy lifted up the wet fabric and used it to wipe the sweat from his shoulders and neck. That there fantasy had given him jerk off material for months.

Enough of those fantasies had driven him to take that fateful month-long vacation to Atlanta. The vacation where he'd met Yi. In hindsight, although he still didn't know why, he was positive she'd spelled him. She'd have had to. His mind had been so full of Russell, he'd been having trouble deciding whether to pick up a rent boy to sate his need. Yi had turned that around somehow, focused it on her. Maybe he'd played into her game. Maybe he'd been so relieved not to think of Russell *that* way, he'd latched onto Yi.

Whatever, it had been a colossal mistake. Letting her into their lives had been a mistake. Perhaps letting two years go by without tracking her down in person had been a mistake. Who knew what she was up to now?

But he could make one thing right. He could bring Russell home. Even without the curse, without Daniel's feelings perhaps being the end of the curse, Russell belonged to the Shifting Sands and it was high time Daniel let him know he was still welcome.

If things progressed from there… Daniel reached down to adjust the start of a boner in his jeans. Well, if things progressed, so much the better.

※ ※ ※

He wasn't Daniel, but he was mighty fine looking in Russell's own opinion. The growl he heard came from his throat, voicing a rumble deep in his belly. Now *that* was just bizarre. Self-conscious, he ducked his head back down over his mostly empty plate of fried chicken, hoping the gorgeous being he'd been checking out hadn't noticed him.

Russell shook his head. What was he doing looking at men? Older men. Cowboys. Men who would almost definitely not welcome the attention of another man. Russell may have grown up in a gay-friendly environment, but he'd learned well that most men did not welcome amorous attention from other men. Or, at least, they wouldn't dream of admitting it.

But, God! The guy was worth looking at. Older, maybe in his late forties or early fifties. Fit and physically powerful. Broad shoulders supporting muscled arms. Short hair without the Stetson that sat on the table next to him, brown with liberal shots of gray through it. He had a great smile, which he used often as he laughed with the friends that surrounded him. Russell really wanted to know the color of his eyes. If they were brown like Daniel's, he'd probably come in his pants, despite jerking off in the shower earlier. They might be brown, he decided. Then he realized he was looking straight into them because he'd got caught looking. *Damn!* He tilted his head down. *Great, just great.* Russell just knew he'd been wearing a hungry look. What the hell was he doing being so obvious? A casual peek up after a few seconds showed not only the gorgeous man looking but two of his friends as well. *Well, fuck a duck. Time to go.* He stared at the half-eaten chicken thigh and the remaining mashed potatoes and wondered whether he should take them home.

The chair at the other side of his table scraped back. Startled, he looked up to see the gorgeous man lowering himself into the chair. Leaning forward on one beefy arm mostly exposed by the short sleeves of his checked button-down shirt, he squinted at Russell. Blue. His eyes were dark blue. Nothing like Daniel's. *Now cut that out!*

"Do I know you, friend?"

"No, sir."

"Then why you keep starin' at me?"

"I, uh…" Russell eyed the two friends standing behind the man's chair. Those were menacing stares if he'd ever seen any and the guys had the brawn to back them up. He swallowed over another growl that threatened the base of his throat. "I thought you looked like someone I know."

Mr. Good-Looking nodded, but didn't seem convinced. A Jack Daniels scent reached Russell's nose and he wondered just how many this guy'd had. "You sure that's it?"

"Yessir."

He grunted, sitting back in his chair. The angle and his spread legs presented his package for Russell's view. *Nice.* Then, *damn!* He got caught looking again!

"I ain't seen you around here before."

"I've been here a few times," he wiped his mouth with his napkin and looked up, hoping to catch his waitress' eye.

"You live around here?"

"Not too far." There she was. He flagged her down, relieved when she started toward the table.

At a glance and a nod from him, Mr. Good-Looking's friends wandered off back toward the bar. Mr. Good-Looking stayed, watching the waitress as she set down Russell's bill and took his plate. "She's a cute young thing, isn't she?"

"Huh?" Russell glanced up from pulling bills out of his wallet. His waitress was, in fact, a knockout with the tight T-shirt and short skirt to show it off. He was more interested in getting away from this dangerous vibe, however. Also, he thought it best to get away from the man's sexy as hell rumble. Obligingly, he glanced after her tight little rump. "I guess so."

The man whistled then laughed. "You guess so? What's wrong, you ain't got *eyes* boy?"

He smiled, standing as he stuffed his wallet back in his back pocket. "She's not really my type."

"What *is* your type?"

Russell froze, realizing that he'd walked into that one. The man was giving him the eye and it was none-too-friendly. "I'm tired," he said, trying a smile. "I'm just gonna go home."

The man nodded. "You do that." He raked a gaze up and down Russell's body. "Boy."

What the fuck? He can't be coming onto me.

The man's eyes met Russell's again and he smiled. Winked.

Confused, Russell decided he just needed to get away. Best to go with his first instinct and not tempt fate. Things were strange enough in his life right now without him inviting more trouble. Keeping his head down, he walked past the bar and out the door.

The night was fresh and cool. Taking a deep breath, he looked up at the clear sky. Dinky little stars hung out up there, almost brighter than the sliver of a moon. He was glad for the chance to walk home, glad for the slight chill in the air. Maybe it would help to clear his head and douse the burn in his gut. He was glad the guy looked less like Daniel close up. If he'd been a dead ringer, Russell would have lost his head for sure. And what the hell was he doing thinking about Daniel for anyway? Checking out another man because he looked a little like him? That was stupid. Beyond stupid. He should be figuring out if he was going to move or not, figuring out how he was going to pay bills.

But right now, he'd just walk. He'd just breathe. Though the streets were mainly dark, this part of town consisting mostly of businesses that were open during the day. The streetlights were bright but widely spaced so that he walked through dim, then bright, then dim patches. Hardly anyone else was around once he turned into a more residential area. Big magnolia trees shaded the streets here, and there were even fewer streetlamps.

Maybe he should call the Sands. Maybe there was a slim chance that he could explain, that Daniel would forgive him. Oh who was he kidding? Even if Daniel did, the others wouldn't. Jud would call him a lot worse than a fucktard if he…

A big truck skidded to a halt right beside him. *What the hell?* He skipped back toward the brick wall of the apartment building behind him as the door nearest him opened. *Oh shit!* Mr. Not-So-Good-Looking and his two buddies spilled out of the truck.

"You live around here, faggot?" the man drawled.

Unfortunately, the answer was yes but Russell wasn't going to let that be known. "What's going on?"

The other man sauntered closer. "Jes wanted to see what you were up to, pretty boy."

Oh shit. Russell tried to keep walking but one of the bullies blocked his path on each side. Together with the apartment building, they had him boxed in. No one else was around and he knew for a fact that this particular building was mostly empty. If he screamed, would someone come running?

"Wassa matter, pretty boy? You was checkin' me out just a little while ago." The older man planted himself right in front of Russell, hands on hips. "Just tryin' to let you get a better look."

Russell couldn't help *but* look. The man's shoulders were half again as broad as his and his arms far bigger. He also had almost a head's height on Russell. His two friends were about the same size. *Great.* The body he'd had cause to admire before wasn't such a turn on now. "That's okay," he said. "I'll just be going now."

He tried, but a beefy hand slammed into his chest, shoving him back against the bricks. The big man leaned into him. "I don't think so."

Russell scowled. "What the fuck's your problem?"

The man's fake genial smile turned into an ugly smirk. "He wants to know what my problem is, Bert."

The man to Russell's left laughed. "Tell him, Chuck."

Chuck leaned in closer to Russell, his forearm now braced on Russell's clavicle. "My problem is little fag pretty boys, *that's* my problem. What the fuck you doin' in my town? Fagging it all up."

Russell literally had no idea how to respond to that. His first instinct was to laugh at the man's absurdity but self-preservation kept him from it.

"You don't *look* at me like that. You don't *think* about me like that!"

Russell winced with each push of Chuck's arm into his throat. "Yeah, okay. I got it."

"You got it."

"Yeah. I got it. Get the fuck off me."

Okay, wrong thing to say. Chuck's eyes narrowed and he snarled. "You need to be taught a lesson, boy."

That's enough. "Fuck no!" He shoved as hard as he could at Chuck.

All four of them were stunned to see Chuck stumble back all the way to the truck idling on the curb. Russell was so surprised he forgot to run. His mistake.

Bert and the other friend recovered first and grabbed his arms. With a drunken roar, Chuck charged forward and planted a fist in Russell's gut. Russell coughed, doubling over in pain, which made it quite easy for the lugs to haul him seven feet aside and into an alley between two buildings. Anger surfaced enough to help him struggle, but the men had him. He tried to shout but another punch to the gut prevented anything but a wheezing moan. He heard the insults thrown at him but nothing registered above the pain and an odd sizzling sensation just below his skin. He twisted, trying to break free. His kicks only succeeded in toppling him over into one of his assailants. A punch to his jaw rattled his brain.

He heard a growl, flexed his fist. One of the men beside him yelped and his hand was free. Snarling, he swung the free hand toward where he knew Chuck would be coming at him again.

"What the fuck?"

His hand met with empty air, then continued on toward the man holding his other arm. His claws sank into a man's shoulder and he used the grip to bring the human body close enough to sink his teeth into the meat of the closest shoulder. A scream burst from the throat near his head.

Daniel parked on the street not far from the main entrance of the small apartment complex. Although he knew the address well, he'd never been there before. Never been to Barston. But Russell was nearby. He could feel it.

Shutting off the truck, Daniel remained seated for a few moments, staring at his hands, waiting for the claws and the iridescent green and blue scales to retreat. Being so far away from the Sands was more unsettling than he'd thought. The farther he drove from his home base, the more the beast wanted to come out. He'd finally allowed the claws and the scales to remain, that little bit seeming to satisfy the dragon for a little while. But he was having a devil of a time keeping his eyes human. His sight kept slipping into that strange shape-sensory sight of the beast rather than normal vision. Not the easiest to drive with since the beast wasn't great at seeing electrical stuff, like traffic lights.

"Damn!" it wasn't working. The black claws and shining scales were still there although the shape of his hands remained mostly human. A weird afterimage to his sight told him that his eyes were half gone. Was this because he was so far from the Sands or was it because he was near Russell? Did it have anything to do with a nagging feeling that he had to get out of the truck *now*?

No help for it. Carefully tugging the cuffs of his flannel shirt as far over his hands as possible, he grabbed his hat and got out of the truck. Luckily, it was a dark night so he might be able to go undetected, at least to Russell's apartment. He'd have to tackle the problem of what to do in the morning, when and if that trouble came.

Something was wrong. The feeling only increased. A definite pull guided him down the street away from the front door of the apartment complex. He shoved his hat onto his head and scowled at the door. *That* was where he wanted to go. But there was no denying the beast's instincts when they were like this and the beast wanted to go down the street. Daniel jumped from the truck, hoping he'd parked in a parking zone, barely remembering to push the button on the key fob that'd lock the door. He forced himself to walk, although at a fast clip, toward the source of anxiety.

He heard them before he got to the corner of an alley between two buildings. An animal growl sank into his skin, shifting his vision completely to shapes and pushing his own anger to the surface. He curled his talons into palms that'd developed the thickly calloused pads of the beast. A curl of smoke drifted from his nostrils as he rounded the corner.

Four men. One on the ground to the side, clutching his arm and crying out. He smelled of blood. One standing a few paces away, staring at the remaining two, who were locked together. Russell was one of the two. He stood out as a shining orange-gold beacon despite the fact Daniel's beast had never seen him firsthand. He was wrapped around the other, bigger man, teeth sunk into the meat of the man's neck, one malformed hand gripping the man's chest. Claws dug into the man's skin. Daniel knew a partial shift when he saw one, having coaxed his men through a few of them over the past two years.

Instinct kicked in. "Russell!" he barked, putting a little of the dragon's musical tone in his voice. It often worked to stun others.

Russell startled, lifting his head. Daniel saw the blood in his mouth as violet fluid running down the orange contours that made up his face. His victim sagged in his grip but Russell barely noticed him, turning toward the sound of Daniel's voice.

Daniel strode purposely toward the men. The one on the ground scrambled to his feet, leaning up against the wall. He was a mixture of reds and blues through to violets to Daniel, strangely detailed enough that Daniel knew he was gaping in shock. The unharmed man turned to face Daniel, his shapes made up of murky reds and ugly greens, but his angry scowl drained from his face at whatever he saw. Daniel grimaced, wondering if his beard was all white yet, and how many scales shone on his skin. He knew his eyes had to be shining gold if he was seeing in emotional shapes. Had the horns sprouted from his head yet?

Daniel dismissed them all, including the injured man in Russell's grasp. He concentrated on Russell, seeing the tiger on the verge of bursting forth. That answered the question about the twelfth animal easily enough. "Russell, let him go."

The younger man's lip curled up in a snarl. It was far enough from the full moon that the fever shouldn't take him this hard, but who knew what Russell was suffering with such an extended absence from the Sands?

"Russell!" Daniel put all the command that he knew in his voice. "Do as I say."

Russell's grip faltered, allowing the injured man to drop from his grasp. His mouth fell open, the shape of his fangs clear in the opening. "Daniel?"

"It's me, Russell."

"What the fuck is going on?" the only uninjured man demanded. He stepped toward Daniel, the stink of fear belying his bravado. "Who the hell are you?"

Daniel grabbed the wrist of the hand that shot out in what might have been a good right hook. Although the man's arm was larger than his, it stopped dead. Angry, Daniel let the man have the full brunt of his gaze, his claws just biting into the other man's skin. "Get. Out. Of. Here." He enunciated properly, letting the beast's angry growl seep from his lips.

All of the man's courage drained from the face before him and the pungent stink of fresh urine overlay the old urine smell of the alley. "W-what the fuck are you?"

"Nothing you'll want to remember tomorrow." Daniel shoved the man's arm away. "Take your friends and go."

Disregarding the men, he turned his head back to face Russell, who hadn't moved. They stared at each other, frozen, as the three men scrambled from the alley. Russell leaned heavily against the stucco wall, knees bent, panting. Daniel's strange vision showed him a superimposition of the tiger barely below the surface of Russell's skin. How long had he been like that, so close to changing?

"We have to go," Daniel said softly, once he heard the other men's truck speed down the street.

Russell didn't move except for breathing, and the wet tongue that slowly snaked out to lap at his lower lip.

Daniel tracked the progress of that wet muscle, trying to ignore what the sight did to fill his cock. He took a step toward the younger man, holding out his hand.

Russell's gaze snapped down, widened. "Daniel?" No doubt he saw the scales and the claws. How much showed on Daniel's face?

The beast demanded that he pounce, that he change so he could wrap his serpentine body around Russell to get the most skin-to-scale contact possible. But the human in him prevailed. He needed to take this slow or else he'd literally have an out-of-control tiger on his hands. Daniel spread both hands, palms toward Russell. He could take the cat, if necessary, but he'd much rather not. "It's me, Russell." He took another step. "Trust your instincts."

A fine tremor shook Russell's body. The claws he still sported dug shallow furrows in the bricks at his back. His own beast's fine instincts spilled scales down his shoulders, neck, back and arms a split second before Russell launched from the wall at Daniel.

Instinct again had Daniel catching him rather than using his own claws to slice open his belly. The smaller man slammed into him, arms snaking around him. Daniel did some arm-wrapping of his own, angling his head to meet Russell mouth-to-mouth just as tiger claws shredded the back of his shirt and scraped over the scales that covered his back.

He disregarded the claws entirely, too focused on devouring the open mouth beneath his. Delectable warm, musky male flooded his senses as the old taste of beer, chicken and Russell filled his mouth. Fangs clashed with fangs as they fought to get closer than they could. Daniel's back hit a wall and his boots slipped on alley sludge but he couldn't tear himself away from Russell's tight, squirming body. He cupped the back of Russell's head, thankful the beast's claws and pads didn't cover his fingers so he could feel the silky softness of Russell's hair.

He braced on the wall behind him as Russell half-climbed his body. Strong arms squeezed his neck and shoulders and one jean-clad leg wrapped around one of Daniel's. The new position put their groins flush together and twin groans of need echoed off the alley walls. His cock was like to burst through his zipper and he found one of his hands squeezing Russell's ass before he even realized it had moved. Hands full of firm denim-covered flesh, he encouraged Russell to rock, to move, to rub that beautiful body and hard cock against his. Never had he felt so desperate, so sexually out-of-control. Never had he been so unable to bring himself and his emotions to heel. The dam had burst on the desires he'd suppressed for so long and he couldn't manage to rein them in enough for him and his frantically pumping tiger to find a better location for this.

A familiar feeling burst forth in his balls, taking him by surprise. Unable to stop grinding with Russell, unable to stop kissing the other man, he was helpless to stop the shot of electricity to his spine or the flood of warmth as he came in his shorts.

🗡 🗡 🗡

Russell shifted the small blue towel back and forth from one of the hands he held between his knees to the other. Rather than watch the bathroom door, he watched the fabric drape the rug beneath his bare feet. He could hear water running.

Daniel. Daniel was here. Something had happened. Weird things had taken over Russell's body. But at the heart of it, Daniel was *here.* Daniel had kissed him. Daniel had come with him. The last had shattered his brain. He'd calmed to find himself wrapped around the man of his obsession with an uncomfortable wetness in his jeans. Luckily, the walk back to his apartment had been quick. They'd managed it without talking much and Russell had given Daniel a clean towel and seen him into the bathroom before going to his own bedroom to change. But Russell was now cleaned up in a T-shirt and flannel pants and he was waiting.

Oh, and Daniel was here.

What the fuck?

The bathroom knob clicked and Russell looked up in time to see Daniel walk out. He'd untucked his black and white check shirt so the length hid his crotch. His hat sat on the kitchen counter so his short, salt-and-pepper hair was fully visible.

No scales. Russell shook himself inwardly. That had to have been his imagination.

"Nice place."

"Yi picked it out."

Daniel leaned down a little to grip the back of the chair catty-corner to the couch. "Where is she?"

Russell shook his head. "Don't know. Haven't seen her for days."

"That normal?"

"Not at all."

Daniel squinted, despite the fact that the three lamps that were on shed plenty of light in the living area, not to mention the overhead kitchen light behind him. So tall and stable. Russell felt more steady just with Daniel in the room. He always had. "You been okay?"

Russell sat back on the couch, still toying with the towel. He held it in his lap to disguise what could be a growing problem. "Since when?"

A little bit of a smile curled the corner of Daniel's mouth, crinkling the sun-worn skin of his cheek underneath a few hours' worth of dark stubble. "Let's start with the last few days."

Russell shrugged. "I'm fine. Don't know how I'm gonna manage the bills or anything, but I'm fine."

The smile morphed into a small, concerned frown as Daniel rounded the chair to sit down. "You been feeling…funny?"

Russell mirrored the frown. "Funny how?"

"What happened tonight? In the alley with those assholes?"

Russell glanced away. "We had a misunderstanding."

"About what?"

Just that fast, Daniel was his guardian again. His replacement parent. That was the *last* thing he wanted Daniel to be right now.

So… "One of them thought I was hitting on him."

"Were you?"

"No." He should have known. He'd been away from the Sands too long. Of course, Daniel wouldn't be fazed by implied or blatant homosexuality. He lived with gay men. Which, come to think of it…he looked up and spoke before Daniel could get out his next question. "Daniel, are you gay?"

The older man blinked, sitting back in the chair. "I believe the answer to that is yes."

"How come you never told no one?"

Daniel lifted one big shoulder then let it drop. "Didn't seem to be anyone's business but my own."

Sure as hell not mine. "Why'd you marry Yi?"

"I think she put a spell on me."

Russell froze. His gaze darted over Daniel's face, searching to see if the other man was having a go at him. But Daniel looked serious. "You know?" he said slowly.

"That she's some kind of witch? Yeah, we found that out when she took off with you."

Russell blinked, fast. "How?"

Daniel leaned forward again, his eyes steady on Russell's face. "Right after you left, we all…changed. Hard to believe, but we came to be what the boys call shape-shifters. Once a month, on the full moon, we turn into animals."

Russell gripped the towel with both hands to keep them from shaking. "A-animals?"

Daniel nodded, still watching him. "Not werewolves. Not like the movies. Ben turns into a horse, Gordy into a bull, Cy into a snake, Michael into a rooster and Jud into a rat."

Russell had to smile. "A rat? Jud must love that."

Daniel gave a small grin. "He's gotten used to it."

"What about you?"

The grin faded. "You ever seen a Chinese dragon?"

Russell's jaw dropped. *The scales. The horns. The beard.* Oh yes, he'd seen tons of Chinese dragons. They were all over a lot of Yi's stuff. "You turn into a dragon?"

Daniel nodded. "That's not all."

"That's not enough?"

Daniel chuckled softly. "There are others now. The boys…" he sat up, wiping his palms on the thighs of his dark jeans, "the boys have all fallen in love. Found their life mates."

Russell shook his head. "What?"

"It's true. Jud has Woody, Cy has Bobby Lee, Gordy has Tristan, Michael has Zan and Ben has Shay."

Russell was torn. His heart warmed to know that the men he cared about most in the world had found their life mates, but this was so much information at one time.

"And the new boys caught the spell. They turn into a monkey, a ram, a rabbit, a dog and a boar."

Russell's reeling thoughts caught a pattern. "Those animals… they sound familiar."

"The Chinese zodiac."

"Yi set this spell?"

"Yes."

"Why?"

"Hell if we've been able to figure it out. I was hoping you might have some idea."

He shook his head. "I knew she was a witch, but I never knew…she wouldn't tell me anything about y'all."

"Russell…she had you under a spell?"

Russell caught his breath, peeking up at Daniel. Was it possible that his fears over the last year were completely unfounded? "At first, yeah. I'm pretty sure she spelled me into sleeping with her." He edged forward again. "She must've Daniel. I wouldn't have betrayed you like that, honest. It wasn't me."

Daniel sat forward enough to reach out and take Russell's hand. "I hoped that's what you'd say, boy."

Boy. No. He didn't want to be relegated to a child. Not now. "Daniel…" He turned his hand over, trying to lace his fingers with the older man's.

But Daniel evaded him. He stood, turning back toward the kitchen. "I think what we need to do is get you out of here."

Russell stood. "Daniel…"

The cowboy was walking toward the hall. "Who knows when Yi's gonna get back. We should get you out of here tonight."

"Tonight?"

"Yes." Daniel turned, halfway down the hall. The light wasn't on above him so only the glows from the kitchen and living room shone on him, the walls casting weird shadows to make him look larger than life. Like the legendary hero of Russell's adolescent dreams. "I want you to come home. *We* want you to come home. You belong on at the Sands."

All other concerns, including the swelling in his flannel pants, subsided in the wake of those words. *Home.* Daniel wanted him to come *home.* He was right. Everything else could wait.

🐴 🐴 🐴

The drive home flew by. Daniel thought he'd known how much he'd missed Russell but he'd been so wrong. Hearing the younger man's voice, his particular way of talking, thoughts as bouncy as a baby colt on its first time in the pasture. It was four a.m. and he'd been up for nearly twenty-four hours but he felt terrific.

Daniel wanted to know more about what had happened between Russell and Yi but he realized as they turned onto the road that led to the Shifting Sands that Russell had managed to keep him talking about the ranch and the hands and the shift for most of the drive. When Daniel turned the truck into the driveway, Russell damn near shut up.

"You all right?" Far up ahead, the main house came into view.

"They hate me?"

The two of them had kept carefully clear of emotions, sticking to facts and funny stories.

"Once we tell them what happened, it'll be fine."

"Will it?"

He reached over and patted Russell's knee. "'Course it will."

A glance over and his gaze caught earnest hazel eyes, all the freckles on his face just coming into view in the pale morning light. A jounce in the road jarred Daniel back to sense and he put his hand back on the wheel and faced forward to pay attention to what he was doing.

"Daniel…"

"Jud's probably got breakfast on the table already. I probably shoulda called to let him know we'd be back this soon."

"Daniel…"

"'Course, that boy'd feed the entire state of Texas daily if we let him. Even Woody can't keep him from mother-henning everyone."

"Hey, Daniel."

He risked another glance over. Russell smiled. "Thanks for bringing me back. For believing me."

His heart flipped at the sight of that smile. "It's where you always belonged."

Thank God they reached the house then, or else the boy might've said something embarrassing. How much did he remember about what they did in the alley anyway? Daniel had been careful not to talk about it, hoping Russell would miss it in the confusion of his first shift. Partial shift, anyway. Daniel had forfeited sleep to bring Russell back to the ranch the same night rather than risk staying the night in that apartment alone with him. He was pretty sure he wouldn't have been able to stay out of Russell's pants and that just wasn't fair to the younger man. This was going to be hard enough for him, coming back home. Daniel didn't need to make it worse by pushing unwanted attention on him.

Bodies poured out the front door as Daniel shut off the truck. "Damn," he called out his open window, "all y'all late to work?"

Ben grinned, stepping up to the side of the truck to peer inside. "Why not? The boss is away."

Daniel glared at him but Ben just grinned harder and looked past him. "Look what the cat drug in."

Daniel glanced over in time to see Russell's door open. He could barely make out the top of Jud's head as the little man reached inside to haul Russell out of the cab.

"You little fucktard!" Russell bent over and Jud's arms appeared to throttle his neck. Daniel would have been concerned if he wasn't certain that Jud was laughing. Also, Cy stood right behind him, laughing. "You fucking little fucktard! Ain't never gonna forgive you for leaving." One arm disappeared and Daniel was quite sure that fist planted in Russell's gut. At least, if Russell's flinch and groan was any indication. "Little shit."

Daniel laughed, opening his door. He exchanged amused grins with Ben. "Good to see some things don't change."

Ben blocked his way from fully standing. He looked at his foreman's now serious gaze. "He all right?"

Shay stood right at Ben's elbow, listening closely.

Daniel nodded. "He knows she's a witch. She as much as told him she spelled him."

With a sigh of relief, Ben stepped back to give Daniel room to leave the truck. "You see her?"

"No. She was gone." He slammed his door shut and looked around. Gordy had Russell up in a big bear hug, with Cy and Michael laughing to either side of him. "I didn't expect this."

"We talked over dinner." Ben put an arm around Daniel's shoulders. "We decided if you brought him back, things must be okay. Hope we were right about that."

Daniel nodded, fighting the swell of joyful tears that warmed his eyes. "You were."

🐾 🐾 🐾

Russell could feel the difference in the air. It had been building for the past week or so, but now it had definitely reached a head. The others told him it was the coming of the full moon. He could only believe them.

They stood in a loose circle in one of the lower paddocks. The space was located in a little valley not far from the house, the land curved so that if they shifted, they wouldn't be immediately visible from the driveway or the road that led through the ranch toward the woods.

If they shifted. From the conversations that had gone on for the two weeks since Russell had been back home, there were high hopes that they wouldn't shift tonight because the number was complete. Shay, their resident magic expert, seemed to think it was very possible the curse was broken. The others believed or disbelieved in varying degrees, but it was obvious the hope was there for everyone.

For Russell…well, it was different. He could only remember bits and pieces of his one partial shift and very little of it involved the shape of a beast. Oh, he'd felt something bestial all right, but he credited that more to lust for a certain man. A certain man who'd kept his distance since Russell had been back at the Shifting Sands.

Daniel stood beside him, dressed similarly to them all in sweat pants and nothing else despite the chilly air. The guys who turned into the bigger animals wore clothing they didn't mind losing in case they didn't get out of them in time for the shift to happen. If it wasn't on the colder side, they'd probably just go ahead and be naked. Russell tried not to be obvious about ogling Daniel's furry chest or toned, flat belly, but it wasn't easy. They were surrounded by couples who were obvious in their affection, even if they weren't overt.

Russell was near out of his mind with want just to be near Daniel. Had been since the night Daniel had come to get him. But the older man kept his distance. Wasn't like he *ignored* Russell or anything, but after a week Russell had figured out that Daniel did everything he could not to be alone with him. In the few times Russell did manage to get him alone, Daniel took charge of the conversation and turned it to anything but what happened in the alley that night. If he wasn't *so* careful to avoid the subject, Russell might have thought he had imagined it all. But Daniel did talk about Russell's partial shift and what it meant to shift, he just wouldn't talk about what had happened between them *during* the shift. Squatting on the ground beside Daniel, Russell thought hard. Maybe he was wrong. Maybe Daniel had said nothing because nothing had happened. But Russell was *sure* he remembered the taste of Daniel's kiss. Sure, and he sure as *hell* wanted to taste it again.

"Almost time," said the voice that haunted his dreams.

Russell glanced up, but Daniel's attention was on the sky. It was still late afternoon, the full moon being one of those that happened during the day. Daniel's salt-and-pepper hair curled around his ears, a little long. *He needs a haircut.* Or was the longer hair and beard like the dragon's? *I wonder what he looks like then?* But if everyone got their wish, Russell would never see it.

Zan and Jud paced in small circles, gaze flitting from the sky to the ground. Michael stared off in the distance and Gordy had his arms around Tristan, both of them looking like they were just waiting for something.

Then Russell felt it. A tingle like nothing else he could explain. Frowning, he stood.

"Do you feel it?" Daniel asked.

"Yeah, I think so."

"Shit!" Russell glanced at Jud, who was staring at his own outspread hands. "It's happening."

Bobby Lee and Cy exchanged a look and a kiss.

Then the world changed.

Russell's body…altered. In the blink of an eye. One second he was watching Bobby Lee draw away from Cy, the next he was on all fours and a buffet of delicious scents surrounded him. Instinct locked his gaze on the tightly curled wool of a ram as the draw of fresh meat filled his nose. Then another scent invaded, overwhelmed, and the sheep was forgotten.

A scaly hide rippled before his eyes, a shiny, almost golden crest marching down a sinuous, undulating back. It looked like a huge snake but he saw legs pass him by. Mesmerized, he didn't realize until he was surrounded that the beast isolated him within the circle of its body. Its trunk was about as big around as a horse's torso but so much more elongated. His lips lifted into a growl as the head came into view, hovering like a snake's just before his nose. Yellow eyes bore into his with an intensity that made the fur on the back of his neck stand up.

Fur? Growl? Instinct melted away, leaving room for shock as

Russell remembered who he was, where he was, even if he could hardly believe *what* he was. A glance down at his hands showed massive white paws. Lethal talons popped out when he flexed the fingers on his right hand. His arm was huge, with orange and black-striped fur taking over for the white on the back of it. A look at his shoulder showed more of the easily recognizable fur. *Hot damn, I really* am *a tiger!*

And…he looked back up. The dragon was still watching him steadily and the body surrounding him hadn't moved. The beast was long enough to completely circle Russell's massively muscled body without nose touching tail. *Daniel.* His scales were mostly blue, but there were green tints to them that shimmered in the waning sunlight. The head that hovered eye level with Russell was everything he'd ever seen in the pictures of dragons in Yi's stuff. The long snout, the vaguely equine nose, the intelligent, round yellow eyes. The beard lining his jaw was fine and snowy white, matching the two tufts of a mustache just below his nostrils. He opened his mouth to display long, sharp teeth that had Russell's tiger instincts wanting to growl again. But then Daniel cocked his head and Russell recognized the smile in the strange face. He wanted to smile and laugh himself but it came out as a strange, rumbly cough. *I guess talking's kind of out.*

Daniel nodded, then flicked his gaze and head toward the road that led to the woods. Even though he'd hoped not to shift, Daniel—ever practical—had made sure to tell Russell that *if* they did shift, Russell would go with him to the woods where they, as the two largest and potentially most dangerous predators among the group, would wait out the shift. Russell nodded his own understanding then watched, mesmerized, as Daniel unwound that long, sinuous body from around him. Unable to help himself, Russell stepped up and brushed his side against Daniel's, wondering what it would feel like for those scales to slide over his naked, human flesh.

Daniel paused and that snake-like neck swiveled around to look at him. Russell watched him, then gave up. There was nothing he could do in this form but follow. So he started walking himself. He'd explore the tiger thing tonight.

Tomorrow was another thing.

※ ※ ※

Daniel led Russell back to the house while they were still in shifted form. It was almost dawn. For whatever reason, even if the full moon happened in the middle of the day, the shift always lasted until the next dawn. The few times when the full moon had occurred just after dawn had been a nuisance, losing them all a full day's work, not to mention explaining to the part-time help that they weren't needed for that day.

He'd watched over Russell all night, enjoying the younger man's exploration of the tiger form. It hadn't been a hardship to watch him. Russell's cat body was a thing of beauty. Even with the dragon's altered vision, he kept losing himself in the colors that were Russell.

They'd just reached the final stretch of dirt road that would lead them up to the house when he felt the dawn start to dissolve the shift. He stopped and turned to face Russell, who had stopped beside him. Daniel stood up on his hind legs as the dragon melted away, his shift causing him to miss the seconds that it took for Russell to change from lethal, orange and black-striped feline to kneeling, naked man. Although, the kneeling man was almost as lethal to Daniel, at least to his heart. Kneeling on all fours, his short orange hair gleaming in the day's first light, the freckles springing to life all over the pale, smooth muscles of his back. Thankfully, Russell faced him rather than away, otherwise Daniel would surely be caught staring at his round, perfect ass.

Get a hold of yourself, he cautioned, breathing deep once his lungs were fully human again. He'd done well keeping himself away from Russell since they'd been back on at the Sands. The boy obviously didn't remember much about that time in the alley and Daniel was determined not to remind him. Let him make up his *own* mind about who he wanted. He didn't have to be slave to the curse. Because, the way Daniel saw it, Yi had manipulated this. She'd somehow figured out Daniel's attraction to Russell.

Why else would she take him? Why else would he be part of the curse, the last animal to complete the dozen? She meant for Daniel and Russell to be together. Daniel was determined that wouldn't happen. Bad enough *he* was caught in an unrequited attraction, Russell didn't need to be caught up in the same.

Even so, he held his hand down to Russell. To his secret delight, Russell gripped his wrist and let Daniel to pull him to his feet. It also gave Daniel a cheap opportunity to glimpse the soft cock sprouting out of a nest of dark orange curls. Put Daniel in the mind of marmalade, and he had to look away before he continued wondering what it'd be like to lick sticky sweet marmalade from Russell's erection. *Down, boy!* Safer, although no less heart-stopping, to concentrate on Russell's wide smile. "How was it?" he asked, with a grin of his own.

"That was fantastic!" He released Daniel's hand in order to dust off his knees and hands. "I never in a million years would have imagined something like that."

Daniel smiled, bemused as they started walking toward the house. "Being a tiger would be amazing," he agreed, "but best not crow about it around Jud or Shay."

Russell thought about it, then laughed. "Yeah, okay, tiger's a little different. Being a horse'd be cool, though. Ben must love that. Oh man, what's it like to be a *dragon*?"

Before he could answer, Daniel heard the others on the front porch.

"...the hell did it happen?" Zan demanded, sounding more frustrated than mad. Of course, it was hard to tell with Zan sometimes. "I thought with Russell here the curse was broken?"

"There were no guarantees," Ben cautioned as Daniel came around the corner of the house with Russell. "Shay only said it *might* break the curse."

The boys were in varied states of dress, some in jeans, some just holding whatever clothing they'd left out on the porch for the morning. All but Michael were bare-chested.

"Yeah, but..."

"All right," Jud said loudly, spying Daniel and Russell. He slapped his thighs with the pants he held in his hand and started for the front door. "Woody, c'mon, let's get some chow on."

The others had caught sight of them now and shut up fast. Daniel quelled an irrational swell of anger. He couldn't very well blame them for hoping. *He'd* hoped last night would be different, too.

He reached over to grab Russell's shoulder and pull him forward toward the house. "Well," he looked to Shay, "looks like we still got some work to do."

Shay nodded, fiddling with the pair of pants he'd had yet to put on. "I'm sorry, boss. I really thought…"

"Not your fault. Not anyone's fault." He gazed around at all of them, making sure they all got the point. "Not like we're any worse off than we already were."

There were nods all around. He looked closely at each of them and was relieved to see varying degrees of disappointment and resignation, but no brimming anger.

"All right then, like Jud said, let's get some chow on and get the day started."

🐾 🐾 🐾

Even though they'd been up all night, no one gave a thought to sleeping. Maybe the others had slept in their animal forms. Or maybe the shifted form had its own energy. Russell didn't know. But he watched and listened carefully during breakfast and it all just seemed to be business as usual. Beyond the dismal reaction they'd had right before coming in the house, everyone just seemed to drop it in favor of going on with their day. At least that's the way they acted on the outside. He guessed he should be thankful that they didn't blame him for not breaking the curse.

But he kind of blamed himself. Okay, he didn't know the details of Yi's curse better than any of them, but thinking he was the key to ending it wasn't a far stretch. They were twelve now, the complete Chinese zodiac, that *had* to be what she was going for, right? So why was it still happening? What did she have in store? Or was it complete? Yes, they were all there, but there was something missing. Besides him and Daniel, the other ten were *couples*. One thing Russell had learned during the two weeks he'd been back was that they were all in love. Very much in love. It was awesome, really. In the past, he'd heard so many complaints about being alone and not having someone to love, it was great to see Jud, Cy, Gordy, Michael and Ben all happy with someone. Even better, in a twisted way, to have the confirmation of that love through the curse. It was enough to make Russell wonder if just his presence was enough. Maybe his being there and sharing the curse was only a part of it. Maybe they were missing something.

Only one way to find out.

Breakfast ended. Jud and Woody disappeared in the kitchen to clean up and the others headed off to the bunkhouse or their cabins to get dressed and go to work. Russell had been sleeping in his old room in the main house since he'd been back, so he alone followed Daniel up the stairs to the second floor. Which suited his purposes nicely. Instead of turning left to his own room, he quietly padded after Daniel into the master bedroom.

Daniel didn't notice he was standing in the bedroom doorway immediately. He wore the old jeans he'd put on before breakfast and an unbuttoned green and blue flannel shirt. The colors reminded Russell of the shine of his scales in dragon form and damned if Russell wasn't imagining what those scales would feel like against his naked skin again. He reached down to adjust his cock where it started to tent his sweatpants.

That's when Daniel looked up and noticed him. First his eyes were on Russell's face, then the hand on his cock, then back at his face. "You need something?"

Daniel wasn't referring to Russell's hand and cock, but damn if Russell didn't make the connection. It made his cock jump again. "Uh, yeah. I need to talk to you."

Daniel threw a pair of socks and a fresh pair of jeans on his bed, then turned to face Russell fully. "We got lots of work to do today. What's on your mind?"

We got lots of work every day, muttered the child in Russell's head. But the adult wasn't going to get put off. "I think I got an idea why the curse didn't break."

The frown on Daniel's face melted to surprise. "Oh?"

"Yeah."

Daniel reached up to scratch at the thick growth of beard on his jaw, thicker than before the shift yesterday. "Maybe you should talk to Shay."

Russell took a step into the room, his bare feet transferring from polished wood to worn carpet. "No, I need to talk to *you*."

Daniel actually backed up a step, which was interesting. "All right."

Just to see, Russell took a few more steps into the room. His own heart started to thud something awful but he was more interested in the signs of nerves in Daniel. The man was normally a rock, nothing fazed him. But right now his eyes were just a bit too wide and his broad shoulders were all drawn up, like he was tensing for a fight. It wasn't like him.

Okay, so here you are. How do you start? Russell took a deep breath, keeping his eyes locked on Daniel's deep brown eyes. "What happened between us in the alley the night you came to get me?"

Those eyes widened just a little more. Did Daniel know he took another small step backwards? "Nothing. You were pissed and you shifted partway. I helped you shift back."

"How?"

Frown. "Does it matter?"

"Yes. We kissed, didn't we?"

The flare of nostrils and the flick of Daniel's eyes gave Russell his answer. "Russell…"

"You've never lied to me, Daniel, not that I know of. Please don't start now."

Daniel's jaw clicked shut. He considered lying, Russell saw it in his face, but his natural honesty won out. "Yes, but…"

Russell took another step, which brought him into Daniel's personal space. "We did more than just kiss."

Daniel tried to step back but the bed was in his way now. Instead, he brought up his hands to grip Russell's bare shoulders. "Yes, we did, but it doesn't have to mean anything."

Russell reached up to grab Daniel's forearms, gripping strong muscle through the flannel. "It means *everything*."

"No!" Fingers dug into his shoulders, keeping him at bay. "No, boy, this is the curse talking."

That surprised him away from getting lost in the delicious warmth of Daniel's nearness. "What?"

"Yi got you caught up in this damn curse and now you're feeling things that aren't true."

He blinked and shook his head. "What?"

Daniel's lips squashed into a thin line, like they did when he knew he had bad news to tell. "I'm sorry you got caught up in this, boy. Yi must have seen my feelings for you and gotten you all caught up in this. It's my fault."

"What about your feelings? What are you saying?"

"She must have put another spell on you, one to make you want me." He shook his head, eyes closed. "But you don't have to. You don't…"

Russell yanked at Daniel's arms to get his attention. "What kind of nonsense are you talking, old man?" When Daniel's eyes focused on his again, he smirked. "I got news for you. Yi had nothing to do with my feelings for you. I wanted you long before Yi ever came to the Sands."

Few times had Russell seen Daniel speechless. This was one of them. Grinning wide enough to hurt his face, he reached up to slide his fingers into Daniel's beard, cupping one side of his jaw. "I've wanted you since I figured out it was okay for a man to want another man." Which, for him, considering his surroundings, was pretty young.

Daniel's mouth opened, his lips worked, but no sound came out.

Russell brought up his other hand to cup the other side of the taller man's jaw. In doing so, he managed to take another step closer, almost bringing their bare chests together. "I knew you couldn't want me until I was old enough. Then when I was, Yi came into the picture." He grimaced. "I don't know what she did to me—" Daniel's hands, which had slid from his shoulders to his waist, gripped just a little bit harder at that "—but it wasn't my idea to sleep with her, or to run off with her." He tilted Daniel's face down so he could gaze hard into those eyes. "Only one I *ever* wanted was you."

Daniel tried to shake his head. "I'm too old for you."

"Are not."

"I'm old enough to be your…"

Russell chuckled. "Uncle? You sure as hell aren't old enough to be my father."

Daniel scowled.

Which just made Russell laugh more. He edged in that last little bit which allowed his chest to brush Daniel's. His eyelids fluttered low as he enjoyed the tickle of soft, curly hair against his skin. "You've always been there for me and you're the best-looking man I've ever seen." Slowly, he pulled Daniel's head down toward his. "How could I not love you?"

Daniel resisted their lips getting any closer, although he didn't pull away. "Love?"

"Yes. Tell me you love me, old man."

The growl as Daniel tilted his head sounded a lot like the sounds he'd made in the woods as a dragon. "Demanding cub."

"You know it."

He would have demanded words of love again but then they were kissing and he didn't care so much. Oh yeah, he remembered that taste, those lips. He opened his mouth and let in the tongue that slid through his teeth, sucking on it to produce another rumbling growl in the chest that was now pressed against his. Strong arms wound around him, big hands pressing his back to hold him close. He slid his own arms up around Daniel's neck, just like he'd always wanted to do, and pressed up against the man like a cat in heat.

Too soon, Daniel pulled his lips away, despite Russell's efforts to keep them sealed to his. He could feel the evidence of Daniel's arousal against his own and was trying to get his addled brain to figure out a way to get them horizontal on the bed.

"Wait," Daniel's breath wafted over Russell's moist lips.

"No."

"Wait." Daniel tilted his head up out of reach. "Stop."

Russell took advantage and tasted the salty skin of Daniel's neck.

Daniel groaned. "Russell."

"Can't stop," he whispered, dragging his lips over the beard growth on Daniel's neck. "Finally got you. Can't let go."

Daniel's hands found Russell's shoulders again, pushing him away. "Stop. We have work to do."

"Fuck work! No, better yet, fuck me."

"Russell…"

"I'm serious. You've been avoiding me since we came back. Don't tell me you don't want me."

"That's not the point."

"That *is* the point, damn it." They glared at each other over maybe two feet of empty space. "What's wrong now? And don't tell me it's work because there are plenty of men out there to do what needs to be done for an hour or so."

Whatever Daniel had been about to say was abandoned. He grimaced, at a loss for words. In Russell's estimation, he'd never seen a better looking confused man.

He planted his hands on Daniel's chest and pushed, catching the cowboy off guard. With a grunt, Daniel fell onto the mattress.

"Wait!"

Russell stayed standing but dropped his hands to the button of his jeans, undoing it. "What?"

"No lube."

Russell paused, then chuckled. Pants gaping, he reached over, opened the top drawer of Daniel's nightstand, and pulled out the tub of Vaseline he knew had to be there. Grinning, he held it up. "Cowboy's best friend." He tossed the tub onto the bed next to Daniel.

The older cowboy stared at it like it was a viper. The sound of Russell's zipper coming down distracted him and his gaze honed in on Russell's crotch. He sat up and grabbed Russell's wrists. He looked up to stall Russell's protest, the smoky look in his eyes shutting Russell right up. "Shut the door."

Russell blinked. He'd completely forgotten the open door. "Good idea." Grinning, he hustled over to close it.

Before it shut, he caught sight of Jud peeking around the corner of the stairwell. The other man winked, then disappeared.

Grinning wider, Russell shut the door and turned back to Daniel, deciding the boss didn't need to know that their first time together would be known by everyone on the ranch even before they'd finished.

Anyway, all thoughts of anyone else flew from his head when he saw Daniel again. Now shirtless, he sat on the edge of the bed, watching Russell with what could only be called a hungry look. Eagerly, he hustled back to stand between Daniel's knees again.

When he reached for his waistband, Daniel caught his wrists again. "You sure about this?"

"More sure than I've ever been about anything in my life."

Daniel's gaze drifted down his neck, his chest, adorably hesitant—and Daniel was rarely adorable. "I've only done this on one-night stands." He shook his head slowly. "And never with anyone I cared about."

Russell sank his fingers into Daniel's soft, curly hair. "I've never done it with anyone. Well, with a guy."

Smiling, Daniel slid his palms down Russell's belly then hooked fingers in his waistband. "We'll go slow." He tugged Russell's pants down his legs.

The frickin' *air* made Russell's freed cock pulse. He groaned. "I don't know if I'll make it if we go slow."

Daniel's gaze fixed on Russell's cock as he left the jeans at Russell's ankles. "We'll see about that."

🐉 🐉 🐉

He wrapped his palm and fingers around the hot, hard stalk of Russell's erection and slid the head past his lips, just like he'd wanted to do all morning. Hell, he'd wanted it longer than that. Russell groaned, his fingers threading through Daniel's hair, guiding rather than pulling. Daniel was willing to be guided, since it followed what he wanted to do anyway. Russell was salty, dark and delicious and Daniel sucked him hard to get him to ooze that sexy moaning. Then the moaning turned into panting and Daniel had to grip Russell's slim hips to keep that hard cock from bruising the back of his throat.

"Shit! Daniel, I'm…" A glance up showed Russell's head tilted down, his eyes screwed shut. "Shit, stop." His shove dislodged Daniel's mouth but not the grip on his hips.

"You okay?"

Sexy-ass hazel eyes cracked open to stare down at him. "I don't wanna come yet."

Daniel licked his lips. "I want to swallow you down."

A shiver rocked Russell's lean body. "Another time. I want you inside me."

Concern quashed some of Daniel's lust. "You might not come. You might not like it."

The stubborn little shit shook his head. "Don't care. I'll like it." His fingers trailed Daniel's beard again. "It's you."

Daniel stood, grabbing Russell's jaw to pull him into a rough, sloppy kiss. "Lie down," he rasped when he pulled away.

Surprisingly, Russell obeyed. *First damn time today.* Daniel's hands shook as he shucked his pants. *Shouldn't do this to Russell,* a voice cautioned in the back of his head, but that voice wasn't near loud enough. Russell had made his wants crystal clear and Daniel was too weak to deny him.

He tossed his pants aside seconds after Russell kicked his own away and lay back on the bed. Russell's gaze locked on Daniel's oozing erection as Daniel reached for the tub of Vaseline.

He paused again. "We don't have a condom."

Russell grabbed his wrist. "So?"

"We need a condom."

"When's the last time you were with anyone?"

"It was Yi."

"If I know you, you were always careful before that."

"Well yeah."

"I've never been with anyone but Yi. We're both clean."

"But…"

Snarling, Russell twisted his arm. "Damn it, Daniel, stop thinking of reasons not to do this and *fuck* me already."

Snatching his arm from Russell's grip, he picked up the tub of Vaseline. "You watch your mouth."

"How about you shut me up by shoving your dick in it?"

That actually made Daniel fumble the plastic tub, which made Russell laugh.

"I got better places to shove my dick right now." He tossed the cap of the tub aside. "Turn over."

If Russell had ever looked greedier for something, Daniel had never seen it. Not a lick of fear showed on his face as he nimbly twisted and got on his belly. While Daniel scooped out a few finger-fulls of jelly, Russell scrambled up on his knees, sticking his ass in the air, legs spread.

"You sure you never done this?" Daniel asked, smoothing jelly on his cock with one hand.

Russell peeked at him over one freckled shoulder, hazel eyes twinkling in the spear of sunlight shining through one of the bedroom windows. "I watched plenty of porn. That count?"

Daniel groaned, scooping up some more jelly. "Next you're gonna tell me you been fingering yourself."

The grin told it all, but Russell answered anyway. "I have."

Daniel put the tub of jelly aside and knelt on the bed. Russell's cock and balls looked delicious dangling between his spread legs, his pucker winking from within the crack of his ass. "You sure you need me?"

Russell sighed, grabbing handfuls of bedspread as Daniel spread open his cheeks to slather the jelly over his entrance. "I need you more'n anything in this world," he sighed, all teasing gone from his voice. "Always have."

Watching Russell's face, Daniel sank one finger into his hole. Russell flinched a little, then sighed and relaxed.

"More."

"Already?"

Russell rotated his hips. "Yes."

Daniel drew back then sank in two fingers. Again, Russell just sighed in pleasure.

Daniel leaned over to kiss the dimple right below the small of his back. "You sure you never done this before?"

"Not with an actual cock." Another twist of his hips. "Let me have yours. Now. Please."

He couldn't help but believe that Russell was ready, not with the clear signs of enjoyment written all over the half of his face Daniel could see. Not with that gently rocking body, pushing back onto his fingers.

He pulled his hand out and grabbed his cock. One internal pause when he remembered that this was the first time he'd ever gone bare with anyone, but it seemed fitting that Russell would be the one. He set the head of his dick at Russell's hole and pushed slowly. Russell's breath hitched, but he gradually pushed back, impaling himself on Daniel's prick. Daniel braced over him, hands on the mattress to either side of Russell's shoulders, having to rope in an overwhelming urge to rut as Russell's velvet heat closed around him.

"God!" Russell shook underneath him, Daniel's cock fully seated inside him. "That's fucking amazing."

"Oh yeah."

"Daniel."

"Yeah?"

"Move."

Daniel groaned, bending over to prop his forehead on the back of one of Russell's shoulders. "I don't think I'm gonna last long. You feel too good."

"You, too. Me, too." Fingers tugged lightly at his hair. "It's okay. Fuck me."

Daniel moaned.

"Fuck me."

Daniel pulled his hips back and cried out at the near painful pleasure that whipped up his spine as Russell's ass squeezed his cock. Beneath him, Russell's "Oh shit, yeah" was nearly lost as he pressed his face into the bedspread. Daniel was lost now. He'd never *needed* to fuck so badly in his life. He could only hope Russell really was enjoying it because his next shove back inside was not nearly as slow or gentle as the first. Russell gasped but rolled his hips, egging Daniel on.

Just one more thing. Forcing himself to pause, Daniel leaned in as far as he could, pressing his chest to Russell's back so he could whisper against the shell of Russell's ear. "I love you," he whispered.

Russell twisted as best he could to look at Daniel with dark, lusty eyes. "I know." His chuckle was raspy, matching Daniel's. He reached back to circle Daniel's neck, pulling them into an awkward kiss. "Now fuck me. Make me feel it."

The words snapped any control he might have mustered. Hardly recognizing the growl in his throat, he rose to his knees, grabbed Russell's hips and started thrusting.

※ ※ ※

Russell buried his face in the mattress to muffle his cries. He'd never *dreamed* it'd be so good! Painful a little at first, sure, and it no doubt would've been more if he'd never played with himself, but once Daniel got up a rhythm it was the best feeling in the world. Russell's entire body sizzled as he braced himself for Daniel's thrusts. When Daniel bent over him, he instinctively arched up, the better to press his whole back against Daniel's chest, needing to feel the soft scrape of chest hair on his sensitive skin. Incoherent muttering spilled from Daniel's mouth, his breath yet another caress over the sweat pooling in the center of Russell's back.

"Shit, Daniel!" he cried, barely remembering to check the volume. Electricity pooled in his gut, leaking down into his neglected cock. "I'm gonna come."

He couldn't help the brief scream when Daniel's calloused fingers closed around his shaft. "Come," Daniel demanded. "Come with…ahhhh!"

He felt it. The falter of Daniel's rhythm, the ragged thrusts that filled his ass. All of that together with Daniel's yank on his cock set him off. Biting his lip over another scream, he shattered, sure that only Daniel's weight and the support of the firm mattress kept him from flying to pieces.

They collapsed on the bedspread, struggling to breathe. Sweat plastered them chest to back and the angle of their hips kept Daniel buried inside Russell for a few more moments.

Russell became aware of sweet little kisses being peppered

over the back of his shoulders and neck. Smiling, he twisted his neck to get a peek of Daniel. At first all he saw was salt-and-pepper curls, then those brown eyes came into view, half-lidded over a satisfied grin. Russell decided to sacrifice the feel of Daniel inside of him for the need to kiss his lover properly. Together they fumbled a little until Russell was on his back with Daniel draped over him like a huge, sweaty blanket...only better. They kissed languidly, not needing words, feeling no hurry. If there was work to be done, it could wait. This was an important moment.

But all moments came to an end. This one with a knock on the door.

Daniel lifted his head, frowning down at Russell at the sound.

"Boss man," Jud's voice came through the wood, "sorry to interrupt but I think you *really* need to get downstairs."

Russell sighed when Daniel jacked up off of him. "What's wrong?"

"Uh, well..."

The uncertainty in Jud's voice set off Russell's bells, even through the pleasant haze of after glow.

Daniel was reaching for his jeans. "What's wrong?"

"Uh...Yi's here?"

"What?"

Both Daniel and Russell were too shocked to mind much when Jud just opened the door to let himself him.

Being Jud, he first had to grin at Woody, who was right behind him. "I *told* you!"

Jeans in hand, Daniel dropped to sit next to Russell on the edge of the bed. "Judson, what the hell is going on?"

Jud snapped back to the matter at hand. "Yi. She's downstairs."

Woody nodded hard. "She just kind of...appeared. Her and this guy who looks a lot like her. They're in the main room."

"The guy said we had to come get you. Get everyone."

Daniel was already on his feet, jeans in hand. "What you do you mean 'appeared'?"

Russell, alarmed, rolled off the other side of the bed and started searching for his pants.

"I mean one minute Tristan was cleaning the living room and the next he rushed in the kitchen and told us these people just popped out of thin air." Jud picked up Russell's pants and held them out to him. "Woody and I went in and it was Yi and this guy. He told me to come get you. That you were..." he cleared his throat, "*finished* now."

Russell froze, pants on, hands holding the open ties. He turned wide eyes on Daniel.

Daniel frowned but stayed thoughtfully silent as he slid on his shirt.

"There's this weird force field around them, too. Can't get real close."

Woody nodded. "They look kinda strange, too. Not see through but..." he looked at Jud, then shook his head.

Jud shrugged, looked to Russell. "Who's the guy?"

Russell shook his head. "I dunno. She's never introduced me to anyone who looks like her."

Daniel sat to pull on his boots. "Where are the others?"

"I sent Tristan to get them."

Daniel nodded, standing to stamp down on his boots. "Let's go see what she wants."

🐾 🐾 🐾

The man didn't just look a lot like Yi, he looked *exactly* like Yi. Same height, same build, same face. Only difference was in the slight curves of her body and the slimmer lines of his hips. His hair was shorter and he wore no makeup. His smile was different, though. Brighter, friendlier, far more open. He turned that smile on Daniel as the Sands' owner came into the living room, but remained beside Yi. As Woody had mentioned, there was a barely visible force field surrounding them, like a bubble. They wavered as though they stood behind flames.

"Daniel. So nice to finally meet you," said the man.

"Finally?"

Heavy footfalls preceded the porch door opening. The men couldn't have gone far in so short a time so it wouldn't take long for them all to re-gather.

Yi's look-alike kept his smiling attention on Daniel. "I've known about you for quite some time but I've never gotten the pleasure of meeting you. Please forgive me, I'd offer to shake hands but—" he indicated the force field around them, "—we're not really here in the physical sense."

Daniel heard the others crowd behind him and stepped closer to the strange pair to make room. "Who are you?"

"I'm Yu. You may think of me as Yi's brother."

Beside and slightly behind him, Yi stood with her profile to the men of the Sands, glaring at the chair beside her. Her red mouth was drawn into a pout and her arms were tightly crossed over her chest. Clearly, Yu would be doing the talking.

"I can *think* of you as her brother?"

Yu laughed. "As we're not human, we've a different standard of relations. I'm closer to Yi's other half than brother, but brother will do."

"Why haven't I met you before?"

For the first time, the smile faltered, but only a little. "You could say Yi and I had a falling out." A few of his words were accented, but otherwise Yu spoke English as fluidly as Yi when she wasn't upset. "A little over two years ago, she managed to... lose me."

Out of the corner of his eye, Daniel saw the others ranged out through the room to get the best advantage for seeing what was going on. Russell's arm brushed Daniel's, the younger man right by his side.

"What does that mean?"

"It means that Yi escaped from me and found you. I can only apologize for the damage she's caused you."

Yi's lip lifted in a snarl but she otherwise didn't move.

"Can you explain what happened to us? Why Yi chose me?"

"Not all of it, no. I can tell you that she found a unique quality in you and your men that attracted her. I can assure you that any romantic feelings you might have had for her were entirely her doing and those feelings won't bother you anymore."

"What about the shape-shifting?"

Yu shook his head. "I apologize about that, too. Even I'm still not sure why Yi would do such a thing. In her anger, she wanted to make you animals to match what she saw of you. Our particular magic is tied very closely to the zodiac. We have some control over it but our mastery is not complete." He laughed. "I assure you, she did *not* intend to unleash the dragon. We are all very fortunate that you are a just and moral man who did not take undue advantage of your transformation." With that, he bowed, a deep gesture of respect.

"So why are you here?"

"We came so that you would know that your curse has lifted. I regret that I couldn't come sooner, but the curse's parameters had to complete before I could. But now those parameters have been fulfilled."

"What parameters?" Russell demanded before Daniel could speak.

Yu smiled at him. "Completion of the zodiac along with each of you finding a mate who truly accepts you for what you are." He nodded. "I'd worried that you wouldn't accomplish it but I can see now that the group of you are very special. I can see why she was drawn to you."

"That doesn't make sense," Jud piped in. "There was only seven of us when she cursed us."

Yu nodded toward him. "Our sense of such things often crosses time boundaries."

Daniel took charge again before anyone else could. "So what happens now?"

"Yi's curse has ended. You are now free to live your lives without our influence."

"No more shifting?"

Yu hesitated, his dark gaze dropping. "Ah, yes, about that. I should warn you...although you will no longer be *forced* to change, Yi's spell has awakened a beast in each of you. Once awakened, we do not have the power to remove them." He cleared his throat, dragging his gaze back up to Daniel. "The beast remains and your souls have learned the ability to shift. You'll retain that power, although your control of it should be much finer. Because of this, you'll be watched by others of our kind. If you try to take undue advantage of your abilities or go public with them, please be aware that we *will* stop you with any force necessary. But, given what I've come to learn of you gentlemen, I don't think that will be a problem."

"What about the tie to the land?"

"Ah, that. Your love of the Shifting Sands is your own, but the beasts' ties to it have loosened. The ability to leave and travel are, once again, yours."

Daniel glanced at the others, seeing his own surprise reflected in many faces. He wasn't quite sure what to think about the shifting thing, too surprised to make sense of it, but some lump of worry that had lived in his chest for two years was rapidly melting. He turned back to Yu to see the two of them hadn't moved. "What are you?"

"That, I can't tell you. It wouldn't make sense. Suffice to say, we're not human and we're not entirely of this world." He chuckled. "And now, having said what needed to be said, we will leave you to go on with your lives."

Which was kind of a shame. Daniel got the feeling he could have liked Yu. But Daniel kept his tongue, as did the others, all of them watching as the pair of non-humans slowly disappeared from sight.

"Okay." Shay stood behind the couch, his back against Ben's chest as the taller man held him. "That was...weird."

"I'll say." Jud stepped across the room until he was right by where the pair had been. He rubbed the spot on the rug with the toe of his sneaker.

Woody was right next to him. "You think we can believe them?"

"Don't see why not," Gordy rumbled from the archway.

Zan marched up beside Jud and knelt to feel the rug. "This whole thing has been weird. Don't see why it wouldn't end that way."

"Is it really over?" Michael asked, eyes on Daniel.

Daniel gave them each a measuring look, all but Russell. Russell he reached for, resting his arms across the younger man's shoulders, taking comfort in the way Russell fit just right against his side. "I think it's probably over. Yes. At least as much as he said."

"But we keep shifting," Cy noted.

"But we control it," Bobby Lee corrected softly.

"So it's not really over," Ben surmised.

Daniel finally glanced down at Russell to find those hazel eyes gazing back. Then he had to smile, a big, warm smile that he couldn't have suppressed if he tried. Happiness burbled in his chest, more than he'd ever felt in his entire life. Still smiling, he bent his neck to brush his lips over Russell's. "No. Not over." He looked up at his men and laughed. "It's better."

About the Authors

KIMBERLY GARDNER has been making up stories for as long as she can remember. As early as the seventh grade, she recalls slashing her favorite rockstars for her own and her friends' enjoyment. It was also around that time that she began a lifelong love affair with the romance genre, devouring category romances as fast as she could smuggle them into the house. So it's not all that surprising that her two passions, romance and putting pretty boys with other pretty boys, would ultimately come together in her writing.

Moliere says, "Writing is like prostitution. First you do it for love, then for a few close friends, then for money."

Kimberly is delighted at long last to be doing it for money. She can be found on the internet at:

http://www.kimberlygardner.com

ALLY BLUE is acknowledged by the world at large (or at least by her heroes, who tend to suffer a lot) as the Popess of Gay Angst. She has a great big penis hat and rides in a bullet-proof Plexiglas bubble in Christmas parades. Her harem of manwhores does double duty as bodyguards and sinspirational entertainment. Her favorite band is Radiohead, her favorite color is lime green and her favorite way to waste a perfectly good Saturday is to watch all three extended version LOTR movies in a row. Her ultimate dream is to one day ditch the evil day job and support the family on manlove alone. She is not a hippie or a brain surgeon, no matter what her kids' friends say.

Ally can be found on the internet at:

http://www.allyblue.com

Erotica Quixotica! WILLA OKATI possesses an abundance of crazy ideas, writes constantly, and drinks an insane amount of coffee. She grooves to the beat of a different marching band and loves coming up with fun, quirky heroes and tales with unusual twists. You can find Willa online at http://www.willaokati.com or on her Google group at http://groups.google.com/group/lovers_and_dreamers

BRENDA BRYCE has been thinking about, learning about, listening to, watching, and reading romance since I was in my early teens...Okay, the watching came later, but you get the idea. A published author since 2005 in both the paranormal m/f genre and the m/m genre, I love it all, as long as it has an HEA. Living in Northern Alabama with her husband, and grown, college-attending kids, I like to keep busy, when not arguing with characters, by knitting, crocheting, reading, and am currently in nursing school. Idle hands, and all that. I love to hear from readers, and will gladly respond if you write me at brendabryce@gmail.com.

J.L. LANGLEY has been talking since she was about seven months old. To those who know her it comes as no surprise, in fact, most will tell you she hasn't shut up since. At eighteen months, she was speaking in full sentences. Imagine if you will the surprise of her admirers when they complimented her mother on "what a cute little boy" she had and received a fierce glare from said little boy and a very loud correction of "I'm a girl!" Oddly enough, JL still finds herself saying that exact phrase thirty-some-odd years later.

Today JL is a full-time writer, with over ten novels to her credit. Among her hobbies she includes reading, practicing her marksmanship (she happens to be a great shot), gardening, working out (although she despises cardio), searching for the perfect chocolate dessert (so far as she can tell ALL chocolate is perfect, but it requires more research) and arguing with her husband over who the air compressor and nail gun really belongs to (they belong to JL, although she might be willing to trade him for his new chainsaw).

You can find JL on the internet at:

http://www.jllangley.com

JET MYKLES has been writing sex stories back as far as junior high. Back then, the stories involved her favorite pop icons of the time but she soon extended beyond that realm into making up characters of her own. To this day, she hasn't stopped writing sex, although her knowledge on the subject has vastly improved.

An ardent fan of fantasy and science fiction sagas, Jet prefers to live in a world of imagination where dragons are real, elves are commonplace, vampires are just people with special diets and lycanthropes live next door. In her own mind, she's the spunky heroine who gets the best of everyone and always attracts the lean, muscular lads.

In real life, Jet is a self-proclaimed hermit, living in southern California with her life partner. She has a bachelor's degree in acting, but her loathing of auditions has kept her out of the limelight.

You can find Jet on the web at: http://www.jetmykles.com